TO OWN THE LIBS

To Own the Libs

Zoe Storm

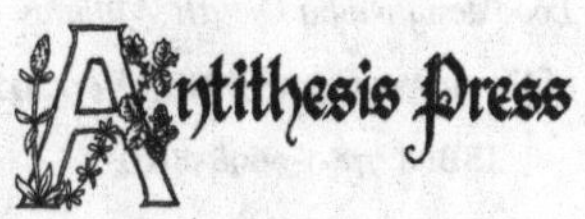

Antithesis Press

Olympia, WA

Foreword

THANK YOU FOR picking up this book.

This story is very dear to me. The idea for it came during a conversation with a friend as we were discussing the current goings-on in politics and society in general, and they mentioned, "At this point, I wouldn't be surprised if a cis man actually tried to transition just to prove it is possible even when he's not trans."

We both laughed at that, but the idea somehow stuck with me: what if someone *actually* tried to transition to prove it's possible even when they're not trans? It's a completely absurd idea, right?

Not so absurd that you can't write a book about it, as it turns out!

But, like I said, this is a story which is very dear to me. It's a story I've poured all my soul and my feelings into writing, and I hope you'll enjoy reading it.

And now, like always, we come to the part where I thank everyone!

I would like to thank my patrons, who keep supporting me day in and day out, and who've created a lovely little community in my Discord, full of friendship and support for each other, and which brought about significant life changes for some of them.

I would like to thank Alyson for being a good friend and an inspiration, and also for allowing me to borrow a line she wrote to put into this book and giving me permission to make a couple cheeky references to her excellent *The Sisters of Dorley* series. (Go check it out, it's extremely good!)

And I would also like to thank Olivia for bouncing a couple ideas back and forth and for helping make sure I got a few things regarding legal issues right.

Thanks are also due to my sister for being there for me and for supporting me, and for her unmatched work on this book's cover – seriously, just *look at it*!

And of course, I have to thank my entire family: I wouldn't be here writing these words if it weren't for their unwavering love and support. Thank you.

A final word before you dive in: this story will contain situations and language which some readers may find upsetting, and therefore a list of appropriate content warnings is available on the Antithesis Press website; this list, however, will by necessity contain spoilers.

Now, without further ado: you may turn the page and start reading. Enjoy!

Prologue
Truth

LAUGHING DRUNKENLY, WE crashed through the door to Nora's apartment. A stumble through the dark, deserted house, then we reached her bedroom where, after fumbling a bit, she flung the door open.

"Welcome to my kingdom, Princess Lily!" she announced, spreading her arms wide. "A glorious 130 square feet of pure chaos! Dare you explore this dangerous realm?" She lowered her voice and whispered, "It's normally not this untidy, I swear."

I giggled and gave a mock curtsy. "Why, Queen Nora, you are much too kind. Would you be so courteous as to show me the sights?"

"But of course," she replied with a grin. "Shall we start with the bed?"

Stepping forward, she swept me up in a bridal carry; I gave a small yelp, blushed furiously, and hid my face with my hands as she carried me past the threshold and flung me on the bed.

"Here we are, my princess, a soft landing." She dipped into a bow. "But I have to say, you shouldn't be wearing shoes in bed."

I pretended to frown. "Will you help me take them off, then?"

I leaned back into the mattress, lifted up my feet, and Nora slipped off my shoes and tossed them to the side.

"Hmm, these are such lovely feet," she commented, giving the left one a kiss.

"No, don't," I protested. "They're smelly."

"The only thing I can smell is you," she rebutted. Dropping onto the bed, she pinned me in place with an arm on each side, and looked down at me. "And you smell like flowers."

My blush deepened, but I smiled at her. "I really love you, you know?"

"I do." She gave that charming smile of hers, then reached up and caressed my chest. "Your blouse is in the way."

"Should I take it off?" I asked, after a moment's hesitation; I still felt uneasy showing someone my bare chest.

"Please do."

I reached up slowly, unbuttoned my blouse, then opened it wide to reveal my bra.

"Mmm." Nora smirked. I arched my back and she reached behind me, expertly unhooking my bra after searching a moment for the clasp, then pulling it down to my stomach. "Cute."

"I'm sorry they're not that big," I said. "They're still growing."

She shook her head. "No, they're the perfect size." She leaned down and planted a kiss on the top of my right breast, sending a shiver down my spine. Then she lifted herself up and looked me straight in the eyes, a mischievous grin on her face. "What do you say? Are you ready to go further?"

I bit my lip, but nodded.

Nora grinned widely and lowered herself onto me. The weight of her lithe body on mine felt warm and reassuring. She made me feel safe.

"Good girl," she whispered in my ear, then kissed me deeply.

Girl.

The word suddenly burned in my mind even through the alcoholic fog that clouded it.

As if from a distant memory, another set of words flowed upwards into my brain:

Rape by deception.

I broke the kiss and turned my head to the side. "Nora. Nora, stop. Please, stop," I said, trying to push her away. "Stop."

Nora pulled back immediately and raised herself to a kneeling position, still straddling me. "Baby, what's wrong? Are you okay?" She had a concerned expression on her face. "Did I do something wrong?"

I felt tears well up as I shook my head. "No, you did nothing wrong. You were . . . You *are* fantastic, Nora."

I looked up and locked eyes with her. "I'm the one who did something wrong. I'm the one who *is* wrong."

Nora's frown deepened. "What do you mean? Lily, what's wrong?"

I tried to take a deep breath, but it turned into a choked sob. "I . . . I've been lying to you, Nora. I've been lying to everyone."

As tears started falling, I admitted the truth.

"I'm not a girl."

1

Seven Months Earlier

"**F**UCK!" Slamming the door behind me, I threw my backpack on my bed. It bounced, hit the wall, and fell to the floor with a loud thud. I swore a couple more times for good measure.

"Whoa there!" Joe pulled down his earphones and turned to look at me. "Everything okay, bro?"

"No, everything is *not* okay," I replied, trying and failing to not sound bitter. "What clued you in to that?"

"The swears, mostly. But let me further my guess — it's a Friday, and your last class today is social studies, which you share with . . ."

I grimaced. "Yeah. Anna."

"As expected. What did she do this time?"

He hadn't moved from where he was lying prone on his bed, and after he'd looked at me his eyes immediately returned to his comic book — the only way I knew he was paying attention was because he hadn't put his earphones back on. To be honest, I kinda hated this part of him.

I flopped onto my bed, sighing. "Well, we were in social studies," I began, "and the professor asked us to debate the pros and cons of self-ID."

Joe frowned. "Of what?"

"Self-ID."

"What the fuck is self-ID?"

"It's when you allow people to declare their own 'gender identity,' whatever the fuck that is. Basically, you say you're a man or a woman and people are supposed to just accept that as fact, without objection."

Joe looked up and gave me a puzzled stare. "That can't be right," he said. "You can't just take what people say at face value without proof. People lie."

"Right," I nodded. "And get this: part of the class — most of it, in fact — said that overall self-ID is a net positive, because it allows a 'transgender person' . . ." Joe visibly sneered at the term, ". . . to have his or her identity recognized without having to jump through bureaucratic or legal hoops." I took a deep breath. "But that's just wrong, isn't it?"

"It is, yeah."

"Sure, a small number of people would benefit from it, but the majority who would self-declare their gender would be . . . perverts. Men trying to get into women's bathrooms and changing rooms." I started to pace up and down the room. "And don't even get me started on all this *non-binary* nonsense. How can someone say they're neither a man nor a woman? There are only two sexes. And I said as much to the class."

By that point I had Joe's full attention, and I saw a deep frown creasing his forehead — mirroring mine, no doubt. "So? What happened?"

"Well, things got heated until it was mostly me and Anna shouting back and forth at each other. She just refuses to recognize the truth! And then . . ." I sighed. "And then Professor Markley said I was being too aggressive, told me to back off, and to come back when I had a more 'cogent argument'."

Joe slowly nodded. "So they wouldn't debate you. *Anna* wouldn't debate you."

"Right." I scoffed. "They had no way to deny what I was saying was true, so they just dismissed the whole thing out of hand. Refused to address my points."

Joe put down his comic and came over to place a hand on my shoulder. "I'm sorry," he said. "I know how it feels. I don't understand how people can just refuse to see the truth for what it is."

"*Right?!*" I spread my arms wide, fingers splayed, palms facing the ceiling. "I mean, everything is plain as day. The best modern philosophers have explained it in very simple terms, and yet . . ." I sighed again. "I can barely stand it any longer."

"Why don't you drop the class?" Joe asked. "After all, they can't recognize the truth when it stares them in the face, and they dismiss your arguments without even addressing them. Why don't you just leave? It's their loss."

"I need the credits," I replied. "I was dumb and didn't pick up enough classes. I really need to pass this one, otherwise I'll be in hot water. I think I'll just fudge it and fake it, pretend I agree with what they're saying to get good marks. But it's *wrong*."

"It is." He smiled in sympathy. "You shouldn't have to pretend."

"But I do."

Joe held my gaze for a moment. "Well, you know what the president said, right? It is what it is."

I hesitated before replying. Joe was absolutely convinced the latest presidential election had been stolen, and the current liberal sitting in the White House (who, ironically, shared a name with him) wasn't the rightful president. I disagreed — there was simply no way to cheat an election on such a scale. We'd butted heads on this a few times, and I knew it was best not to press the issue.

"That bitch Anna really got to you this time," Joe said.

"Yeah." I huffed the word out. "Sorry for coming in here and getting you down too."

"No biggie." He shrugged. "I know how these things are — it's no use letting them get to you. And I know how to cheer you up, bro. There's a party at the Theta Omega Tau frat house tonight. Wanna go? There'll be booze."

"Will there?" I asked. When Joe nodded, I smirked. "I'm in, then."

That was one positive thing about college: even though we were both freshmen, alcohol was always readily available to us in ample amounts. And though I was no stranger to booze, having drunk regularly since my freshman year of high school, since starting college I'd gotten used to drinking every evening. It helped me to drown out the constant low-key emotional noise I always felt and to fall asleep more easily, so I could spend the following day focusing on my studies. I honestly had no idea how I got through high school when I could only drink on the weekends.

I was careful, of course. I never got so drunk I couldn't pass for sober if I knew there was a chance of someone in authority spotting me — my RA, Darrell, was particularly strict about that — and I never brought booze into the dorm. Getting busted for underage drinking was the last thing I wanted.

"Alrighty then," Joe said, looking at his watch. "Let me just get changed, then we'll head out."

"It's a shame, though, that tracksuit looks comfy."

"Well, unlike *someone*, I wanna wear something classier. You know, in case there are any ladies at the party."

"I wouldn't worry about that. Theta Omega Tau's parties are

always boring sausagefests," I replied. "Anyway, what's wrong with jeans and a sweatshirt?"

"They're ugly," he said. "They make you look like a formless blob."

I crossed my arms in front of my chest. "Well, maybe I like looking like a formless blob."

"Suit yourself." Joe shrugged, shed his tracksuit top, and started pulling off his T-shirt; I turned to avoid having to look at his naked chest. For whatever reason, seeing male bodies, even my own, always sent me into a depressive mood. I'd noticed this soon after starting junior high and, as a consequence, I avoided looking at naked — or half-naked — men. I'd also become very good at changing clothes with my eyes closed.

When I first explained this to Joe, he told me I was weird because there's absolutely nothing wrong with men being naked in each other's presence. ("What are you going to do when you're in a changing room, at the gym, or at the pool?" Well, for starters, I just don't go to those places. In the end, however, he stopped mentioning it.

"Ready," he said, and I turned back around. He was wearing his best jeans and shirt, and I watched as he put on the fedora he always wore when he was out and about, carefully adjusting its position as he looked in the mirror. "Alright, this is fine. Shall we go?"

"Let's."

☰

"Cheers!" I clinked my bottle against Joe's, who immediately chugged his beer down. I frowned, because he was already on his seventh and we'd been at the party for less than an hour. I was on my third, already quite buzzed, and planned on getting roaring drunk by the end of the evening. But even through my slightly fogged mind, the speed with which Joe drank worried me.

"You sure you shouldn't slow down a bit?" I asked.

He shrugged. "Nah, why should I? There's no harm in getting drunk." He grabbed another bottle. "You know what they say, ninety-nine bottles and everything. Beer is made to be drunk."

I disagreed; while I enjoyed getting a nice buzz and drowning out my emotions, I knew how to pace myself. Joe didn't, and he would probably get sick as a dog, as he had all the other times we'd been out — almost every Friday and Saturday since we'd moved into our dorm room a couple months earlier. But I knew from experience that pointing this out would be useless, so I just shook my head and didn't comment.

"So what are your plans for the weekend?" I asked instead. "It's already Friday, we should decide if we want to go somewhere or just spend it on campus."

"Way ahead of you," he answered. "I'm going away with some guys from my physics class. I'll be back on Sunday evening. What about you?"

"Nothing, really," I said. "I think I'll just stay and study, since I'll have free rein of our room."

"Why don't you come with us? So you can be among men and have some fun for once in your life."

I very briefly considered it. *Very* briefly. Spending two days with a bunch of dudes, most of whom I barely knew and some not at all? Sounded like a recipe for awkwardness. No thanks.

"I'll take a rain check."

If Joe was disappointed by my answer, it didn't show. "Your loss."

"Well, hello, *boys*," a voice came from behind me. "Fancy meeting you here tonight."

I felt my blood run cold.

"Oh, hi, Anna!" Joe said, looking over my shoulder, his lips curling into a slight smile as he glanced at me to see my reaction. "How are you?"

"I'm quite well, thank you."

Joe was still looking at me, so I turned around. "Anna. Hi."

"Hi yourself," she replied, her cool, steel-gray eyes looking down at me from her full six feet.

Anna was a stunning woman. Tall and lean, with close-cropped hair dyed a deep violet. She was also dressed in her usual all black, mostly leather along with several chrome accessories which were polished to a mirror sheen. Every time I looked at her I wished I could be brave enough to try out something like that with my looks, or at least something different from my usual jeans and sweatshirt.

The first time we'd met in class I'd even asked her out, but she very quickly shot me down. That's how I found out she was a liberal-brained, PC-poisoned lesbian.

"How are you doing?" Anna asked. "Have you thought about what we talked about this afternoon?"

I gritted my teeth. "I did, yes."

She smiled at me. "So how about it? Are you enlightened yet?"

"I was *already* enlightened, I—"

"Guess not. It's a shame, really. You're not nearly as dumb as you look, and you would be a cool dude if you just learned to respect other people."

I bristled at her words — how dare she call me *dude*? "I can respect people just fine," I said.

"Really?" she said, completely deadpan.

"Yes, really. I respect people for who they are, though, not for their opinions."

"Well, let's put that to the test, shall we? Let's make a bet." She crossed her arms and smiled teasingly. "Ten bucks."

"Interesting," Joe said. "A bet on what?"

"On whether you can *actually* respect people for who they are. I'm going to introduce you to someone, and if you can manage to hold a conversation without insulting them, you win."

"Deal," I said.

"Good." Anna pulled a ten-dollar bill from her pocket and placed it on a nearby table, then looked at us expectantly. After a moment I realized what she was waiting for, and I took two fivers from my wallet.

"Spot me?" Joe asked. I frowned at him, but pulled out ten more dollars, and set all twenty on the table.

"Alright, let me call my theyfriend over," Anna said. "I think you'll like them."

Joe tilted his head to the side. "*Theyfriend?*" he asked. "What's a theyfriend?"

"You'll see." Anna looked around the crowd and waved at someone. "Hey, Elanor! Over here!"

I turned to look at the person approaching us, and gave a start of surprise.

They were taller than Anna due to the heels they were wearing — with a large, muscular frame, blonde, shoulder-length, carefully styled hair, and wide hazel eyes framed by makeup which had clearly been meticulously applied. They were wearing a dress that went down to their ankles.

"This is Elanor," Anna said, gesturing at the newcomer. "My theyfriend. Don't they look nice?" She leaned over and gave Elanor a peck on the lips.

I stared at Elanor for a moment, then my mouth — fueled by booze — moved faster than my brain.

"Are you a man or a woman?" I asked.

Elanor's eyebrows pinched together momentarily. Then, in a deep voice, came the answer: "Neither. I'm non-binary."

"Ha!" Joe scoffed. "As if!"

Anna looked at him, her expression unreadable. "What, we got a problem?"

"Yes, we do," Joe replied. "That's not a real thing."

"Well, plenty of people seem to think it is." Anna scowled. "And it's been *a real thing* for literally millennia; there's clear historical proof of non-binary people in ancient civilizations."

"Maybe such things should be left in the past," Joe said.

"Or maybe it's just you being a small-minded bigot," Anna shot back, a smirk forming on her lips.

I could see Joe's face go red. The insult had clearly sent him over the edge, and while he normally would've been able to mostly keep his cool, he was too drunk not to lose control. "Shut the fuck up, you dyke!" he shouted.

Too loudly. Everyone in the room turned to look at us, the only noise the slowly pulsating background music.

"Would you look at that," Anna said. "Guess I win." She scooped up the thirty dollars and stuffed them into her pocket.

"Well done, dear," Elanor said, smiling and giving Anna a half-hug.

Joe seemed to realize what he'd done. "I . . . Uh . . ." He looked around, clearly embarrassed.

As I'd done a few times before, I took charge. I set our beers on a nearby table, then grabbed him by the arm. "Come on, let's go," I said as I guided him out of the frat house. As an afterthought, I turned back on the threshold and looked at Anna and Elanor. "Excuse us," I finished, then closed the door behind us.

⣿

"I honestly can't believe it," I slurred as we half-stumbled into our room. "*That* was supposed to be a woman?"

"Nuh . . . Not a woman," Joe drawled. "You heard him. He's non-binary or sumthin'."

I waved my hand dismissively. "Saaaaaaaaaaame difference. Remember Joe, there's only men and women. Nothing else. And she clearly wasn't a man, so she must have been a woman."

Joe's eyes stared into the void for a second, completely unfocused as he tried to concentrate, before finally grasping the thought he'd been chasing. "Nah again, bro. Remember what we talked about earlier?"

I took off my shoes, almost tripping in the process, and flopped down on my bed, turning my head to look at Joe. "What are you talking about?"

"Y'know. The thing. A man pretending to be a woman. To get into women's changing rooms," he explained.

Right, I remembered, and I felt my forehead crease in thought. "Someone should do something about it."

"Nothing we can do about it. He says he's a woman . . ."

"Non-binary," I interjected.

"Same difference. He says it, and no one can disprove it. In fact, we could get in trouble for doubting him."

". . . It's not fair."

"It's not," he replied. "But it is what it is."

Joe closed the door. Since we hadn't bothered to turn on the lights, the room was filled with darkness. I heard a muffled shuffling — Joe taking off his clothes before going to bed. A small part of my brain wondered if I should do the same; a larger part was thinking about something else.

It wasn't fair. Someone could just say they were a woman, and everyone was supposed to believe it? Just like that?

It wasn't fair. You couldn't just become a woman. You couldn't just be a woman. That wasn't *how it worked.*

Men were men, and women were women. There was no way to change that simple fact, no matter how desperately someone wished foit. No matter how bad they felt about themselves.

Yes, of course, there must be *some* people for whom gender . . . dysplasia? Dyslexia? Dysmorphia?

Dysphoria.

There must be some people who suffered from gender dysphoria, but those were most certainly few and far between. I was absolutely sure most of the so-called *trans women* and *trans-feminine non-binary people* I sometimes spotted on campus were just pretending. Just . . . doing it to get ahead.

After all, life is much easier for trans people than it is for men, right? People always tell them they're so brave.

People practically worship the ground they walk on.

Someone had to do something. There had to be some way to prove that someone who wasn't trans (*cis*, I recalled the term) could just transition out of the blue, without needing to have gender dysphoria. Just *pretend to be trans.*

What if someone actually did it, I thought. Transitioned. To prove it was possible. Someone who had never thought about becoming a woman before. Someone who didn't suffer from gender dysphoria. Someone like . . . like . . .

"Joe, you still awake?" I asked the darkness.

"Hwuh? Yeah," came the sleepy answer. "Whassup?"

"Tell me a girl's name."

There was a long pause.

"Dude, what the fuck?"

"Tell me a name. A girl's name."

"What the hell, man?"

"Just do it, please."

"Okay. Anna."

". . . What the fuck? No!"

"What? You asked me for a girl's name!"

"Not *that* one!"

"Okay, okay. What then?"

I thought for a moment. "I dunno. What are girls named after? Flowers, maybe?"

Silence once again.

"Dude, did you fall asleep on me?" I asked.

"Nah man, just thinking. What about Rose?"

"Rose's an old lady name. Do I look like an old lady to you?"

"Uh . . . What?" Joe said. "Why is this suddenly about you?"

I gestured dismissively, even though he couldn't see it in the darkness. "Never mind. Come on, tell me another."

"Okay. Iris."

"Isn't that a part of the eye?"

"Also a flower," he replied, but the last word was cut out by a yawn — Joe was clearly about to fall asleep.

"Pass. Tell me another."

"Amaranth."

I turned my head and frowned in the direction his voice had come from. "The fuck's an amaranth?"

"A flower. Isn't that what you asked for?"

"Pass."

The silence stretched longer this time.

"Dude? You still awake?"

"Bwuh?"

"I said 'pass'. Give me another."

"Fiiiine. Lily."

All the names Joe had said so far had bounced off my brain. 'Lily' though, floated right in, settled down, and made herself a comfortable nest deep inside my mind.

I turned to lie on my back and stared at the darkness above me.

Joe began to snore softly.

"Lily," I whispered as I fell asleep.

2
Coming Out

Tʜᴇ ᴡᴀʀᴅʀᴏʙᴇ ᴅᴏᴏʀ slammed shut. I lurched to a sitting position, then groaned as pain pierced my head.

One thing I hated about drinking on the weekends was that I'd get too drunk and the following mornings were always terrible. Every time this happened, I'd think about quitting booze for good.

And then the background noise my mind always produced would start up again and I'd reach for another beer just so I could sleep without the constant ringing in my ears.

I squeezed my eyes shut for a few moments to dispel the pain, then forced them open. Joe was bent over the bottom drawers of his wardrobe and was rummaging inside them.

"What the fuck, man, can't you be quiet? It's not even . . ." I glanced at my bedside clock, then continued, "It's not even eight and it's a Saturday. Why are you being so loud?"

"I'm late! he yelled over his shoulder. "Overslept a bit. I'm supposed to meet my bros in five minutes, and I haven't even had breakfast." He pulled out an undershirt, a pair of boxers, and a pair of socks, hurriedly stuffed them in a duffel bag, and slammed the drawer shut.

"You're *always* late," I protested. "And you always make too much noise when you're getting ready for something. Maybe I would've liked to sleep in, you know?"

Joe kept gathering his things, not looking at me or even acknowledging my complaint, and my eyes narrowed as my glare bore a hole in his back. This was another part of him I hated: he never, *never* apologized, even when he was clearly in the wrong.

"And maybe if you hadn't drunk so much last night you'd have woken up in time," I continued. Yeah, I was being a little snippy — plus, glass houses and stones and everything — but my head was throbbing and I was honestly quite annoyed at his behavior.

In response, Joe just laughed. "What are you, my mother?" he replied. "Why do you care about how much I drink?" I opened my mouth to answer, but he preempted me. "Don't bother, I'm in a hurry. I can't be here talking to you right now."

He picked up his duffel bag and rushed out the door, slamming it behind him without so much as a "goodbye" or "see ya".

I stared at the closed door for a few moments, then wordlessly grumbled in my throat, shaking my head.

Why did I have to be assigned such an ass as a roommate? Yes, Joe could be cool sometimes, and I liked having someone I could vent my frustrations to, but on many — most? — occasions he was *the source* of those frustrations: an abrasive jerk who drove me crazy.

I pulled open my nightstand, took out a bottle of painkillers, and popped two pills. Then I flopped back down, closed my eyes, and tossed and turned for an entire hour as I tried and failed to fall asleep again.

How did Joe even *do* it? I was used to drinking and I'd had only a few beers — how many had I drunk again? I honestly couldn't remember, but I was terribly hungover: every muscle in my body ached, and my head felt like it was being squeezed in a vice, despite the ibuprofen. Joe'd had quite a few more, yet he'd seemed entirely fine. God, if it weren't for the fact that alcohol was the only way I'd found to keep my anxiety and emotions at bay, I would gladly have stopped drinking altogether — the side effects were barely worth it.

I turned onto my back, opened my eyes, and stared at the ceiling again as I tried to remember what we'd done the previous night. We'd gone to Theta Omega Tau's frat party, drank a bit, chatted among ourselves, and then . . .

Oh. Right.

Anna. And Elanor.

And all of a sudden, I was angry again. At Anna. At Elanor. At the world in general.

Everything I'd thought about before falling asleep last night came flooding back. Even though he'd been drunk, the me from the previous evening had been on the right track.

It wasn't *fair*. You couldn't change your sex just like that. It wasn't fair to the rest of us.

No, sir, I did *not* like it. I would see to it that they were put in their rightful place. (*Who are 'they'?* a voice in the back of my mind said, but I quickly and expertly shut it up.)

I dragged myself out of bed, sat down at my laptop, and fired up Google. I had some reading to do.

≣

One hour later, my stomach was trying to bring attention to the fact that I hadn't put anything in it besides beer since lunch on the previous day. However, I didn't notice, since I was staring at the screen in puzzlement.

Judging by all the searching I'd done, it seemed that self-ID was . . . good, actually? I'd gone on a deep dive through a mixture of liberal and conservative websites and besides the really fringe, far-right ones (which I knew were not to be relied on — no one who uses slurs while making an argument is worth paying attention to) they all agreed that trans people's ability to just declare their gender was a net positive.

For trans people.

While the liberal sources I'd read made no mention of it, the more conservative ones made it very clear that self-ID would also allow people who *weren't* trans to say they were a different gender than their real one, and this would allow them to get ahead in life in a variety of ways. Gaining access to women's toilets and changing rooms, for one; but also, if a man were to say he was a woman he would suddenly be included in "all-women" categories for stuff like employment, awards, diversity quotas, and sports.

Any man could do it just to progress in life. And meanwhile, he would get a rush, a thrill of excitement, whenever someone told him how brave and strong he was for coming out as trans.

It wasn't *fair*. They got to be women (no, to *behave* as women, I quickly corrected myself), and they gained society's respect. *It wasn't fair.*

The idea I'd had the previous night, the idea I'd half-remembered that morning, floated upwards through my brain, spread out, and settled in.

From the outside I looked like the perfect candidate for being a trans girl deep in denial: much like the women I'd read about, I was going nowhere in life — I was struggling in school, I had very few friends and a limited social life, and I had very few prospects after college. I was, if the liberal websites were to be trusted, a textbook example of someone who could majorly benefit from transition.

Suppose I said I was trans? That I was a woman? That, after a lifetime of feeling bad about myself, after years of dysphoria and depression, I'd finally figured out I was actually a girl?

I could just . . . *pretend*. Just go along with it for a while, until finally I would reveal that — psych! It was all a trick! Joke's on you, I was just pretending! I had you all fooled!

That would prove it. Definitely. Without a shadow of a doubt. After all, I was a cisgender man. True, I wasn't very manly to begin with, but still: if someone like me could convince everyone they knew I was actually a girl — a trans woman — it would be a clear demonstration that anyone could do it and, indeed, that many other men *had* done it.

The thought of having everyone refer to me as a girl, of going around dressed in skirts and dresses, of being called *Lily*, sent a thrill of excitement down my spine and gave me a weird sensation in the pit of my stomach.

A lot of people would be surprised at first: after all, my political beliefs didn't exactly align with the left. But during my research that morning, I'd read that one thing commonly said about trans people was, "There were no signs." Even people who were closest to a trans person didn't realize he or she (or they?) were trans until the person actually came out.

So I could do that.

At first the idea sounded remote. Far-fetched. Unbelievable. Crazy. Insane.

But the more I thought about it, the more excited I became: besides the whole prove-cis-people-can-transition-too bit, spending time as a woman sounded really enticing. I'd often wondered what life was like on the other side, and this was a good chance to experience it.

And then I would reveal I was just pretending.

This was great. It was clearly the best idea I'd had in quite a while, the best idea ever, maybe. I would handily prove a point which had been argued back and forth for years, and show everyone what I was capable of doing when I put my mind to it.

Anna was the linchpin. The key to everything. She and I had butted heads over politics and social issues several times since we'd first met; the previous day's discussion about self-ID had been the latest in a series of arguments. If I could convince Anna, I was confident I could convince everyone.

I had to act then and there. I had to meet up with Anna and put my plan into action. There was just one problem: finding Anna.

We weren't even remotely friends, and I had no idea where she lived. I couldn't wander around aimlessly hoping to meet her: Bradford McKinley wasn't a big college, but it was still home to several thousand students. There was no way I would run into someone I knew out of the blue.

I would have to wait until Monday when I would see her in class. I would ask to talk in private and get things rolling.

That thought made me sad. The idea of having to wait two full days before I heard someone call me Lily bummed me out: I'd been looking forward to hearing that name said out loud, and now I had to put everything on hold, to be my usual self for two days more.

But it couldn't be helped, could it?

Unless . . .

Bradford McKinley was known for the variety of cultural events it hosted on campus, and student life was lively. Not for me, however: after a full week of being forced to socialize in class, I was utterly exhausted and, most of the time, shut myself in my room to be alone — Joe having gone some place with his buddies. Surely this weekend there'd be an event someone like Anna would like and show up for. I could go and look for her.

I opened another tab and checked the day's events. Yeah, there it was. That afternoon there would be a queer poetry bash in the quad. I had no idea what a poetry bash even was, but if it was *queer*, it was surely something Anna would like.

I would find her there. Probably. Maybe.

Honestly, I had no idea, but it was worth a shot. It was certainly better than waiting two more days for someone to see me as a girl.

Yes, definitely.

I would go to the queer poetry bash, find Anna, and tell her I was actually trans and a woman. And . . . Well, then I would have to go from here. But I was sure I could improvise.

I was clearly a genius.

Before I could get too satisfied with myself, my stomach growled, and I decided it was time to eat. It was early for lunch, but I could always go for a late breakfast.

Absent-mindedly, I lifted my arm, sniffed my armpit, and grimaced.

Shower first, a change of clothes, then breakfast. Even though I was a guy, I still cared quite a bit about my personal hygiene.

≣

". . . And this concludes our queer poetry bash, y'all," the speaker announced into the microphone. "Thanks for coming, and have a good evening."

Well, that had been . . . fun? Fun-ish? Question mark?

To be completely honest, the meaning of most of the poems (were they even poems if they were apparently ad-libbed by whoever wanted to walk on stage?) went right over my head, and I wasn't really paying attention anyway. At first I'd been trying to spot Anna in the crowd — which hadn't been hard, since she was quite tall and her violet hair was very noticeable — and then I'd been thinking about how to approach her once the show was over.

In the end, I decided the best thing to do was to just be completely honest and upfront.

(A loose definition of "honest" and "upfront", anyway.)

Taking a deep breath, I sped up and weaved through the crowd until I was close to her. But not too close, I didn't want to startle her.

"Anna. Hey," I said.

She turned around, a puzzled expression on her face, but when she saw me her gaze turned stern.

"Oh, it's *you*," she replied. "What are you doing here?"

I flashed her my best grin. "Hey, can't this be a coincidence? Maybe I'm the kind of person who enjoys a queer poetry jam."

"Bash."

I blinked. Right. "Jam, bash. Same difference."

Anna didn't say anything, but from the look in her eyes she definitely didn't buy that I was there for the event.

"Where's Elanor, anyway?" I asked. "Isn't she with you?"

"*They're* not here," Anna said pointedly. "They had to study, and this type of thing isn't really their jam anyway, so I came alone."

"Bash," I said.

She gave me a curious look. "Excuse me?"

"You said it's not her . . . *their*, sorry," I said, raising a hand in apology. "It's not their jam, but it's not a jam, it's a bash, right? Right?"

I'm sure I looked like that meme where a moray eel has just told a particularly bad joke, but still Anna smiled — very briefly, I almost missed it — before she resumed staring sternly at me.

"What are you doing here?" she asked again, then when I opened my mouth to speak, she held up a finger. "And don't try to say you enjoy this kind of show again, this *clearly* isn't your thing." She paused. "Wait, have you been following me? Because that's—"

"No, no, I haven't been *following* you." I held up my hands. "Not really. I . . . Well, I was looking for you. I wanted to talk to you, and I read about the queer poetry jam . . ."

"Bash."

". . . and I thought I might find you here, so here I am."

Anna pursed her lips in thought. "And *why* did you come here to find me? Do you want to continue the argument we had in class? Well, too bad. I don't have time for that; I have better things to do."

"No, I don't want to continue the argument. But it's actually related to that," I said. "I . . . First of all, I wanted to apologize. For what happened yesterday evening." She gave me a puzzled look, so I continued, "You know, with the bet. After you introduced Elanor I asked what was probably an impolite question, and Joe . . ." I drifted off and gulped. "So, yeah. Sorry."

Anna's expression softened a bit. "You don't have to apologize for that."

I looked at her in surprise. "I don't?"

"No, you don't," she said. "You weren't the one who called me a dyke: Joe did that. And he was also the one who dismissed Elanor's gender identity. Your question was far from polite, true, but who hasn't put their foot in their mouth at one time or the other? I know I did. And you do recognize that what you said was wrong." Again, she paused for a moment and her mouth quirked pensively, before she continued, "Apology accepted on one condition."

"And that is?"

"You have to repeat the apology to Elanor when you see them next."

I nodded. "I can do that, yeah."

"Good." Anna smiled another brief smile. "So, what else?"

"What do you mean?" I asked.

"Well, you said, 'First of all, I have to apologize,' which implies there's something else. So, what else do you want to say?"

"I . . ." I began, and looked around. The crowd had thinned and dispersed, but there were still several people who could overhear us if they wanted to. "About that — can we speak in private?"

Anna looked around too. "Is that really necessary?"

"Yes, it is," I answered. "I'm not going to be all dramatic and say, 'What I have to say is for your ears alone,' but . . . I'd prefer to tell you without anyone else hearing it."

She held my gaze for a few moments, raising a questioning eyebrow, then nodded. "Alright. Come with me."

She turned and strode away. After a moment's hesitation I followed, struggling a bit to catch up — she was walking very briskly, and her legs covered more ground than mine because of her height. In a short while we'd reached some benches, which were unoccupied and set off to the side of the quad, away from the usual avenues of traffic but still in plain view of the crowd: no one would be able to hear us talking there, but we were still visible. We were still in public.

Anna clearly didn't trust me enough to be alone with me.

That made me feel a bit bad, but then again I did deserve it, didn't I? She was right to distrust me, judging from how I'd behaved with her so far.

I suddenly felt a pang of guilt at the idea of deceiving her. My throat felt tight.

She plopped down on a bench and gestured for me to sit too.

"So?" she asked.

Alright. Moment of truth.

"Okay. So." I took a seat, keeping some space between the two of us. "Well, you see . . . yesterday you asked me if I'd given some thought to what we'd talked about in class." Anna nodded in acknowledgment, and I took it as permission to continue speaking. "Truth is . . . I *have* been thinking about it. Very much so. All of yesterday, and this morning too.

Something about what you said just . . . clicked. And I couldn't get it out of my mind. I did some reading. Lots of reading. Lots of research. And . . ." I paused. My mouth suddenly felt dry.

When I didn't continue Anna looked at me, frowning slightly. "And? What do you mean? What are you trying to say?"

I licked my lips. "What I'm trying to say is . . ."

I paused again and looked at the ground. *Why is this so hard? Just tell her.* I clenched my fists.

But somehow, I just couldn't get the words out.

God, was I really going to go through with this?

Suddenly I was doubting myself. Was this really right? To pretend to be a girl? And what for? To get back at someone? And who was that someone? Yeah, right, "the libs", but what did that even mean?

The silence stretched for several seconds until Anna huffed impatiently. "Come on, out with it. What is it?"

I looked up at her and frowned a bit. Something about her attitude really ticked me off and spurred me to continue my plan despite my doubts.

"I think I'm a girl," I quickly blurted out before my courage could fail me again.

There. I was committed.

There was another moment of silence as Anna looked at me; first her eyes widened in surprise, then she regarded me carefully. Then, after what felt like hours but was probably ten seconds at most, she spoke.

"Okay!" she said brightly. "What are your pronouns?"

I blinked in surprise. That's it? "That's it? You believe me? Just like that?" Was it really going to be *that* easy?

"I believe you, just like that," Anna nodded. "I'm not in the business of doubting someone's stated gender: if you say you're a girl, then you're a girl. And, *God*, this makes so much sense!"

I tilted my head to the side, puzzled. "It does?"

"Yeah, it really does. From how you behaved . . . Well, let me tell you, I've met many a spiky egg in my time."

"I'm sorry, what's a 'spiky egg' again? I think you've lost me."

"Well, I guess that's one thing that didn't come up in your research," she said, smirking. "An 'egg' is a trans person who has yet to realize they're trans, like you were until a while ago. And a spiky egg is an egg with spikes, of course: to cope with their dysphoria, they lash out at the world around them. Like you did until a while ago."

"Yeah, that makes sense."

"It does, doesn't it? But that's beside the point. So, what are your pronouns?"

I'd done enough research to know how to answer that question. "Uh . . . she and her, please."

"Cool, cool," she said, smiling encouragingly. "And do you have a name yet? It's okay if you—"

"Lily."

I hadn't meant to blurt out the name, but when she asked the question, my brain got ahead of itself and it just happened.

Her eyes widened, but then she smiled again. "You *have* been thinking about this a lot, haven't you? And it's a beautiful name, too." She paused and inclined her head slightly to the side. "Oh, cute, you're blushing."

"I am?" I touched my cheek — it *did* feel warm.

"Yep, you are. And with that, I think it's only fair we start over." She scooted closer to me on the bench, closing the gap between us, and extended her hand. "Hi, I'm Anna!"

I hesitantly took her hand and shook it. "Hi, I'm Lily."

Anna gave my hand a reassuring squeeze. "It's really nice to finally meet you, Lily."

And despite the fact I was going to be deceiving her for the foreseeable future, when Anna said my name I couldn't help but smile.

3

Both Sides

"**M**AN, I WILL never get tired of this." Anna inclined her head slightly and looked at me carefully.

I raised a questioning eyebrow. "Of what?"

"Seeing trans people's expressions when you use their chosen names for the first time," she replied. "Their faces light up, like yours just did. It's actually incredible. One of the wonders of the world."

My other eyebrow raised too. "You mean . . . you've done this before?"

Anna let go of my hand and leaned back into the bench. "Only a couple times," she said. "With Elanor, and another friend of mine. You don't know them. You're the third one, but your reaction was the same."

Really? I'd had the same reaction when she called me "Lily" as when she called Elanor, well, "Elanor?" And the same for another of her trans friends?

Huh.

Weird.

I very briefly wondered what that meant, but didn't have time to think about it before Anna spoke again.

"So, who else knows?"

Even though I was determined to be careful — I'd probably have to start taking notes, to make sure I didn't contradict myself — that question was easy enough. "No one," I replied. "You're the first person I've told."

"Really? You haven't told anyone?" she said, seemingly taken aback. "Not even Joe? Or your parents?"

Her question gave me pause. She was right: apparently Lily, a young trans girl, had first disclosed her identity to someone she didn't see eye to eye with instead of someone she knew and trusted. And that thought brought another consideration to the surface right away: did Lily — did I — actually trust Joe, or my parents for that matter, to not hate me if I came out to them?

For Joe, the answer was clear as day: no. No, Joe was someone who would never accept having a trans person as a friend, or even as an acquaintance. So I needed to be careful around him, and decide when and where to tell him I was trans. Maybe I'd do it in public, so he would think twice about his reaction, to avoid—

No, wait. Hold on. Why would I even tell Joe I was trans in the first place? After all, I wasn't really trans, I was just pretending, right? I could just tell him that. Tell him the truth. I'm sure he would think it was completely hilarious; maybe he would even volunteer to help me somehow.

Yeah, I should probably tell Joe about my plan the next time I saw him. To avoid any misunderstandings, and to have someone to talk to and bounce ideas off as my plan progressed.

But that's not what *Lily* would have said, was it?

I sighed — or pretended to sigh, at least. "No, I haven't told Joe," I said. "Simply put . . . Well . . . You know how he is. He's a bigot. You said as much yesterday."

I felt a small pang of guilt at having to insult Joe behind his back, but Anna just nodded. "Yeah, I did. But still, aren't you two friends? Do you really think he would hate you for being trans?"

"I don't know." I shook my head. "Sometimes I wonder what goes on in his head; one moment he's really friendly and the next he cold-shoulders me. And since I have to room with him for the foreseeable future . . .'

"You can't risk it," Anna said.

"Right, you get it," I said, spreading my hands. "As for my parents . . . I don't know about them, honestly. They were good parents as I was growing up, only . . . distant. I've never really talked at length with either of them, they had a very hands-off style of parenting. But I've heard them bad-mouth people for being different several times and I know for a fact that every time they've voted, they've marked the R option. I mean . . ." I looked up at Anna. "I'm sure they love me, but that's the problem: they love *me*. Will they love *Lily* too? Or will they—"

I stopped talking as I realized something. I hadn't needed to lie about my parents. I'd given a perfect description of the two people who'd raised me, and for the first time ever I was forced to wonder: would they still love me if I was different somehow? I don't mean if I was trans — wasn't trans — but if I somehow disappointed them? Let them down? If I was less than the perfect golden boy they thought me to be? If they found out about my drinking, for instance, or if I made a life decision they didn't approve of, like dating or marrying someone they thought was different?

Would they still love me, or drop me like a hot coal?

No, I told myself firmly. This was not the time to be having these thoughts. I would have to examine them in detail later.

"I mean, I will have to tell them eventually," I said. "This isn't something I can hide forever. But . . ." I sighed. "I would very much prefer to wait until I really *have to*." I locked eyes with Anna. "You know what I mean?"

"I do," she replied. "My parents were the same."

"They were?"

"Oh yeah," she said. "I told them I was gay when I was fourteen, and let me tell you, they did not take it well. At all. It took several months before they even started speaking to me again, and several *years* before we were on cordial terms." She smiled ruefully. "They accept it now, of course, but it took some work. Lots of work. And they were very much like your parents, except for the fact that they always voted Democrat instead of the GOP."

"Huh," I said. Surprising. I had no idea. I thought all Democrats — all liberals — were automatically accepting of gay and trans identities, but apparently this wasn't the case.

"Look, I should really be going," Anna said, glancing at her watch. "It's getting late, and I have to meet up with Elanor." She smiled at me. "Thank you for trusting me with your secret, Lily. I promise I won't tell."

When she said the name I felt my cheeks warm up a bit again, but then I realized I still had to put another part of my plan into motion.

"Actually, before you go there's something else I want to ask you."

"Ask away."

"Well, like I told you, I only realized this . . . *this*, over the past few days. And to be honest, I don't know left from right at this point." Which was true. I mean, I'd read lots of things on the internet, but knew you should never believe what you read online without cross-checking it. And it was better to ask someone you trusted anyway. "So I was wondering if you had any resources about how I should handle this," I said. "Something that could help me. Anything at all."

Anna put her finger to her chin and thought for a bit. "Well, actually, there *is* something," she said. "Our college has a counselor, I heard she's really good about this stuff. Saunders? Sanders? Something like that. I have a couple friends who've talked to her when they were figuring stuff out."

"Okay, I'll look her up."

"And also . . . Well, there's a queer club. I'm part of it, actually. It's a GSA, we meet once a week."

"GSA?"

"Genders and sexualities alliance," she explained. "It's a safe space where everyone is free to express themselves without fear of being judged or outed. I'll ask one of the coordinators if I can bring you to the next meeting."

I mentally scoffed. A *safe space*? Really? What do they need to be safe from? But I didn't say that, of course. "Alright." I stood up. "Thank you, Anna."

"Any time, Lily." She offered me her hand and I yelped, startled, when she pulled me into a tight hug.

"Don't let the world tear you down, girl," Anna whispered in my ear. "Remember, you are worth it, and there are people who are willing to help you."

She released me and stepped back. "See you on Monday," she said with a smile, then turned and walked away.

I looked at her for a few seconds, then at my watch. It was almost five, so I decided to get back to my room to study before heading to dinner.

As I walked toward the dorm building, I thought about my conversation with Anna. It had been . . . pleasant? Yeah, that was the correct term. Pleasant. Which was surprising, because the day before we *really* didn't agree on things and she barely gave me the time of day. This time she'd listened to me carefully, and I'd really enjoyed talking to her. She'd been warm, caring, and supportive.

Yeah, but she's only being caring and supportive because she thinks you're a trans girl, said a voice in the back of my mind, and I realized it was completely true. If she knew I was really a cis guy, she would never have treated me like that.

Typical liberal.

I gave a wave to the RA, sitting behind his desk, on my way into the dorm. When I put the key in my room door lock, I realized it was unlocked. Weird.

I pushed down the handle and walked in.

"Dude!" Joe exclaimed. "Welcome back!"

"Joe?" I said, freezing in surprise. "What are you doing here? I thought you weren't supposed to be back until tomorrow."

"Change of plans. Meet my pals!" Joe waved in the general direction of two other people who were holding open cans of beer — and sitting on my bed, I realized with some irritation.

"Eddie," one of them said.

The other one waved. "Tommy."

"Nice to meet you," I said, deciding to be polite. Then I turned back to Joe. "What happened? Why are you back so soon?"

"Nothing much," he said, swigging from a can. "We had some differences of opinion with the owner of the hostel we were supposed to stay at."

"Kicked us out, that's what he did," Eddie commented.

"What? Why?" I asked.

"Something about us being too loud and talking back when he said we weren't allowed to bring booze inside the building," Joe said. "Gonna sue him to get our money back."

"We don't need to get our money back," Tommy said. "We hadn't even paid in the first place."

Joe shrugged. "Whatever. Maybe I'll sue him for breach of contract then, for canceling our reservation with no warning. Let's see if I can get a couple hundred out of it."

Tommy laughed. "Oh, come on, Joe, we all know you're loaded."

"Wait, you are?" I looked at Joe: this was the first I was hearing about it. Usually he borrowed money from me, like he'd done to cover his share of the bet at the party.

"You don't know?" Eddie said. "His old man is a bigwig back home. Oil money, apparently."

"Which I can't touch," Joe replied. "My parents monitor my expenses very closely. Got caught buying something I wasn't supposed to one time too many."

"That means booze, if it wasn't clear," Eddie said.

Joe nodded. "That it does. But booze is good." He raised his can, and Tommy and Eddie hit their own against it.

I looked at them for a moment, then sighed. Well, there went my peaceful Saturday evening and Sunday morning. "Okay, alright. But could you tell your friends not to sit on my bed, please?"

Joe quirked an eyebrow at me, but when I held his gaze he nodded and waved at Tommy and Eddie, who dutifully sat on Joe's bed instead.

"Here, have a drink," Joe said, reaching into a duffel bag and lobbing a beer at me, which I caught in mid-air.

I looked at it for a moment and briefly considered opening it and taking a sip. But I remembered I still had to study, and drinking alcohol isn't very conducive to that. And besides, for whatever reason, the "buzz" — the background emotional noise I always felt — was way less loud than usual. It had been ever since I'd talked to Anna, I realized, and wondered why that was.

"Nah, I'm good," I said, tossing the can back to Joe. "I'm gonna do some studying before dinner."

I sat down at my desk, opened my laptop, and typed in my password.

The words, "So you've realized you're transgender" appeared in big bold letters on my screen.

Shit.

I hurriedly closed the page I'd left open before heading out, and glanced at Joe and his friends. They were talking among themselves, not paying attention to me, so apparently hadn't noticed. I let out a small breath of relief. Even though I'd decided to tell Joe about my plan, it was better to do it before he noticed anything, to avoid any possible misunderstandings.

I focused back on my computer, pulled up the document I transcribed my class notes in , and then opened my textbook and notebook and got to studying.

Ten minutes later, I was annoyed.

Joe, Tommy, and Eddie were still chatting and drinking. And not quietly either: they were making it all but impossible for me to focus.

At first I gritted my teeth and tried to bear it — this was Joe's room too — but after yet another crass joke-uproarious laughter combo, I turned in my chair to look directly at them.

"Can't you guys be quiet?" I said. "I'm trying to study here."

Joe looked at me, eyes slightly unfocused but widening in surprise, but then he laughed again. "Oh, come on!" he said. "We're just talking!"

"Yeah, but your *talking* is really loud," I rebutted. "And I can't concentrate. Could you . . . I dunno, go somewhere else? The common room, maybe?"

"Nah, no can do." Joe shook his head and held up his beer can. "Can't go to the common room with this."

"Well, leave it here!" I snapped. "Or better yet, throw it away. Seriously, guys, it's not even six and you're already drinking? What the hell!"

Joe stared at me. This was the first time I'd talked back to him like this. I had no idea why I did it either, but I was particularly on edge that evening — maybe it was a result of starting my plan to pretend to be transgender.

Eddie and Tommy, for their part, just laughed. "Oh, look, he's angry!" Eddie said. "Cute, he's so tiny and scrawny, it's adorable!"

I glowered at him. "Don't fucking call me *scrawny*."

"But you are," Tommy added. "Do you even work out, bro? Maybe we should check your man card, make sure it's not a fake."

I blinked. Did he just . . . ?

"Okay. Get out," I hissed.

The three of them looked at me in surprise. "What?" Eddie said.

"You heard me. Out. I don't want you in my room."

"Hey now, this is my room, too!" Joe said. "I have a right—"

"You can stay," I replied. "But they can't. Get lost."

Tommy started to get up. "Listen here, you . . ." he began to say, but Joe raised a hand to stop him.

"Okay," he said. "Okay, they're going. We're going. Come on, guys."

He drained the last of his beer and tossed the can in the waste bin, then stood up and pulled a football from his wardrobe. Following his friends, he started walking out of the room, but then stopped and looked back at me. I just quietly met his gaze, and he turned and left, closing the door behind him.

The room was quiet.

For a second.

Then just outside of the door, I heard Joe shout, "Hey, Ed! Go long!"

The shout was followed by a loud crashing noise and a grunt of pain.

"Yeah, boy!" Tommy shouted. "That was awesome, dude!"

I marched to the door and opened it, looking into the corridor. Eddie was lying on the floor a few meters away, surrounded by pieces of plastic which were the remains of what had probably been a small folding table; flyers and pamphlets were scattered all around, and he wasn't moving.

"Dude, are you okay?" Tommy asked.

Eddie grunted, but then rolled over onto his back. "I'm fine!" he shouted, throwing a double thumbs-up. "Super okay! Doesn't hurt one bit! Please tell me you caught that on video!"

I shook my head in disbelief. What even the hell? I hadn't had many friends growing up, so I couldn't help but wonder: was this how men normally behaved?

"Alright, what the hell is going on here?" a voice called from down the corridor. I looked up and saw Darrell jogging toward us. "What happened? Did you do something again, Thompson?"

"No sir," Joe said. "Not at all. It was just an accident; my friend tripped on that table."

"Table?" Darrell surveyed the scene for a moment, then bent over and picked up one of the flyers. "The Bradford McKinley Libertarian Association," he muttered under his breath. "Fucking *hell*, I keep telling them they can't just leave their shit lying around without clearing it beforehand, but they think the rules don't apply to them." Then he offered his hand to Eddie, who grasped it and pulled himself to his feet. "Sorry, man, the table wasn't supposed to be there. But still, how did you not see it?"

"Well, um . . ." Eddie began, but Darrell's eyes darted around the corridor and he spotted the ball.

"How many times do I have to tell you, Thompson?" he said. "No ball games inside the building. It's in the dorm rules. You *know* that."

Joe shrugged. "Sorry, man. I forgot."

"How do you forget that?" Darrell asked. "In fact . . ." He sniffed loudly a couple times, then leaned toward Eddie and sniffed deeply again. "Have you guys been drinking?"

". . . No?" Tommy said.

"Alright. You, and you," Darrell said, pointing at Tommy and Eddie. "Get lost, the both of you."

He didn't need to say it twice; Joe's friends exchanged one look, then turned on their heels and quickly started walking toward the exit.

"As for you," Darrell continued, turning toward Joe, "give me the beer."

Joe hesitated. "But . . ." he began.

"Give me the beer," Darrell repeated. "I'm not going to ask a third time."

Joe looked at him for a moment, then nodded. I stepped aside to let him pass and he walked in, followed closely by Darrell. After rooting in his duffel bag, he pulled out a half a six-pack, which he handed to the RA.

"All of it," Darrell said. Joe hesitated, but complied. As I looked on, he sullenly pulled out another six-pack, and then another one. He gave both to Darrell.

"Be thankful I don't report you," he said. "Next time I catch you with booze in the dorm, I absolutely will."

"Yeah," Joe replied quietly, and Darrell left.

There was a moment of silence, then Joe turned to me.

"This is all your fault," he said.

"Um, excuse me, what? How is this my fault?"

"If you hadn't been such a pussy about having to study, Tommy, Eddie, and I wouldn't have had to leave the room, and Darrell wouldn't have caught us," Joe said. "But you did, and now I'm out twenty bucks for the beer, and that idiot will be watching me closely. I hope you're happy."

I just stared at him, at a loss as to what to say, for a moment, then shook my head. "You're unbelievable."

I sat at my desk and started studying again. Joe and I didn't exchange another word for the whole evening.

By the time I went to bed that night, telling him about my plan was the farthest thing from my mind.

4
Safe Space

JOE AND I still hadn't patched things up when I left the room on Monday morning. Yeah, maybe I was being stubborn in not letting the whole thing go, but on the other hand he still blamed me for Darrell taking his beer away: we'd exchanged roughly five words on Sunday, and they'd all been about that.

Truth be told, I was mad at him. I could understand his train of thought: he and his friends getting caught had directly stemmed from me asking them to leave the dorm room. But everything after that had been a result of their own actions. I wasn't the one who'd brought beer into the dorm, breaking the rules (and the law). I thought Joe would get it; I thought trying to shift the blame would be an initial reaction brought about by irritation and booze, and after he'd calmed down he would see he was wrong.

No such luck.

He didn't have classes on Monday mornings, so when I left he was reading a textbook at his desk, still in his pajamas. "See ya," I said. Perhaps it was the chilly tone in my voice, but he just grunted in response and didn't bother to look up. I frowned, but closed the door behind me and headed to class.

As I walked across campus, I thought about our fight. One thing specifically: the fact that, despite being wrong, he was refusing to back down from his position. What was up with that? If someone realizes they've done something wrong, they should try and make amends, right?

And yet.

I wondered if this was something specific to Joe, or if all men — all "bros" — behaved like this.

But for now, I had to put my head back into the game and concentrate on the role I was playing. I was about to see Anna for the first time since I'd "come out" to her — my first class for the day was social sciences, and she would undoubtedly be there.

I paused briefly in front of the classroom, took a deep breath, and lightly slapped my cheeks a couple times.

Alright, Lily. Showtime.

Anna spotted me immediately. She was talking with a few of her friends, but when she saw me cross the threshold her face lit up with a smile. She excused herself, and made her way over to me.

"Good morning," she said, still smiling. "How are you today?"

"I'm good," I replied. "Though I didn't really sleep that well. You?"

"Oh? Why's that?" she asked, eyebrows pinching together.

"I had a fight with Joe on Saturday, just after I met up with you."

Anna's frown deepened. "Ah," she said, in a tone indicating she'd already decided who was to blame. "Wanna talk about it?"

I considered it for a moment, then nodded. "Yes, actually. You see, Joe was . . ." I glanced around, checking no one was within earshot — I didn't want to completely ruin his reputation — then continued, ". . . He had been drinking with some of his friends, and the RA caught them and took the beer away. And now he's mad at me."

"Wait, what? Why would he be mad at *you?*" Anna said in surprise.

"Because they were drinking in our dorm room. Mine and Joe's, that is. They were being loud and annoying, so I asked them to leave, and they did. Then they started playing football in the hallway, caused some damage, and the RA found out about their drinking. So Joe says it's my fault they got caught."

". . . How would it be *your* fault? I don't get it."

"Because, and these are Joe's exact words, if I hadn't been such a pussy about having to study, they wouldn't have left the room, and they wouldn't have been found out."

Anna looked at me for a moment, mouth open in disbelief, then she scowled and shook her head. "Ugh. *Men,*" she said, almost spitting the word out. "Honestly, I can't believe them sometimes. Always acting so entitled, like the world revolves around them. Absolute trash."

"Hey now," I replied with a small laugh. "I could be offended by that."

She gave me a curious look. "Why?" She hesitated and, like I'd done earlier, glanced around before continuing. ". . . You're not a man, Lily."

Oh, right. The whole pretend-to-be-a-trans-girl thing. It had almost slipped my mind; I needed to be more careful about that.

"... Right," I said. "Sorry. I guess old habits die hard."

"Ah, don't worry about it," Anna said, squeezing my arm. "You'll get used to it in no time." She paused, as if thinking about something. "Oh, by the way, yesterday I sent a text to the people who manage the GSA. And they gave me the all clear to bring you to the next meeting. It's the day after tomorrow, after classes are over."

"Great." I smiled. "I'm looking forward to it." And that wasn't a lie; I really was curious about seeing what gay and transgender people got up to when they were in a safe space with no one but their own people around. It would be a learning experience, and maybe something I could use when I exposed the whole trans conspiracy for the world to see.

"I think it will do you good," Anna nodded. "You'll be able to meet other people like you. Having a community and support structure behind you is really important, especially nowadays with everything that's going on in this country."

"Right. So—"

"Good morning, class," Professor Markley said, stepping into the room. "If you'll take your seats..."

He stopped speaking when he saw me talking to Anna, and frowned at us — or, rather, at me.

"Are you giving Miss Suarez a hard time again, Mr. O'Connor?" he said, a tone of reproach in his voice. "Trying to continue Friday's ... discussion?"

I quickly shook my head. "No, not at all. We were just talking."

He seemed entirely unconvinced. "Were you now?" He looked at Anna.

"Yes, we were," Anna confirmed with a nod. "O'Connor is actually really nice once you get to know him."

She shot me an apologetic glance out of the corner of her eye — so brief I don't think anyone noticed it — and I realized, with some surprise, that she was silently apologizing for referring to me using a masculine pronoun.

Huh.

"Alright," Professor Markley nodded, after a moment's consideration. "Let's begin today's lesson."

"I'll text you later," Anna said, then clicked her tongue. "Uh, I just realized I don't have your number."

"Here, put yours in here." I pulled out my phone. "I'll message you so you know it's me."

She typed her name and number into my contacts, then smiled and rejoined her friends.

⧉

Glancing at the clock in the corner of the screen, I saw it was almost time to head out. The GSA meeting was going to start soon, and I had to leave to arrive there in time. I saved my homework, closed my laptop, and grabbed my keys, wallet, and phone.

"I'm leaving for a bit," I told Joe. "I'll be back later tonight."

He looked up from his book (I couldn't quite make out the title, but it had an American flag prominently displayed on the cover) and glanced at me. "Where are you going?"

I hadn't expected him to talk to me — we were still in a kind of cold war, mostly ignoring each other unless it was absolutely necessary. "To meet up with friends."

"You have friends?"

I suppressed my first instinct, which was to give him a snippy answer, and instead said, "Yeah, of course."

"Huh." He looked back down at the book.

I decided not to press the issue; instead I just left the room.

"Hi there!" Darrell said when he saw me walking toward the exit. "Heading out?"

"Yeah, just for a couple hours," I replied.

"Alright. Is everything okay with Joe?"

". . . What do you mean?"

"I know his type," he said. "I've been an RA for a few years now, I've had plenty of guys like him in the dorm. The kind of person who blames everyone but themselves for what happens to them. And considering what happened on Saturday . . ."

I thought about whether to tell Darrell about Joe blaming me for his booze getting confiscated, then decided against it. Joe wasn't doing anything truly bad anyway, he was just being his usual self. "His usual self" being an abrasive jerk, true, but I could deal with that, no problem.

"Everything's good," I said. "No problem at all."

"Okay." He paused for a moment, then continued. "Got your keys? I don't wanna have to come unlock the door for you again."

"Come on, it only happened the one time." I laughed, showing him my keyring.

"One time too many," Darrell laughed along. "Remember: 10 p.m., front door gets locked."

"Yeah, I'll remember."

"Good. See ya, then."

I stuffed my keys into my coat pocket as I left the building. As I did so, I idly thought about how unwieldy it was to carry all my stuff: my phone and wallet were in my pants pockets, and the keys would be joining them come spring when I would be going around without a coat or jacket. That was uncomfortable and looked ugly, so maybe I could buy a bag? I knew there were some men who wouldn't be caught dead with what they called a man-purse, but I wasn't one of them.

≡

When I arrived, Anna and Elanor were already waiting for me. Anna greeted me with a wave and a smile, while Elanor gave me a look halfway between annoyed and pissed off. I hadn't expected to see them — Anna hadn't told me they'd be coming — so I was momentarily taken aback, but then I remembered what I'd promised Anna I'd do.

I licked my lips.

"Elanor. Hi. I don't know if Anna spoke to you about this, but I wanted to apologize for what happened the last time we met." I paused, waiting for a reaction. Elanor just crossed their arms and inclined their head slightly, but didn't say anything, so I continued. "I recognize that what I said was wrong, so I just want to say I'm sorry. It won't happen again."

Elanor was silent for a few seconds more, then nodded. "Apology accepted," they said.

"Thank you."

They turned to Anna. "Is this all?" they asked.

"No, it's not," Anna replied, shaking her head. "We've a meeting to go to."

As Elanor looked at her in surprise Anna knocked on the door, which was opened by a tall girl with shoulder-length hair wearing a deep blue ankle-length dress and a black leather jacket. She smiled when she saw Anna.

"Anna, hi," she said. "Elanor. And . . ." She turned to me.

"Hi, Allie," Anna said. "This is the new person I told you about."

Allie nodded. "Of course. Come right in."

"The group used to be open to everyone," Anna explained as we entered. "But there were some issues with some . . . *unsavory* types attending and making trouble. So starting this year, all new people have to be introduced by a current member, to have a minimum of vetting."

"I get it." I felt a bit bad at having infiltrated the meeting — after all, it was supposed to be for gay and trans people only. I didn't really belong there.

"Anna, what's this?" Elanor asked. "What's he—"

"Alright, I think everyone's here," Allie said, raising her voice above the quiet hubbub filling the room. "And it's about time for the meeting to begin anyway. Shut up and sit down, y'all."

I looked around and saw there were at least fifty people there: the GSA had filled up the classroom they'd borrowed for the meeting. Apparently there were many more queer people at Bradford McKinley than I'd thought.

We sat in a wide circle. Allie stepped in the middle to stand next to a girl with long brown hair and a tall man with skin a few shades darker than the other two.

"Welcome, everyone. Since we have a few new people, let us introduce ourselves again. We're Allison, Lena, and Patrick." She motioned to the other two. "And we're the coordinators for the GSA meetings." She paused and looked around. "The main purpose of the GSA is to have a place where we can discuss queer issues freely, without any fear of being judged. Or just have a chat, that's good too. You can talk about anything you like, no issue is off-limits, but please do be mindful of other people's feelings and boundaries. Are we clear on that?"

She waited until she received a few noises of acknowledgment before continuing. "Since there's a lot of people here, I think we should split into smaller groups — say five to six people? Just grab a few folks, make a circle with your chairs, and start talking."

There were murmurs of agreement, and we started shuffling chairs around. Anna, Elanor, and I ended up in a group with three other people: a short, chubby girl wearing a knee-length black dress, black tights and white trainers, who had jet-black, shoulder-length hair; a tall, lithe blonde girl, who looked comfortable in a tan jumpsuit; and a brunette who had her hair tied back in a tight bun.

"Alright," Anna said, when we'd settled down. "I know all of you, but there are some people who've not been to a meeting before." She pointed at me. "So let's go round and say our name and pronouns. I'm Anna, and my pronouns are she and her."

She looked at the blonde girl, who'd ended up sitting on Anna's right. "Nora. She and her," she said, raising a hand in greeting.

"Jillian," the brunette said.

After a few moments, Nora prodded her in the shoulder.

"Alright, *fine*. She and her," Jillian added.

"There. Was that so hard?" Nora asked.

"I just don't see the point, Nora."

Nora pursed her mouth as she looked at Jillian, eyes narrowing slightly, but didn't say anything.

Next was the black-haired girl: "Victoria," she said. "She and her."

Suddenly it was my turn.

I looked around the circle and gulped nervously. I felt really exposed, sitting there with everyone looking at me. What should I say? I could have introduced myself with my old name and male pronouns, but the thought made me feel a bit queasy, as if they were somehow wrong. Anna smiling encouragingly at me gave me the final push.

I gulped again.

"Um . . . Lily. She and her, please."

". . . Oh," I heard Elanor say; I turned to face them, and gave a weak smile.

"Yeah — surprise," I said.

"See?" Nora said. "I never would've guessed. That's why doing this is useful."

I turned back to face her just in time to see Jillian scoff, though she didn't say anything. I gave her a puzzled look, but turned my attention back to Elanor as they said, "Elanor, they and them."

"Alright!" Anna said brightly. "Now that we're all on the same page, does anyone have anything they'd like to talk about?"

She looked around expectantly, but I understood she was giving me an opening to ask a question.

"Yeah, I do, actually," I said, raising my hand. "How do you know if you're *really* a queer person? Like, is there a particular feeling, or what?"

"That's easy to answer," Jillian said. "You're queer if you're in love with people of your same sex."

"I think Lily was asking specifically about being *trans*, Jill," Nora said, once again quirking her lips.

Jillian shrugged. "No clue then. Don't know shit about it."

"Be *nice*," Nora said, giving Jillian a light slap on the shoulder.

I was a bit startled by the dismissive and aggressive reply, but let it slide. "What I meant was, is there a way of telling for sure if someone is trans or not? Like, a test or something?"

"Sadly, there isn't," Elanor replied. "There's no way to make a diagnosis, it's something that you have to feel deep inside yourself. Some people figure it out when they're young, while for others it takes quite a while. And it's difficult to identify the exact flavor of trans you are, too," they continued. "I knew I was transgender at a very young age, but I only realized I'm non-binary over the past year, year and a half."

"Right," I said, biting my lip in thought. "And this . . . this 'feeling deep inside,' is it something continuous, or does it come and go?"

Elanor shrugged. "Depends," they said. "For some it's just a background buzz throughout their lives. Others feel serious distress, even if they don't know exactly what the reason is." They paused. "And it causes them to lash out."

They gave me a significant look, and I glanced at them sheepishly. ". . . Yeah. Sorry about that."

"Lily only figured out she's trans less than a week ago," Anna explained. "I knew her before then, and I can tell you she was *remarkably* spiky."

The group nodded in acknowledgment, except for Jillian, who frowned.

"Sorry about that," I repeated.

"I know that feeling, girl," Victoria said, briefly touching my arm. For some reason, I felt a fuzzy, fluttery sensation deep in the pit of my stomach. "I realized I was trans, like, a good half dozen years ago, but I tried to keep it hidden away. That lasted until the very end of high school, and let me tell you, I was *supremely* toxic to everyone." She took a deep breath, then let it out. "Like, holy shit. I was garbage. It was probably due to my family environment — my parents still don't know — but I did plenty of stuff I'm not proud of. It took another trans girl coming out to make me realize there was a different way to go about it."

"Right. So I guess you'd never worn a dress until you came out?"

"Yeah, it was pants only until I came to BMK," she replied with a smile. "But skirts feel much better, I always wear them. That's another thing: you have to figure out what kind of woman you are." She paused. "If you *are* a woman, of course."

I turned her words over in my mind. "So you're saying I have to figure out *my* way to . . . do gender?" I asked.

"Right," Victoria replied. "You need to find out what works for you. You can be binary or non-binary, you can be a complete butch or a femme or whatever, all that stuff. There is no wrong way to go about it. Try things out, see how they feel."

"For example, I'm a total butch," Nora said, raising her hand. "I wear skirts sometimes, but very rarely. Though I'm cis. But I think you get what I mean."

"And I'm a one hundred percent certified femme," Victoria said. "But there are infinite variations between these two extremes. Every person is unique, cis or trans."

Jillian snorted a half-laugh through her nose. "As if," she said.

We all turned to look at her. "I'm sorry?" Victoria asked.

"I said, *as if*," Jillian repeated. "All of this? It's just playing dress-up. It's not real."

Victoria's eyebrows knit together. "What are you talking about?"

"What I'm talking about is that gay, and lesbian, and bi people have been fighting for our rights for decades, and now you people come along and try to claim we're the same," Jillian spat out.

"We *are* the same," Anna said pointedly.

"Are we?" Jillian replied. "This new thing about 'gender' is a fad anyway, and even if it weren't, gender is not attraction — they're separate things. There's all this talk about 'queer spaces' and 'LGBT spaces,' but where are the spaces for LGB people? They're gone!"

"Jill," Nora said quietly, eyes narrowing, an edge to her voice.

"You think we don't need safe spaces too?" Victoria said. "I haven't come out to anyone in my family. My dad would literally kill me if he knew I was trans!"

"Honestly? You have it easy. I can't opt out of being a lesbian," Jillian snapped.

"I can't opt out of being *trans*," Victoria rebutted.

"Sure you can," Jillian said. "It's all clothes and presentation anyway. You just put on a pair of pants and—"

"JILLIAN!" Nora said, grabbing her arm.

All noise in the room stopped; everyone turned to look at the scene unfolding in our group.

"Enough," Nora said, more quietly. "That's enough."

Jillian hesitated. "What do you mean?"

"I mean I can't put up with this anymore. I can't put up with you anymore. I'm done," Nora replied, letting her hand drop. "*We're* done."

Jillian went pale. "You're not . . . ?"

"I'm breaking up with you, Jill. I'm sorry," Nora said. Then after a moment, she added, "No, you know what? I'm *not* sorry, actually."

Jillian was on the verge of tears. "But . . ." she began.

"Is something the matter here?" One of the coordinators, Lena, said, approaching our group.

"Yeah," Victoria replied. "Jillian doesn't believe trans people are real, and she's being stubborn and offensive about that."

Lena turned to the rest of the group. "Is it true?" she asked. "Jillian?"

"Well . . ." Jillian said, but then stopped.

"Care to repeat what you said about 'playing dress-up?'" Nora said. "About how trans people are just pretending and can stop being trans any time?"

I felt a pang of guilt at Nora's words, but didn't say anything.

"I . . ."

Lena looked directly at Jillian, crossing her arms. "Is that what you said?"

Jillian hesitated for a long moment, and then wordlessly nodded.

"I see," Lena said. "Alright. Will you apologize for saying that?"

The silence in the room was deafening.

Lena's eyes hardened. "I think you should leave, Jillian."

Jillian looked at her in surprise. "Leave? But . . ." she said.

"No buts," Lena replied. "Leave."

Jillian looked around, tears in her eyes. Her gaze stopped on a number of people, apparently looking for support, but she found none. She took a deep breath and threw her head back.

"Fine," she hissed. "*Fine.*" She picked up her bag, stood up dramatically, and made her way to the door. "You know what? Fuck you. Fuck *y'all.* Homophobic freaks." She threw the door open, turned around, and left walking backward — showing us the finger on both hands — then she slammed the door behind her.

Lena slowly exhaled. "Oh, I always hate having to do this." She turned to us and continued, "Are you all okay?"

"Yeah, we're okay," Anna said, and Lena went back to her group.

"Sorry, you three," Nora said. "I knew Jill had . . . weird ideas about trans people, I just hadn't realized how weird." She took a deep breath, then smiled. "So, what were we talking about?"

As the conversation resumed and shifted to other topics besides trans issues, I was bewildered; what had that all been about? I thought all gay and transgender people were on the same page about everything, but that was apparently not the case. And it hadn't been a simple disagreement: Nora and Jillian had broken up as a result of their differences in opinion.

This was *bizarre*.

≣

I stretched and looked at my watch as I stood up: almost dinnertime — the meeting had run much longer than I'd expected. Surprisingly, I'd found lots of things to talk about with my group.

"So how was it?" Anna asked as she and Elanor approached me.

"It was . . . interesting," I replied. "Especially the first bit, I didn't expect that."

Anna laughed. "Yeah, things aren't usually *that* contentious. I'm sorry, I didn't want your first exposure to the queer community at large to be like that."

"No big deal. So you'll let me know when the next meeting is?"

"Yeah," Elanor chimed in. "And about that, we were planning on going to dinner with Vicky and Nora now; wanna come with?"

I looked at them, surprised: were they really inviting *me* to join them? "If it's not a bother ..."

"No bother at all," they said. "After all, us queers must stick together, right?"

"Right," I replied with a smile which I hoped didn't betray the guilt I felt at seemingly having successfully completed the first part of my infiltration. "Let's go."

5
Key to Her Heart

"WHERE WERE YOU?" Joe asked, looking up as I opened the door. I'd tried to be quiet, thinking he would be asleep since it was already midnight, but he was still awake reading a book with an American flag on its cover — *another* book with an American flag on its cover: it was at least the third one I'd noticed him reading. "Out. With friends," I replied, puzzled.

He looked at me skeptically. "Didn't know you had friends. You didn't before."

I dropped my phone, wallet, and keys on my desk and grabbed my PJs before answering. "What's that supposed to mean?"

"This is the third time in as many weeks you've gone out on Wednesday afternoon and come back late. You never did that before." He shrugged. "So I was wondering what was up."

It's the third time in as many weeks I've gone to the GSA and pretended to be a trans girl in front of everyone, then been to dinner with Anna, Elanor, Vicky, and Nora. The foursome I'd found myself hanging out with were surprisingly good company. I'd never noticed just how sharp and witty Anna could be, and I'd gotten to know the other three really well: Elanor was wicked smart, and seemed to have an encyclopedic knowledge of mid-2000s Nintendo games; Victoria — Vicky — always had a warm smile and a kind word for me; and Nora was cool, attractive, and fun to hang out with, as well as being the one to go to for tech support.

It was actually incredible: I'd thought liberals were all uniformly boring people who didn't talk about anything except politics, but we'd hardly ever broached the subject — most of our time was spent shooting the shit. They were much more fun to hang out with than Joe had ever been.

But I wasn't about to tell him that, so I just shrugged.

"I made some friends in class, and started hanging out with them," I said. "Simple."

From his expression, Joe didn't seem to be entirely convinced by my explanation, but he nodded. "Alright. Okay. Happy for you."

"Thanks."

He held my gaze for a few moments, then continued. "Listen, bud, there's something I've been meaning to tell you."

I inclined my head to the side and looked at him. "What's up?"

"Well . . ." he sighed. "I feel like I have to apologize. For what happened with Tommy and Eddie. The thing with the ball, I mean."

Huh. Surprising; never thought I'd see the day. "Go on."

"At the time I blamed you, but I've come to realize I've been wrong," Joe continued. "It's not your fault Darrell was around. And, if anything, it's the libertarians' fault for leaving a table out where there shouldn't have been one."

My eyes narrowed a bit. So he was still blaming someone else instead of himself.

"So, I'm sorry," Joe concluded.

"Okay," I said. Even though he'd reached the wrong conclusion, I wasn't about to look a gift horse in the mouth: thawing the chill that ran between us was good enough for me.

"So we're cool?" he asked.

"We're cool."

"Okay."

He didn't say anything else, so I turned around and walked into the bathroom, where I quickly shed my clothes — keeping my eyes closed, as I always did — and put on my pajamas.

When I got out to go to bed, Joe was already asleep.

≡

"Evenin'," I said, closing the door behind me.

Joe looked up from his textbook. "Hi, bro."

I hesitated for a moment. Always with the 'bro' and 'buddy' and 'man' and stuff. It felt terrible, the way he never used my name. I didn't much care for *that*, either — it always felt too stuffy and oppressive, carrying too many expectations — but it was a whole lot better than what Joe called me. I briefly debated whether to tell him, but in the end decided not to. We'd just become cordial again and I didn't want to risk ruining it: Joe could be *weird* regarding some things.

"How was your day?" I asked.

"Oh, same old." He shrugged, then smirked. "How about you? Did you have fun at social studies? Had any more fights with Anna?"

"No, actually," I replied. "It's been fine since, oh, about three weeks ago?"

Joe's eyebrows lifted slightly. "It has?"

"Yeah," I nodded. "I apologized to her, and she accepted."

"… Why the hell would *you* apologize?" He gave me a bewildered look. "She was clearly in the wrong, *she* should have been the one to say sorry."

Was she really in the wrong? Joe and I had been complete asses to her and Elanor, and even if I didn't agree with Anna's politics, that didn't justify being insulting. But I couldn't tell Joe that. "Well, you know how I need the credits for social studies?" I asked. "It's much easier to concentrate on studying when you don't have someone glaring at you from across the classroom the whole time."

Joe was silent for a moment. "Yeah, I see your point. But I still think you shouldn't have apologized. As a man, you shouldn't bow down to anyone. You should have pride."

I smiled. "It is what it is."

"You're right about that," he replied with a laugh. "Oh, by the way, that reminds me: Theta Omega Tau is having another party tonight. You in?"

I thought about it. Joe and I hadn't hung out in quite a while. And he was basically my only friend at college besides the people from the GSA. It would be good to spend some time with him again. "Okay."

"Give me a few minutes to get changed, then we'll go."

While I was waiting for him, I set my backpack on my desk and pulled my phone and wallet from it. I was about to grab my keys too, when Joe said, "Ready."

I turned to him and chuckled. "Still with the hat, huh?"

"Hey, it suits me, doesn't it?"

"Yeah, it does. Come on, let's go."

≣

As Joe chugged his fifth beer of the night, I took a sip from my first and made a face: it tasted *awful*. The booze that's usually offered at frat parties is hardly top-shelf stuff, but I didn't remember it being this bad. I probably hadn't noticed, since I was too focused on using it to numb myself. And that made me realize I hadn't drunk even a drop since the previous party. I hadn't gone that long without drinking since I was fourteen. It was weird: I no longer felt the need to reach for a can just to help me sleep. Huh.

"It's good to get out of that stuffy room once in a while," Joe said, breaking my train of thought. "Do something fun."

"Don't you do 'something fun' every weekend? I mean, you're rarely in our room on Saturdays and Sundays."

"'Course," he replied. "Why should I stay cooped up? This is college, man. We should enjoy it while we're here, we'll never get these moments back."

"You're right about that," said a voice behind me. I turned and felt the smirk freeze on my face. Eddie and Tommy were walking toward us, looking as if they didn't have a care in the world.

"Tommy!" Joe exclaimed. "Eddie! Buddies! It's good to see you!" They embraced briefly, and when they separated Joe grabbed two bottles from a nearby table and handed them over. "Here, have a drink with us!"

"Gladly," Eddie said, then took a deep swallow. "Here's to the end of another boring week, and the start of a weekend of fun!"

"Hear, hear!" Tommy cheered, lifting his bottle toward the ceiling before taking a swig. "Here, pal, have one! Enjoy your college life!"

He grabbed a bottle and offered it to me; I declined by raising the bottle I still had in my hand. "I *am* enjoying my college life," I said. "I'm just not a party beast like you are."

"Youuuuu don't get it!" Joe slurred. "College is supposed to be about having fun! About celebrating life!"

I inclined my head and smiled mildly: he never changed. "I thought college was supposed to be about studying?"

He scoffed. "Yeah, also studying. *I guess*. But above all, it's about fun! And girls!"

"Yeah!" Tommy and Eddie agreed as one. "Girls!"

My smile disappeared as my eyebrows knit together. This, I realized, was starting to look like a repeat of what had happened a few weeks before: me being completely ignored as the three of them got drunk, loud, and annoying.

"Look at the tits on that one!" Eddie said, motioning with his bottle.

"Nice, nice," Tommy agreed. "But I prefer her friend, I'm more of an ass man."

Really annoying.

"Excuse me." I cleared my throat, and Eddie, Joe, and Tommy turned to me. "Could we please just have some fun, talk among ourselves, without acting like horny apes?"

Tommy scoffed. "Oh, come on, we're just having some fun. Enjoying the scenery."

"Well, can we enjoy the scenery without any crass comments?"

Joe shook his head, apparently in disbelief. "What the hell, man. Sure, I've only known you for a few months, but you could've told me you were gay."

As Joe's friends laughed, I bristled. "I'm not gay," I protested, feeling the need to defend myself. "I like girls. And the point I was making is that you're objectifying those girls. You can appreciate someone's beauty without demeaning them; you're being misogynistic."

Joe blinked in surprise: he'd never heard me use those words before. And a few weeks earlier, I probably wouldn't have. I guess it was my hours of hanging out with my friends from the GSA, of being educated in the mysterious queer way of *respect*, that were rubbing off on me and teaching me new words to express myself.

"Misogy-what?" Tommy asked. "What's 'objectifying' mean?"

Against my better judgment, I launched into an explanation:

"It means you're focusing on just the parts of those girls that you can see and like, without considering them as a whole. You're viewing them only as a sexual object, as a thing, rather than a person."

He looked at me curiously. "Guess I am. So what? Are you going to say that's bad?"

"Yes, that *is* bad," I replied. "I mean, what would you say if a girl decided to approach you just because she thought you had a nice butt?"

"I would think 'score!' HEYOO!" Tommy shouted. He turned to his friends, and raised his hand, seemingly waiting for a high-five. They obliged, repeating his obnoxious shout.

My mouth fell open in disbelief. Suddenly the atmosphere felt oppressive; I needed to get some fresh air.

"I can't believe you guys," I muttered. I set my half-finished bottle on a table and walked away.

"Hey, what?" I heard Joe call. "What the hell, man? Why you gotta be like that? We were just talking!"

No, you *were talking, and I was dumb enough to think you were worth listening to.*

≣

Well, *that* had been a waste of a Friday evening.

I could kick myself. Joe and I had barely made up two days before, after three weeks of him not speaking to me over something that had been entirely his fault. And I knew from experience how he could be, especially when he had a bit too much to drink.

I'd been an idiot thinking I could enjoy myself with him.

Fuming, I made my way back to the dorm. As I walked, I bundled myself up in my coat — it was especially chilly with that scent in the air that suggested it was going to snow soon. It was surprising that it hadn't snowed yet that year, actually: it was already early December. Still, it was the kind of weather that made you want to get into bed and stay there until you've warmed up, and that was what I was planning on doing.

After about twenty minutes of walking through the cold, I reached the dorm. I walked up the three steps out front and pushed the door.

It didn't budge.

Of course, I thought, looking at my watch — a few minutes past eleven.

I hadn't brought my keys with me.

I'd grabbed my phone and wallet before I left, but then Joe'd distracted me, and grabbing my keys had slipped my mind. Maybe, subconsciously, I'd been counting on Joe to let me in when we returned together.

I hadn't been anticipating throwing a tantrum and leaving the party early.

The stress of the week and the exhaustion I felt at having to deal with Joe and his friends caught up to me and I sat down heavily on the steps. I thought about calling Darrell, but decided against it: yes he was our RA, but I'd be bothering him if I called at 11 p.m. on a Friday. And for such a stupid reason, too; he'd be very annoyed with me.

I just had to sit and wait for someone to come back and open the door for me. No, I realized, I had to wait for *Joe* to come back: even if someone who lived in the dorm happened to come by, I'd also need someone to open my dorm room, and only Joe and I had the key to that.

I bundled myself up tighter into my coat, which wasn't really keeping the cold out, and I watched as my breath painted billowing clouds through the air. It was *really* cold. I just had to hope Joe wouldn't take too much time.

"Lily?"

Startled, I looked up. I hadn't expected someone to call my name, especially since not many people knew it. And that voice sounded like . . .

"Nora. Hi," I said, looking around — we were the only ones nearby.

I'd asked my friends from the GSA to only call me Lily if nobody else was in earshot, so Nora using my name wasn't a big deal. I knew I could trust her — and Anna, Elanor, and Vicky, for that matter — to be careful.

"Hi," she replied with a small, bashful smile.

"What are you doing here?" I asked.

"I was just passing by, saw you, thought I'd say hi. I'm coming back from a movie night." Nora wrapped her arms around herself and shivered. "What are *you* doing here? It's freezing, why are you sitting out here?"

"Oh, I live here," I said, motioning to the dorm behind me. "But I was a dum-dum and didn't bring my keys with me when I went out tonight. I'm locked out. So I'm waiting for my roommate to come back and let me in. He shouldn't be long."

"How long did he say he would take?"

I hesitated a moment. "Ah . . . I don't know," I replied. "I kinda got mad at him and stormed out of a party we were at. I have no idea when he's coming back."

I shivered, and her eyes turned worried. "You can't just sit out here in the freezing cold, you'll catch your death. Call him, or something."

I shook my head. "I can't just *call him*. We've had a fight. And it's *his fault.* Calling him would be admitting I need his help, he'd be really smug about that." I stuck my hands deep in my pockets and rubbed my legs to warm up. "I don't mind sitting in the cold if it means I don't have to ask him for help."

Nora grinned at my words. "You're headstrong, girl. I like that."

I blinked, taken aback: of all the things I'd been called in my life, *headstrong* was a new one.

"Let me handle this," she continued. "Come on, up we go." She offered me her hand and pulled me to my feet, before moving to the door and crouching in front of it. "This should be just a moment," she said, slipping something out of her purse. "You keep watch, make sure no one's coming."

I looked at her, puzzled. "Why, what are you going to do?"

"Keep watch, I said." I spun on my heel and looked around: the street was still as deserted as it had been a few moments before.

"There's no one here."

"Quiet, please," Nora muttered under her breath. "I need to listen for the pins."

The what? I thought, but continued keeping watch.

After half a minute or so, I heard a loud click.

"Hah, got it." Nora said, sounding as if she'd just scored the decisive touchdown at the Super Bowl.

I turned back around and saw her pull the door open, step back, and give me a bow.

"After you, my lady."

I felt my mouth fall open. "Wh– How? How did you do that?"

Her lips curled into a playful smile. "Magic. Deep, dark magic, passed down my line through generations." She paused. "No, actually I used lockpicks. See?"

She held up two pieces of metal, one flat and bent at one end, the other curved like a small hook.

"*Lockpicks?*" I said, bewildered. "You know how to pick locks?"

"Sure do, it's a small hobby of mine."

I looked from the picks to her. "Um, aren't lockpicks illegal?"

"No, they're not." She shook her head. "*Breaking and entering* is illegal. That is, opening locks that aren't yours to open." She inclined her head and put her finger to her cheek, still smiling that charming smile of hers. "Though I suppose since I don't live here, what I did is a liiiittle bit illegal. Just a tad." She winked and, in a whisper, added, "Don't tell anyone."

"That . . ." I began. *Whoa. What a girl.* "Well, thank you. That was amazing. Thank you."

She quickly touched her forehead in a mock salute. "Glad to be of service, ma'am. I'll be on my way, then. See you at the next GSA meeting."

She turned around and started to leave.

"Actually," I called out. Nora turned back and gave me a questioning look. "Actually," I repeated, "could you do my dorm room door, too? I don't have the key to that either."

"Ooh, *more* breaking and entering," she said, grinning and rubbing her hands together. "Fun. Show me this door that's keeping you from your room, and I'll see to it that it's opened forthwith."

I guided her down the corridor to my room. There was no one around, but I still kept watch as she fiddled with the lock, probing and prodding it with her lockpicks. It took her only a minute or so to get it open.

"Ta-da!" she exclaimed, as the door swung open. "One lock picked, as requested."

I found myself smiling at her showmanship. "Thank you, Nora," I said. "I'm really grateful. And this was a fun way to end a horrible night."

"Was it so bad?" she asked.

"Yeah. It seems I have bad luck with Friday nights. Every time I've gone out in the past month, it turned out to be terrible." I didn't mention I'd only gone out twice, and both times with Joe.

Nora hummed pensively. "Tell you what, why don't you come with me next Friday?"

I blinked in surprise. "With you?"

"Sure," she nodded. "I said I was on my way back from movie night — we do them regularly at Vicky's place. We started a couple weeks ago, after I broke up with Jillian. Needed something to do with my weekends, and she mentioned she watches movies with her roommates, so . . ." She shrugged.

I hesitated for a moment. "Won't I be in the way?" I asked.

"Aw, nah," Nora said, waving her hand dismissively. "Vicky knows you, and her roommates are in the GSA, they've seen you around. But if you're nervous because you won't know many people there, we can invite Anna and Elanor too."

"In that case … Okay," I replied. "Thank you, Nora."

"Great!" she exclaimed. "I'll let you know the details at the next meeting."

She reached forward, put a hand on my shoulder, and gave it a friendly squeeze. Then she leaned in.

"Have a good night, Lily," she whispered in my ear, before walking away.

I stood there, watching her go.

What an interesting girl.

6
Free Your Mind

I COULDN'T SEE any mistakes.

I hummed to myself as I scrolled through the document, ran it through spell-check again, then reread the four pages one last time. The social studies essay was my last piece of schoolwork for the year, and would be sure to get me a good grade. Just as planned.

I'd read lots of feminist theory to write the paper — asking Anna for some sources, which she helpfully pointed me toward — and I had to admit I'd been a bit surprised to find most of what I read was quite reasonable, actually. There were some parts I didn't agree with, but many others — like the need for intersectionality in addressing gender-related inequalities — seemed like common sense. I didn't know why I hadn't realized it before.

Ah well. That was one thing done, and I could focus on my other research. My *secret* research. My master plan.

I was in a good place regarding that. I'd made several queer friends and I was slowly gathering material, mostly based on my experience as an actual cis person pretending to be trans, so I could get to writing an exposé as soon as my ruse was complete. I wondered what I should title the article. 'I have earned the queers' trust: they still don't realize I'm cishet'?

No, that was too on the nose.

I still had lots of time to think about it. For the moment, I had to get going or I would be late for movie night.

I grabbed my coat, phone, wallet, and keys — *especially* my keys — and glanced at Joe. As usual he was lying on his bed, watching a video on his phone with earbuds plugged firmly in his ears. When he noticed I was looking at him he briefly returned the stare, but almost immediately focused his attention on the screen again, as if I wasn't worth paying attention to.

We had exchanged exactly zero words since I'd left the Theta Omega Tau party; the cold war between us now a nuclear winter. We did not speak to each other. At all. Not even a "hi," or "good evening," or "bye."

But I didn't mind that one bit. Like the first time it was entirely Joe's fault, so I saw no reason why I should offer him an olive branch. We were roommates, yes, but I didn't need him as a friend; I had several others — from the GSA — I could rely on.

I felt a pang of guilt, thinking about them.

Were we *really* friends? I mean, they seemed to think of me as one. I, on the other hand, was just using them for my own ends. What was I even doing? They all seemed like cool people, and here I was deceiving them.

For the first time since I'd begun my ruse, I started to have serious doubts. Was I in too deep? It had been a month since I'd come out to Anna; I couldn't well say, "Hey y'all, I'm not actually trans, you know. I was just pretending, ha ha! But I would still like to be friends with you, if you don't mind."

My life — my social life, at least — would probably end right then and there.

That was one more reason to keep pretending. Keeping up the act meant that, besides gathering material, I could have some friends at college. People I could talk to, besides Joe.

I still felt guilty about it, though.

Best not to think about it. Following the directions Nora had sent me via text, I reached Vicky's place. I looked at it: a normal, two-story house in a residential neighborhood just off campus, which wasn't unusual. Bradford McKinley had been growing recently, admitting more and more students, and they couldn't all fit in the dorms or frat houses. Many of them rented apartments nearby — or entire houses, splitting the cost among several people, which was what Vicky had done.

I took a deep breath. Okay, Lily. Stop overthinking things.

Game face.

I walked up the stone-paved path and rang the bell; the door opened almost immediately to reveal Vicky. Her face was carefully made up, and as was usual she was wearing a dress — come to think of it, I'd never seen her wearing anything other than a dress or skirt, which contrasted with the other three girls in our friend group: Nora, Anna, and I all seemingly lived in pants.

"Hi, Lily," Vicky said with a smile, and drew me into a brief hug. "Nora told me you were coming. You're a bit early, the others aren't here yet. Come in."

I followed her into the living room, where two couches and an armchair had been arranged in a semicircle in front of a wide-screen TV which was showing a quiz show. There were two girls I recognized from the GSA meetings, who waved when they saw me.

"Lily, this is Mel and Katie, my housemates," Vicky said, pointing at each of them in turn. "I think you've seen them at the GSA, but this is your proper introduction. Girls, this is Lily."

"Hi, Lily," one of them said. "I'm Melanie, nice to meet you."

"Katie," the other added. "Hi."

"Hello," I replied. No matter how many times it happened, someone new accepting me as a girl at face value still gave me a happy, fuzzy feeling deep in the pit of my stomach, like a mug of hot chocolate on a cold winter afternoon, especially since my *actual* face was a man's.

They still don't realize I'm cishet.

"Make yourself comfortable, I'll get some snacks." Vicky walked off toward the kitchen, and before I'd settled in she was back with a tray of bowls containing salty and sweet snacks, soda, and beer.

"Do you have any allergies?" she asked me.

"No, none."

"Good, then you can eat all of this." The doorbell rang. "Oh, that should be the others." She opened the door, and we heard from the hall-way: "Hi girls! And Elanor! Welcome!"

I gave Anna, Nora, and Elanor a wave as they filed into the room.

"You look very nice." Elanor complimented Vicky. "Where did you get the dress?"

"Thrifted it."

"Oh, lucky. All I find in thrift stores in my size are pants."

"I know a few stores that are good for that, I'll bring you next time."

Elanor chuckled. "And I'll bring you where I buy my pants."

"She doesn't wear pants," Melanie piped up. "It's always a dress or skirt with this one."

"I don't think I've ever seen her wear, like, a tracksuit," Katie added. "Girl, you *can* have a slob day once in a while."

"No, I can't," Vicky snapped, closing the door.

Her voice was surprisingly harsh, and my eyebrows rose in surprise. I looked at her, puzzled: if I'd learned one thing over the past few weeks, it was that being trans wasn't about clothes. I'd also never seen Vicky react like that.

Probably against my better judgement, I decided to press the question. "Why?" I asked. "It's not like you need to wear a skirt to be a girl."

Vicky stopped, her hand on the door handle. After a moment she turned to look at me. We locked eyes and I could sense her hesitation, as if she was debating something with herself. Then she sighed.

"Sorry. I'm sorry for reacting like that," she said. "Sometimes my temper still gets the best of me. It's that . . . You know." She paused, and her eyebrows scrunched together. "I think I told you how I wasn't a good person before . . . *Before*. Right?"

"Right." I recalled her mentioning it the first time we'd met.

"This dress?" she continued, motioning at herself and at the clothes she was wearing. "It's something *he* would never have worn, not to save his life. It's a clean break. It's armor." She looked off to the side. "It means I'm no longer *him*," she finished, in a whisper.

There was a moment of silence in the room, then Nora stepped forward and spread her arms wide. "Alright, come here," she said.

Vicky blinked at her. "What . . . ?"

"Shush," Nora said. "No words. You're always kind and caring, Vicky, always ready to comfort people. Well, now *you* need it. You look like you need a hug. So." She took another step toward Vicky and opened her arms even wider. "Bring it in, girl."

After a moment's hesitation, Vicky stepped into Nora's embrace and they hugged tightly. I felt a bit jealous, but I pushed that feeling down as soon as it surfaced. *Just be happy for your friend, Lily.*

"Thank you," Vicky said, her sad expression gone.

"Any time." After a few moments Nora broke the embrace, and continued, "So what do you say we stop thinking about bad memories, and watch a movie?"

After a bit of finagling, we managed to fit everyone on the couches, sitting somewhat comfortably.

"Whose turn was it to pick tonight's movie?" Nora asked.

"Mine, actually," Vicky replied.

She grabbed a Blu-ray case and held it up so we could see the title.

"*The Matrix*," I read. "Huh. Never seen it."

"Seriously?" Anna said. "You don't know *The Matrix*?"

"I know *of* it," I answered. "But I've never seen it. It always seemed like it was, you know, a dumb action movie. Not really what I would pick."

Vicky and Elanor exchanged a knowing glance. "Oh, I think you'll be surprised," Elanor said. "This movie has *an effect* on some people."

I raised an eyebrow at them. "An effect," I repeated. "Okay then."

"Anyone using a veto," Vicky asked, "or should we go ahead?"

"Veto?" I questioned.

"Some movies can be . . . contentious," Nora said. "If someone really doesn't like someone else's pick, they can veto the choice. We always pick a backup movie, just in case."

"If there are no objections, let's get movie night officially started!" Vicky popped the disc in the player.

The Matrix. I wonder what this will be like.

☰

"Whoa," I whispered, two hours and change later, as the credits started rolling. "That was . . ."

Nora turned to me and smiled. "Did you like it? Come on, I really want to hear your thoughts."

I realized everyone was looking at me. "I take it you've all seen it before?" I asked. "Okay. So, first of all: it was excellent. I really enjoyed it."

Elanor leaned back into the couch and smiled widely. "And what was your favorite part?"

"Well, the action was absolutely fantastic," I said. "It was probably very innovative back in . . . When did this come out?"

"1999, I think it was," Anna replied.

"Yeah, 1999," Vicky said.

"Right. But what stood out the most was just how . . . relatable it was. Like it was looking deep into my soul."

Mel lifted an eyebrow. "Do tell."

"I mean . . ." I paused, bit my lip, and thought back to the plot. "It's the whole thing about feeling that someone is controlling your life, that some-how you're just playing a part without even knowing it," I continued. "It's like that thing Morpheus says when he meets Neo. 'It's why you lie awake at night, as if there's a splinter in your mind.' Stuff like that." I knew that feeling very well, even if it had faded to the point I didn't need to quiet it with booze anymore. I sighed. "I dunno, maybe that doesn't make sense."

"Oh, it makes *perfect* sense, Lily," Vicky said.

Elanor nodded. "It does," they agreed. "I honestly feel the same way about this movie, as do a whole lot of people."

"Right. There are some people who *really get* this movie, Lily, and you're one of them, my girl."

I blushed at her words. But still, I wondered: "Who do you mean by 'some people'?"

"It was made by two trans women," Nora said.

I blinked. "It was?"

"Yup," Katie confirmed. "They hadn't come out when they made it, but they've spoken about how they put lots of their own experiences into it while they were writing it."

"Huh," I said. It was strange: the movie had been gripping and engrossing and I'd been really taken in by it, and now they were telling me it was a mirror for trans experiences. So perhaps cis and trans people had more in common than I first thought. "They made some sequels, right?" I asked. "Maybe next time we can watch them and see how they compare."

"The sequels are no good," Anna said dismissively.

"What!" Katie exclaimed. "The sequels are fantastic! The action is even better, for one."

"Yeah, but they don't go as deep into the metaphysical, like this one."

"They absolutely do," Elanor said.

"They do not," Anna insisted.

Elanor looked at her for a moment, then huffed. "You're lucky you're hot, otherwise I might break up with you because of this take."

"You know you love me," Anna said, and leaned over to peck them on the lips.

"Oh, get a room you two," Katie said, grabbing a handful of popcorn and tossing it at them.

"Hey! Quit it!" Elanor said with a laugh, picking up a cushion and tossing it at Katie . . . missing completely and beaning Nora right in the face.

Nora grinned. "Now you've done it," she said.

A few minutes later, the battle was over: with the dust settled, it wasn't exactly clear who was the victor. Luckily most of the food had managed to stay in its bowls, so there was only a little to clean up.

"I'll go get the vacuum," Mel said.

"I'll help." Katie followed her. "I started it, so it's only fair I help with the cleaning."

While we waited for them to come back, Vicky turned to me. "Lily, listen, there's something I've been meaning to ask," she said in a low voice.

I hesitated for a moment. What did she want to ask? Had she somehow realized I wasn't really trans?

I barely managed to keep my voice steady as I asked, "Sure, what is it?"

"I'll get straight to the point: are you on HRT?"

"HRT . . . You mean hormone therapy, right?" Vicky nodded, and I continued, "No, not yet."

"Okay. Do you have any plans regarding that? How are you going to go about it?"

Was I going to go about it? After all, I was a perfectly normal cisgender man: the idea of taking hormones, *female* hormones, made me more than a bit nervous. But I wanted to see where she was going with this conversation, so I shrugged. "Not really? I think I'll probably ask around, see if there's a clinic nearby that takes my insurance."

"That, ah . . ." Vicky hesitated. "That might not be ideal."

"Why's that?"

"You said your parents don't know you're trans. That you haven't come out to them yet."

"Yeah."

"Are you planning on telling them any time soon?"

When hell freezes over. I mean, pretending to be trans was already a dicey proposition: coming out to my family, only to have to take it back months down the line? No, thank you.

"No, I'm not," I said. "Not for a while still. Not until I *have* to."

"Well then, your insurance is no good," Vicky explained. "If you're still on your parents' insurance, they'll be able to see what was paid through it and where. They won't be able to see *what it was for*, but I know a girl who had to come out to her mom because she noticed she'd been to Planned Parenthood and asked why."

". . . Okay," I said slowly. "Good to know. So, what do you suggest?"

"During Christmas break I'm going to drive up to Canada to buy my HRT. I know someone near Ottawa who's willing to turn a blind eye to the fact that I don't actually have a prescription for it. That's how I get it, since I'm in the same situation as you and I *definitely* don't want my parents to find out. I'm buying it for some other people, too."

"Like me," Elanor interjected. "My parents know about me being non-binary, but they refuse to let me use their insurance for HRT. If I tried that they'd kick me off the insurance entirely, and you can see how that would be bad."

"So I was wondering," Vicky continued. "Do you want me to hook you up?"

I hesitated for a moment; there was one sticking point about her proposal which was immediately apparent to me. "Is this . . . um . . . legal?"

"Strictly speaking?" She looked away. "Not entirely, no. But it's the only way some people here can get hormones; we have no other choice. Of course you run basically no risk, since I'll be the one making the purchase and bringing it over the border." She looked at me again, her eyes determined. "So how about it? You in?"

To say I was surprised by Vicky's offer — and her admitting to what was at least a misdemeanor, and probably a felony — was very much an understatement. I honestly had no idea it was *this* difficult for people to get on hormones. I thought all you had to do to start HRT was ask for it, and you could get it almost immediately after coming out. But Vicky was willing to run a significant risk to obtain her meds, and she was offering to help another trans girl get them too. (Well, someone she *thought* was another trans girl. I wasn't actually trans.)

The conversation cleared any lingering doubt I had in my mind: while I was still certain there were some cis men who were pretending to be trans women, Vicky was clearly not one of them. She was absolutely, one hundred percent, a trans girl, and I looked at her with renewed respect.

So now the question was: was I going to be buying hormones? After all she'd told me, it felt bad to refuse. She was running a serious risk just telling me about it.

Also, maybe I could write something about this in my exposé. Mention that many trans people have difficulty getting on hormones. Not what they had to do to get them, specifically — I was certainly not going to snitch on Vicky — but I could mention that people often had to resort to less-than-legal means to obtain healthcare. This would surely ingratiate me in some left-wing liberal circles: if I both-sided the issue, it added credibility. They wouldn't be able to attack my writing as purely right-wing screed against trans people.

"Okay," I nodded. "Sure. What are you going to buy?"

"Estrogens and antiandrogens," Vicky replied. "But we'll go over what exactly you need some other time. It'll take a while and it's already late."

"Sure. After the next GSA meeting, then?"

"Yeah, let's do that," Vicky agreed.

After that, we finished cleaning up and said our goodbyes. Anna and Elanor walked off in one direction, and Nora insisted on walking me home. "I need to pass your dorm to get to my place," she said.

We walked all the way in silence, enjoying the quiet. Even though it was a Friday evening it was still December and there weren't many people out, especially in this sleepy residential neighborhood.

Nora didn't speak again until we reached my dorm.

"So. HRT, huh?"

"What, did you eavesdrop?" I laughed.

"Overheard. Are you nervous?" she asked.

"A little bit." It was the truth, although I was nervous about the risk Vicky would be running, not about the hormones themselves. It wasn't like I was *really* going to take them.

"I don't think you have anything to worry about," Nora said. "I know plenty of people who are on HRT, it doesn't have many side effects. If anything, it's just going to make you look cuter."

She paused and flashed me a grin.

"Though personally, I think you're already one of the cutest girls on campus."

Wait, what?

I felt a blush creep up my face, but Nora didn't seem to notice. She just waved to me and said, "Good night, Lily."

And then she turned around and walked away, leaving me standing there, dumbfounded.

7
Pilled

JOE WASN'T IN our room when I came back from Christmas break. I was glad: it would save me a few hours of awkward, uncomfortable silence — though probably not as awkward as the days I'd spent at home.

It had been good to be back in my old room up north, especially after the many hours I'd spent on the bus. I'd also been happy to see my parents again, but our interactions were still of the cordial-but-distant type, same as they always had been. The only time we'd exchanged more words than necessary had been at Christmas dinner and then when exchanging presents, which I had, surprisingly, enjoyed. No, the problem was that after a month and a half of hearing everyone — everyone I cared about anyway — call me Lily, being referred to by another name and by masculine pronouns felt uncomfortable: every time they said those words I found myself squirming. My parents had noticed, and after a couple days my dad had taken me aside and asked me outright if I was okay, because apparently, "You've been acting weird, son."

I'd felt myself cringe at his words, but I forced myself to put a smile on my face and reply, "I'm just a bit stressed and anxious because of college stuff, Dad. Don't worry, I'm okay."

Dad didn't seem convinced, but he nodded, and neither he nor Mom had broached the subject again. And just as well: I loved my parents, and I had good reason to think they loved me back, but I didn't want to bother them without good reason. That weird feeling I had whenever someone called me by my birth name instead of Lily was probably due to anxiety anyway, a minor lapse due to having stopped drinking recently, coupled with being back home and forced to interact with my parents.

As I unpacked, I once again wondered what my mom and dad thought of LGBT issues. I'd talked to a few trans people besides Vicky and Elanor at the GSA meetings I'd attended, and from what they'd told me a parent's reactions to their child coming out varied wildly from immediately and enthusiastically supportive and accepting to Vicky's situation: "They would literally kill me if they found out I'm transgender."

Suppose I told my parents I was trans. How would they react? Would they still love me? Would they support me, or would I have to cut ties with them?

I would probably never find out. I had absolutely no plans on coming out to Mom and Dad; and this whole "pretending to be trans" thing was going to disappear completely after the school year was over and I'd gathered enough material.

Overall, things were going perfectly fine. There was no need to worry about anything.

As usual, I carefully avoided looking at the mirror as I changed into my sleepwear: the anxious buzz I'd always felt might have gone away, but seeing my reflection still made my stomach turn.

My last thought before falling asleep was a drowsy, *I sure hope my parents aren't like Vicky's.*

≣

"I know you'd all like to stay and chat some more," Patrick, one of the GSA coordinators called out. "But time's up. Sorry!"

It was my first meeting since coming back from vacation, and I hadn't realized how much I'd missed it. Being able to sit and chat with friends without being guarded, without having to watch myself, without being careful about what I said, was a wonderful feeling. It probably also helped that I was feeling quite relaxed owing to Joe's absence: weirdly, my roommate had yet to return from Christmas break. But I didn't mind; it meant I had the dorm to myself without having to walk on eggshells.

"Well, that's that for today," Nora said, approaching me. "What do you say we head to dinner?"

I looked at the rest of our small group. "Are you coming?" I asked.

"Of course," Anna said; Elanor nodded in agreement.

"I'm coming, too," Vicky said, closing the gap between us. "Especially because I have something to give you." She motioned to her backpack.

It took a second before I realized what she was getting at. "You mean . . . ?"

"Yes. Come on, let's go."

It didn't take us long to move to our favorite café, Giovanni's, and find a table. Once we'd placed our orders Vicky reached into her backpack, pulled out a large brown paper bag, and handed it to me. I found myself laughing: it was as if she were an old-time bootlegger handing over the alcohol she'd smuggled over the border — which wasn't too far from the truth. Holding the bag, I felt a thrill of excitement and anticipation.

"Here you go," she said. "Sorry I didn't come find you right away, but I didn't know when it would've been safe, what with you not being out and all. And I didn't do it at the GSA meeting because there are some people there who don't approve of DIY-ing HRT. Best not to arouse any suspicion."

I opened the bag, pulling out two cardboard boxes from a dozen or so in there.

"Estradiol valerate," I read off one box, then looked at the other. "Cypto . . . Crypto . . ."

"Cyproterone," Elanor said with a smile.

"Thank you," I said, smiling back. "Cyproterone acetate. So I guess this is the antiandrogen, while the other is the estrogen?"

Vicky nodded. "Precisely."

I looked at the box of antiandrogen. "I thought you used spironolactone; that's what I read, at least."

"You've done your research, I see," Vicky replied. "You're right, you'd normally use spiro, but that's because cypro isn't available in the US. They don't sell it here, even though as an antiandrogen it's much better than spiro. But since we get ours from Canada . . ."

"Okay, yeah, that makes sense," I said, as I continued staring at the boxes, then when no one said anything, I looked up. They were all looking intently at me. "What?"

"Well?" Anna said.

"Well what?"

"Aren't you going to take them?" Elanor said.

I blinked. "Right here? Right now?"

"No, hold on, wait a second," Vicky said, waving her hand to draw attention to herself. "There's something very important I have to say first. Thanks," she added, as the waitress set our food down.

"Okay," she said, when the waitress walked away, and cleared her voice. "Two of those per day, one in the morning and one in the evening."

She pointed at the box of estrogen. "And half of one of those per day, evenings are best," she continued, pointing at the cyproterone. Then she grinned. "Okay, *now* you can take them."

I looked down at the hormones — *my* hormones, I realized. I gulped. "Uh . . . Um . . ." I mumbled. I looked up again, and saw that Elanor, Anna, and Vicky were looking at me expectantly.

"Um . . ." I repeated. I looked back down at my hormones. "Er . . ."

"Come on, y'all, don't pressure her," Nora said. She put an arm around my shoulders. I jumped, startled by the sudden touch since I'd been focused on the boxes, but I found myself enjoying the closeness. "It should be Lily's choice when to start hormones. Ease up on the peer pressure a little bit, will you?"

There was a moment of silence. I felt the mood shift around the table as the other three realized what they were doing.

"Yeah, you're right. Sorry, Lily," Anna said.

"Yeah, our bad," Elanor added. "I guess we were a bit too on the enthusiastic side of things."

"You were," Nora said. "Please don't do that."

There was a murmur of assent around the table, and Vicky, Anna, and Elanor started eating, looking a bit chastized. Nora tightened her grip around my shoulders and smiled her charming smile at me. My stomach suddenly felt like it had a million butterflies dancing around inside it, but I managed to smile back. "Thank you," I whispered.

≣

Well past 11 p.m., I crept up to my dorm room, but stopped just outside. There was no way I could easily hide the bag I was holding. Joe hadn't been in our room when I'd left, but what if he'd come back in the meantime? How would I explain the bag? Did I even *need* to explain the bag? We weren't talking to each other, and he still hadn't apologized. So if he asked, I could just say, "None of your business," and leave it at that.

Would he accept that explanation? Because if he didn't, and he decided to look in the bag while I was out of the room, I had no idea what his reaction would be.

Best to be safe. I set down the bag in the hallway, out of sight of the door, and slowly opened it. I let out a small sigh of relief when I noticed Joe's bed was still empty: that was a confrontation avoided.

Once inside, I pulled out two boxes — one of estrogen, and one of anti-androgen — and placed them on my desk, before hiding the bag behind a pile of clothes in my wardrobe.

Slowly, deliberately, I went about my nighttime routine. I brushed my teeth and changed into my pajamas. It took me longer than usual, since I was concentrating on every movement, taking as long as I reasonably could.

Then, instead of going to bed, I sat at my desk and stared at the boxes.

Cyproterone acetate and estradiol valerate.

The boxes were small. Innocuous. But the more I looked at them, the more menacing they seemed: after all, the chemicals they contained were able to change a person.

Well, not *literally* change a person. The person was the same. But their outward appearance changed radically. I knew it. I'd seen the time-lines people had posted online — all part of my research, of course — and the results were incredible. Night and day. The people depicted in the "before" and "after" pictures looked similar, but like siblings or cousins: not even remotely the same person.

What if … ?

I got up from my desk, walked to my wardrobe, and with a supreme exertion of will, I forced myself to stare at my reflection.

Ugh.

No matter how many times I saw my face, I *still* didn't like it. I never had, not since I'd been thirteen or fourteen. I ran a finger over my fore-head and traced down to the tip of my nose; I brushed the back of my hand against my cheek, felt the stubble, and frowned. My electric razor didn't give me nearly as close a shave as I would've liked. An actual razor would be better, but I couldn't use that without looking in the mirror.

Cute, Nora had called me. One of the cutest girls on campus.

I really didn't see it.

I wonder what effect the hormones would have on me.

I blinked. The thought had passed, unbidden, through my mind.

Where the hell had it come from?

This whole thing was really starting to get to me. I should get to bed: I had no idea how long I'd spent thinking about the hormones, but it was probably well past midnight.

I took one last look at my face in the mirror, grimaced, and closed the wardrobe door, fully intending to go to sleep right away. Yet despite my best intentions, I found myself sitting at my desk and looking at the boxes again. *Staring* at the boxes again.

I stared hard. For a long time. I stared, refusing to avert my eyes, willing myself not to blink, until my eyes started watering. Then I blinked, and stared again.

I wonder what effect the hormones would have on me.

There. That thought again, there it went.

It was a bad thought. It was a terrible thought. It was a thought I shouldn't have had. It was a thought I wasn't *supposed* to have had. Not in a million years.

But somehow, it was a thought I couldn't avert my mind from.

I couldn't help but be curious. What effect *would* the hormones have on me?

I'd looked up the list: softer skin. Redistribution of fat. Some hair regrowth, maybe. That one, I had to admit, would've been nice — I was already starting to thin out a bit on top, which was weird since my dad still had a full head of hair.

But I was sure the results wouldn't be that great. I'd seen the timelines, sure, but most of those people were starting from a good place. They already looked feminine, even before HRT.

What effect would the hormones have on someone who looked *like me*? A person so terribly masculine, so incredibly *male* that you couldn't mistake them for anything else?

"Two of those, morning and evening," I whispered, almost mesmerized. "So one right now. And half of one of those per day, evenings are better."

Without thinking, I opened the boxes, popped two pills out of their blisters, then broke one in half and put one half carefully back where it had come from.

I looked down at the pill-and-a-half, cupped in the palm of my hand. Estradiol and cyproterone. Light blue and white. Small. Innocuous.

Menacing.

Why shouldn't I try it?

Just for a while, to see how it felt.

What was that if not gathering more material for the article I was planning to write? Real life experience: can't beat that.

I could stop any time I wanted. I'd done the research: it would take several months before the effects mounted to the point that they weren't easily reversible. Taking estradiol and cyproterone for a couple weeks — or a couple months — was no big deal.

I chuckled to myself, remembering how startled I'd been to learn *The Matrix* had been written by two trans women. Later on my friends had explained to me that the red pill was a stand-in for Premarin, the estrogen of choice when the movie was made. It was quite ironic: all those idiots on the internet who proudly declared themselves to be "red-pilled" — how many of them knew what that really meant?

I looked down at the pills again: cyproterone and estradiol.

White and light blue.

The instrument of change for many trans people.

Could they be my instrument of change, too?

You take the blue pill, and I show you just how deep the rabbit hole goes.

...Was there a reason to *not* take them?

Let's think about this carefully, Lily. You've always been a logical person, put the two things on the scale and see how they balance out.

Pros of taking the pills: I would get first-hand experience of what being on hormones felt like, and be able to use it when writing my exposé.

Cons of taking the pills: my body might change a bit, but the changes wouldn't be permanent until several months in. I might become a bit cuter, maybe.

Probably not, given the starting material.

(Ugh.)

But possibly? Well, whatever.

Why would I want to become cuter anyway?

My mind flashed to Nora for a moment.

No, don't get distracted. Keep going.

Pros of not taking the pills: none that I could think of, really.

Cons of not taking the pills: having to explain to my queer friends exactly why I wasn't taking them. And it's not like, "I don't feel it's the right moment for me" was going to cut it — all trans people want to get on hormones as soon as possible, so not doing it would be weird. It might arouse some suspicion. They might even discover that I was just pretending to be trans. And then I would have to stop.

So, yeah. Summing everything up, I had a clear picture in my mind.

Taking the pills: one big pro and one small con. Not taking the pills: no pros, one big con.

Once again, I looked at the hormones in my hand.

My other hand moved, almost without me thinking. Almost automatically.

I quickly popped the pills in my mouth and chased them down with a big swig of water from a bottle on my desk. Then another one. And another one, until the half-litre bottle had been completely drained.

Then, before I could think about what I'd just done, I tucked myself into bed and turned off the light.

Sleep didn't come easy to me that night.

8
Clothes Make the Girl

MY CELL PHONE buzzed.

Shaken from my unsatisfying slumber, I reached over and tried to slap it to shut it up. I missed cleanly, my hand hitting the nightstand's wooden surface with a thump. I tried a few more times, but to no avail, so I focused my gaze on the device, which took a few seconds — then a few seconds more — before I could turn off the alarm.

I turned over again and stared at the ceiling for a few moments, then pulled myself up to a seated position, my mind protesting all the way. I felt really drowsy; that night had been the worst sleep I could remember. It almost felt like a hangover, but my head wasn't hurting, I was just really tired. I almost considered skipping the morning's lessons, but decided against it. I might not have been a straight-A student, but I still cared about my studies. Plus, Professor Markley would probably give us back the essays we'd turned in just before Christmas break, and I was anxious to see how I'd done.

I yawned, blearily rubbed my eyes, and looked around the room: I was still alone. Joe hadn't come back during the night, not that I expected he would. Where *was* he anyway? He'd missed almost a full week of class. Not that I cared, but still, I wondered if he'd dropped out.

I stretched and looked around again.

And my eyes fell on the two boxes sitting on my desk.

The memory of the previous night came back to me.

Oh. Right.

I'd done that, hadn't I?

I'd begun taking hormones.

Weirdly, the thought didn't alarm me. It hadn't been a spur-of-the-moment thing, after all; I'd carefully thought about it. It had been a deliberate act.

I briefly took stock of the situation, tried to grasp the sensations my body was broadcasting to me, but I really didn't feel any different.

You've only taken one dose, said a voice in the back of my mind. *Trans people say hormones are magic, but in the end they're just medicine. It takes time for them to have an effect.*

What effect would that be, anyway?

Only one way to find out.

I walked to my desk and popped an estradiol pill out of its blister and put it in my mouth. My water bottle was empty, so I took a drink from the tap to help me swallow the hormones.

I straightened up and felt the pill slip past my throat and down to my stomach. Two down, an unknown number to go.

An unknown number, but not high. I was going to stop before anything permanent happened: counting two pills per day for a few months amounted to a couple hundred at most. Any more and the changes would become permanent, which was probably best avoided — how would I explain it to my parents?

I'd better take notes.

I opened my laptop and brought up a blank text document.

Day one, morning, I wrote. *One estradiol and half a cypro last night before bed, and one estradiol this morning. I don't feel anything yet. Will continue to monitor for changes.*

I stared at the words on the screen for a moment, then giggled. I felt like an archaeologist spelunking deep into the unknown, exploring ancient ruins and dodging deadly traps, keeping a log of her travels, wondering what—

I frowned.

Her travels? Where had that come from? I tried to push away the drowsiness and concentrate: why had *her* been the pronoun to pop into my brain?

Think about it, Lily. When you imagine famous archaeologists with a knack for adventure, who comes to mind first?

Lara Croft.

Yeah. That's right. That's who I'd pictured myself as. That's why the female pronoun had come naturally to me. That made sense. *Tomb Raider* was one of my favorite game series. I'd played the most recent ones to completion and found all the secrets, and I'd even gone back and played the ones that were released in the nineties before I'd even been born. Lara was a really cool protagonist, someone I could relate to, so it was natural for my mind to associate her with archaeology.

That was one mystery solved, at least.

✲

"O'Connor," Professor Markley called. I stood up and nervously walked the short distance to his desk. He was looking at my essay as I approached, a tiny smirk on his lips, and when I reached him he looked up.

"I have to say that this was actually really surprising," he said, handing me the paper. "From how you behaved at the start of the year, I wouldn't have bet a dollar on you passing my class, but instead ... Well, see for yourself."

I took the essay from him, looked down at it, and felt my eyes widen; I looked up at him, completely stunned. "An A-plus?" I asked. "Are you sure?"

He nodded. "Quite sure. Please do realize I don't give out such a grade lightly: in all my years of teaching I can count on one hand all the times I have. But this was, without a doubt, one of the best things ever written for this class. You did an excellent job. Congratulations, Mr. O'Connor."

I felt a weird sensation in my stomach, and I gulped. "Thank you, sir," I replied.

I walked back to my seat, still bewildered. An A-plus? Unbelievable. I'd worked really hard and read a lot of theory, true, but I never thought I would get this kind of grade in a social studies class. Not in my wildest dreams.

Maybe I'd internalized the conversations I'd had with my friends from the GSA so well that I'd managed to put them down on paper. I looked around the class searching for Anna, and when our eyes met she was grinning widely and giving me a thumbs-up, even as Professor Markley called her surname and she got up from her seat. I realized I should probably thank her: if she hadn't been so stubbornly set in her social-justice-warrior ways I would never have thought to pretend to be trans, and probably never gotten an A-plus — or even passed the class.

But despite being surprised, I was feeling very happy with myself.

✳

"Aw, come on, Anna," I told her once again. "A B-plus isn't the end of the world."

"Yeah, I know," she said. "*I know*." She sighed deeply. "But . . . I was really expecting a better grade."

"What did Markley say?" I asked. "You went to him after class to ask for an explanation, didn't you?"

"Yeah. He said that while most of my points were sound, I put too much emphasis on how men are holding back feminism. Also, apparently I was forgetting that in many cases men are victims of the patriarchy too, and can often be really good allies." Her eyebrows scrunched together. "I really don't see it. Trans and gay men, sure, but cishet men? Trash, the lot of them."

My mouth quirked pensively. I'd heard her talk like this once before, but I still didn't like it. Even though I had come to realize that toxic masculinity could be a real problem — just look at Eddie, Tommy, and *especially* Joe — I wasn't so convinced that men couldn't be made to reject it. I had, and I was a completely normal cishet man like the ones Anna had just dismissed as trash. The thought of being lumped together with the likes of my roommate made me feel a bit queasy.

But I couldn't say all that to Anna; I was trying to cheer her up.

"I'm sure you'll do better next time," I said. "What do you say I buy you lunch?"

Anna looked up at me with a small smile. "Yeah, sure. Let's text the others and see if they can join us."

We assembled our small gang and made our way to Giovanni's. As we sat down to eat, though, Anna was still unhappy about her grade.

"It's unfair, that's what it is," she said, slumped over the table.

"I know, sweetie, but you just have to accept it." Elanor soothed her, rubbing her back as she grumbled into her drink. "Unless you wanna challenge Professor Markley's decision and ask for a review?"

Anna turned her head to look at them for a moment and I could tell she was considering it, but after a moment she sullenly shook her head.

"Didn't think you would," Elanor continued. "Come on, after all it's just a momentary bump in the road. It's not that serious."

"Yeah, but . . . it's a B-plus. I was at least hoping for an A-minus. I mean . . ." Anna motioned to me. "I mean, *look at her!* She's just barely gotten started into feminist theory, and apparently she's already at the point where Markley considers her his star pupil!"

I speared a shrimp with my fork. "Jealous much?"

"Little bit, yeah. At least *you're* happy."

"Yep," I replied. Then I remembered something, and added, "And not just because of that."

Nora inclined her head slightly toward me. "What do you mean?"

"Well, I . . ." I took a deep breath. "I began taking my hormones. Last night, in fact."

"Oh, hey, that's great news!" Vicky said. "Congrats!"

"Yeah, that's awesome!" Elanor added. "We need to celebrate. Dessert's on me!"

"Good, so I won't be paying anything today," Anna quipped, "since Lily is already buying me lunch."

I felt a hand grab mine and squeeze it. When I looked to the side, Nora was smiling warmly at me.

"Congratulations, Lily," she said. "This was a big step. I'm so proud of you."

I felt my cheeks warm up, and I smiled back. "Thank you, Nora."

She kept looking at me for a few moments, a twinkle in her eye, then said, "So what now?"

I looked at her curiously. "What now?"

"Yeah. What are your next steps? Regarding transition, I mean."

"I . . ." I hesitated. "I don't know, really. I've done so much in so little time. Coming out, choosing a new name, starting hormones . . ." I paused. "I mean, what's left?"

"Changing your presentation. Different clothes, makeup, new hairstyle. Maybe getting your ears pierced," Vicky replied. "But only if you want to. There's no rush, and nothing is mandatory."

"Really?"

"Really," Elanor said. "If you say you're a girl, then you're a girl. Simple as that. You don't even need to be on hormones. It's certainly more common among enbies, but there are some binary trans people who don't take HRT, and that doesn't make them any less valid."

". . . Seriously? But I thought every trans person wanted to take hormones."

Vicky shook her head. "That's a common misconception," she answered. "Didn't Nora tell you yesterday?"

I thought back. Yeah, Nora *had* said something about that. Something about a choice to start hormones.

Huh.

"But still," Vicky continued. "What's next?"

"Ooh, I know," Nora said. "Clothes shopping!"

"Clothes shopping?"

"Yeah. Such a cute girl can't go around wearing jeans and sweatshirts all the time." She grabbed hold of my hoodie, pinching the cloth between her thumb and forefinger, an expression of distaste on her face. "Seriously, Lily, what are you even doing? This doesn't fit you at all."

"Do you have something against sweatshirts?" I asked.

"The fact that I've never seen you wear anything but sweatshirts aside, I have something against *this* sweatshirt specifically," she replied. "Seriously. Look at it."

I gave the cloth a long, critical look. It was one of my favorite hoodies: I'd bought it in my second year of high school, and it still fit me fine. But it *was* quite old and well-loved — almost threadbare in places, in fact.

Nora was right: I was in sore need of some new clothes. A wardrobe change.

But . . .

"I don't know," I replied. "I can't just start wearing girls' clothing. How will I even explain it to Joe?"

"Who's Joe?" Nora asked.

"Lily's roommate," Anna explained. "He's a chud."

"Oh," Nora said. "Well, that's not really a problem. You don't need to start wearing skirts and dresses. Not right away, at least. You can go for jeans, maybe a nice shirt, and no one will be the wiser. Except us, of course." She grinned roguishly at me — her usual grin, the one that made me feel a bit weak in the knees. "And you'll still be cuter."

I looked at her as she smiled at me, I found I just couldn't resist her.

"Okay. Fine." I laughed. "If you really insist, let's go shopping. But I won't promise I'll buy anything."

"Good girl."

≡

"Alright, now try this on," Vicky said, stuffing a pair of shorts into my hands.

"And these, too," Anna added, holding up two shirts. (Blouses? Maybe? But they could pass for men's shirts.) "I think they'll go nicely with the pants you tried earlier."

"You're enjoying this, aren't you," I said, shooting them both a look; it wasn't a question.

"Yep, they are, and so am I," Elanor said. "Try these too." They handed me two pairs of pants — the same model in two different sizes.

"My vengeance will be terrible and prolonged," I muttered before retreating into the fitting room and sliding the curtain closed.

I quickly took off the pants and shirt I was wearing, and passed them through the side of the curtain to the girls (and enby) standing outside. "These don't work, so you can put them back," I said as someone grabbed them from my hand.

"Ah, just leave them lying around, someone will get to it," I heard Anna say.

"Put them back, please," I insisted; we were making too much work for the shop assistants, who were probably minimum wage and not paid nearly enough to clean up after us. I pulled on the shorts and one of the shirts, before posing in front of the mirror.

They actually fit fine. Both of them.

A bit on the snug side, but this was how women's clothing was, wasn't it? They fit the body much more closely than men's clothes. I knew that from my high school days — I'd spent most of my first year staring at girls and checking out what they were wearing. (I stopped doing that once I realized I was creeping them out, and that being interested in women's fashion was a weird hobby for a guy to have.)

Okay, these go in the 'maybe' pile. The ever-growing 'maybe' pile. I would need to decide what to get; I couldn't spend hundreds of dollars on clothes I would never wear again after a few months.

Or maybe I could? After all, clothes were just clothes. Pants and shirts especially: if I bought a skirt or a dress, that would be a different matter, since men don't wear those. But pants and shirts are unisex.

I shook myself: I was getting sidetracked. I still had two pairs of pants to try on. I slipped the shorts and shirt off, and spun around to grab the clothes Elanor had given me.

As I turned I caught sight of myself in the mirror, and what I saw made me pause.

I was only wearing a pair of panties and a simple camisole, which my torturers had insisted I put on — after all, girl's clothes don't fit right if you're wearing men's underwear. But I didn't feel the usual repulsion, the usual disgust I experienced when I looked at men's bodies, including my own.

In fact, I quite liked what I saw.

It was *bizarre*. For years I'd avoided staring at myself so I wouldn't feel bad . . . and somehow now that whole thing had just gone away?

Slowly my hand drifted to the hem of my camisole, and I started pulling it up . . .

"How are you doing in there, Lily?" Nora said. "Everything good?"

I jumped and shook myself again. "Yeah!" I replied. "I just need to try on a couple more things!"

"Alright," she said. "Take your time. I have something else for you when you're done with those."

I quickly pulled on the last two pieces of clothing — they fit fine and went on the 'maybe' pile too — then pulled the curtain open.

"What do you have for me?"

They all looked at me without speaking, making me a bit nervous.

Nora looked nervous too as she took a deep breath. "Alright, I know this isn't exactly what you've asked for," she said. "It's not something you can wear without outing yourself. But I thought you might want to try it."

She held up a long-sleeved teal dress with an asymmetric, blue-and-yellow flower pattern splayed all over it.

I felt my breath catch in my throat; it was beautiful.

But . . . A dress? I couldn't wear a dress! How would I explain it to Joe? How would I explain it to everyone who didn't know I was trans?

It was impossible. I should've refused to try it on. Said no right away.

But I couldn't take my eyes off it.

I nervously bit my lip. "Nora, I . . ." I began, then stopped. I what? What was I going to say? What did I *want* to say? I couldn't just try on a dress. I couldn't just *wear* a dress.

And yet, I really wanted to. Just to see how it fit.

Nora made the decision for me. "Just try it," she said, pushing the dress into my hands. "You don't have to buy it. Just try it on."

I looked at the dress, then back up at her. Our eyes locked together, and the warm look I saw in her gaze gave me the final push; I found myself nodding.

I retreated into the fitting room and slowly, taking care, slipped on the dress. Shaking a bit, I turned and looked at myself in the mirror.

And I audibly gasped.

It was a completely alien sight. The dress fell down to just below my knees, and hugged my body snugly. Even the shoulders, which were a sore point in quite a few of the shirts lying in the 'maybe' pile, looked perfect.

It was beautiful.

The dress was beautiful.

I was beautiful.

How can you be beautiful? Girls are beautiful; men aren't. Men can't be beautiful. And you're a man. You're a guy who's pretending to be a girl. You're not beautiful. You can't be beautiful. What the hell do you think you're doing?

I grimaced. I felt the bottom of my stomach drop to somewhere below my feet. Gone was the happy feeling that had filled me only a few moments before: I felt *awful*.

What the hell do you think you're doing?

My breathing became labored.

This was never going to work. I had to take off this dress. I had to get out of there. I had to—

"How's the dress?" Nora asked.

Hearing her voice grounded me. *No*, I firmly told myself. *This isn't the time to make a scene.*

All I had to do was smile and pretend I was fine. I could do that. I was an expert at it: I'd done it for years.

I plastered on a smile I sincerely hoped looked genuine, took a deep breath, and pulled the curtain open. "See for yourself."

"Whoa," Vicky said. "Lily, you look . . ."

"Yep, I knew it," Nora said, nodding in satisfaction. "Cute. No, not even cute: *beautiful*."

"Yeah, holy shit," Anna added. "You have a very good eye, Nora."

I felt a bit better. "You . . . you really think so?" I asked hesitantly. "You really think . . ."

I paused and bit my lip.

"You really think I look beautiful?"

"Yes, we do. Right, folks?"

There were murmurs of agreement, and my spirits lifted a bit more. I found myself smiling — genuinely smiling, unlike the fake smile I'd sported a few moments before. "Thank you," I mumbled. I took a deep breath. "You know what? I think I'll take this."

Anna looked at me in concern. "Are you sure, Lily? If Joe sees it . . ."

"I'll keep it in my room," Nora said. "So there's no risk. Lily can come over to wear it whenever she wants."

She winked at me, and I felt my face go deep red.

"I . . . I'll get changed so we can pay for everything and go." I returned to the fitting room and quickly took off the dress.

I put my jeans and hoodie back on and paused. After the clothes I'd spent a couple hours trying on, my boy clothing felt . . . weird. Odd. Uncomfortable. I briefly wondered why that was, but didn't have time to think about it.

"Ready," I announced, sliding the curtain back open.

"Good," Elanor said. "Now let's sort these clothes out, decide what to buy. You're getting the dress, right?"

I hesitated for a moment again, but nodded. "Yes, the dress and—"

"Excuse me, are you done with this fitting room?" a girl's voice asked.

"Oh, yeah, go ahead, please," I said, looking up.

The girl who'd spoken gave a start, but immediately afterward pierced me with an icy glare. I almost unconsciously took a step back as I shrank under her gaze: why was she looking at me like that? She looked familiar; where had I seen her before?

Nora solved the mystery: "Jillian," she said, her voice flat.

Jillian. Of course. That's who she was: Nora's ex-girlfriend.

"Nora," Jillian said, turning to look at her. "What are you doing here?"

"We're helping Lily pick out some clothes," Nora replied. "For her new wardrobe."

Eyes full of contempt, Jillian looked at me like I was a disgusting insect, just waiting to be squashed by a rolled-up newspaper and thrown out with the trash.

"I see," she said. "So you're still humoring him."

I felt the pit in my stomach swallow me up.

Yes, that's right. Thank you for the reminder, Jillian. What the hell am I even doing here, trying on girls' clothing?

I was a man.

Tears welled up in my eyes, and my breathing sped up.

"*Her*," Vicky said, a dangerous edge to her voice. "Do *not* make that mistake again."

Jillian scoffed. "Why should I—"

"Because otherwise it could be a problem. For you." Vicky cut her off, straightening to her (admittedly modest) full height.

Jillian looked at Vicky for a moment, not even bothering to hide her contempt, and then turned her gaze around to look at each of my friends in turn, almost as if she was sizing them up.

"I would help her, you know," Nora said. "We might have dated once, but if you insult Lily again I will not hesitate to lay your ass flat."

My gaze drifted to Nora; our eyes met, and she smiled at me.

The pit in my stomach deepened, feeling bottomless. I was frozen in place. Was I still breathing? I had no idea.

Jillian focused her glare on me. "Alright," she said. "But I still need to use the fitting room, and *she*—"

She put a significant emphasis on the pronoun, and never before had I heard a word spoken with such venom.

"—said you were done. May I?"

I gulped, trying and failing to swallow the dense, heavy lump that had formed in my throat, and nodded weakly.

"Good," Jillian said. She marched inside and slid the curtain closed.

I seemed to have forgotten how to breathe: each time I inhaled, I had to force myself not to pass out.

"Lily? Hey," Elanor said. "Don't mind her, okay?"

"Yeah," Nora added, placing a hand on my shoulder and squeezing it in reassurance. "Don't let her get to you. You're a girl, no matter what that bitch thinks or says."

But you're not a girl.

What the hell do you think you're doing?

You're not a girl, Lily. You're a man.

Stop pretending.

I looked around at my friends, then shook my head.

"Let's just pay for these clothes and go home."

9
Consent

I COULDN'T STOP thinking about the encounter we'd had with Jillian at the clothing store.

It was as if she could see right through me: somehow she'd said the exact words to needle my guilt. To make me feel bad. To make me feel like an impostor.

Jillian had, unknowingly, hit the nail on the head. She'd stopped short of saying it outright, but the implication in her words had been unmistakable: Lily O'Connor is not a real girl. Lily O'Connor is just a man who's playing pretend for the purpose of deceiving everyone.

But that was what I was doing. I *was* just pretending. I wasn't a real girl.

I *was* an impostor.

I'd thought I was over my feelings of guilt about my plan: it had been months since my 'coming out,' and I'd comfortably settled into the role of the newly-out trans girl trying to navigate life. I'd even almost stopped thinking about it all being a ruse and started to enjoy it, but Jillian had blown the whole thing back open, and now I was dwelling on it.

But it was my fault, wasn't it? This was the bed I'd made for myself, and I would have to lie in it sooner or later. In a few months I would have to confess to everyone that I'd just been pretending. And then I would probably lose all my friends. Anna, Elanor. Vicky. Nora. They'd immediately stop talking to me. No doubt at all about that.

Which sucked a whole lot.

While hatching my plan I hadn't considered how much I would come to enjoy hanging out with my little queer friend group. They were all excellent people, and I seriously disliked having to lie to them. Maybe in the future, when the dust had settled, we could start over and be friends again.

Doubtful.

At least I could still enjoy the time I was spending with them. I'd just finished my classes for the day, and I'd come back to my room to drop off my school stuff and take my hormones before heading out to movie night. I was running late because Professor Markley had stopped me to tell me about a research project he wanted me to participate in; something about toxic masculinity.

. . . But maybe I could take a few more minutes and dress up. Wear some of the girl clothes I'd bought. They'd been locked in my closet for the past two weeks, which was a shame.

Yes. I should definitely—

As I turned the key, it didn't make the usual noise. Almost as if . . .

It was unlocked?

Weird. I always made sure to lock it when heading out; there was no way I'd forgotten.

I pushed the door open and went in.

"Hey! Buddy!" Joe exclaimed, springing to his feet a bit unsteadily. "It's good to see you!"

"Joe? What are you doing here?" I asked, wrinkling my nose: I could smell him from six feet away. The whole room stunk of booze. Ever since I'd started hormones my sense of smell had become much more sensitive: Vicky told me it was a side effect many trans women experience. I normally thought it was neat, but at that moment I seriously wished I'd been an outlier — the smell of cheap alcohol emanating from my roommate was making me a bit queasy.

"What d'you mean?" Joe spun in a circle, almost losing his balance as he gestured expansively to encompass our surroundings. "This is my room too."

"No, I mean, where have you been?" I said. "It's nearly February. I was expecting to see you after Christmas break."

Joe turned to me and waved my question away as if it wasn't worth thinking about. "Oh, that. It's no biggie, really. I was just locked up for a while."

"Locked up?" I repeated.

"Yeah, funny story." He got up and started pacing around the room. "I was about to come back to college and just went out for one last night of partying with my buddies from high school. We had fun, drank a bit, became a bit loud — just a bit — one thing led to the other and before I knew it, this fag was getting in my face."

"This . . . Wait, who did what again?"

Joe stopped dead in his tracks and nodded dramatically, his head bobbing up and down comically. "Yeah! It turned out there was a group of gays at the bar, and one of them didn't take kindly to something I said, so he walked up to me and said something, I don't even remember what." He paused and scrunched his face in concentration, trying to remember. "Something about respect? Whatever. But long story short, we got in a fight. I punched him, he punched me. See here?"

He turned his face to the side and pointed at his cheekbone: there was a bruise there, fading but still visible.

"Yes, I see," I said. "So you got locked up for that?"

"Nah, not for that. When the cops came over and broke the fight up, the fag decided not to press charges. And a good thing he did, or he'd have got what was coming to him." His face screwed up in disgust. "Seriously, some people. They act as if they're worthy of respect. One of these days . . ."

"Joe?" I cut him off. "You were saying?"

"Hm?" he replied, coming back to the moment. "Oh, right. He didn't press charges, but it turns out I had an outstanding warrant from last summer."

"An outstanding warrant for what?"

"Punched a dude in a bar? I think? I forget," he said dismissively, as if him assaulting someone was a completely normal thing not worth thinking twice about. "But the cops decided to enforce that — entirely unfair, if you ask me — and I got three weeks in the county jail. Plus a fine." He scowled. "The fag got off scot-free, of course."

"Oh," I said.

"Yeah, 'oh.' The system is rigged, I tell you. Rigged!" He took a deep breath, then unexpectedly stepped forward and crushed me into a bearhug. "Man, there are so many freaks out there, you wouldn't believe it. I'm glad you're not one of them, my man."

The stench of booze assaulted my nose and I grimaced, but at the same time the hair on the back of my neck rose and an icy chill ran down my spine

Shit. This was bad. This was *seriously* bad. If Joe somehow found out I was trans — or, rather, that I was *pretending to be* trans . . .

I honestly had no idea what his reaction would be. I mean, he'd just admitted to being homophobic, and to punching someone on at least two occasions — that was besides being a misogynistic ass, which I already knew about him.

I could still probably explain everything. If I could just sit him down and talk to him, man to man, he'd understand what I was doing. He'd probably think it was hilarious, but there was no way I could do it then — he was way too drunk. I would have to do it some other time.

And avoid him finding out on his own before that. Because if he did . . .

I gulped, thinking about how he would react.

"Uh . . . Joe. Buddy. Think you can let go?"

"Oh!" Joe exclaimed. "Of course, of course." He released the hug. "Don't want nobody to think we're some kind of homos, after all. You get what I mean."

I plastered a fake smile on my lips. "Yeah, don't want that."

"But anyway," Joe continued, plopping back down on his bed. "Circling alllllllll the way back to your first question: that's why I was so late coming back."

"Yeah, I get it. And, speaking of late." I looked at my watch for effect. "I really have to go now."

His eyebrows rose in surprise. "Oh? Where you going?"

"I'm meeting up with friends," I said. "I just came to drop off my school stuff and pick up something before I head out."

Joe nodded and let himself fall back on the mattress, face toward the ceiling. Keeping watch on him out of the corner of my eye, I pulled my school stuff out of my backpack and set it on my desk, then opened my wardrobe and, keeping my body between it and Joe, grabbed the paper bag which had my hormones in it and stuffed it in the backpack. "I'll be out late. Don't wait up," I said, turning back around.

"Alright," he said, raising an arm and waving without looking at me. "Have fun!"

I didn't exhale the breath I'd been holding until I'd closed the door behind myself.

Jesus *Christ*. Just when I'd thought Joe was gone for good, there he was again; and this time, I would have to tread even more carefully around him.

☰

"Hi, Lily," Vicky said, opening the door; then she frowned. "What's wrong? You don't look so good."

"I'm fine," I said, giving her a weak smile and walking into the house. "It's just . . . Well, it's Joe."

"What did he do now?" Anna asked from the couch. "Wait, I thought he still hadn't come back."

"He came back today, actually," I replied, taking off my coat and plopping down on the other couch next to Nora. "Tonight. He was in our room when I came back from social studies."

"Okay," Nora said, putting an arm around my shoulders. "So your chuddy roommate is back. What about it?"

I took a deep, shuddering breath and leaned into Nora's embrace before launching into an explanation, recounting what Joe had told me about his Christmas break, where he'd been and, more importantly, what he'd done.

There was a somber silence in the room. Nora pulled me closer to her, holding me reassuringly, and I found myself smiling.

Then Anna spoke up.

"Lily, this . . . Wow. I knew he was an idiot, but I didn't think he would . . . *Damn.*"

"Yeah, me neither," I said. "And that . . . Well, that makes me real nervous. If he finds out about *me* . . ."

I let the sentence hang in the air.

"Do you think he would *attack* you?" Elanor looked at me, wide-eyed.

"I'm not sure. But I'm also not sure he wouldn't," I replied with a grimace.

"But . . . you're roommates!" they exclaimed. "You're friends!"

I gave a brief laugh. "No, we're not friends. Nowhere close, actually. I really tried being friends with him at first, but . . . Nope. Which brings me to this," I continued, waving my hand toward my backpack. "My hormones are in here. Can I ask one of you to keep them in your room? So I don't run the risk of Joe finding them."

"Of course," Nora said. "Since I already have your dress, I can absolutely keep your hormones too. You can count on me for this, Lily."

She smiled at me, and I felt warm inside. "Thank you," I said, smiling back.

Anna's brow furrowed. "I think you should tell someone. About Joe, I mean."

"What would I even say?" I replied. "Do I just go up to the RA and tell him, 'Hey, I'm actually a trans girl, surprise! And my roommate said something that made me go, ha ha ha, I'm in danger, can you do something about it?'"

"Yes," Anna said. "That's exactly what I'd do."

"As would I," Nora supplied.

I thought about it for a moment. Yeah, that was probably the wisest course of action, wasn't it? But on the other hand, it would mean telling someone at college — someone who had authority — about me being trans. And that would make it even more real. So far I'd just told other students, but if I told faculty or some other employee, like Darrell, that would be something I wouldn't easily be able to walk back.

And besides, it wasn't like I was in real danger anyway. I mean, I probably would be if Joe found out about me before I could talk to him, but with the hormones safely out of the room, that was now unlikely. I just needed to find a moment when he wasn't drunk or mad at me to sit him down and explain everything, and then it would be fine.

But I couldn't tell my friends all that — the real reason. So I made up an explanation on the spot. "No. Joe doesn't deserve this."

Anna looked at me in disbelief. "Are you kidding me right now? He's a bigoted asshole! And he *assaulted* someone, Lily! *Two* someones! At least!"

"That was probably only a misdemeanor assault, though," Elanor commented. "The first one, I mean: three weeks in jail is a misdemeanor, not a felony. Either he didn't hurt the other guy too much, or he got off lightly somehow. And the second one was *definitely* a misdemeanor, otherwise the cops would've arrested him even without the other guy pressing charges. The *other* other guy, I mean."

Everyone turned to look at them. There was a moment of silence.

"That was not helpful, dear," Anna said.

"Sorry, it just came out," they replied, looking sheepish. "I studied this just this afternoon. Forgot to turn off Lawyer Mode."

"That's even more reason," I said. "He did something wrong, true, but it wasn't too bad and he paid the price. And he hasn't done anything to me yet. There's the fact that he's a . . . a bigoted asshole, yes . . ."

"And how," Anna commented snidely.

". . . but you can't just lock men up to cure them of toxic masculinity. It doesn't work that way. If I went to Darrell it would ruin Joe's life. I won't do it."

"I agree with you," Vicky said.

Well, *that* was unexpected. Vicky had been about to throw hands with Jillian when she'd misgendered me: for her to defend *Joe*, of all people . . . "You do?"

"Yes. I mean, we can't condemn someone for something they might do in the future. It's not that simple. Maybe he'll come around and see what he did was wrong." She looked around the room, and I was surprised to see her eyes were pained. "I believe people can change. I *have* to believe people can change."

There was a moment of silence, which I then filled. "See? This is the right course of action. I won't do anything for the moment, and keep my guard up."

"I'm sorry, Lily, but as your friend I have to tell you I disagree with you on this," Anna said.

"As do I," Nora said. "You're putting yourself in danger for no good reason."

I sighed. "Yeah, probably," I conceded. "But I'll be careful. I promise."

"You do that," Nora said. "I care about you, girl. Don't make me worry."

I felt butterflies flutter in my stomach as she stood up from the couch and retrieved something from her purse.

"I want you to have this." She handed me a can of pepper spray. "Don't hesitate to use it. And if you need help, call me. I'll come running."

"Thank you," I said, and patted my pockets, realizing there was no way the spray would fit in there: I would need to think of some way to carry it. For the moment, I slipped it into my coat pocket before sitting back down.

"Oh, this reminds me, I haven't taken my hormones for tonight yet. Couldn't take them in front of Joe, obviously."

I fumbled in my backpack, pulled out my usual pill-and-a-half, popped the hormones in my mouth, and chased them down with a swig of soda.

"Hold on," Victoria said. "You're just swallowing them?"

I looked at her, puzzled. "Yeah? Is that not how I'm supposed to take them?"

"No you're not." She shook her head. "You swallow the cypro, but you put the estradiol in your mouth and let it dissolve under your tongue. There's a whole technical explanation about it, but you get much better effects if you do it like that."

Weird. The thing about dissolving pills under your tongue hadn't come up in all the research I'd done. I wondered if there were other important things I'd also missed.

I was shaken out of my thoughts when Anna asked, "Anyway, whose turn was it to pick the movie?"

"Mine," Elanor said, showing us the DVD case: *Revenge of the Nerds*.

"Nope," Nora snapped. "Absolutely not. I'm using my veto. Fuck that movie."

We all looked at her, surprised at the venom in her voice.

"Why?" Elanor replied. "I mean, it's no problem, it's the rules after all. I was just wondering."

"I refuse to watch a movie that normalizes rape by deception," Nora said.

I gave her a curious look. "What's that mean?"

"You know how consent is the basis for a relationship? That everyone has to be on the same page, everything has to be done by mutual agreement, especially when it comes to having sex?"

I nodded: I'd read about it online, and it made sense.

"In this movie there's a scene where one of the protagonists dresses up in a mask for Halloween or something like that. I forget what the occasion is, exactly, but that's beside the point. The point is, he's disguised, and he has sex with the antagonist's girlfriend while he's disguised," she explained. "But the girl doesn't know who the person under the mask is: she thinks it's her boyfriend. So she didn't consent to having sex with the protagonist, he's tricking her into it. He's *deceiving* her. Which makes it . . ."

". . . Rape by deception," I said. "Yeah, I get it."

"And the worst part is, the movie treats this as no big deal. Later on she says she enjoyed it, so it's fine," Nora continued. "So, again: fuck that movie."

"Okay," Elanor said, "I see your point. Here's my backup."

"*The Lost World*," Vicky read the case. "That's the second *Jurassic Park* movie, isn't it?

"Yep," Elanor said. "It's one of my dad's favorites; we always watch it when I go home."

"I've seen it before, but it'll be fun watching it again." Melanie spoke for the first time that night. "And I know a game we can play with this movie."

"Oh?" Katie perked up, suddenly interested. "I love games. What kind of game?"

"Hold on." Melanie went to the kitchen, returning with three six-packs of beer. "Drinking game." She grinned. "The rules are simple: take a drink whenever a new dinosaur appears on screen, and take a drink whenever someone gets eaten."

Elanor gave her a skeptical look. "That's not nearly enough beer for this," they said.

Mel shrugged. "There's more, but I think that's enough if we pace ourselves. I didn't say how big the drink has to be. And you don't have to play if you don't want to."

I thought about it: a drinking game wouldn't hurt, would it? It would be a good way to distract me from the ongoing weirdness with Joe. I could loosen up a bit, really: I hadn't drunk any booze the whole month — I was a bit startled to realize that the last time had been when I went out with Joe and his friends before Christmas break.

"Alright, I'm in," I said, grabbing a can.

After all, how bad could it be?

≣

I woke to the smell of cooked bacon.

Cracking open an eye, I looked around. It took me a few moments to recognize my surroundings; I was still in Vicky, Mel, and Katie's living room, lying on a couch with a blanket draped over me. The curtains were drawn, but some light still filtered in.

What the hell had happened?

I tried to pull myself up to a seated position and immediately regretted it, as a lancing pain shot through my head and I fell back on the couch with a groan. I instantly recognized the symptoms of a hangover, but they were really intense: probably the worst I'd felt in my life.

"Oh, you're up," a voice said. "How are you feeling?"

I looked at Nora as she crouched next to the couch. "Terrible," I mumbled.

"Understandable. The booze really did a number on you yesterday, like holy shit. Here, take this, it will make you feel better."

She handed me a pill and a glass of water, and I gladly swallowed it — my throat was parched. I tried to think back: I could barely remember someone rubbing my back while I was bent over the toilet puking my guts out, and then being laid down gently on the couch.

"But still, it's weird," Nora continued. "The drinking game was tough, but you didn't drink *that* much."

"It's the hormones," Vicky said, walking into the living room in a nightgown and a pair of leggings. I felt a weird sensation in my stomach as I took in just how feminine she looked even in such simple clothing: maybe I could look like that, too. Or maybe it was the hangover talking. "They absolutely tank your alcohol tolerance. You're lucky it happened here among friends, and not somewhere public. That might have been dangerous." She wrinkled her nose. "Do I smell something burning?"

"Oh, the bacon!" Nora exclaimed, and she rushed to the kitchen.

"She was by your side all night, you know," Vicky said, lowering her voice. "When she saw how you were looking, she got really worried. And then you said something like, 'I don't wanna go back,' and she asked us to let you both sleep here. She even popped out to the store this morning to buy eggs and bacon for breakfast since we didn't have enough in the house." She winked at me. "You're very lucky, girl."

Maybe I was too addled from the previous night, but I didn't understand what she meant.

"Saved it!" Nora called from the kitchen. "Come on, breakfast's almost ready! The Nora Hangover Special!"

"I'll go call Mel and Katie," Vicky said. "You take your time."

Slowly, carefully, I pulled myself up to a seated position, then stood up. Every muscle in my body aching, I dragged my sorry self over to the kitchen, where Nora was sliding fried eggs onto five plates with crispy bacon on them.

Mel, Katie, and Vicky joined us. The bacon and eggs were cooked perfectly: as I gulped them down and chased them with plenty of coffee and orange juice, I felt like I was coming back to life.

"Now, Lily, you really should try to be careful," Mel chided me. "I can understand drinking, but that was way too much."

"Hey, it was *you* who thought to make it a drinking game," Katie rebutted. "So if anything, it's your fault."

"We all stopped when the velociraptors showed up." Mel shrugged. "Lily was the only one who kept going. Ah well, we got free breakfast out of it, at least."

After we'd had our fill, Nora and I thanked the trio for letting us stay overnight, then slowly, walking side by side, we made our way back home. As she'd done a few times before, Nora walked me back to my dorm. When we arrived, I turned to her and smiled.

"Thank you, Nora," I said. "I'm really grateful for what you did."

"You're welcome, Lily." She paused for a moment, then continued, "But there's one more thing I'm going to do right now."

I looked at her, puzzled. "Oh?"

"You know how we talked about consent yesterday? How it's the basis of a relationship?"

I nodded, still wondering what she was getting at.

"I would really like to kiss you right now, Lily. I'm *going* to kiss you right now," she said confidently. "You can stop me if you don't want to, but if you don't stop me I'll take it as a sign that you consent to it."

Wait, what? She was going to *kiss* me? What? What?! Hold on, why did she want to kiss me? I probably looked like death warmed over, not exactly someone you'd want to kiss. Was Nora sure about this? I wasn't entirely sure myself. What if—

Nora leaned in.

I didn't say anything or try to stop her.

Our lips met. She pulled me into the kiss, her tongue snaking past my lips to touch mine and flick against it a few times. By the time we came up for air, my mind was in the clouds, enveloped by a happy, fuzzy, light-pink fog.

Nora pulled back and smiled impishly as she licked her lips. "Hmm, tastes like bacon. I like it," she said, grinning at me. "Did you like it too?"

I looked at her, wide-eyed. In my mind, the little Lily who controlled my speech looked around desperately, flipping open books and manuals, trying to find the correct response and coming up empty: in the end, she resorted to just smashing a few keys.

"Sfhaadhvkafs," I mumbled.

Nora laughed. "I'll take that as a yes." She leaned forward and gave me another peck on the lips.

"Have a good weekend, Lily," she said, turning around and walking away.

I watched her go for several minutes, until she was out of sight, then, still dazed, I walked to my room, not even reacting to Darrell's greeting. Joe wasn't there; he'd probably gone off somewhere with his friends. I lay on my bed and looked at the ceiling for what felt like several hours, a stupid, contented grin on my lips.

10
Getting It Together

BY THE TIME late morning rolled around, my grin had turned into a frown.

My mind kept going back to the kiss. It had felt amazing. Incredible, even. It was my first kiss, and one of the best things I'd ever experienced.

There was just a slight hiccup: why, exactly, had Nora kissed me? We were friends, true, but that wasn't really a friendly kiss. Far from it. (Do friends kiss each other on the lips, even?)

But if it hadn't been a friendly kiss, did . . . Did it mean Nora liked me? Like, as in *like* liked me.

My first instinct was to dismiss the thought right away. After all, who would like someone like me? Someone who could barely hold it together at the best of times. I was a complete disaster, not even remotely worthy of being loved.

Some people *liked* me, true: all my friends from the small queer group we'd accidentally put together. But they liked me as a friend. No, thinking about it, not even that: they liked *Lily* as a friend. They liked the persona I put on when I was with them. They liked someone who didn't even exist. They liked a phantom. They didn't like *me*. No one did.

Just like no one would ever love me. My parents loved me, true (probably), but that was familial love; romantic love was entirely out of my reach.

That was a conclusion I'd come to when I was in high school, after years and years of trying and failing: every time I'd tried to get close to someone in a romantic way, every time I made advances, I'd invariably been rejected. And the few times I hadn't been, nothing really came of it and they broke up with me after one or two dates, before we'd even kissed.

So that was the conclusion I'd circled back to: no one would ever love me. Not romantically, anyway.

But if that were the case, Nora's actions — her kissing me — didn't make any sense. On one hand: it had been the kind of kiss you give to someone you really like. To someone you love, even. But on the other: it was clearly, plainly ridiculous. No one loved me, ergo Nora didn't love me.

But why had she kissed me, then? Why had she kissed me *like that*? What—

I took a deep breath and shook my head to clear it. I was getting nowhere, my thoughts were getting wound up in a tight circle, which was starting to resemble a spiral with each passing second. There was no way I could reason myself out of this, not without more information.

I needed a second opinion. And maybe a third and a fourth.

I sat up in bed and grabbed my phone, which was charging on my nightstand. With a few taps I opened WhatsApp, and added three people to a group chat — Anna, Vicky, and Elanor.

Hey, y'all, I typed. *Sorry to bother you, and sorry for the short notice, but can we meet for lunch? At Giovanni's. I have something to ask you.*

The first one to respond was Elanor. *Sure, what's up? Is there a problem?*

I don't think so, I wrote. *I just need to talk.*

Sure, no prob, they wrote back. *I'll tell Anna, we're together right now.*

I'm good with it too, Vicky answered. *Oh, Nora isn't in the chat. Hold on, I'll add her now.*

No! I immediately sent, then took a deep breath and, more calmly, continued, *No, I don't wanna talk to her for the time being. Just us four for now.*

...Okay, Vicky replied. *Alright, is noon fine?*

Works for me.

It's okay with me and Anna too, Elanor replied.

See y'all in a few. I closed the chat. Looking at my watch, I saw I had just enough time to brush my teeth, wash my face, and change my clothes before heading out.

I was confident my friends would help me make sense of all this.

≡

"Sorry I'm late."

I approached the group at a jog. I'd gotten distracted picking out my clothes: since the shopping trip, my wardrobe had significantly expanded and sometimes I had trouble deciding what to wear. I'd gone for an androgynous ensemble of a long-sleeved shirt and a pair of black pants, plus my coat since it was still late January. I'd been careful, though: it was still an outfit that could pass for men's clothing, so I would hopefully get no raised eyebrows or probing questions from Joe.

"No worries," Anna replied. "So, what did you want to talk to us about?"

"What do you say we talk about it in front of some food?" I asked. "I'm famished."

"Surprising, given how much you ate this morning," Vicky said.

"I have a fast metabolism." I grinned. "Somehow I seem unable to gain weight, no matter how much I eat."

"We'll see about that," she replied cryptically, but before I could ask what she meant she'd pushed open the door to the café and gone in, followed by Anna and Elanor. We sat at a table which was a bit more isolated — no one within earshot. The waiter came over and took our order, but I barely paid attention. I was busy figuring out what to say.

"Okay," Elanor said. "So?"

"So." I took a deep breath. "When Nora and I left this morning, she walked me back to my dorm, and . . ."

I paused. Despite having prepared myself, I was still incredibly nervous. The silence stretched.

The waiter came back with our food.

The silence stretched further.

". . . And?" Anna queried. "What happened?"

I gulped and took a deep breath.

"And Nora kissed me."

There was a brief moment of silence as my friends digested what I'd said.

"Hey, congrats, that's really—" Elanor began, but they stopped talking when Vicky held up her hand sharply.

"And?" she asked. "You wouldn't have called us here if there wasn't a problem."

Typical Vicky: she was always the perceptive one. "And . . . and I don't know what that meant. What the kiss meant," I said. "It clearly wasn't a friendly kiss. I mean, there was tongue and all."

"Bragging, are we?" Anna said under her breath; Elanor swatted lightly at her.

"But . . . but if it wasn't a friendly kiss, what *was* it? I . . ." I carefully studied the wood grain of the table. "I mean, Nora hadn't shown any interest in me before, right? And besides, she can't be in love with me. That's just impossible. No one can be in love with me, because . . . Well, who would like me? I mean, you like me obviously, but as a friend. You're not in love with me. So if Nora isn't in love with me, what did that kiss mean? Because . . ."

I realized I was rambling. There was dead silence, punctuated only by the far-off noise of conversation at other tables, the hissing of the coffee machines, and crockery being moved around.

I was still looking at the table — I'd got lost in my head and spaced out a bit — so looked up at my friends.

Elanor was staring at me in clear disbelief, as was Vicky. Anna, on the other hand, had put her face in her hands and was mumbling softly to herself.

"Um, what?" I asked. "What's up? Why are you all so shocked? What's wrong?"

"Oooooooooooh God," Anna said. "Oh. *My. God.* Lily! You're just . . ."

"I'm just what?"

"You're so dumb," she groaned, face still in her hands. "I mean, holy shit, girl. Seriously."

Elanor shook their head. "Yeah, *seriously.* Like. *Wow.*"

"I don't get it." I spread my hands. "What's wrong?"

Vicky shook herself; she pierced me with a stare, her brow furrowing. Then she sighed.

"Nope. No, absolutely not," she said, and she started rooting in her purse. "*Absolutely* not. I'm not dealing with this. I'm not letting you do this to yourself. I'm nipping this in the bud *right now.*"

She pulled out her cell phone and held it to her ear. It took only a few moments for whoever was on the other side to answer.

"Yes, hi, it's Vicky. Yeah, hi," Vicky said into the phone. "Sorry to bother you. Okay, you see, I'm at Giovanni's, I'm having lunch with the others. Yeah, Elanor, Anna, and Lily. Yeah. Lily told us what happened this morning. Yep, she did. Yes, she told us about that. Yes. Congrats, by the way. Okay, you see, the reason I'm calling is that Lily is being a dumb baby and her brain is bullying her, so can you maybe come over and talk to her? I feel you really should. Okay." She tapped the screen to end the call. "Nora will be here ASAP."

I blinked. "That was Nora?"

"Yep," Vicky replied.

The thought of facing Nora so soon, without having had time to prepare myself, made my stomach drop and the blood drain from my face. I started to get up from my chair. "I'm sorry, I'm really sorry, I have to—"

"Oh no you don't, missy," Anna said, reaching across the table and grabbing my wrist to prevent me from escaping. "You ain't going nowhere."

I looked at her, then at Vicky and Elanor. "I know it's scary," Vicky said, "but this is when you put on your big girl pants and talk to Nora."

Elanor put a hand on my shoulder, pressing down on it, inviting me to take a seat again. "Sit down, eat your food, and prepare yourself," they said. "This is a conversation you need to have."

I still resisted a bit, but my three friends gave me three identical looks of disapproval, so in the end I sat back down and after a few moments, when she was sure I wasn't going to bolt, Anna let go of my wrist.

As we ate our meals in silence, I ruminated as I chewed each mouthful. What was I even going to say to Nora? Were we going to talk about the kiss?

Yes, of course we are going to talk about the kiss. This is kinda what it's all about. Don't be dumb, Lily.

And then what else were we going to talk about? The reason she'd kissed me? It couldn't be the fact that she loved me — I'd figured out that much by myself, but then *why* had she kissed me?

Was I overthinking all of this?

Yes, I probably was. Best to stop trying to figure things out by myself. Until I'd talked to Nora, at least.

Less than ten minutes later there was a loud jangling from the bells above the café door, and Nora burst through it, red in the face, hair unkempt. It was obvious she'd run all the way there.

She frantically looked around until her gaze landed on us. She took a half step forward, then paused and, after a moment, ran her hand through her hair, attempting to get it under control, and inhaled sharply

— so sharply I swear I could hear it from all the way across the café. Suddenly her panic was gone, and she was the confident, self-assured Nora I was used to seeing. She strode over to our table and absolutely *beamed* a smile down at me.

"Lily. Hi," she said, breathlessly. "Fancy finding you here. What an amazing coincidence."

Despite my feelings being in turmoil, I couldn't help but giggle. "Oh, come on, no need to pretend. I know she," I jerked a thumb toward Vicky, "called you here."

Nora nodded. "Figured as much. Vicky said you wanted to talk to me?"

"Hmm. Not *wanted* to talk, really. But I think we kinda *have* to talk."

"Alright." Nora pulled a chair from a nearby table and sat down. "Let's talk."

"And that, I think, is our cue," Vicky said, standing up and turning toward Anna and Elanor. "Let's go, you two."

The three of them — Anna quite reluctantly, it looked like she *really* wanted to listen in to what Nora and I would say to each other — left. Once they'd disappeared out of the door, Nora turned back to me.

"Okay. What did you want to talk about?"

"Well." I paused to gather my thoughts. "I wanted to talk to you about . . . the kiss."

"Okay . . . ? What about the kiss Did you not like it?"

"I did, but what I wanted to ask is . . . What did it mean, exactly? Was it a friendly kiss? Because—"

"Lily." Nora cut me off. "Come on. It wasn't a *friendly* kiss. Not at all." She paused. "I mean, did it *feel* like a friendly kiss? There was tongue. If that's a friendly kiss to you, I really wanna know what a passionate kiss looks like."

"I . . ." I said, then paused, blushing at the memory. "Okay. Next question, I guess is . . . What did it *mean*? If it wasn't a friendly kiss . . . ?"

Nora grinned roguishly. "What do you think? It means I *like* you, Lily. I like you a lot. I don't kiss just anyone like that."

My blush intensified. "I would hope not. How many girls have you kissed *like that* anyway?"

"Not that many," she replied. "And that's not the point: the point is, the only girls I kiss *like that* are girls I can see myself dating." She paused and, seeming suddenly nervous, looked me in the eye. "And I wanna date you, Lily. I seriously do."

I just looked at her, losing myself in her eyes. Nora was beautiful, and I . . .

"So," she continued, bringing me back to the moment. "Do you want to date?" There was an undertone of unsteadiness behind her smile, but it was still charming and irresistible. "I mean, you know. Go out together, see places, hang out . . . That kind of stuff."

I decided I wanted to tease her a bit. "Weren't we already doing that?"

"Yes, actually," she replied. "But this would be different." She leaned forward, grabbed my hands, and whispered conspiratorially: "This would involve *more kissing*."

I giggled. "Well, if it means more kissing, I'm in. Absolutely."

"Good," Nora said. She leaned further forward and our lips met.

This kiss was different. It wasn't anything like the kiss she'd given me that morning: our tongues weren't involved, it was more chaste but much more passionate. And I enjoyed it a lot.

"So this is it?" I asked, after we'd separated. "We're officially dating then?"

"Yep," Nora replied. "We're together, an item, and all that jazz. But don't worry, if you're not comfortable with something, just tell me. Consent, remember? We're not going to do anything either of us doesn't want. We'll take it slow. I can wait for as long as you need. I care about you, Lily."

She reached out with her hand, squeezed my shoulder, and smiled at me; I smiled back.

Well. I'd gotten myself a girlfriend.

But I was still puzzled. I still couldn't tell why anyone, much less an amazing girl like Nora, would want to date *me*.

11

Growing Pains

"Come on, what are you waiting for?" Nora said, a bit impatiently. "I've shown you how to do it plenty of times."

"Um . . . okay," I nervously replied. I licked my lips, then slowly, carefully, slipped my tool inside the hole. "Like this?"

"Exactly like that." Nora nodded in satisfaction. "Now move it around, try to get a feel for it. Find the spot."

I shifted positions. Pushed around. Everything was surprisingly pliable, I expected it to be more . . . rigid, somehow. Not that I had much experience.

"Good," Nora said. "Try twisting a little."

I found some unexpected resistance: no matter what I did, it just wouldn't budge, so I stopped. I was unsure whether to keep pushing forward — if I did, I risked bending or breaking something. "Is it . . . is it supposed to feel like this?" I asked. "I can barely move it."

"No, it's supposed to slide around without any problem," she replied. "Hold on. Try to pull back. Just a tad."

I did as I was told, and immediately heard the rapid-fire *click-click-click* of the pins falling back into place; I sighed deeply, and pulled the lockpick out of the keyhole.

"I'll never get this," I complained. "It's too hard."

"It's absolutely not hard, you're just not used to it." Nora held out her hand. "I'll show you again. Give it here."

I handed the padlock and lockpicks to her, and she immediately got to picking. "See, you turn the tensioner slightly, just a little bit. Not too much, or it'll be difficult to push in the pins. And then you feel for the pins," she said, sliding the lockpick in the keyhole. "You move it around a bit, listen for the clicks, and . . ."

The keyhole turned and, with a loud *clack*, the padlock popped open. "See? Nothing to it."

"You make it look easy," I said sullenly.

"I suppose," she replied. "But then again, this is a particularly shitty padlock. It's good for practice, but I wouldn't use it for its intended purpose. It's easy to open and I've picked it probably hundreds of times, so I know exactly where the pins have to go. Muscle memory." She smiled warmly at me. "You'll get it eventually. All it takes is practice."

I shook my head. Nora had talked me and a few of our friends into giving lockpicking a try; after just one hour of this, though, I was getting ready to give up.

"But even if you don't get it," Nora continued, "you can just call me. I'll come right away and open any lock you need me to."

She leaned forward in her chair and gave me a peck on the cheek, which went red — along with both my ears.

Even after two weeks, I was still not used to being the object of someone's affection, since I'd never been in a serious relationship before. Nora and the others delighted in teasing me endlessly, and seemed to revel in my embarrassed reactions. I definitely didn't dislike this, I was just completely unused to it. It was an awkward feeling of wanting to be loved, but not knowing how to react to it at the same time.

"Oh, look at that blush," Vicky commented from the next table over. "Cute."

"Isn't she?" Nora said. "The cutest girl on campus."

Case in point: my blush, if at all possible, became even deeper.

"Don't be mean to me," I mumbled, covering my face with my hands. "I may cry."

"Oh, really?" Nora said. I felt her lean in, then she sent shivers down my spine by whispering in my ear, "I'd really like to see that."

I made a noise. It may have been a squeak.

"Alright, I'm going to grab the spray bottle," Anna said. "Seriously you two, get a room."

Peeking between my fingers, I saw Nora look around in pretend confusion. "But we're already in a room."

"You know what I meant."

"Mmhmm," Nora mused. "Okay. Shall we get a room, Lily?"

"I . . ." I began; then gulped. "I don't think I feel ready for that yet. We've only been dating for what, two weeks now? And besides . . ." I trailed off.

What did I even want to say? That I didn't want to be intimate with someone? That I didn't *feel comfortable* being intimate with anyone? I could barely stand to look at myself in the mirror in the first place: the thought of someone seeing me naked or, worse, touching my naked skin, made me feel almost physically sick.

"I get it," Nora said, shaking me out of my thoughts. "Don't worry, we'll wait until you're ready." She brushed my hair aside and planted a kiss on my forehead. "Take your time."

I managed to stammer a "thanks" to Nora.

"Speaking of time," Anna said. "Lily, we should really be going, class is about to start. We don't want to be late."

"Yeah, okay," I said, getting up from my chair.

"Hold on," Nora stopped me. "I want you to have these."

She handed me the padlock I'd tried to open earlier, and a small pouch containing a beginner's set of lockpicks.

"So you can practice when you're on your own," she explained. "But I'm always available to give you some pointers regarding that, or if you need anything else."

I thanked her, then patted my pockets, wondering where I should put what she'd given me. My coat pockets were full with my wallet, keys, phone, pepper spray, and hormones — while I'd given most of them to Nora for safekeeping, I still kept a box of estradiol and one of cyproterone on hand at all times. And now I had the lockpicks and padlock too. Where . . . ?

"I have something else for you," Nora said.

"What?"

"Hold on," She fished in her backpack and pulled out what looked like . . .

"A purse?"

"I've noticed you've been having trouble carrying everything around, so . . . yeah. I got this for you."

My blush returned. She'd noticed I needed something? Without me having to say anything? She was incredibly thoughtful. Still . . .

"I'm sorry, Nora," I replied, shaking my head. "I'm grateful, I really am, but . . . I can't go around with a purse. You know. Because of Joe."

"I don't think that's going to be a problem," she said. "Look at this. When the purse is like this, you put it over your shoulder. Like, well, a purse." I nodded, and she continued, "But if you pull this strap out, you can wear it cross-body, and it looks like the things men use. A man purse."

She pulled on the strap to lengthen it and slung it over her head, demonstrating how to wear it.

"Yeah, I guess that makes sense," I said. "And it *does* look like something a man would wear." I didn't particularly like having to pretend, but at least I would be able to keep it after going back to being a man, so Nora's thoughtfulness wouldn't be wasted.

"Here, try it." She handed me the purse, and I passed the strap over my head, arranging it diagonally across my chest. As I did, it brushed briefly over my nipple. Ow.

. . . Ow?

That had hurt. Not a lot, but it had been a weird, unexpected pain. My chest had never hurt like that before. What . . . ?

"I still don't get why they have to call it a man purse," Anna said, distracting me from my thoughts. "I mean, why not call it a purse, period? I can't believe how fragile men are: so fragile they need to specify that something is made for men, and is absolutely not feminine at all, no sir, my masculinity is definitely not threatened at all, why do you ask?"

Nora laughed. "You know how men can be. Not all of them, but some are very . . . *defensive* of their masculinity."

"I can definitely attest to that," I replied; living with Joe had given me ample proof of it. Come to think of it, it was weird *I* wasn't more defensive of my masculinity: maybe it was the whole pretend-to-be-trans thing? Or maybe not having had many friends as I was growing up had shielded me from the worst of toxic masculinity, so, as a result, it wasn't a learned behavior.

Yeah, that was probably it.

"In any case," I continued, "We really gotta go now. Thank you, Nora." I rose on my tiptoes and gave her a peck on the lips.

"You're welcome, my dear," she replied.

Anna and I waved goodbye to our friends and began the trek to the social studies classroom.

"I'm surprised Elanor wasn't here today," I said as we walked. "Aren't you two always together?"

"You say that like we're a pair of conjoined twins." Anna laughed.

"But yeah. Normally, we are. But today they took some space, said they wanted to prepare a surprise for me for tomorrow." She smiled. "I really can't wait to see what they've cooked up."

"Oh? Is tomorrow a special occasion?" I lifted a questioning eyebrow.

"Oh yeah. Our first Valentine's Day together."

I stopped dead in my tracks, and she walked a few steps more before turning back and giving me a curious look. ". . . Fuck," I swore under my breath.

"Lily? Is something wrong?"

"I'm a complete dumbass," I said. "I can't believe I've forgotten Valentine's Day. Nora will never forgive me."

"Ah, I wouldn't worry," Anna said, dismissing the thought with a wave of her hand. "She's not the type. And besides, you still have time until tomorrow."

"Yeah, I guess so. I better think of something."

Anna smiled and put a hand on my shoulder. "Don't worry about it, Lily. You'll figure it out. You're a really smart girl."

I gave her hand a squeeze. "Thanks, Anna."

"Any time. Now, let's get to class."

≡

"And that's all for today," Professor Markley said, as the bell rang. "Remember you have to turn in your assignments by the end of next week. Have a good evening."

There was a general shuffling around as everyone got up and moved toward the exit.

"Mr. O'Connor, a word?" the professor said, catching my eye. I felt my mouth quirk slightly — he was always so formal, did he *have* to call me *Mr.*? — but I approached him as everyone else filed out.

"Yes, sir?" I asked.

"I want to talk to you about the research project I mentioned," he said. "The one about toxic masculinity and the effect it has on both the person holding those beliefs and those around them. Have you given it any thought?"

Yeah, I had given it some thought, actually: he'd asked me if I wanted to take part in it, it was meant to be a group effort. It was a good opportunity for me, and a surefire way to pass the class with an almost-perfect grade . . . But I had other plans.

"I'm sorry, sir," I answered, "but I was thinking of doing something else as my final project. There's something I've been working on for a while."

His eyebrows rose in surprise. "Oh? And what would that be?"

I hesitated for a moment, thinking of how to put my thoughts into words. "I don't have a title for it yet, I'll have to decide on it later down the line. But it's a project I started way back in November. It's about . . ." I stopped for a moment: I couldn't just come out and tell him I was pretending to be trans, so I adjusted course. "It's about trans people. And transition. And the effects transition can have on cis people."

The professor looked at me curiously. "I'm sorry, but how does transition affect *cis* people? Is this something about how trans people have to relate to a cissexist society when transitioning? Because there's been plenty of research done in the field."

"Not that. I . . . It's kinda hard to explain, actually," I replied. "But I can promise it'll be a very interesting read once I've completed the whole thing. I hope so, at least. I think you'll be surprised."

"I see," he said, giving me a pensive look. "Alright. Well, the last thing you wrote for the class *was* really interesting. You're an excellent student, so I can't wait to see what you come up with."

"Thank you, sir," I said, beaming at the compliment.

"Though it's a shame, really," he continued. "I was looking forward to having you work on the toxic masculinity project. It's a really interesting subject."

I suddenly thought of something. "Why don't you ask Anna to do it?" I said. "Anna Suarez, I mean."

"Miss Suarez?" Professor Markley asked. "Why her?"

"I think she'd be a good fit for the project. I know she's had problems with toxic masculinity before, and we both know someone who's chest-deep in the stuff, giving us both trouble because of it." Mainly me, I thought, but Anna too: every time she'd met Joe they'd been seriously at odds.

"Indeed? I thought you two didn't see eye to eye."

I waved the thought away. "No, not at all. We had our differences at first, but after I tried to listen to her, to what she had to say, we ended up becoming friends. Good friends. She's been helping me with some stuff, actually."

"… Stuff?"

"Stuff."

The professor's half-smile indicated he was curious, but he understood that I wasn't willing to elaborate further. "Alright, I'll give this some thought," he said, looking at me carefully. "Thank you for your time. Have a good evening, O'Connor."

I blinked, surprised at the lack of title, but replied, "You too, sir. Thank you." I left the room, passing my purse's strap over my head as I did.

Once again, it brushed across my chest and, like earlier that afternoon, I felt a bit of pain.

I stopped walking.

This was *weird*. Why was my chest hurting like this? I carefully poked and prodded it with my finger, and sure enough it felt a bit tender. On both sides, actually, in a very specific area. It was as if …

Realization dawned on me.

Oh.

※

"Hey, bro, welcome back," Joe greeted me, looking up from his textbook when I burst through the door. "What's wrong? Why the rush?"

"It's nothing," I replied, and then I looked at him, puzzled. "Wait, are you studying?"

"What's it look like? Of course I'm studying," he replied. "What, you have a problem with it?"

There he went, always aggressive. "No problem," I replied. "I just can't remember the last time I saw you study."

"Have to," he said simply. "The administration is already on my ass because of Darrell, don't wanna give them an excuse to kick me out."

"Wait, hold on," I said. "What was that about Darrell? What did he do?"

Joe shrugged. "What do you think? He ratted me out to someone high up. About the beer." The gaze he leveled my way said he still blamed me for that whole debacle, but I ignored it.

"But he said he wouldn't report you."

"He must have. Otherwise, how do you explain the fact that since I've come back I've had nothing but failing grades?" The annoyance was clear in his voice. "They have it in for me, I tell you. Of course if I were a woman, or black, or gay, or non-binary — whatever that is — they'd go easy on me. But normal white men get the short end of the stick."

I pursed my lips at his use of 'normal' to describe being cishet — it didn't sit quite right with me. And, in fact, I could think of several reasons why he was failing: that he hadn't bothered to study nearly as much as he should have in the first place; that he'd missed three full weeks of class after Christmas break; that he had a *terrible* attitude if the way he talked to me was any indication of his general behavior; that he spent all weekends partying, without bothering to get ahead on schoolwork. And a couple more.

But I didn't tell him any of that. Best not to antagonize him.

"Sorry to hear that, buddy," I said, walking toward my bed and dropping my backpack and purse on it.

He shrugged in response. "Nothing I can do about it except study at this point."

I opened my wardrobe and grabbed my towel, pajamas, and bag of toiletries from it. "I'm taking a shower, today was tiring and I'm all sweaty," I told Joe, then added in a joking voice: "No peeking."

"What, you think I'm some kind of homo?" he replied with a laugh. "Don't worry, I really don't wanna see your dick."

I smirked at him, then moved to the bathroom and closed — and locked — the door behind me. I set down my things on the toilet, then quickly disrobed, turned around, and looked at myself in the mirror.

It wasn't full-length, so checking myself out wasn't easy — I had to stand way back against the door to get a full view of my body, and that made me miss some details. But by alternating the two positions, far away and close in, I got a pretty good idea of what I looked like.

And I looked . . . different?

To be fair, I didn't have a good baseline for what I looked like before. I'd never liked to look at my body, so I couldn't really remember my exact shape, but I seemed to be . . . rounder, somehow. Softer. My hips were fuller, maybe? Just a little bit? Or maybe it was just my imagination.

The main thing that caught my eye, though, was my chest. I hadn't really noticed it before, but there seemed to be two small, raised bumps just behind my nipples. I experimentally tried to probe them with my finger and found they were quite sensitive. That settled the deal.

I was growing breasts.

It was funny, but the thought didn't alarm me nearly as much as it probably should have. After all, it was just one of the effects of the hormones, and like I'd read online as long as I stopped taking hormone replacement therapy before the six-month mark, everything would go back to the way it was before. So I didn't see it as a problem, rather an opportunity to see firsthand the very early stages of breast development in a trans woman.

Or a cis man on feminizing HRT, anyway.

But as I showered, I found out there *was*, in fact, a problem with me growing boobs: they were *way* too sensitive. I had to be careful about washing them under the stream of warm water, because they hurt if I just rubbed at them the way I'd always done when I showered. And when I put on my pajamas, the cloth felt so rough on my nipples I could barely stand it.

I had to do something about this.

I wrapped a towel around my head to dry my hair — which was halfway to my shoulders, I would have to get it cut soon — and grabbed my cell phone.

Hey, I texted Nora. *Are you free tomorrow?*

The answer came almost immediately. *Yeah. What's up?*

Can we hang out?

Of course, she replied. *Any particular occasion?*

It's Valentine's Day.

You remembered!

I smiled. *Of course I remembered. I thought we could maybe go shopping? In the afternoon?*

Sure, was the reply. *Anything you're looking to buy?*

I hesitated for a moment before typing out the next message, but in the end there was nothing to it.

Yeah. I need to buy a bra.

12
A Tightness in the Chest

NORA WAS WEARING a dress.

It instantly made me forget the annoyance I'd felt at the Uber driver telling me, "Have a good day, man," when he'd dropped me off. It was the first time I'd seen my girlfriend not wearing pants, and she looked *amazing*. Considerably less butch than she usually was, which made me a bit jealous that she could effortlessly pull off both butch and femme (or femme-y, since she was wearing sneakers and a backpack along with her dress).

Nora waved me over excitedly, then walked halfway across the mall's food court to meet me.

"Hi, Lily!" She leaned over to give me a peck on the cheek. "Happy Valentine's Day!"

"Happy Valentine's," I replied with a smile. "You look really good."

"Don't I?" she said, twirling in place. "It's not what I would usually wear, but considering what today is, I borrowed this thing from one of my roommates. Thought I'd impress you a bit."

"Consider me impressed," I said. Compared to my girlfriend I felt seriously underdressed, even though I'd worn one of my best outfits. But all my outfits were androgynous, since I couldn't risk arousing Joe's suspicion. To be honest, they looked quite ugly when compared to a dress.

"Why don't we head to Victoria's Secret? It's just over there." Nora said, pointing.

"Just a moment before we go," I said. I rooted inside my purse and pulled out a box. "Happy Valentine's Day," I said again, handing it to her.

Her face brightened into a wide smile. "You've bought me a present?" she asked. "Aw, Lily, you shouldn't have."

"I should, actually," I replied, as she opened the box of chocolates — the fanciest chocolates I could find on short notice. "You're my girlfriend. And this is Valentine's."

"Thank you," Nora said, popping one in her mouth. "You know, I actually have a present for you too."

"You do?" I asked. I was puzzled: usually it was the girl in a relationship who received a present, wasn't it?

As soon as that thought ran through my brain, another followed it: *of course she bought you a present, you idiot. She thinks you're a girl. Her girlfriend, to be precise.*

I felt a pang of guilt.

"Why the frown? Of course I have. Why wouldn't I?" Nora said. "But if you don't mind, I'm going to wait until a bit later to give it to you."

"Huh," I replied, shaking my head to chase away the bad thoughts. "Alright then. When you're ready." I motioned toward Victoria's Secret. "Shall we?"

We joined hands — a perk of having a girlfriend; it had been years since I'd last walked hand-in-hand with someone — and strolled over, stopping on the threshold to look inside.

I hesitated. The thought of stepping foot inside a lingerie store made me nervous. It felt almost like the point of no return, like an event horizon — almost like there would be no coming back from this.

Nora sensed my hesitation. "Do you want me to handle this?" she asked, with a kind smile. I nodded wordlessly, grateful she was taking charge.

Still holding my hand, she gently guided me inside. It was quite big, I didn't expect there to be so many choices of lingerie. Nora spotted a shop assistant and waved her over.

"Good afternoon," the assistant said with a professional smile. "May I help you?"

"Yes, I think you can, actually," Nora said; she leaned forward and lowered her voice, even though there was no one else within earshot. "You see, *my girlfriend*," she continued, nodding her head toward me, "is looking for her first bra. We need some help with sizing, and in figuring out what works best."

The shop assistant's eyes flickered toward me, widening in surprise for a brief moment, but then she smiled and nodded. "Of course, that's no problem at all. I'm Astrid, and I'll be glad to help you."

"Thank you, Astrid," Nora said, and I felt her squeeze my hand in reassurance.

"Let's just go to the back, away from any prying eyes," Astrid continued. "This way we'll have a bit more privacy."

As we followed Astrid to the back of the store, I found myself giggling a bit. It may have been weird, but I was sort of looking forward to the experience of being fitted with a bra. It was probably going to be a once-in-a-lifetime thing.

My brain added, almost as an afterthought: *And something you can use when writing your article.*

"Alright," Astrid said, stopping in front of a changing room. "Do you know what size you are?"

"No," I replied, shaking my head.

"We'll have to get you measured then." She paused. "Uh . . . You have to strip to do that, though. Show me your bare chest. Are you comfortable with that?"

I felt my cheeks go slightly pink. "Uh . . . Um," I mumbled. "Can't we do it over my clothes?"

"We could," she replied. "But we probably wouldn't get the correct size, and it'd be difficult to find the right bra. But if you want to . . ."

She let the sentence hang in the air, and I looked at her, then at Nora who was beaming a reassuring smile at me. "Don't worry, Lily," Nora said. "We're all girls here. Nothing to be ashamed of."

She was right, wasn't she? We *really* were all girls there. As far as she knew, at least. And it wasn't like I was going to see *her* bare chest.

And, what the hell! I was a man! There was no shame in showing someone my bare chest!

I just had to let two people stare at me topless for a while: a shop assistant and . . .

And my girlfriend.

I gulped.

"I don't want you to see," I said reflexively.

Nora blinked in surprise. "Wait, what?"

I realized the words had just come out without me meaning to, but this was what I felt. "I'm okay with her seeing." I nodded toward Astrid. "But not you." I paused, looked away, and added, in a small voice, "You're my girlfriend. It's embarrassing."

There was a moment of silence, then Nora giggled softly. "Oh my God, Lily, you're so precious," she said. "I love you so much."

I looked up at her in surprise: wait, what? I was almost expecting her to be angry at me for refusing to show her my boobs, but she wasn't. Instead, she seemed . . . amused.

"Don't worry, I won't look," she continued, giving me a peck on the cheek. "You two go in there and do your thing, I'll stay out here and wait. Shoo, shoo." She motioned me and Astrid toward the changing room.

"It's a bit of a shame, though," Nora added. "I was looking forward to it. Ah well, I'll have to be satisfied with my imagination."

I blinked. "No, wait, hold on, what are you imagining?"

"Oh, you know . . . things," Nora replied, and I swear I could *hear* her smirk.

I blushed furiously. "Oh, go away, you!" I exclaimed. "Go browse in the store or something! We'll call you when we're done!"

"Okaaaaaaaay!" she called back. "See you later!"

I heard her step away from the changing room, and Astrid said, "She seems like a really nice girl."

"She is, I don't know what I did to deserve her."

"You clearly must have done something right. I can tell she cares about you very much," she said. Then, she added, "Now, let's get to it. Strip, please."

I quickly removed my coat and top, which I hung on the hook.

"Camisole too," Astrid said; with some trepidation I took it off.

Astrid was extremely professional: she didn't comment on what I looked like, just made me turn around, my back to her, and got to work placing a tape measure snug across my chest, just under my breasts.

"Thirty-six . . ." she said. "Alright, this might be a bit uncomfortable, but bear with it for a moment."

She moved the tape so it ran right over my nipples, and pulled it taut. I shivered as my tender chest reacted to the cold — it was a completely new experience.

"You're a 36A," Astrid said. "Just barely, but it *is* an A. Okay, I'll be right back."

When she returned, she was carrying half a dozen different types of bras. "You could probably make do with a training bra for a couple months still, but I'll give you a proper one instead," she said. "This way you'll have room to grow."

She had me try each bra on until I found the one that fit me best — a simple, skin-tone bra that cupped my budding breasts. It felt a bit tight across my chest, but I was sure I would soon get used to it.

I gave my reflection a good once-over. I looked . . .

Well, I looked like myself.

Wearing a bra.

I was satisfied with what I saw. When I moved, it supported my breasts and made them stick out a bit from my body — I was sure they'd be noticeable even under my clothes, unless I went back to wearing my baggy hoodies, which I really didn't want to do.

"I'll take this," I said. "And . . . do you have, like, a sports bra? Or something that can flatten my breasts and not make them show as much?"

"We do," Astrid nodded. "But why? You look very nice in that. You should be proud."

Her words did make me proud, actually, which was a bit of a weird feeling — what man is proud of how he looks wearing a bra? But I explained, "I'm not out, except to a small number of friends. And if someone figures me out, there could be issues. So I have to hide these," I motioned to my boobs, "for the time being."

"Alright, hold on a second."

She fetched a couple of sports bras, and I picked the one that fit best.

"Do be careful, though," Astrid warned. "Don't wear this too much. You're still growing, and if you're too constricted it could cause damage."

"I'll keep that in mind." I took off the sports bra, then hesitated, looking at the other one I'd picked. The cute one.

What would be the harm in wearing it a bit more? Just for today, around the mall. I could always duck into the bathroom before leaving to take it off. Yeah, I could do that. And this way I would get more experience in what being a trans girl is like that I could use for my article.

Excellent idea, Lily.

Fumbling a bit, I put the bra on — Astrid had helped me before, but

I insisted on doing it myself: after all, I had to learn how to do it on my own, since once I got home there'd be no one to help me wear it and take it off. Then, once again, I looked at myself in the mirror.

Yeah. Cute.

"I'll bring the sports bra to the register," Astrid said. "You take your time."

I reached for my clothes as she left.

"I guess you're done in there?" Nora called from outside. "It's getting a bit late, and we have an appointment after this."

An appointment?

"Yeah, I'm done."

There was a moment's pause, then Nora said, "Can I see?"

I couldn't help but smile. "Not right now, but I'll show you eventually. Let me just get dressed, and I'll be right out."

"No, hold on a bit," Nora said. "Here."

The curtain slid back a couple of inches and Nora's hand poked through, holding a dress. *The* dress, actually, the one she'd picked out for me and kept in her room.

"Uh . . . Nora? What's this?"

"It's your dress,"she replied, matter-of-factly.

"And you want me to wear it?" I asked.

"Of course. That's why I brought it in the first place."

I bit my lip looking at the dress. It looked incredible, the flower motifs complementing the teal background. It was a shame I'd only worn it once back when I'd bought it, and only briefly at that: I really wanted to wear it, if only to see what it looked like on me again. Still . . .

"I can't wear it, Nora," I said. "What if someone sees me?"

"What *if* someone sees you, Lily? They'll think you're cute."

"No, I mean, I'm not out yet."

"Ah, no one gives a crap. It's a liberal college town, trans and gender non-conforming people are a dime a dozen here. No one will look at you twice. I promise."

I nervously bit my lip again. She was right, wasn't she? A newly-out, mid-transition trans girl wasn't an unusual sight around these parts. And the chances of someone I didn't want to know about me seeing me were near zero — when I'd left my dorm room Joe was studying intently, trying to catch up on everything he'd missed while he was on his short stint in jail.

"I haven't shaved my legs," I protested weakly.

"I brought tights," Nora said. "So, are you going to wear the dress or not?"

She really thought of everything. "I'm going to wear the dress."

Nora chuckled. "Good girl. Take your time, but not too much."

"Yeah, you said we have an appointment?" I slipped the dress on and grabbed the tights. "What's that for?"

"It's my Valentine's present for you."

I slid the tights up my legs. "Oh, right. What is it?"

"You'll see."

"Okay, I'm ready," I said, opening the curtain and being rewarded by Nora's warm smile.

"What do you think?" I asked, spinning around and making the skirt flare out.

"Cute," she said, nodding approvingly.

The top of my ears started to feel warm, but luckily they were hidden beneath my hair. "Thank you," I said. "What should we do with my other clothes?"

"I'll put them in my backpack."

"Oh, you've changed," Astrid said when she saw me at the register. "You look great."

Nora put an arm around my shoulders and pulled me close to her. "Doesn't she? My girlfriend is the cutest."

I giggled and disentangled myself from Nora's embrace. After I paid for the bras — "Thank you, and come back any time," Astrid said with a smile —we left.

"Okay, that's one thing done," Nora said, turning toward me. "Now it's time for your present."

She offered me her hand, which I took. "Lead the way."

13

A New Face

Nora was right: even though I absolutely didn't pass, and everyone who passed me in the mall saw a trans girl (or someone who *looked like* a trans girl), no one cared.

And why *should* they care? As long as everyone minded their own business, I was sure trans and cis people — no, make that queers and cishets in general — could get along just fine. The only slight hiccup was cis people pretending to be trans for their own purposes, whatever those might be. I was yet to meet one — I now knew Vicky, Elanor, and the other trans members of the GSA enough to be sure they weren't just pretending — but I was sure they *had* to exist. Otherwise, it just wouldn't make sense.

After all, wasn't that exactly what I was doing?

"We're here," Nora said, bringing me back to the moment: she'd guided me to a side corridor just off the main area of the mall, and we were standing in front of ... a salon.

"Surprise!" Nora exclaimed. "Happy Valentine's Day, Lily. This is your present."

"My present?"

"Yup," she nodded. "Not the salon, I'm not nearly rich enough to buy you a whole store. But I've made an appointment, and they're going to make you cute. Well, *cuter*. You're already cute."

I never got tired of her telling me that, it always gave me a fuzzy, happy feeling deep in my stomach.

"But yeah, you're getting a haircut, a mani-pedi, they're going to do your makeup ... the works."

"This will be an experience."

"The first time of many, I'm willing to bet." Nora smirked. "Every girl wants to get pampered once in a while."

Taking my hand once more, she guided me inside where a worker rose to her feet, grabbing a small book.

"Hi there, and welcome," she said with a polite, business-like smile. "Do you have an appointment?"

"We do, it should be under Hartley," Nora replied.

The girl nodded, opened the book, and looked through it. "Hartley . . . Oh, yeah, here you are," she said. Then, louder, she called, "Molly, your four-thirty is here!"

"Coming!"

Another girl — about as tall as me, with long blonde hair tied back in a ponytail and a face speckled with freckles — made her way across the store. "Hi, I'm Molly," she said when she reached us. "Nora Hartley and Lily O'Connor, right?"

I gave Nora a look. She'd actually told Molly my name when making the reservation? I wasn't sure I was entirely comfortable with that, to be honest: the more people knew me as Lily, the more difficult it would be to eventually go back to being a completely basic, run-of-the-mill, 100 percent boring cisgender and heterosexual man once I was done with this whole thing.

Neither Molly nor Nora seemed to notice my stare. "Right," Nora nodded.

"Perfect," Molly replied. "Right this way, I've got everything set up in the back."

We followed her into a wide room filled with mirrors and sinks and comfy reclining chairs. I sat down in one, and Nora in the one next to it.

"Okay, you're getting The Works today," Molly said, and I swear I could hear her pronounce the capital letters. "Both of you."

"Wait, you too?" I asked, looking at Nora.

"Of course," she replied. "What did I tell you? Girls want to be pampered every now and then, even me. And doing it with a girlfriend is part of the experience," she concluded with a wink.

"Okay," I said.

"Now sit back, relax, and enjoy," Molly said, reclining our chairs all the way back. She looked at me for a moment, then narrowed her eyes. "Excuse me, Lily, is it alright if I touch your face?"

". . . Yes? Of course," I replied, puzzled.

Molly ran her hand across my cheek. I grimaced as her fingers caught on my stubble — the noise was slight, but it seemed remarkably loud to my ears, as though she was rubbing a piece of coarse sandpaper.

"When was the last time you shaved?" she asked.

"This morning."

"What with?"

"An electric shaver," I said. "Why?"

Molly shook her head. "Can't work like this," she muttered; she walked over to the door, and called out, "Jules, get in here please. And bring your things."

"Be right there!" a male voice called back. It was followed, a minute or so later, by a tall, middle-aged man with black hair and a bushy gray beard.

"Lily, this is Giuliano," Molly said. "He's going to give you a shave."

Giuliano smiled. "Pleasure to meet you."

"Wait, we didn't ask for a shave," Nora said, her forehead creasing.

"Oh, I'm throwing it in, free of charge," Molly replied. "We can't do most of the rest unless she's clean-shaven." She looked at me. "Are you comfortable with that, Lily?"

I glanced at Giuliano, who was setting his tools — including a long, menacing, straight-bladed razor — on a nearby sink. I nervously nodded. "Let's do this."

He grabbed a hot, moist towel, which he wrapped around my face. "This is to soften the skin and open the pores," he explained. "I'll leave this on for just a minute, and then get to shaving. You can close your eyes if you're nervous, I know some people don't do well with a blade next to their face."

"No, it's alright." I relaxed and sat back, looking at the ceiling as he used a brush to slather my face in shaving cream, then grabbed his cut-throat razor and got to work. I glanced at him a few times while he was doing his thing, but I was careful not to move my face. The whole experience was surprisingly pleasant, albeit brief: after less than ten minutes spent maneuvering his razor across my chin and cheeks and around my nose like an expert sailor steering a ship, he had managed to remove every trace of hair from my face.

"Done," he said, wiping what little shaving cream remained with a towel. "What do you think?"

I ran my hand over my cheek: it felt completely smooth. I honestly couldn't remember the last time I'd had such a close shave; never, probably. The last time my face had been fully free of hair had likely been before puberty. "Wow," I said, rubbing my chin: the feeling was incredibly pleasant.

Giuliano smirked at me. "Like a baby's bottom, right?"

His voice sounded like it was coming from very far away, I was so mesmerized by the alien feeling of my hand touching my cheek, skin against skin, with nothing between, so I just nodded.

"You may consider permanent hair removal, though," Molly interjected. "It'll take a while, but that way you'd never have to shave ever again."

"Aw, girl, do you really wanna put me out of business? Just like that?" Giuliano said, his voice teasing.

"Shush," Molly replied, lightly slapping his shoulder, but something she'd said had caught my attention.

"Hair removal?" I asked.

"Yeah. For you, it's probably going to be electro. You're a ginger with very light skin, so laser would just be a whole lot of pain for very poor results," Molly said. "A friend of mine had to do electro too, and she has light brown hair, so her beard is also light. Well, *was* light. She doesn't have any now."

"Huh," I mused. "Alright, I'll consider it." And I *was* considering it, quite seriously in fact: I'd never liked having a beard, and the thought of not having to shave again was enticing.

"Until you get to that, I recommend a safety razor," Giuliano said as he gathered his things. "You can get a much closer shave than with those modern plastic-y things, and the blades are much cheaper."

"I'll keep that in mind."

"Thank you, Jules," Molly said. "Can you please send Mary in now?"

"Of course." He left the room, and a couple of minutes later the girl who'd greeted us at the door walked in and introduced herself as Mary.

"Let's get to the main course," Molly said. "I'll do Lily, Mary. You do Nora. The Works."

"Just remember," Nora interjected. "Lily is not quite out yet, so let's not do anything that can't be easily hidden or reversed."

I smiled my thanks to her as Molly took on a pensive expression. "Hm, that means no eyebrow threading and no nail polish on her fingers," she mused. "Can we put polish on your toenails, though?"

I thought about Joe. I almost always wore shoes or slippers when I was in my room, so the chance he'd notice my painted toenails was slim, but it was there. I couldn't risk it.

"No, better not," I replied.

"Okay, I'll give you a rain check on the polish," Molly said. "Let's get to work."

"How long will this take?" I asked.

"It'll take as long as it takes," she replied cryptically.

'As long as it takes' turned out to be quite a while. Molly put on some relaxing music and, after asking for permission, she slipped my tights off my legs and put my feet and hands to soak in basins of scented hot water. I closed my eyes and took in the experience as she steamed my face with a towel again, then softly scrubbed it with a coarse paste before washing that off and replacing it with a floral-scented cream. Then she quickly cut and shaped my hair: there wasn't much to do with it since it was still only just halfway to my shoulders.

I heard both her and Mary walk off, leaving Nora and I alone to give the various concoctions time to act. I found myself smiling: before getting embroiled into this whole trans thing, I'd often found myself wondering how exactly girls managed to keep their skin so smooth and radiant. There had to be a secret, right? Well, now I had the answer — and it felt like witchcraft. A coven of magic practitioners, passing down mysterious secrets through generations.

This was seriously bliss. I felt as if I was floating on a fluffy cloud. As if every trace of stress was leaving my body.

"Lily?" Nora whispered. "Are you awake?"

"Hm? What's up?"

"Nothing, really," she said. "I just wanted to hear your voice."

I blushed under the heavy cream that covered my face. We were quiet for a while, until I spoke up again. "Nora?"

"Yeah?"

"Thank you."

A moment's pause. "What for?"

"For being here for me. I've been under . . . under a lot of stress recently."

"Understandable."

"Today has been wonderful. It's the best day I've had in quite a while. So thank you."

"You're welcome, Lily."

We sat for a while in silence, enjoying the music, the pleasant smells, and each other's presence, until Mary and Molly walked back in.

"Alright, we're almost done," Molly said.

"Almost?" I asked.

"Just need to do the actual mani-pedi, nail polish, and makeup. And don't worry," she added. "I haven't forgotten. No polish for you."

"Thank you."

Did I say the experience had been pleasant? I was a fool. I still hadn't experienced true bliss: someone gently massaging your hands and feet while carefully trimming your nails and scrubbing away all the rough skin and calluses. There weren't many, true, I'd never been one to use my hands for physical work, but they felt incredibly soft when Molly was done. It was amazing.

"Now for your makeup," Molly said, wiping the remaining cream off my face and rubbing what she called 'primer' into my skin.

"Be gentle with her," Nora interjected. "This is her first time."

Molly's eyes glinted. "Oh, is it?" she said, a mirthful tone in her voice. "Well, well, well."

I looked at her warily. "Um. Should I be worried?"

"Oh, no, not at all," Molly said, waving her hand dismissively, but with a grin on her face. "There's nothing to worry about. You just sit here," she swiveled my chair around to face away from the mirrors, "and let me work. This will be *fun*."

I gulped. "Alright, I guess."

Molly was incredibly professional. She carefully explained what everything she used on my face was — as well as the primer there was foundation, powder, blush, lip pencil, lipstick, eye pencil, mascara, eye shadow, and a couple more things whose names I instantly forgot. Once or twice I tried to look at myself in the mirror, but Molly was quick to pull my head back into position. "No peeking," she chided me with a soft smile.

"Oh, this was fun," Nora said, standing up from her chair — Mary was done with her makeup. She walked around my chair to stand in front of me.

I took one look at her, and I blinked.

She looked amazing.

I'd never seen her wear that much makeup; she usually only put on a bit of eyeliner and lip gloss. But everything she'd had done to her face complemented it beautifully: she looked . . . *more*. More adult, more beautiful, more confident, more attractive. As I looked at her, I found myself squirming in my chair.

"Well? How do I look?" Nora struck a pose. Her fingernails had been painted a deep red and I felt a bit jealous at not being able to put on polish. "Do you like it?"

"I really like it," I replied truthfully. "Nora, you look . . . Well, you look incredible."

"Thank you. You're coming along nicely too, if I can say so."

"I am?"

"Yep, you are."

"Okay, I'm done," Molly said, putting down her brush. "Want to see?"

Molly and Nora together turned my chair back around. I looked at myself in the mirror.

And I gasped.

Reflected in the mirror was a girl. Her face was a girl's — I could barely see the makeup it was so subtle — and she was dressed like a girl, and had a startled, deer-in-headlights expression on her pretty face.

At an unconscious level I recognized that the girl had to be me. I was the one sitting in the chair in front of the mirror. Unless this was a trick somehow . . . No, if I moved my head, turned it this way and that, she mimicked my movements. It was amazing. Molly had done an incredibly good job: she'd somehow taken a horribly masculine face and managed to disguise it as a girl.

. . . No, not disguise. That wasn't the right word. I was still recognizably *me*: anyone who knew me would've instantly been able to tell who I was. But somehow the makeup (and maybe the facial and lack of beard) had managed to uncover a lot of femininity where I'd thought there was none.

I kept looking at myself for a long time, examining every detail of my face, looking for a 'tell' that would dispel the illusion, but there was none to be found.

I was a girl.

No, *I looked like a girl*, I quickly corrected myself. I wasn't *actually* a girl. Don't forget that, Lily. It's important.

"I think she likes it."

Those words shook me from my reverie, and I looked over my shoulder. "Uh? What?"

"I said, I think she likes it," Molly repeated. "I never get tired of seeing this reaction. When they see themselves for the first time, their face just lights up."

"Right?" Nora leaned forward and put a hand on my shoulder. "You look amazing. Happy Valentine's Day, my dear." She planted a kiss firmly on my cheek.

I blushed a bit, and smiled at her. "Thank you, Nora. Again."

She smiled back, and gripped my shoulder for a moment before letting go.

"Alright," Molly said. "I think we're done here."

"Thank you, Molly," Nora said, offering me a hand and pulling me up from my chair. "You've been great."

"Yeah, this was an experience I won't forget that easily," I agreed. "I'm already looking forward to next time."

"Thank you. Do remember I still owe you nail polish on both your hands and feet, and be sure to recommend me to your friends," Molly said, with a smile and a wink.

Nora paid for The Works we'd been put through, then we thanked Molly, Mary, and Giuliano — who winked at me too, and said, "Best of luck, girl" — and left the store.

"I think we still have some time until we have to go home," Nora said. "Should we take a tour of the mall? I've never been here before."

"You haven't?" I asked, puzzled. "Then how did you know about Molly's salon?"

"I asked someone at the GSA," she explained. "She came highly recommended, in fact. Shall we go?"

The day had already been wonderful: that final hour and a half was the capstone of it all. We ducked inside every store that caught our eye, browsing and looking around. A few salespeople approached us, asking, "Can I help you ladies?"

"No, we're just browsing," we'd reply, but the way they talked to us —
as if we were a pair of normal girls having fun on a day off from school
— always made a thrill of excitement run down my spine.

Nora and I also took the occasion to sneak a kiss or two. Or three.
Or four.

Or five.

God, I really loved this girl. I just couldn't get enough of her. And,
apparently she couldn't get enough of me. I'd never dated anyone for so
long, and it was wonderful to be able to connect to someone like this.

Afternoon turned to evening, and we had to go home. After all, it was
the middle of the week: we'd both played hooky, taking a day off from
school that afternoon, but we'd have to study to catch up on the lessons
we'd missed and to prepare for the following days.

"This has been a wonderful day," I said, as I kissed Nora one more
time. "Thank you."

"No, thank *you*," she replied, smiling brightly at me. "I'm really glad
to have you in my life."

I blushed, and smiled back. "Let me just call for an Uber . . ." I said,
rooting into my purse for my cell phone.

"Um," Nora said.

I looked up at her. "Yes?"

"You're going home . . . like that?" she asked, gesturing at me.

I looked down at myself. "Oh, good point," I said. "Can't go home
wearing a skirt. Come on, let's find a clothing store, so I can borrow their
changing room and switch back."

"And the makeup?" Nora asked. "Aren't you going to take that off?"

Her words made me hesitate. I walked up to a shop window. The
reflection was faint, but I could see my face.

I bit my lip, the girl in the window mimicking the expression.

Did I *have* to take the makeup off? After all, Nora had paid for it.
Molly had put lots of work into it. And it looked really good. Why
couldn't I keep it on? For a while, at least. Until it was time to go to bed.
Yes, that's it. I would have Nora show me exactly how to remove it, and
then I'd take it off when I got back to my dorm room—

My train of thought screeched to an abrupt halt.

Fuck. Of course. My dorm room. I'd almost forgotten. That was why

I couldn't go back looking like this, wearing a dress and makeup. That was the problem.

Joe.

"Yeah, I'm going to take it off. I kinda have to, you know," I said, in a small, tired voice.

Nora smiled sympathetically. "I know. Wait here."

She ducked into a store and came back with a small plastic bag. "Makeup remover and cotton pads," she said. "And moisturizer. Since we forgot to get them from Molly."

I let her guide me to the bathrooms, hesitating just a little before going into the girls' toilet, but in the end no one looked at me twice.

Nora showed me how to wash off the makeup, which wasn't complicated. You just had to wipe the liner and mascara from your eyes, then wash your face with warm water and the correct cleansing product, and moisturize afterward.

I dried my face with a wad of paper towels and looked at my reflection.

Plain old me again.

After that, we found a clothing store where I ducked into a changing room and quickly shed my dress, replacing it with the clothes I'd worn that morning.

Plain old me again.

This was a bad end to a good day, but I still managed to smile as I said goodbye to Nora. We kissed — with tongue, she was apparently feeling very passionate — and separated.

I pulled out my phone and called for an Uber.

Time to go back to my boring, everyday life.

14

A Voice in the Choir

"**Y**OU DON'T HAVE to go home, but you can't stay here!"

"You said that last time!" someone in the crowd called back.

"Did I? Well, hire me a speechwriter if you don't want me to repeat myself," Patrick replied, causing laughter to ripple through the room.

"Oh, before I forget," Lena added, raising her voice above the noise, "we have something to tell the trans and enby folks, so if y'all could maybe stay a moment longer? It'll just take a few minutes."

Nora, Anna, Vicky, Elanor and I exchanged perplexed glances, but Nora shrugged.

"We'll wait outside for you." She and Anna left, while the rest of us gathered in the middle of the room where Patrick, Lena, and Allie were waiting.

Lena waited until the hubbub had died down so she wouldn't have to shout, then she spoke up. "Alright, I'll make this brief. I have a friend — I met her through my sister — who's a vocal coach with quite a bit of experience in helping trans people find their voice. And she offered to come over here and do a few group lessons for free." She paused and ran her eyes over the crowd. "Then if any of y'all wanna continue training with her, she'll give you a discount."

I turned her words over in my mind. "I'm sorry, what do you mean 'help trans people find their voice?' How is she going to do that?" I asked.

"There are some tricks you can use to sound more feminine," Allie replied. "Or more masculine, but that's rarer because testosterone does a lot for transmascs. Once you learn the technique, it's all a matter of training and practice until you get it down, and your voice becomes . . . well, yours." She shrugged. "It's not that hard."

"Huh. Okay."

"So yeah, like I said," Lena said, "Let us know if there are any takers, and we'll set up group lessons." She smiled. "Alright, class dismissed. Go home, y'all."

There was a murmur of assent and we rejoined Anna and Nora. Together we made our way toward Giovanni's, chatting as we did.

"What did Lena want?" Nora asked as we entered.

"She said she knows a vocal coach who can give us some pointers regarding our voice," I replied, sitting at our usual table. "Asked if anyone was interested."

"Hm," she mused. "Do you think you'll go for it?"

"I don't know," I replied. "Voice training sounds bothersome, to be honest. I think I'll wait and see what effects I get with HRT." I turned to the waiter who'd approached our table. "I'll have the chicken sandwich with fries and a Pepsi, thank you." When I turned back to my friends, I saw Vicky was giving me a weird look. "What?"

"Lily, HRT does nothing for trans girls' voices," she said.

It was my turn to give her a weirded-out look. ". . . It doesn't?"

"No," she replied. "Testosterone enlarges your throat and makes your voice deeper as a result. Once that's done, once you've gone through puberty, estrogen can't turn it back. That's why voice training is less critical for transmascs — they get a natural change from their HRT, while we have to work for it."

"That's not what I've read," I protested, frowning. "I did some research . . ."

"And where did you do that research?" Anna asked.

"On the internet."

"Well, there you have it," she said.

Elanor and Nora both nodded in agreement. "You can't believe everything you read on the internet, Lily," Elanor said. "There's lots of misinformation going around. You'd be better off asking people who know what they're talking about."

"Like us," Vicky said. "I've been going through transition for two years now, so I'd like to think I know a few things."

"Still," Nora said. "Are you going to do voice training?"

I quirked my mouth pensively. "I don't know, to be honest. I mean, I really don't like my voice, but changing it seems like a lot of effort." I looked at Vicky. "What about you?"

"Already done," she replied. "On my own, even."

I looked at her in surprise. "What? Really?"

"Really," Vicky nodded. "What, did you think this was my natural voice?" She put a finger to her chin. "Well, it kinda is now. I've been using it for so long it comes naturally to me. I have to concentrate if I want to go back to a male voice. Which isn't even my previous voice, I couldn't find that to save my life. It's entirely different."

"Huh," I said in amazement. "Can you show me? Use your male voice?"

The answer was brief and curt: "No."

I blinked. "No?"

"No," Vicky repeated. "Using a male voice gives me a whole lot of dysphoria, I don't do it unless I have to. Like when I'm talking with my parents, for example. So no." She smiled. "Sorry."

"No need to apologize." I turned to Elanor. "What about you?"

Elanor shook their head. "No, I'm not going for voice training either. I actually like my voice, it's deep and powerful. I see no reason to change it."

I looked at them in amazement. Huh. I'd thought all trans people hated their voice. (And some cis people, too — I did, for one.) But apparently I'd been wrong.

"You know what?" I said. "I think I'll go for it. The free group lessons, at least. To get an idea of what I can get out of it. Thank you," I added, smiling at the waiter as he put our plates on the table.

"And then if you need some help, I can give you some pointers," Vicky supplied. "I mean, been there, done that, all that jazz. I know how to do it. A professional voice coach may be better, true, but friends are also good."

I reached across the table and gave her hand a squeeze. "Thanks, Vicks."

"Anytime, girl," she smiled back.

I bit into my sandwich and frowned.

"Something wrong?" Nora asked, her sandwich halfway to her mouth.

"They got my order wrong," I answered. "This is a beef burger, not a chicken sandwich. Ah well."

I brought the burger to my mouth again, but Nora stopped me by putting a hand on my arm. "Excuse me!" she called out, turning around and waving the waiter over.

"Nora, what are you doing?" I asked.

She turned back to me. "I'm having them replace the burger."

"What? No, there's no need to," I said. "It's not a big deal. I like beef, too."

"But you wanted chicken tonight, didn't you?"

I hesitated for a moment. "Well . . . yes. But—"

Nora held up a finger, stopping my objection in its tracks. "No buts, Lily." She turned to the waiter and said, "Yes, her order was wrong, she asked for chicken and got beef; can you have them make another one, please?"

"Of course." The waiter took my plate, leaving the basket of fries on the table, and carried it away.

"See?" Nora said. "There's no need to make a scene, it was an honest mistake. But you have to tell people when they get something wrong."

Truth be told, I'd never liked to make a fuss, except when someone really annoyed me like when Joe brought his asshole friends to our dorm room, or when I'd argued with Anna in social studies. (Even though I now recognized that, in that case, I'd been mostly — *mostly* — wrong.) I'd never liked to cause a scene, I always tried to avoid confrontation instead, even if it meant backing down from something I believed in. But as I looked around at my friends, I saw they were clearly in agreement with Nora.

And after all, why not? Why shouldn't I be a bit bolder? Not too much, of course, I didn't want to be overbearing. But why should I be passive all the time?

As the waiter put the new sandwich down in front of me — along with another basket of fries as an apology — I resolved to put my foot down more often.

And the chicken sandwich tasted really good.

☰

It wasn't unusual for Joe to still be awake when I got back. What *was* unusual was that instead of reading a book or watching a video on his phone in bed, he was sitting at his desk, reading a textbook with notes scattered everywhere. I realized he'd been at it for a while — he was studying when I'd left to go to the GSA, and he was still studying now. I was reasonably sure it was the same textbook too, so he'd been on the same subject for several hours.

Joe looked up at me and grunted as a way of greeting, and even in the dim light of his desk lamp I noticed his eyes were red.

"Evenin'," I said. "Are you alright?"

He scoffed and looked back down at the textbook. "What do you even care?"

I bit back a snappy response and took a deep breath instead.

Relax, Lily. Don't let him get to you. Don't antagonize him.

"I do care, actually," I replied. "You're my roommate."

And you become incredibly cranky and outright insufferable when you're upset, and you take it out on whoever's nearby — most often me,. So if I can nip that in the bud . . .

He looked back up and locked eyes with me.

"What?" I asked.

He kept staring for a few moments, apparently in surprise: he seemed genuinely puzzled that I would want to talk to him, and for a few seconds it looked like he wanted to say something but then he just shook his head. "Nothing," he replied, his gaze returning to the book.

His reaction, weirdly, made me actually worried for him: he hadn't snapped back at me like I'd expected. "Have you even taken a break since I left?"

He shook his head again without looking at me.

"Alright," I said, deciding to take matters into my hands. "You're done for tonight. Go to sleep."

"No," he replied under his breath.

"Yes," I said. "Joe, the human brain can only absorb so much information at a time, and you're clearly too tired to retain any of it. Go to bed and start back up tomorrow."

Even though I couldn't see his face, Joe seemed to hesitate; he stiffened, like a tightly-wound spring ready to uncoil. But then his muscles slackened as he untensed. "Yeah. Yeah, you're right. It's just . . . Yeah. I'm being too stubborn, trying to wrap my head around this stuff. Physics can be maddening, and I missed the professor explaining this whole thing," he gestured at the textbook, "so I gotta do it by myself."

He stood up from his desk. God, he looked terrible. Which was weird considering how much attention he usually paid to his appearance: this was the worst I'd seen him. He looked so vulnerable, almost as though he was going to cry — bloodshot eyes, hair ruffled, unsteady smile. Falling behind in his studies must have been getting to him, even though it was almost completely his fault.

Joe clapped me on the shoulder and walked past me to his bed. "Thanks for talking some sense into me, buddy. Good night."

Without even bothering to change out of his day clothes, he stuffed himself under the covers; it took him only a few moments to start snoring.

I turned off his desk lamp and got ready for bed.

☰

Joe was still asleep when I changed into my day clothes the next day — in the bathroom, as had become my usual, since I didn't want him to notice I was growing boobs and I'd started shaving my legs. That was unusual: he was an early riser by nature. And while I knew he didn't have any classes on Thursday morning, it showed how tired he'd been the previous evening.

I felt a bit bad for him; I wished I could help him somehow, but we had two entirely different majors: I was in social studies education, while he was studying aerospace engineering. There was no way I could even begin to understand the subjects he had to learn.

Like physics. Before I headed out I glanced at his textbook and notes, still scattered on his desk. I'd never had a head for scientific subjects, so all those equations, those mathematical symbols, they . . .

I stopped dead in my tracks as I looked at them. To my enormous surprise, I found that I . . .

. . . I kinda understood them? They looked remarkably familiar, in fact.

I picked up a page and ran my eyes over it. It was a bit chaotic — he really needed to be more organized when writing things down — but I did somewhat understand it. It was almost as if . . .

Realization dawned on me as I remembered exactly where I'd seen the math Joe'd been studying before.

I turned on my heel and grabbed my laptop before heading out.

That morning I paid very little attention in class: I could afford to as I was a bit ahead — ever since I'd stopped getting drunk every weekend (and drinking every week night) I'd found studying came much easier to me. And I didn't need to drink any more: the constant buzz I'd felt my entire life was almost gone now, so I could concentrate on things without having to numb myself. That meant I could neglect my lessons for a day and spend a few hours putting together several pages of notes — complete with diagrams and simplified explanations — for Joe.

Just after lunch I excused myself from hanging out with my queer friends, stopped by the computer lab to print out what I'd typed up, and made my way to the dorm room. Joe was at his desk, poring over his textbook and notes.

"At it again, I see."

He just grunted in response.

"It's past one. Have you eaten anything?"

"Had breakfast," he muttered.

"This is for you, then," I said, placing a sandwich and a can of soda on his desk. Joe looked at me, surprise evident in his face. "What?" I asked.

"For me? Seriously?"

"Joe, I know we're not friends, but, like I said yesterday, you're my roommate. I care about you, if only a little bit." I smiled at him. "So take a break and eat your lunch."

After a moment's hesitation, he grabbed the sandwich and began unwrapping it. "Thanks."

"Also, I made this for you." I pulled the printout from my backpack.

"What's this?" Joe asked.

"Read it."

He took a bite of the sandwich and looked down at the sheets of paper, chewing pensively as he read.

After a few moments, he stopped chewing. He stared at the writing, apparently transfixed, for a few moments, then looked up at me and swallowed.

"This is . . ."

". . . some notes on orbital mechanics, transfer orbits, delta-vee, engine efficiency, specific impulse. That kind of thing. I saw you were studying them and thought you could use the help."

He looked at me, flabbergasted, for several seconds. "I'm sorry, but . . . what the fuck?" he said, finally. "How do you even *know* this stuff? You're in an entirely different major which has nothing to do with this! How . . . ?"

"I played video games a lot in high school," I said, trying and failing to keep the mirth out of my voice.

Joe was still staring at me like I'd grown another head, so I thought I'd better explain.

"You see," I said. "There's this game. You play as the manager of a space program, and you have little green men build rockets to try and get off their planet and explore their solar system. And while it's a bit different from real life, the makers of the game made a point to put a physics system in it. A Newtonian physics system. Do you follow?"

"Yeah."

"So you can try to fudge things a bit at first. To just point the rocket where you want to go, open up the throttle, and go at full blast. But because of the limitations, sooner or later you find yourself having to make plans. To study orbits, to manage your fuel, to balance efficiency with transit time — because there's also stuff like limited life support to take into account. Or maybe that's a mod? I forget. But still." Joe nodded and I continued. "So you need to actually study orbital mechanics. Because otherwise you'll get nowhere. Or you'll end up lithobraking or going into rapid unplanned disassembly." I smiled. "So that's why I understand this stuff."

"Lithobraking?"

"That's when you stop because you've hit the lithosphere. The ground."

"Right, that makes sense." The corner of his mouth twitched upwards. "And rapid unplanned disassembly would be when this force," he tapped a formula in the notes, "becomes too large, and the rocket breaks apart."

"Precisely."

"Yeah, I see. Alright."

"But besides what's on there, don't count on me for anything else," I said. "What I've written down there is literally the extent of my expertise. If you need anything else you'll have to study it yourself."

"Alright," Joe repeated. "Still, this is really very helpful. Thanks, man."

I cringed a bit at him calling me 'man' — why couldn't he just use my name? "Don't mention it. And now I'd better get going."

"Hey," Joe said, as I turned to leave.

"Yes?"

"Think you can show me that game? It sounds interesting." He grinned. "And maybe it'll help me with my studies."

"Yeah, of course. See you, roomie."

"See ya."

As I started down the corridor, I smiled to myself. I'd actually managed to connect with Joe! Only a little bit, but still. Maybe I could talk to him some more, and we could actually become friends.

And then I could maybe somehow convince him his attitude — especially about queer people and other minorities — was wrong. Perhaps. Maybe I could breach his thick, toxic-masculinity shell.

I could try.

Maybe things were looking up.

15
Rules for Life

"Miss Suarez, a word?"

As the class began the slow after-lesson shuffle through the door, Anna turned to me. "Can you wait for a minute?" she asked. "I won't be long."

I left the room to wait for her in the corridor; it was only a few minutes before she rejoined me.

"What did Professor Markley want?" I asked as we started walking.

"To check in with me about how the work he's got me doing was coming along," she replied.

"Oh, you agreed to work on the toxic masculinity project? That's great!"

Anna smirked. "I knew it."

"Knew what?"

"It was you. You told the professor to give me this chance."

I stopped walking and turned toward Anna. "How did you . . . ?"

"When he offered me the position he said he'd asked someone else, but they couldn't do it because they were already working on some other stuff; however, they'd recommended me instead."

I shrugged. "It could've been anyone in our class. You have plenty of friends."

"But Professor Markley really likes you, Lily, so you're high up on the list of suspects. And also, and I'm not saying this to put anyone down, none of my other friends are as smart as you."

"I'll take that as a compliment," I said, a smile forming on my lips.

"Good, because it was. But also, you knew what the project was about. I never told you."

"I hope you don't mind."

"Why would I mind?" she replied. "This is a great opportunity for me to get started on research in the field, so I'm really grateful you thought of me. Thank you, Lily." She put a hand on my shoulder and squeezed it affectionately.

"You're welcome."

"It's amazing, though. I was talking about you with Markley a few days ago, and we commented on how far you've come. No, don't worry, I didn't out you," she quickly said, noticing the look in my eyes, "but you remember what you were like at the start of the year, right? You were mired so deep in toxic masculinity, you were hanging out with *Joe* of all people . . . and look at you now." She rubbed my shoulder. "A top student, and a really lovely girl. I wonder what the you from back then would say if he could see you."

"She," I replied. When Anna gave me a puzzled look, I explained. "I mean . . . I'm trans, so I was always a girl, right? So it was 'she' even back then."

"You're right," Anna replied. "Sorry."

"No need to apologize," I said, waving her words away. "I used to be a horrible little shit, so it's natural that you see me as a completely different person now."

By then we'd reached the exit, so we said goodbye to each other and went our separate ways. As I walked back to my dorm, I thought about what Anna and I had both said: it was true, I had changed a lot. For one, I'd been immersed in queer society for so long that referring to myself as a trans girl was natural. Pretending came to me as easily as breathing, and it felt weird to think about myself as 'he', even in the past tense.

I'd also completely stopped believing in that toxic masculinity stuff. I'd been totally honest with Anna: I *had* been a horrible little shit, to her and to several other people. But by hanging around my friends, I'd gradually come to recognize everything that had been drilled into me by society since I was very young, everything I was told about what 'being a man' meant — strong, hides his emotions, always ready to fight — was completely wrong.

If only I could make Joe see the light . . .

I'd already made some headway: I'd managed to mostly reconcile with him, and while we weren't exactly the closest of friends, we also were no longer at odds. At first we'd started talking about video games — I'd shown him how to build a rocket and get it into orbit without crashing — and then we'd chatted about our life stuff. He was still quite bummed by the fact he'd had to miss three weeks of school, and angry at the people who'd 'made him miss' them; I had yet to find a way to broach the subject that what had happened had been almost entirely his fault.

But still, I was hopeful.

I stepped into the dorm to see Darrell sitting at his desk in the entry hall. I waved to him. "Hi, how's it going?"

He looked up from his laptop and smiled at me. "Oh hey, hello there! I'm good, you? Everything alright?"

"Everything's alright," I replied. "Just got done with classes for the day, now I'm thinking I'll get some studying in before bed."

"Good," he said. Then he glanced around, as if to check no one was nearby, and beckoned me over. "Listen, I . . . I wanted to talk with you for a sec, if you don't mind."

"Yeah, sure. What's up?"

"How are things between you and Joe? Everything okay?"

I was puzzled by his words, and I'm sure it showed in the look I gave him. "Yes, of course. Everything's fine, why wouldn't it be?"

"Well . . ." Darrell began, then paused to gather his thoughts. "I know how that guy can be. I haven't been around him nearly as much as you have, so I'm sure you know how he's . . ."

He paused; when he didn't continue, I spoke instead: "He's . . . what?"

He hesitated before answering, "I really don't want to badmouth him too much, but . . . he's a bigot. I've heard him talk with his friends a few times, and the way he speaks about queer people or people of color . . ."

He let the sentence hang in the air. "Yes, I know how he is," I said. "Sadly. I'm . . . working on it."

". . . You're *working on it*?"

"Yes, I'm trying to talk to him. Reason with him, make him see that some of the things he thinks and does are out of line. That kind of stuff."

Darrell seemed unsure, but slowly nodded. "Okay," he said, a slight edge to his voice. "Alright. Good. Just . . . be careful. Take it slow, and try not to do anything that would put you in danger."

"Hold on, what?" I laughed a bit. "Why would I be in danger?"

"I don't know. No real reason, I guess," he said, shrugging. "It's just a feeling I get. Hey, did you know we had a boy and a girl share a room in this dorm two years ago?"

I did a double-take at the sudden non sequitur. "I'm sorry?"

"Yeah, it was the weirdest thing," he said. "They roomed together from the very start of the year, it just took a while for any of us to notice."

"Really? That's quite the feat, keeping it hidden from you. You're usually on top of things. How did they even do it?"

"I dunno really. Things just fell into place that way, I guess." He smirked. "It was a headache for me when I found out, too, having to wrangle things so they could finish the school year without having to find another place. Good ol' Pat and Allie."

I blinked again. Pat and Allie? As in Patrick and Allie, two of the three coordinators of the GSA? He probably meant them, but why? I had no idea where he was going with this conversation.

"Why are you telling me this?"

Darrell shrugged once more. "No real reason," he said again. "Maybe I just wanted you to know that if you need my help with anything, I've got your back." Then, after a brief pause, he continued, "And that if you want to talk to me about anything, I'm right here."

About anything?

What was the *anything* he was referring to? No matter how much I wracked my brain, no matter how many scenarios I ran through, I just could not figure it out. What exactly was Darrell implying? What did he *know*? Why would he mention Allie and Patrick out of the blue? As if they had something to do with me. I knew they were both bisexual and in a relationship with each other. (And with Lena, too, which was a bit weird, but hey, as long as they were all happy about it.) And that Allie was trans. But beyond that we had nothing in common—

Hold on.

Was...

Was Darrell implying I was in love with Joe?

If that was the case, he was way off the mark. I was a completely heterosexual man. Hell, I even had a girlfriend, which was still a new experience for me. But I didn't like men, either romantically or sexually. Never did. So there was no way I could have that kind of relationship with Joe.

Sorry, Darrell, but you're completely mistaken.

"Alright," I said. "I'll keep that in mind. Thank you, Darrell."

"You're welcome," he replied. "Have a nice evening."

I waved goodbye and made my way down the corridor to my room. I took a moment to steady myself and catch my breath, then I went in. Joe was bent over his bed, straightening the covers.

"Hi," I said.

Joe glanced over his shoulder and gave me a brief nod. "Hello," he said, then turned back to making the bed.

"Hold on, are you tidying up?" I asked.

"Yeah?" he replied. "What else could I be doing?"

It was weird. I'd never seen him make his bed or tidy up his side of the room in all the time we'd been rooming together.

"Well, this is a first," I said, carefully keeping my tone neutral. "What prompted it?"

Joe finished making the bed, before straightening up and turning to me. "I just thought I'd do some self-improvement. You know, work on myself. To become a better person." He screwed his thumb over his shoulder at his bed. "This is part of it. Rule six."

I looked at him in puzzlement. "What's rule six?"

"Set your house in perfect order before you criticize the world," he recited.

"That sounds like a direct quote. What's it from?"

He picked up a book from his nightstand and wordlessly tossed it to me. I turned it over so I could see the cover.

"*Twelve Rules for Life*," I read aloud. "By … Wait, isn't this the lobster guy?"

Joe frowned at me. "Lobster guy?"

"Yeah, the guy who says human brains work on the same chemicals as lobster brains, so natural behavior in lobsters is also natural behavior in humans," I replied. "Or something like that. My friends told me about him, apparently he has dodgy opinions on several things."

Joe walked toward me and snatched the book from my hands. "Dr. Peterson is one of the foremost experts on human behavior as it pertains to the relationships between people, i.e. society," he said. "And I will not have you besmirch his name."

Before I could help myself, a burst of laughter escaped me. "Excuse me? 'Pertains?' 'Besmirch?' Since when do you use those kind of words?"

"Since I started reading Dr. Peterson's book," he replied with a huff. "Like I said, I'm trying to improve myself."

We locked eyes and I saw that he was, surprisingly, actually offended. "Alright, I'm sorry. I apologize, I shouldn't make fun of you. My bad," I said, to defuse the situation.

The apology had the intended effect: Joe's eyes softened and he nodded. "Apology accepted. And I should apologize, too, I was getting too defensive," he said. "I should have waited for you to finish what you were saying. Assume the person you're listening to knows something you don't."

"That's another rule, I assume?"

"Rule nine."

"That's a good one," I said. And I meant it. After all, I'd become aware of several things I hadn't known until after I actually started talking to queer people and listening to what they said in turn, instead of judging from appearances and preconceptions.

"Isn't it?" Joe replied. "I'll let you borrow the book once I'm done with it, I think you'll like it."

Speaking of books, that reminded me: "Oh, by the way, how did your physics test go?" I asked. "Weren't you supposed to be getting the results today?"

"Oh, right!" Joe brightened up. He rummaged in his backpack for a few moments, then handed me a sheet of paper.

"A B-plus?" I said. "Joe, this is great!"

"It is," he agreed. "I was hoping for something a bit better, but it will still bring my GPA up. And look at this!" He grabbed the test from me and turned it over. "I got a perfect score in the orbital mechanics section. This is all thanks to you!"

"Well, thanks to me and video games."

My joke prompted a laugh from him. "Yeah, you're right. I should play games more often, really." He paused. "Still, thank you. I really appreciate it."

"You're welcome."

Joe slapped me on the shoulder. "What do you say we go out this Friday? Grab a few drinks, celebrate. Like old times."

I thought about it for a moment, but shook my head. "I'm sorry, but Friday's no good for me. I'm meeting with friends for a movie night."

"Alright," he nodded. "Saturday, then?"

"No, I have a date on Saturday," I replied without thinking.

And I instantly regretted it.

Joe's eyes widened. "A date?" he asked. "Like … a *date* date? With a girl?"

"With my girlfriend, actually."

"DUDE!" he spread his arms wide, making me flinch — both from how loud he'd been and from using the word 'dude'. "You have a girl-friend?!"

". . . Yeah, I do," I said. "We've been dating for just over a month. Maybe six weeks."

"That's great!" Joe said. "It really is. I was getting worried for you, my man."

I cringed at his choice of words again, but managed to smile. "Thank you."

"So, what's she like?" he inquired. "What's her name?"

"Nora," I replied. "And . . . Well, she's tall. Taller than me. And she's smart, and clever, and—"

"No, that's not what I meant," Joe cut me off. "Is she *hot*?"

My eyebrows pinched together. After learning about me having a girlfriend, the first thing Joe had thought to ask about was her physical attractiveness; he couldn't be more superficial if he tried.

"Yeah, she's … She *is* hot, I suppose," I said. "But more than that, she's really warm and caring. When we hug or kiss, it's like I can forget the world. It makes me feel . . . protected. Like I could rely on her for anything." I saw Joe was giving me a weirded-out stare. "What?" I asked.

"It makes you feel 'protected?' Really? I didn't think you were one to have those kinds of mushy feelings. What, are you turning into a girl?"

His words stopped me dead in my tracks. I looked at him in disbelief for a moment, then shook my head. "You know what? Forget it," I said. "You're making me regret telling you. I'm going to take a shower."

I pulled out my PJs, toiletry bag, and another small pouch from where I'd hidden it at the very bottom of my wardrobe under my old hoodies, and wordlessly made my way to the bathroom. As I walked in I heard Joe say, "What the hell, man? We were just talking! Why you gotta be like this?"

I stopped, my hand on the door handle. "Think about what you said, and why that could make me mad," I said, without looking at him.

I closed the door behind me and locked it. Then I took a breath and let it out in a deep sigh.

God, talking with Joe was exhausting. I always had to be careful about what I said, and I had to bear him being a complete idiot about things. I knew he had some good buried somewhere in his heart, but bringing it out would require a lot of deep digging. For what was probably the millionth time, I wondered if he was really worth the trouble or if I should just leave him alone again.

I'd have to think about it later; I had other stuff to do.

I quickly stripped down to my panties, camisole, and sports bra — and looked at myself in the mirror. My curves were really coming along now, even though it was less than a month since I'd noticed the first changes. I wondered if I could somehow manage to keep this shape (slender, but with a bit of heft around my chest, thighs, and hips) once I went off hormones later this year. I quite liked how I looked; it would be a shame to have to go back to my previous body type.

The only thing I really didn't like was my face. Even though it seemed to be getting a bit rounder, less rough around the edges, it was changing noticeably more slowly than my body was.

On the other hand, my face was the one thing I could change most easily. Following Giuliano's suggestion, I'd taken to shaving carefully with a safety razor close to the skin every morning. Luckily my beard didn't grow very fast, so my face was still almost completely smooth by the time bedtime rolled around.

And, of course, there was makeup. My tiny pouch contained a small assortment of eyeliner, mascara, foundation, and lipstick, which I used every evening. Just to get some practice with them and to enjoy how I looked in the mirror for a few minutes, before showering everything off.

That was another thing I was considering continuing after going back to being a guy. Makeup isn't exclusive to girls, after all, plenty of men wear what they call 'guyliner'. Why call it *guyliner*, anyway? Calling it eyeliner was perfectly fine. Once again, I wondered at how amazingly fragile men's masculinity could be.

Working slowly and deliberately, like I'd done a few times before, I carefully applied the products. It only took a few minutes, but I really liked the final effect. It made me look … softer. Cuter. But more sophisticated at the same time.

It was a shame I couldn't look like this all the time. How could I explain it to Joe? Maybe I would be able to when I managed to make him recognize the pitfalls of toxic masculinity. But with how things were going, that would probably be way into the future.

I sighed and got into the shower to wash away the makeup and the day's tiredness.

When I got out of the bathroom Joe swiveled his chair around and looked at me.

"I think I've figured it out," he said, sheepishly.

"So?"

"I'm sorry for implying you're a girl."

I shook my head. "Close, but no cigar."

"Wait, what?" he said in clear surprise. "That's not it?"

"That's not it."

" …Then what?" he asked. "What is it?"

I sighed deeply. "Joe, feelings aren't exclusive to men or women. A man could have what you describe as 'mushy feelings,' and still be secure in his masculinity. Because that masculinity is not toxic."

"Dr. Peterson has some things to say about that so-called 'toxic masculinity,'" he said, straightening up in his chair, clearly getting ready to launch into a speech. "Like—"

"You know what? I don't want to hear it right now," I said, raising a hand to stop him. "We'll talk about it more tomorrow if you want. Right now I have to study a bit, and then I'm going to sleep."

Without waiting for his answer, I marched to my desk, pulled out the day's notes from my backpack, and started reviewing them. After a moment, out of the corner of my eye I saw Joe turn back to his desk.

One step forward and two steps back.

16

Complacency

"Touch your chest. Try to say something."

"Something like what? What do we say?" someone to the left of me asked.

"A normal sentence is fine," Skylar replied. "What you've just said works perfectly, actually, though I usually go for the classics."

"Classics?"

"Heat from fire, fire from heat," Skylar recited, then smiled mysteriously as if she'd just let us in on a secret. "It's one of the best sentences for testing resonance."

"Okay," I mused. "Heat from fire, fire from heat." The others in our group — a bit over a dozen people — imitated me.

"Now, did you feel your chest vibrate?" Skylar asked.

"Yes, actually," I replied.

"This is called 'chest resonance,' and is typical of male-coded voices. It's the timbre, the sound quality, for those of you who know that term. Female-coded voices, on the other hand, have what is called 'head resonance', which means that instead of vibrating mostly here," she touched her chest, "they vibrate mostly here." She touched her throat, just below her chin, and looked around the group. "In music terms, this is similar to the difference between a flute and a violin: even when they play the same pitch, the same note, you can immediately tell which is which by their timbre."

I thought about what she'd just said. "So raising your pitch is useless?" I asked. "If it's all about resonance . . ."

"Raising your pitch *can* help, since female-coded voices tend to be higher than male-coded ones," Skylar answered. "But it's resonance that does most of the work, resonance is what differentiates between male and female voices. Plenty of women have a deep, low voice, yet you'd never mistake them for men. Look up Gianna Nannini sometime."

"Who?" someone piped up.

"Italian singer."

"Or Shohreh Aghdashloo?" I said.

"I see someone likes *The Expanse*," Skylar said, smiling.

"*Arcane*, actually," I replied. "But don't ask me to pronounce her last name again, I'm surprised I got it right on the first try."

She laughed. "Alright. Now, try to raise your pitch just a little bit. Find a tone where you're comfortable speaking, but still have chest resonance."

There was a cacophony of voices, as we all tried to find our tone. After a little bit, I thought I'd found it. "Like this?" I asked, in a pitch which was maybe two notes up from my normal speaking voice, my hand still on my chest to feel the resonance.

"Exactly like that," she said. "Now, here comes the tricky part. One hand on your chest and one on your throat, and slowly go up in pitch, like this. E-E-E-E-E," she sang, raising the pitch of her voice by several notes each time, "until you're just about to break into falsetto."

"Falsetto?" someone asked.

"The stereotypical *squeaky Minnie Mouse voice*." Skylar demonstrated what she meant with her voice. "Do you understand? Okay, all together. E-E-E-E-E-E."

The class imitated her until we'd all reached the same point.

"Good," she said. "Now, hold that note. EEEEEEE, feel the resonance. You have it?"

I nodded, as did several people around me.

"Okay. Now, the trick is: you have to lower your pitch again, reaching the same note you started from, your baseline. E-E-E-E-E-E," she demonstrated, lowering the pitch of her voice. "But you have to keep the resonance you have now, and you may think it's easy, but it's not. So I'll make you a bet: I'll buy dinner for anyone who manages to do it on the first try."

There was another jumble of sounds as each of us tried to follow her instructions. I was feeling confident at first: it didn't seem that hard. But after lowering my pitch just a little bit, I found that it automatically dropped back into chest resonance, no matter how careful I was.

We all gave it several more tries and I got a little bit better, but in the end I still couldn't manage to do it.

"Guess I don't have to buy dinner this time," Skylar said, laughing.

"This is too hard," someone complained.

"Of course it's hard. It's called voice *training*, after all," Skylar replied. "You're meant to keep at it. You don't run a marathon right after being a couch potato for several years, and you don't speak like a girl right after speaking like a boy all your life." She smiled. "But I know you'll get it. I have faith in you all."

Feeling someone affirm their trust in my abilities made me feel warm inside.

"So, what do you say I show you a few more exercises?"

≣

Although my 'girl voice' still sounded like a toad choking on a frog at the end of the lesson, I was confident I would get it down sooner or later – probably sooner, since I'd improved noticeably over the hour-long session. And there were still two free group lessons to go. After that I could always pay Skylar for one-on-one lessons or practice on my own, maybe with Vicky's help since she'd been down the same path as me.

I waved goodbye to Skylar and the class and started down the corridor.

"Hi."

I turned around in surprise: Nora was leaning right beside the door I'd just come out of, smiling at me.

"Nora! Hi," I walked forward to meet her, lifted myself onto my tiptoes and gave her a peck on the lips. "What are you doing here?"

"I was lonely and wanted to see you."

"But we saw each other at the GSA yesterday," I said. "And we're going out to lunch tomorrow."

"Two days is a long time, Lily," Nora said, shifting her smile into a grin. "I wanted to see you now, so here I am. You look lovely, by the way. Did you do something with your hair?"

I felt a blush creep up my face, from my neck to my ears, but I nodded. "I combed it to the side, used a bit of hairspray to hold it in place." I tilted my head to give her a better look. "I've been practicing. Is it really that noticeable?"

Nora leaned forward and whispered in my ear. "It is for me. I notice every tiny difference in you, since I look at you all the time. I know I probably shouldn't, but you're so cute I can't help myself."

I looked away and stammered a few words in protest, along the lines of me not being that cute at all, but Nora just looked at me with an amused smirk.

"You should really learn to control your reactions, Lily," she said. "When you're like this, it only makes me want to tease you even more."

I pouted. "Did you come all this way just to make fun of me?"

"Oh, no, absolutely not. I wanted to talk to you, about this weekend. There's a concert at the Chip, the dive bar near the quad. Wanna come?"

"Yes, of course," I answered without hesitation. "When? Saturday or Sunday?"

Nora hesitated. "Uh . . . Friday, actually. Tomorrow evening."

"Okay, let's do it."

"Are you sure? We have movie night on Friday."

"Like every Friday," I shrugged. "I'm sure the others won't mind us missing one night. It's fine. Let's go to the concert."

"Great!" Nora exclaimed. "It's a date."

"I'm already looking forward to it."

She offered me her hand: I knew from experience this was her way of telling me she wanted to walk me back to my dorm, and I readily accepted the invitation.

We walked in silence to my dorm, hand in hand, just feeling the closeness with each other. When we reached the building, we let go reluctantly after exchanging a kiss.

"Can I pick you up tomorrow?" Nora asked. "So we can walk to the venue together. If you don't mind, that is."

"Why would I mind?"

"Well, you know . . ." she began, then glanced around before leaning forward. "Since you're not out yet, I don't know if you want to risk running into *someone* when we're together."

I immediately understood she was talking about Joe. "It's not a problem," I said. "I'm not out to him or to anyone else outside the GSA, but I've already told him I have a girlfriend."

"You did?" Nora said, taken aback. "How did he take it?"

"As well as he could, I guess. He was his usual self: the first thing he asked me was if you were hot."

"Am I? Hot, I mean."

I saw her grin and groaned. "Yes, Nora, you're hot," I rolled my eyes and jokingly nudged her in the shoulder. "But that's beside the point: we don't have to worry about him seeing us together. You can even wait for me in the lobby if you want. We just need to be careful about how you refer to me. You can't call me Lily in front of him, for one."

"And what should I call you?" Nora asked. "I don't even know your deadname."

"It's—" I began, but stopped myself just in time. "You know what, it doesn't matter. Just call me darling, or honey, or something along those lines."

Nora looked at me, a dangerous glint in her eye. "How about 'princess'? Would that be okay?"

"Absolutely not," I replied, shooting her a look. Truth be told, however, the idea of Nora calling me 'princess' was quite enticing.

Nora laughed. "Sorry, it was just a joke. Alright." She leaned forward and gave me a peck on the cheek. "See you tomorrow, babe."

"See you tomorrow, Nora."

When I walked into the dorm, it was right into an argument.

"Come on, man!" I heard Joe's voice coming from the corridor leading to our room. "It's not fair!"

"I already warned you several times, Thompson," Darrell's voice came in response. "No ball games inside the building."

As I walked toward the hallway Eddie and Tommy rushed past me without even sparing me a glance — evidently Darrell had ordered them to get lost, like he'd done before.

"Oh, come on! It only happened twice!" Joe protested.

"What only happened twice?" I asked.

"Hello there," Darrell said. "This guy broke a lamp playing with his friends." He pointed along the corridor, and I saw the glass on one of the wall lamps had been smashed.

I frowned. "Wasn't it a table last time? A table that wasn't even supposed to be there?"

"Yeah!" Joe exclaimed, jabbing a finger toward me and nodding enthusiastically in agreement. "You tell him!"

Darrell shook his head. "Even if it only happened twice, that's two times too many. I was lenient last time, but now I'm confiscating this." He held up Joe's football and walked to a closet, which he opened with a key hanging from his belt before tossing the ball inside. "I'll give it back in a couple weeks, if you're on your best behavior until then." He turned back toward Joe. "And don't even think about buying a new one: if you keep playing ball games inside, I'll just keep taking your balls away."

"Fuck you, man," Joe snapped. He stormed into our room, slamming the door behind him.

"That fucking guy," Darrell muttered; then, looking at me, he added, "Sorry."

"For what?"

"Even though it's my job, I made him angry. I hope he doesn't take it out on you."

"I'll be fine," I said with a smile. "The worst he's ever done was being grumpy in my general direction, and I know how to handle that."

"Still, be careful."

"I will," I replied, though I had no idea why I needed to be careful, exactly. As Darrell returned to the lobby I walked to my room.

Joe was pacing back and forth, obviously fuming. At least he couldn't blame me this time. I sat at my desk, pulled out my notes, and began studying, but I just couldn't concentrate as Joe kept pacing up and down, mumbling to himself.

Finally I set down my pen and turned around. "You alright?" I asked.

"No, I'm not alright. Obviously," he hissed through clenched teeth. "It's just . . . that goddamn fucker. Who the hell does he think he is?"

". . . Our RA?"

Joe made a face. "Yes, I do know he's our RA. Thank you," he spat out. "How dare he take my ball away?"

Suddenly I thought of a way I could ingratiate myself with Joe. Connect with him, if only a little bit.

"Come on, let's go get it back," I said, standing up from my chair and grabbing my purse.

"Get it back . . . how?" Joe gave me a puzzled look. "You heard him, he's not going to give it back for two weeks."

"Then we'll *take* it back," I replied, smiling at him. "Where . . . oh, there it is." I pulled my lockpick set from my purse. "Come with me."

I walked to the closet Darrell had put the ball in; Joe followed me, clearly puzzled. "What are you doing?"

"Keep watch, and tell me if anyone's coming," I replied, as I started fiddling with the lock. "Alright, now, let's see . . ."

It took me some minutes to get it: while I'd kept practicing, I was nowhere near as good with locks as Nora. But in the end I managed to set the pins, and the lock turned smoothly, the latch rolling back with a satisfying click. "Here," I said, opening the door and picking up the football.

Joe looked at me in surprise. "Wait, why do you know how to pick locks?"

"My girlfriend taught me," I said, tossing the ball to him and closing the door.

"Huh. She sounds cool."

Thinking of Nora made me smile. "She is."

"Anyway. Thanks," Joe said, gesturing at me with the ball. "I'm really grateful."

"If Darrell catches you, though, remember: you didn't get it from me," I said, raising a finger in warning, but smirking at the same time.

≣

I stared at the screen for a moment, then put my face in my hands and massaged my temples. I had some free time to work on my paper, and I was completely stuck. I just didn't know what to write.

Scratch that. There were several things I could write: about my experiences with transition, for instance, or how I found relating to queer people to be easier than to cishets, or how, despite being a cis man, HRT had done wonders for my mental health — I'd almost completely stopped drinking, and I was doing much better with my studies.

But none of those were things I *wanted* to write. None of those things would lead the reader of the paper to the conclusion I wanted to make: that a lot of people only transitioned for clout and to improve their social standing. I'd spent nearly five months immersed in queer society, and yet, out of all the trans and non-binary people I'd met, there were none who fit the bill. After talking to them extensively, I was sure every single trans or non-binary person I'd met was really trans or non-binary: none of them were pretending.

It was as if I was the only person at Bradford McKinley who was transitioning without actually being trans.

But that couldn't be the case, right? It was impossible. *Surely* it was impossible.

I'd simply not gone deep enough. There were still things I hadn't done. Things I could do. Things which would lead me to a deeper understanding of the issue, allowing me to see the truth.

Things like . . .

I closed the text editor and brought up a browser window. I typed a few words in the search bar, clicked on the link that seemed most likely to yield the answer I was looking for, and started scrolling through the page. There it was: how you went about—

"Changing your legal name in New York State?" Joe's voice said from behind me. "What's this about?"

I jumped and swiveled my chair around to face him; I'd been so focused that I hadn't noticed him walking up behind me.

"Nothing!" I exclaimed, and flinched a bit: too loud. Then, recovering from the shock, I repeated more calmly, "Nothing. Just some research for social studies."

"Huh," he mused. "Is this still about that whole transgender stuff?"

I nodded.

"Okay. Listen, I'm going away for the weekend."

"With Tommy and Eddie?"

"Yeah. I'm leaving right now, I'll be back on Sunday afternoon." He paused. "Do you want to come?"

"No, thank you. Kind of you to offer, but you know I don't like that kind of stuff. And anyway, I have a date tonight."

"With your girlfriend? What was her name again?"

"Nora."

"Nora, right," Joe said. "Okay. Have fun."

"I will. You too."

"Just one thing: can I borrow ten bucks? I need to pitch in for gas. I'll pay you back on Sunday."

"Just like you paid me back the last time and the time before?" I asked, and then smirked in response to his frown. "No, it's fine, don't worry. It's just a few bucks." I pulled out my wallet, extracted a ten-dollar bill, and handed it to Joe. "Here you go."

"Thanks, buddy," he said, clapping me on the shoulder. "See you on Sunday."

He picked up his duffel bag, waved goodbye to me, and left the room.

I looked at my watch; it was time for me to get ready too. I closed my laptop, grabbed my toiletries, makeup pouch, and a clean set of underwear (including my good bra), and made my way to the bathroom.

As I showered I thought about Nora. God, I really loved her, and I was really looking forward to our date. It would be my first concert. I didn't really enjoy live music to be honest, but the company more than made up for it.

I toweled myself dry and put on my underwear. My bra felt a bit snug; I'd probably need to buy a new one soon. I briefly wondered what size my breasts were now — the bra was an A cup, and I was just about filling it completely. I'd definitely grown.

I dried my hair, styled it, then carefully applied my makeup. Looking at myself in the mirror, I smiled. Cute.

I looked around the bathroom, realizing I'd forgotten to bring my clothes in.

I opened my wardrobe and looked at the treasure trove inside. Over the previous few months I'd been expanding my clothes collection, and now I could put together several outfits I really liked. Not that I had much occasion to do so, what with not being out to Joe. But now he was gone for a couple days . . .

My lips drew into a smile as my eyes fell onto a pair of skinny leggings. I could pair them with a cute top, and they'd make a very nice outfit. Unmistakably feminine, but I had no reason to worry.

I pulled the leggings on and passed the top over my head, flattening the wrinkles until it sat perfectly.

I was confident I looked really cute. Nora would surely—

The door opened.

I turned around just in time to see Joe walk in.

"Sorry, man, I forgot my—"

He froze, staring at me. I stared back.

His eyes widened.

". . . What the *fuck* are you wearing?"

Finding Out

The LOOK IN Joe's eyes slowly turned hard.

His jaw set into a tight grimace.

"I see," he said.

I didn't reply. Fuck, this was really bad. The situation I'd feared most had suddenly come true. But then again, Joe and I were friends.

Were we friends? Maybe? Question mark? Probably. We'd connected quite a bit over the previous few weeks. We'd had our differences, but we were probably closer than we'd ever been. So maybe if I could just talk to him calmly and—

"Well then. Yes, I get it," Joe said casually, almost amiably. "How long has this been going on?"

He stepped fully into the room and clicked the deadbolt shut.

I gulped. "Joe, listen—"

"How long has this been going on?" He cut me off. "When did it start?"

I debated with myself whether I should answer truthfully, before finally answering, "November."

His eyes widened. "November? That far back?"

I nodded.

"Alright, so that makes it, what? Five months ago?" His voice was still calm and casual.

"Four and a half. It started . . . It was the day after we met Anna and Elanor at the frat party. The day you brought Eddie and Tommy over for the first time."

"Okay, yes, I see. That makes sense," he said. "It means you've been lying to me the *whole time*."

The last few words he hissed through his teeth. I felt a chill run down my spine.

"Joe, I wasn't—"

"And you're still lying RIGHT NOW!" He punched the door; I jumped at the sudden noise.

"No!" I protested, taking a step away from him. "I didn't—"

"You don't even have the courage to say it," he said, chuckling and shaking his head. Then he looked straight into my eyes. "You've been. Lying. The. Whole. Time." He paused. "ADMIT IT!"

He balled up his fist and took a step toward me; I took another step back and raised my hands in what I hoped was a peaceful gesture.

"I . . ." I began; I looked at him, saw the furious glare in his eyes. "I've kept this from you, yes. I'm sorry. But I didn't lie!"

"A lie by omission is still a lie," he said, and sighed deeply. "Ah, man, to think I've been rooming with a fag all this time."

I bristled at the insult. "I'm not a fag," I said. "First of all, that's a slur. And second, it means 'homosexual man', which I'm not."

"You're not what?" Joe answered. "A man?"

"Homosexual," I replied. "I like girls. I even have a girlfriend, I told you."

"Ha! A girlfriend, right. I've never seen her. Does she even exist?"

"She does. Her name is—"

"Nora, I know," Joe cut me off again. "See? I pay attention when you talk to me. Because I care about you! While you clearly do not."

"That's not true," I said, unconsciously taking a step toward him. "I mean, we're roommates. We're friends! Aren't we?"

"Do friends lie to each other?"

"I didn't lie! Joe, I never told you a single lie! Not ever!"

He scoffed. "That may be true, but you didn't tell me the whole truth, did you? A lie by omission is still a fucking *lie*. I've been sitting here, unaware of everything, while you were running around like . . . like a sissy, together with those fags and dykes you call friends. Like Anna, you're friends with her, right?" I nodded and Joe pointed a finger at me. "See? Anna. Nora, if she's even real. And I bet you even hang out with that tranny monster. What was his name? Elanor?"

"*Their* name," I said. "And you fucking take that back."

Joe laughed loudly. "Or what? You're going to punch me? You're going to fight me, to defend the honor of those degenerates?"

"You fucking take that *back*!" I repeated, louder this time. I took a step toward Joe, raising a finger in warning. "Elanor is one of the best people I've ever met. They're warm, caring, and willing to live their truth even if it means having to deal with people like you every waking moment!"

"People like me?" Joe hissed. "People like me?! You mean normal people?"

"No, I mean people so poisoned by toxic masculinity they aren't content with just living their lives, they want to tell other people how to live theirs!"

"Toxic masculinity is a liberal invention. It's a woke code-phrase used to make young men feel guilty and keep them down," he rebutted.

"GOD!" I shouted, throwing my hands up. "Are you even listening to yourself?! You have your head so far up your own ass that I wonder how you even manage to breathe, let alone talk! Try to listen to someone outside your own camp once in a while!"

Before I could move, he took a step forward, and suddenly his face was inches from mine. "Like you did?" he said.

"Yeah, exactly like I did. I had my head up my ass too, at least until I took off the blindfold and earplugs and decided to start learning."

"So that's how you became a degenerate."

"I didn't."

"You didn't what?"

"I didn't become a . . . a *degenerate*, as you put it." I chose not to bring too much attention to his choice of word. "I'm not gay. I'm not trans. I'm still a man. I'm still . . . still *normal*."

"Are you kidding?" Joe said, and he smirked. "Have you taken a look in a mirror lately?"

"What, this?" I said, taking a step back and gesturing at myself. "This doesn't mean anything. I'm just pretending."

"You're just . . . pretending?"

"Yes, this is all fake. The clothes? I can take them off. The boobs? They'll go away once I stop taking hormones. I can cut my hair, remove my makeup. And I will, in a few months."

Joe was clearly puzzled. "Are you serious?"

"I am."

He paused for a few moments. His face scrunched in concentration. "But . . . why? Why would you do this?"

"To prove that being trans is just a fad. That it's not true. I mean, if just anyone can transition, even someone 'normal,' it means people aren't doing it for the reasons they say. They're just doing it for . . . for clout. To get ahead in life." I spread my arms wide. "And I did it! I've proven it!"

"You've . . . proven it?"

"Of course! Don't you see? I successfully transitioned, deceiving everyone, but I'm still me. I'm still a cishet man."

Joe looked at me, bewildered, for a few moments. Then he started laughing — a deep, bitter laugh that only lasted a few seconds.

Before I could react, he'd stepped toward me and seized my wrist.

"Do you think I'm fucking stupid?!" he bellowed. "Who would even believe such a story?"

I looked up at the fire and fury roiling deep in his eyes. "Joe . . . Joe, please. You're scaring me."

"Good."

His other hand smacked me clear across the cheek, throwing me off balance. I landed sprawled on my bed, beside my open purse.

Joe grimaced as he flexed and shook his hand. "Ow, fuck. Look what you've made me do."

My ears were ringing from the blow, and I realized just how bad the situation was. Alone, locked in a dorm room with someone who refused to listen to reason. A *violent* someone who'd assaulted people before, and who'd just assaulted *me*. How was I going to get out of this situation?

I blinked the tears away, and as I did so I spotted something.

"Still, I think we can turn this into a teaching moment," Joe said, pacing back and forth. "I think you can learn something from all this."

My hand moved. Snaked across the bed and into my purse.

Joe turned toward me. "You want to be a tranny so bad? Well, so far you've been in . . . in a safe space," he spat. "I'll fucking show you what being a tranny is like in the real world."

He stepped forward.

"I have something to fucking show you, too," I hissed.

As fast as I could, I pulled my hand out of the purse, straightened up, and pressed the button.

The pepper spray didn't hit him directly in the eyes — in my haste, I hadn't aimed carefully enough — but he still got plenty of it. He howled in pain and clawed at his face as he stepped back.

I dropped the can as I sprang up from my seated position and barreled into him, hitting him shoulder-first. He lost his balance and tumbled backward to the ground, while I barely managed to keep my footing.

I made a beeline for the door and fumbled with the deadbolt.

"You bitch!" Joe roared, as he got up. "How fucking DARE YOU!"

I clicked the deadbolt open, and ran into the hallway without a moment's pause. "Help!" I shouted.

"Get back here!" Joe was already stumbling after me.

"Help!" I repeated as loud as I could.

For such a big guy, Joe was surprisingly quick — and good at football, apparently. He dove after me and managed to grab my feet. I fell to the ground, barely managing to soften the blow with my arms.

"You fucking whore!" Joe screamed, struggling to get a better hold of me and getting a kick in the teeth for his trouble. He grunted in pain, but tightened his grip.

"Let fucking go of me!" I said, kicking him again. "Help!"

"Alright, what is—"

Darrell jogged into view from down the corridor. He stopped dead in his tracks and looked bewildered at the scene in front of him. A few moments later, Nora appeared right behind him.

I locked eyes with her.

"Help me."

Darrell moved first. He ran forward and shouted, "Get the fuck away from her!" as he tackled Joe off me.

I scrambled away from the two of them, crawling across the floor. In seconds, Nora was beside me, helping me up.

"Lily," she said. "Lily, what happened?" She looked at Darrell and Joe, who were grappling with each other and cursing loudly. "What did he do?"

I looked at her, wide-eyed and breathless. "He . . . I thought he was gone . . . and then he came back . . . and he saw me . . . and . . . and he . . ." I sucked in a deep breath. "He hit me," I said, pointing to my cheek. "And then . . ."

"Stop," Nora said quietly, wrapping me in a hug. "There's no need to say anything else."

I melted into her embrace. "I—"

"Shh," she soothed me. "I got you. You're alright now."

Just as suddenly as it had surged up in me, I felt the adrenaline leave my body. My breathing became labored. My vision clouded.

And I started crying.

I wept and wept, tears pouring out of my eyes, my breath coming in ragged gasps and deep sobs. I cried, completely unaware of anything apart from Nora's warm embrace, the feeling of her arms around me.

I slowly got control of my lungs again, and I took a deep breath. I wiped my eyes and was startled to realize I was sitting on one of the couches in the entrance hall. How had I gotten here?

Nora was sitting beside me, an arm wrapped around my shoulders. Vicky, Elanor, and Anna were standing a short distance away, looking worried.

"How are you feeling?" Nora asked.

"Here, I have some water." Anna handed me a plastic bottle. "Drink. It will make you feel better."

I grabbed it with shaking hands. "What . . ." I began, then hiccoughed. "What are you all doing here?"

"I called them," Nora said. "Thought we could use some backup."

"And we came as soon as she called," Vicky said.

I squeezed the bottle tightly — fortunately it was still capped or I'd have made a mess. "Thank you."

"Don't mention it."

With a start, I realized something. I turned my head toward the corridor that led to my room. "What about . . . ?"

"Darrell managed to put Joe in a choke hold," Nora said. "He held him until he passed out, then dragged him to a closet and locked him in. He's making a phone call now."

She nodded her head toward the doors: they'd been propped open, and through them I could see Darrell pacing back and forth on the phone, clearly agitated. He was shouting.

". . . It's bullshit, that's what it is!" he said. Then he paused, listening to the other end. "It's a fucking stupid decision, and I want it put on the goddamn record that I am absolutely not in agreement with it!" He paused again. "No, I won't let you talk to her, I'll tell her myself. You've done enough. Have a good fucking night."

He hung up and hung his head. Then he looked toward our group, shook his head, sighed, and walked over.

"Hi," he said, crouching in front of me so our eyes were level. He had a red mark, the beginning of a bruise, just below his right eye.

"Darrell . . ." I whispered, motioning to my own face.

"This is nothing," he replied, shaking his head. "I do MMA, I've had much worse. Rather, how are you feeling?"

"Terrible."

"I'll bet. Alright, listen . . . it's Lily, right?" I nodded. "Okay, Lily. First of all, I'm truly, deeply sorry for what happened to you. And I have some news. Some good, and some bad."

"Good news first," Nora said. Darrell looked at me to confirm.

"Okay," he said. "Good news is: Joe will absolutely be punished for what he's done tonight. There will be a disciplinary hearing next week, which will decide what exactly that punishment will be, but that's just going to be a formality. I guarantee he will be expelled. No ifs, no buts. What he did was way too serious."

I nodded.

"And the bad news?" Vicky asked.

"The bad news . . ." Darrell began; he paused, and then sighed. "Like I said, the hearing is next week. The school won't do anything about him until then."

There was a moment of silence, which was broken by Anna.

"Are you fucking kidding me?" she shouted. "He assaulted Lily, and he gets away scot-free?"

"He's not getting away scot-free," Darrell replied. "There will be a hearing, and he will be expelled."

"That is bullshit," Anna snapped.

"It is," Nora said and my friends nodded in agreement. "Assault is a serious crime, and this isn't the first time Joe has done something like this. Or the second, for that matter." Darrell looked at her in surprise and was about to say something, but before he could Nora continued, "Why don't you call the police?"

Darrell bit his lip. "Look, I'm going to give it to you straight: I agree with you, and I absolutely would. If it were up to me, I'd have had the cops here right away. But I just can't."

"What do you mean?" Elanor asked.

"I was on the phone with Dean Anderson just now. He's Dean of Housing, and he's also responsible for discipline and disciplinary hearings. And since the . . . the *incident*," he said, screwing his mouth in clear distaste, "happened on campus, it falls under his jurisdiction. And he said, and this is a verbatim quote, 'We don't need that sort of negative publicity.' He's planning on making the entire thing go away quietly: not mention it at all outside the school, expel Joe as soon as possible — which, like I said, is next week — and just forget all about it."

"That's complete . . ." Anna began.

". . . Bullshit," Darrell said at the same time as her. "I agree with you, and I told the dean that. But besides yelling at him, there's nothing I can do. I'm your RA. I'm a school employee. If I go against his orders, I could get fired." He leaned in, lowered his voice, and continued, "But to be honest, there's nothing stopping one of you from calling the cops. I could just say you went against my advice. It would become a whole thing, of course: a trans student assaulted on campus, in the dorms even. Can you imagine? The press would have a field day with it. But you can do it if you want."

Suddenly a picture of a newspaper with my photo and my name — Lily O'Connor — splayed on the front page flashed through my mind. It would be in print, it would be on news websites . . .

I quickly shook my head. "No. I'm not out to my parents yet. If they found out like this . . ." I took in a deep breath and let it out slowly. "I just can't."

Nora squeezed my shoulder reassuringly.

"I understand. What this means, however," Darrell continued, "is that Joe is absolutely free until Monday. So you better do your best to avoid him. And move out of your room, since he'll be free to use it."

"I'm sorry, what the fuck?" Anna exclaimed. "Joe is the guilty party, and you're asking Lily to move out?"

Darrell closed his eyes and bowed his head. "I'm sorry," he said. He looked up at me. "We have a couple of free rooms here, but I'm guessing you don't want to be in the same building as Joe?" I shook my head. "Understandable. Do you have a place to stay?"

I locked eyes with Nora, but she gently shook her head. "I'm sorry, Lily, but I don't even have a couch at my apartment, just a few armchairs, which are hardly ideal for sleeping."

"She can stay at my place," Vicky said. "My room's a double, but I'm using it as a single. We'll have to rearrange the furniture a bit and reassemble the bed frame I've stashed in the closet, but that won't take long."

"Are you sure? I don't want to be a bother . . ."

She smiled warmly at me. "You're not a bother, Lily. And I'm not leaving you high and dry. Not if I can help you."

I smiled back. "Thank you."

"Alright, that's settled then," Darrell said, getting to his feet.

"No, it's not settled at all," Elanor said.

Darrell turned to look at them. "What do you mean?"

"This is a college dorm. Lily has paid good money for a place here. And now she's being forced out because of something the college did. That's hardly fair." They paused. "Not unless there's some sort of compensation, that is. Like . . . giving Lily back the money she spent?"

"You studying law?"

"Pre-law."

"I'll call Dean Anderson, see what I can do."

Elanor smirked. "Do remind him that the college doesn't need 'negative publicity'."

"I might just do that." He turned to me. "You better go pack your bags now. I have to let Joe out sooner or later, so you should be gone by then."

I hesitated. "I . . . I really don't want to be in that room right now."

"I'll pack your bags for you," Nora said. "Can you help me, Anna?"

"Of course."

"My wardrobe and desk are on the left, all my stuff is there," I said. "And thanks."

Nora and Anna nodded in acknowledgment and walked away. Vicky pulled out her phone and walked off too, leaving me with Elanor and Darrell.

"Will you be alright?" I asked him. "With Joe, I mean."

"He's had enough time to cool off, so he shouldn't give me any trouble when I let him out," he replied. "But if he does . . . well, I told you I do MMA. I can handle myself."

"Maybe you should smack him around a bit in any case," Elanor said. "God knows he deserves it."

"Trust me, if he tries anything I won't hesitate to lay him flat."

Vicky returned, closely followed by Anna and Nora carrying my suitcases, which looked remarkably fuller than they had been months earlier, probably because of all the clothes I'd bought since then.

"Here we are," Anna said.

"You're just in time, the car's here," Vicky said.

"Car?" Nora asked.

"I called a friend."

We walked outside to see a beat-up old car there. A girl I'd never seen before, but who looked familiar, was in the driver's seat, and she rolled down the window and waved at us as we approached.

"Hi, Lexi," Vicky said. "Sorry for calling you here this late."

Lexi waved her hand dismissively. "That's what friends are for, right? Come on, get in."

☰

"Just sit on my bed, Lily," Vicky said when we finally got to her room. "We won't be a minute."

I watched as Nora and Vicky screwed the legs to the spare bed frame, set it down on one side of the room next to the wall, put a mattress on it, and made the bed.

"Everything's ready, my princess," Nora said with a bow. "You should really get to sleep, you've had an . . . eventful evening."

"Thank you."

She kissed me on the forehead. "Good night, Lily."

She turned to leave.

Before I could stop myself, my hand shot out and grabbed her by the wrist.

"I don't want to be alone."

Nora smiled kindly at me. "You won't be alone," she said. "Vicky will be sleeping here too."

I shook my head. "I . . . I don't want to be alone."

The full weight of what had happened that night hit me like a sledge-hammer, and I found myself crying again. I hugged myself, shivering.

I looked up at Nora, tears in my eyes.

"I—"

"Shh," she said, wrapping her arms around me. "It's okay. It's okay. I won't leave you."

"Neither will I," Vicky said. "We're right here for you, Lily."

A sob escaped me. "Thank you," I said in a small voice.

"Come on, give me a hand here, Nora," Vicky said, and they pushed the two beds against each other, then rearranged the covers.

They quickly changed into their sleepwear, Nora borrowing some PJs from Vicky, then we lay down with me in the middle and Nora and Vicky on either side of me.

They held me until I stopped crying and shaking and, finally, fell asleep.

18
Full Time

J OE DIDN'T EVEN show up for the disciplinary hearing. In fact, he'd all but disappeared. According to Darrell, Joe had emptied out his room, packed everything, and left for parts unknown without telling anyone where he was going. At that point I didn't even care whether he went home to Texas, or backpacking for a couple years to find himself, or disappeared into a torture basement somewhere: it was all the same to me as long as I didn't have to deal with him anymore.

I still had to show up for the hearing, however. Bradford McKinley had a whole process set up. It was basically a small-scale trial: the person who was being accused of breaking the school's rules had to attend, as well as any victims. Witnesses were called, and there could even be lawyers of a sort — other students who could assist during the hearing if anyone needed it.

In this case, though, almost everything was moot since Joe was gone and had therefore given up on defending himself. In fact, besides Dean Anderson (a bald man in his mid-sixties who seemed to have a stern look permanently affixed to his face), the only people who spoke at the hearing were me, Darrell, and Nora. I testified about what Joe had done; Darrell and Nora corroborated my version of the events, telling the dean what they'd witnessed when they'd answered my call for help. With no one available to rebut what we'd said, the dean banged his gavel and expelled Joe from the college, also barring him from setting foot on campus for three years for good measure. When we heard his words, we all breathed a sigh of relief.

It was almost a nonevent, except for one detail.

I showed up for the hearing wearing a dress.

It had been a difficult decision. After the assault I spent the whole weekend hiding in Vicky's house with her, Mel, Katie, and Nora providing moral support. Anna and Elanor also visited a few times a day, with information and gossip that was going around the campus. And from what they said, the chances of me keeping up my charade didn't look good. Several people had witnessed the attack and despite the dean trying to do damage control, within a day the whole campus was abuzz: "One of the guys living in the dorm was actually a closeted trans girl, and when her transphobic roommate found out he assaulted her."

They had me sit down before they told me this. Once I learned that basically everyone at the college knew who I was — or who I was pretending to be — I felt the world drop away from me.

But then I thought about it carefully.

This was a good opportunity. Until that point I'd been going about my day being able to hide my pretend transness from anyone who didn't know: which meant the majority of people at Bradford McKinley didn't treat me any differently from your average cis boy.

How would they treat me now that I was actually out?

I could now experience what being a trans girl was actually like, and use what I learned to further my understanding of queer issues and as material for the paper I was writing. It would also make an even bigger splash when, months down the line, I would reveal that I was just pretending.

Equally as important, there was my mental health to consider. Over the previous few months I'd noticed that I was much happier, much more relaxed, when I was with my queer friends and pretending to be a trans girl than when I was out in the world as the cis man I was. The tension I'd felt since I was thirteen or fourteen, was just . . . gone. I could enjoy myself, I could just be me and not have to be careful about what I said and did.

So why couldn't I start pretending to be a trans girl everywhere all the time? Before now there had been two layers to the deception: I was a cis man, who was pretending to be a trans girl, who was presenting as a cis man with everyone she wasn't out to. I could just remove the second layer: be a cis man pretending to be a trans girl, period. This way I could stop being careful about what I said to whom. It would be much easier. Much more relaxing.

I got a first practice run when I showed up *en femme* to the disciplinary hearing, but it wasn't that difficult: the only people there were the dean, my friends, Darrell, and a stenographer who wrote everything down into the official record. And the dean, to his credit, was completely professional — he didn't even blink at how I was dressed, and he called me 'Miss O'Connor' on the occasions he needed to address me.

The biggest challenge came a day later when I had to show up for class again. That was the moment I'd been dreading: having to endure looks from my classmates, some of whom, I was sure, would be judging me for being trans. Despite Bradford McKinley being a very liberal college, it certainly had its share of bigots in the student body.

I decided I had to go all out. To make everyone see me for what I was: a girl.

After the disciplinary hearing, I went with Nora to Molly's salon to cash in my rain check for nail polish and to have extensions put into my hair, lengthening it so it fell to just below my shoulders. Molly dyed and styled it for good measure, and the result was absolutely breathtaking, a far cry from my old haircut. The next morning I had Vicky do my makeup, and I put on the dress Nora had bought me a few months earlier.

Wearing the clothes she'd picked out for me boosted my confidence. It was also the only dress I owned; I would have to go shopping soon, since I couldn't borrow from my friends forever. While they were more than willing to lend me their clothing, nothing they owned fit me right. The only one of them who wasn't at least two inches taller than me, Vicky, was instead two sizes bigger. She absolutely rocked every look she did, but when I tried on her clothes I felt like I was swimming in them.

Despite all my preparations, though, I was still extremely nervous when I showed up at the social studies classroom side by side with Anna and Nora. Even though we didn't share any classes, Nora had insisted on walking me there, and I was extremely grateful to her for it.

"Alright," I said. "This is it."

"Remember," Nora said, "you got this." She beamed a smile at me and gave me a peck on the cheek.

I nodded. I took a deep breath, and slowly let it out, staring at the door to the classroom as if it was the gate to hell. Abandon all hope, ye who enter.

"Well . . . see you later."

"I'll wait at Giovanni's."

I exchanged a glance with Anna, who smiled at me reassuringly, took another deep breath, pushed the door open, and walked into the room.

I'd barely taken two steps in when the hubbub that filled the classroom before the start of the lesson died out and everyone turned to look at me. I felt as if I was naked, their stares on every square inch of my skin. Looking at me, examining me.

My breathing started getting faster. What was I doing? Why did I think this was even remotely a good idea? I had to—

"What the fuck are y'all looking at?" Anna said loudly, stepping up beside me: she wasn't shouting, but she managed to make her voice carry to every corner of the room. "Have none of you ever seen a woman before? Seriously."

At her words almost everyone looked away in shame; whispered conversations started filling the room again, and I was certain they were talking about me, but at least I was no longer the object of everyone's direct attention.

Anna patted me on the shoulder. "See? Nothing to it."

"Thank you."

"You're more than welcome," she replied. "Shall we take our seats?"

I started walking toward my usual spot.

"Where are you going?" Anna asked.

I turned back toward her. "Um . . . to my seat?"

"No you're not." She shook her head. "You're not sitting on your own any longer. Come here."

She gently but firmly grabbed me by the arm and pulled me to the front of the classroom toward the group of girls she usually sat with.

"Hi girls," Anna said. "This is Lily."

"Hi," one of them said. "I'm Lauren."

"Brie," added another.

"Lydia."

"Sequoia, but you can call me Essie," the last one said.

"She hates her name, and wonders what her parents were even thinking," Brie explained.

Essie smiled. "I guess that's one thing we have in common. Nice to meet you, Lily."

"Nice . . . nice to meet you, too," I said. I turned to Anna and saw she had a wide smile on her face — she'd clearly planned this. "Thank you," I whispered to her, as Professor Markley entered and called for us all to quieten down.

"You're welcome."

I had a huge smile on my lips until the end of the lesson.

⫶

"Miss O'Connor, may I have a word, please?"

I started to get up from my chair, but Anna stopped me by putting a hand on my shoulder. "Want me to come with you?"

"No, thank you, I'm sure I'll be fine. I'll see you outside."

She left the room as I walked up to Professor Markley.

"How're you doing, Miss O'Connor?" he asked. "I know about..." He paused, thinking about how to formulate the next few sentences, then he spoke again. "I've heard about what happened on Friday. Are you alright?"

I was honestly thankful to him for worrying about me — and for being careful with his words. "Mostly. I'm not completely okay, I still have a few things I need to work through. But I will be. I'm sure of it."

Professor Markley nodded. "Glad to hear it. Next question, then. About the paper you're writing, the one on how transition affects cis people."

"Yes?"

"Do you still feel comfortable writing it?" he asked. "I don't know what you were planning to cover, but considering what happened to you, I think some parts might be ... triggering."

I didn't say anything, so he took that as his cue to continue.

"Of course, if you want to switch tracks and make your final project about something else, I'm sure I can find something for you to discuss. And I'll be lenient in grading, since you'll have just a couple months to gather material and write it. What do you think?"

I shook my head. "Thank you, sir, but it's fine. I can keep going, no problem."

Professor Markley gave me a long, hard look, appraising my response; for a moment, I was afraid he would *order* me to switch projects, out of misplaced concern for my mental well-being. But then he said, "Alright. But if you need to switch, just tell me. I'll figure something out."

"Okay. Thank you again."

"Of course," he said. "Have a good day, Miss O'Connor."

I was met outside by Anna. We made small talk as we started walking to Giovanni's, but she quieted when she saw I clearly had a lot on my mind.

She was right. I was thinking about the exchange I'd just had with Professor Markley.

I was on the verge of rethinking writing my paper. After all, who would benefit from it in the end? Certainly not trans or queer people: my paper was about how cis people could pretend to be trans to access the spaces reserved for the other gender, and to get ahead in life.

But as I'd experienced, trans people were not better off than cis people, not by a long shot. Joe thought I'd been trans and he'd assaulted me because of it, which wouldn't have happened to a cis man. And there was also the stress of having to actually transition, of getting on HRT, of having to be closeted for a significant amount of time, of buying an entirely new wardrobe, of doing voice training . . . The only thing I'd proven was that, all other things being equal, the life of a trans woman was significantly more difficult than the life of a cis man.

I had also found exactly zero proof of cis people pretending to be trans and transitioning. The only person who was doing that, as far as I could tell, was me. If I wrote my dissertation the way I was originally planning to, I would put lots of trans people in a difficult situation: suddenly they'd have their lives examined closely for any 'proof' that they weren't actually trans. And no one would gain anything from it either. I'd originally thought the entire point of the exercise was to expose 'fake' trans people, but there was no one to expose.

Besides me, of course. I was the only one who was faking being trans.

Was it really worth it to risk ruining the lives of countless trans people just because someone had been an enormous idiot who had gotten a dumb idea into her mind one day because she was drunk and angry at the universe?

No. Probably not.

And Professor Markley had given me an out, which I didn't have before: I could say I didn't feel comfortable writing my dissertation because of what had happened with Joe. That would be the end of it. No more thinking about it. No more agonizing over things.

But there was one thing I knew I had to try before calling it quits.

I sighed deeply as Anna and I sat at a table where Nora, Vicky, and Elanor were already waiting.

"That sigh didn't sound promising," Nora said. "Did it really go that badly?"

"What? No, no it didn't," I replied. "It's just . . . I have lots of things on my mind."

"Such as?"

I hesitated. "Well . . . I was thinking. Now that basically everyone here knows I'm trans . . ." I looked around the table. "There's no real reason for me not to change my legal name, right?" I paused for a moment, but before anyone could talk me out of it — before I could think myself out of it — I continued. "I mean, originally I was planning on waiting until the school year was over before getting to it." Which meant never getting to it, since I was planning on going back to being a man just before summer vacation. "But now . . . Why not just do it? I mean, might as well."

My friends were smiling at me. I was a bit surprised: I'd expected them to advise me to be cautious, but once again they were nothing if not completely supportive of my choices.

"This is a very big step," Nora said, reaching for my hand and giving it a squeeze. "And I'm proud of you for taking it."

I was warm in the pit of my stomach at her words and her smile, but at the same time I felt guilty: here I was, deceiving Nora yet again.

I dismissed the thought. I would have to face the music sooner or later, but that moment was yet to come. "Thank you," I said. "The problem is . . . I don't know how to go about it. I mean, how do you even change your name?"

"It's complicated," Vicky replied. "I haven't changed mine yet because I don't want to risk my parents getting wind of it, but I've looked into it a lot, obviously. It mostly depends on where you were born, each state has its own rules." She paused. "Which reminds me, I don't even know where you're originally from."

"Oh, I'm a local," I replied. "Or almost a local. I'm from New York, up near the border with Canada."

"Alright then, I'll help you look into it," Vicky said. "I think I know who to ask, actually: a girl who was born near here and who's had a legal name and gender change. I'll send her a text."

"That would be great," I smiled. "Thank you, Vicks."

"No need to thank me, Lily," she replied, smiling warmly back at me. "I'll always be here for you, girl."

⧃

According to Vicky the process to change your legal name was simple, requiring just two steps. Step one: file with the court for a name change and attend a hearing to confirm it. Step two: publish the details of the name change in a newspaper within sixty days. That's it. Done.

There was no problem with either action, really, not even the second one. Even if I had to declare I was changing my name publicly . . . who even reads newspapers anymore? Especially the classifieds section. My parents sure didn't, they got all their news from the internet, so there was no danger of them finding out that way.

The real problem was that doing the whole thing required proof of birth: to change my legal name I had to send in a certified copy of my original birth certificate.

Hence why I was sitting on a couch in Vicky's living room, staring at my phone: I had the contacts app open and my mom's number was displayed.

I had to call her. Either her or my dad. That was the only way I was going to be able to get a copy of my birth certificate.

God, what was I even going to tell them? "Hey, Mom and Dad, it's me, ya girl. I've been pretending to be trans, and I need you to send over a document so I can further that deception!"

Yeah, right. They'd probably disown me or have me committed. Who would believe such a wild tale? Some days I could hardly believe it myself.

My hand moved toward the call button.

Then stopped, as I realized something.

Hold on. I was an adult, wasn't I? Just barely, since I was eighteen, but I was a legal adult. Did I really need to go through my parents to get a copy of my birth certificate? Why couldn't I do it myself?

I put down my phone and grabbed my laptop, did some quick Googling and, sure enough, New York State had a website from which I could request a copy of my birth certificate and have it overnighted to me. It would be just a couple of days before I had it in my hands.

I breathed a sigh of relief. It was lucky I'd realized there was no need to phone home: it had saved me an uncomfortable conversation with my parents, one I really hadn't been looking forward to.

Okay then. Let's do this. Let's order the birth certificate and get the ball rolling on that name change. Let's do this, Lily.

I clicked the link.

19

By Any Other Name

THE BAILIFF LOOKED at the paper in his hand, then back at us. "O'Connor?"

"Here!" I replied, as I stood up from the bench on shaky legs. "That's me."

"Right this way, miss." He motioned to the open courtroom doors.

I turned to my friends, who remained seated. "See you later, folks."

"You got this, Lily," Nora said, smiling reassuringly. I smiled back, and made my way through the doors.

As I walked up to the judge, who was high in his imposing chair behind the bench, I was a bundle of nerves. The turnaround for getting here had been surprisingly quick: the copy of my birth certificate had arrived the day after I'd ordered it, and the court had had an opening for a hearing for two days later. So almost before I knew it, a week to the day after I'd been forced to move out of my dorm room, I was about to change my legal name.

I was almost expecting the judge to see right through me, to instantly realize that I was faking it, and to call for someone to lock me up. I imagined him staring at me sternly, the word GUILTY appearing out of thin air in capital letters.

When I stood in front of him, however, he smiled kindly at me. "Don't be nervous," he said warmly. "You're not on trial here."

I gulped, and – despite what he'd just said – nodded nervously.

"Let's see now," the judge continued, reading from a sheet. "Petition for change in legal name. So your new name will be Lily O'Connor. Is this correct?"

"It is, sir."

"Nice name. Now, has all the necessary paperwork been filed?"

"Yes, your honor," a clerk seated to his right answered.

The judge nodded. "And have all relevant fees been paid?"

"Yes, your honor."

"Good." The judge turned to me. "Do you swear you are not changing your name to evade debts or in order to defraud?"

That question gave me pause.

I'd been expecting it. According to Vicky, judges often asked this and it made some trans people very nervous. Thanks to impostor syndrome, trans folks often feel like complete frauds. I did feel nervous to be put on the spot, since I was technically a fraud, but that wasn't what 'defraud' meant in this circumstance.

'Fraud' has a very specific legal definition, which I'd looked up: it's intentional deception to secure unlawful gains, or to deprive someone of a right. What I was doing wouldn't make me gain anything material, and would not deprive anyone of any rights, so while I often felt guilty about it, it didn't count as fraud. And also, I didn't have any debts, so . . .

"No, your honor. I mean, yes. Yes, I swear," I said, trying to sound surer than I was.

The judge nodded again, and banged his gavel. "Name change approved. You will be required to publish notice of this in a newspaper before it becomes official: you'll be instructed as to which one, and the wording you'll need to use." He smiled. "Have a nice day, Miss O'Connor."

I was a little stunned. That was it? The whole thing had taken barely five minutes, I'd expected something . . . *more*. Still, I replied, "Thank you," and walked back out to my waiting friends, stopping only briefly to receive the publishing instructions from another clerk.

"That was quick," Nora remarked. "Is everything okay?"

I nodded, still a bit out of it. "Yes. Yes, everything's okay." I looked over the paper I'd been handed, then back to my friends. "According to this, I just need to publish notice of the court order in a newspaper within sixty days, and the ruling will become official. They'll mail it to me once it does."

"So it's done," Anna said. "You're Lily. Really for real."

Vicky nudged her lightly in the shoulder. "She was *already* Lily really for real, this was all just to make bureaucracy recognize the truth."

Anna looked sheepish. "Yeah, you're right. Sorry."

"No harm done," I said: she'd always been very careful not to misgender or deadname me, so I could easily forgive a small slip-up like that.

"Alright, we have to celebrate!" Elanor exclaimed. "Let's go shopping!"

Now there was a thing I could not do, unfortunately. "Um . . . I'll come with to keep you company, but I think I'll pass on buying anything," I answered, trying not to deflate their enthusiasm.

Elanor looked at me questioningly. "Oh? Why's that?"

"This whole thing wasn't exactly cheap," I began. "Between the copy of the birth certificate, filing fees, and now the cost of publishing a notice in a newspaper . . . This is setting me back nearly five hundred dollars. I'll have to watch my expenses for a while."

"Oh, don't worry, I'll pay for anything related to your legal transition," Vicky said.

I turned to look at her. "What? Vicky, I can't—"

"Yes, you can," she replied. "I've already been paying for your HRT, I can pay for this too."

. . . Hold on. What?

I thought back, and I realized that while she'd been giving me box upon box of estrogen and testosterone blocker, no money had changed hands.

I closed my eyes. "Holy shit," I said under my breath. "Vicks, I'm so sorry. How much do I owe you?"

"Like I said, don't worry about it," she said, waving away my offer without even pausing to consider it.

I just looked at her, at a loss as to what to say. "But . . ."

"But what?"

"It's a lot of money!"

"It's *my parents'* money," she rebutted. "Whenever I need some cash, I just phone home. They never ask what I use it for; frankly, I doubt they care. And I'm going to milk them for transition money, for me and other people, for as long as I can." She grinned. "Call it a bigot tax."

☰

"Lily, what do you need?" Nora asked, turning to me as we walked into the mall.

My answer was instant: "Dresses. And skirts. I mean, I've slowly built up my wardrobe, but I haven't dared buy anything particularly feminine. In fact, the only dress I own is the one you bought me."

"And you look really cute in it," Nora said, grinning at me; I tried and failed not to blush.

"I think I have to buy a new bra, too," I continued. "The one I have is starting to feel a bit tight."

"Already?" Vicky seemed surprised. "When did you start hormones again?"

I thought back. "It was . . . mid-January, I think? About that."

Vicky's eyes flicked to my chest a couple of times. "I think this store has a lingerie section," she said. "Come with me."

She grasped my arm and dragged me toward the back of the store, where she approached a shop assistant.

"Hi, may I help you?" the assistant asked, with a polite smile.

"Yes," Vicky replied. "I think my friend has had a growth spurt recently, she may need a new bra."

"Of course. Come right this way, and we'll get you measured."

She led me to a changing room. Like the first time I'd been measured, nearly two months earlier, I stripped to the waist; this time I barely hesitated, though — the thought of someone staring at my naked skin didn't faze me anymore.

"Alright, let's see here," the assistant said, wrapping a tape measure around my chest. "You're a thirty-six . . ." She paused, readjusted the tape measure, and continued, ". . . A, but a bit on the large size. Nearly a B, actually."

"What!" I heard Vicky shout indignantly from outside.

"Vicks? Is there a problem?" I asked.

Vicky's head poked through the curtain: she had a mock-scandalized expression on her face. "Yes, there is, in fact, a problem! You've been on hormones for less than three months, and you're already a full A, maybe a B? How actually *dare* you!" She reached in, and slapped me lightly on the shoulder. "You have *no idea* how lucky you are!"

"What, are you jealous?" I laughed.

"You're damn right I'm jealous," Vicky responded, laughing along with me. "I would've paid damn good money to be as big as you are after three months, you bitch!"

From outside, I could hear Nora, Elanor, and Anna trying and failing to hold back laughter.

"Um," the shop assistant said; at that moment, I realized she was looking at me weirdly.

"Yes?" I asked.

"... You're trans?"

Oh, right. Vicky and I had accidentally outed ourselves to her. Shit, this could be bad; the last time I'd been outed to someone, they had *not* taken kindly to the revelation.

"Um ... yes," I warily replied. "I hope it's not a problem."

"No problem at all. I'm just a bit startled; I honestly couldn't tell." She paused for a moment, then continued. "I'll get some bras for you to try on, I'll be right back."

"I'll come help you, I know what style she likes," Vicky said. "Hey! Nora! Come help me pick out a bra for your girlfriend!"

They left me standing there dumbfounded.

... She *couldn't tell*? Seriously?

Did that mean I ... *I'd passed*?

I'd been told about passing, of course: it's when a binary trans person is automatically perceived by someone as their true gender — a woman for trans women, and a man for trans men.

But that couldn't be right. I'd been on hormones — *medically transitioning* would be the exact term — for fewer than three months: there was no way I could've passed. The shop assistant was just being considerate.

And yet the thought of being seen as a girl — not as a *trans* girl, as a *girl* — made me feel warm and fuzzy, deep in the pit of my stomach.

Was this ... euphoria? And if so, what did it mean? Why was being seen as a girl making me so happy?

Did it mean—

"Here we are." The assistant walked back in with an armful of bras and derailed my train of thought. "Let's try these on, shall we?"

≣

I was indeed a large A, nearly a B, much to Vicky's envy-tinged amusement. After I'd picked a bra, it was time for clothes. Like the first time we'd gone shopping together, my friends basically turned me into their dress-up doll. Not that I minded — they were very knowledgeable about women's clothing, while I was still a newbie.

We spent the best part of the afternoon flitting between various clothing stores — mostly low-end, nothing pricier than a Zara — and emerged laden with several bags. Mine were filled with dresses and skirts, as well as some tops and pants — I just couldn't resist. It was a hit to my wallet — even though Vicky gifted me some, I insisted on paying for what I could myself: I'd *really* have felt guilty otherwise — but worth it.

Before we went back to Bradford McKinley, Nora insisted on making one last stop, and led us to a shoe store.

"I've looked this place up," she said, showing me her phone. "Apparently it has a good selection of shoes, even in large sizes. Perfect for you."

"But I already have shoes," I protested.

"You have men's shoes," she rebutted. "The most feminine of them are the Converses you're wearing, and those are unisex. A lot of the clothes we bought today need something a bit more sophisticated: a classy pair of flats, or even heels."

Heels? Seriously? I'd always thought they made girls' legs look great, but I'd never thought I would wear a pair.

"I'm not sure about this," I said, nervously biting my lip. "Heels are very different from what I usually wear."

"That's the whole point," Anna said.

"It's totally the point," Elanor agreed. "Women's shoes are much more varied than men's, same as clothes. But one pair of heels can go with almost everything."

I glanced around and saw my friends looking at me expectantly. "Okay," I nervously said. "But nothing too high; I'm afraid I'll break my ankle."

"You won't. You'll get used to them in no time," Nora said.

"You gals have fun," Vicky said. "We're going to check that shop over there." She turned around and pointed, seemingly at random.

Anna looked at her in surprise. "What? No, we're not."

"Yes, we are," Elanor said, and they grabbed Anna's arm. "Come on."

"They're not being subtle, are they?" I noted with a giggle as Vicky and Elanor dragged Anna away.

"No," Nora replied. "I asked them to leave for a while, actually."

"You did?" I queried. "Why?"

"With everything that's happened lately, we haven't had time to be alone," she said. "I've been missing this. Being able to be with you on our own."

I felt myself blushing a bit. "You're right, I'm sorry, I—"

Nora quickly shook her head. "You don't need to apologize. You've been through a lot. I . . ." She sighed. "I just want you to know I'm here for you. Feel free to lean on me for anything you need."

"Thank you, Nora." I grabbed her hand.

We looked at each other for a moment, then my girlfriend squeezed my hand. "So. Let's get you a new pair of shoes."

Soon I was sitting on a stool, barefoot, staring down at a pair of heels on the floor in front of me.

"Try these on. Take your time, I'll be back soon," the assistant said, and went off to assist someone else: the shoe store wasn't that busy, but she was apparently the only one on duty.

I looked down at the shoes and gulped. They had a modest heel, barely an inch, yet they looked like skyscrapers to me. Would I even be able to balance in them?

"Um . . . little help?" I asked, looking pleadingly up at Nora.

"Here, let me," she said, kneeling. "Your first pair of heels is an important milestone, something every girl goes through, and I want you to enjoy the experience." She took one of the shoes and gently slipped it onto my foot. "How does it feel? Does it fit right?"

"It does." I turned my foot this way and that to get a better look, then I giggled. "I almost feel like a fairy-tale princess right now. Like Cinderella. Only my transformation wasn't quite as fast."

"Even though it wasn't as fast, it was still amazing," Nora replied, slipping the remaining shoe onto my other foot, then standing up. I took her hand and gingerly rose to my feet, finding my balance. "I mean, you were cute when I met you, but now? You're not cute anymore. You're absolutely beautiful, Lily." She gave me a peck on the lips. "My princess."

I gave her a mock curtsy, almost losing my balance — I had to lean on her hand to avoid falling over. "Why, thank you, Queen Nora."

She blinked. "Queen Nora?"

"Of course," I said, straightening up. "If I'm a young, naïve princess taking her first steps into the world, you're a wise queen, expertly guiding her subjects through the perils of life." I smiled. "And I'm really grateful for everything you've done for me, Nora. I love you."

Nora's face turned deep red and she looked away from me.

"What's the matter?" I asked, puzzled.

"I'm sorry, give me a sec," she said, still not meeting my eyes. She brought a hand to her mouth and sniffled loudly as though she was about to cry.

"Nora? What's wrong?" I was suddenly concerned. "Did I do something wrong?"

She quickly waved her hand. "No, no. You absolutely did nothing wrong, it's just . . ." She sniffled again. "It's just . . . this is the first time you've said you love me."

My mind raced. I thought back to every moment I'd spent with Nora and realized she was probably right. While I did love Nora with all my heart . . . I'd never actually said it out loud.

"Then I'll say it again. And again. Over and over, as many times as it takes," I said, unsteadily stepping up to her and grasping her hands. "I love you, Nora."

She had tears in her eyes, but was smiling widely.

"And I love you, Lily."

She leaned forward and we kissed. It was quite chaste, but I felt a connection with Nora I had never experienced with anyone. At that moment, I couldn't picture my future without her.

God, I really loved her.

We separated just in time, as the shop assistant came back.

"How do they fit?" She motioned to the heels. "Are they comfortable?"

"Very," I nodded. "More than I was expecting, actually. But I'm having a bit of trouble finding my balance."

"That will come with time and practice," the assistant replied. "So, how about it? Want to try on another pair?"

I grabbed Nora's arm to keep my balance and lifted one leg behind me, turning my head to look at the shoe. It was beautiful, the unblemished black leather contrasting with my light skin, and it made my legs look longer and more slender.

"No, I think I'll take these."

"Great," the assistant said with a smile. At the register, Nora insisted on paying.

"They're a gift, Lily," she said. "To celebrate your name change."

"Thank you," I said with a smile.

We left the store, and found our friends waiting for us. "So, how did it go?" Anna asked. "Did you enjoy yourself?"

Nora and I exchanged a glance, blushing slightly. "Yes. Yes, we did," Nora said.

"Okay then," Vicky said, with a knowing grin. "Are you ready to go back to college? It's getting a bit late."

I nodded. "Yes, of course. Let's go home."

20
Close Encounters

K ATIE SWORE LOUDLY as I walked through the door, and I laughed: it was good to be home.

Nearly two months had passed since my name change hearing and I was still sharing a room with Vicky; I would be for the foreseeable future. I'd tried to go back to the room I'd shared with Joe, but it had been a harrowing experience: when I found myself standing in front of the door the memories had come flooding back, and I almost had a panic attack. Thankfully Nora and my friends were there, and their presence managed to calm me down enough to get control of my breathing, but the thought of sleeping there was unbearable. Vicky agreed to let me stay with her, which I would be eternally thankful to her for —though I'd insisted on paying my share of the rent, which I could afford since Elanor had talked the school's administration into giving me back what I'd spent on the dorm room.

I'd only gone back to my dorm once since then to pick up a few things Anna and Nora had accidentally left behind while packing, and had been extremely nervous the whole time. Sometimes I woke up in a cold sweat, the memory of a nightmare fading in the back of my mind, leaving me trying and failing to fall asleep again. It had happened a lot during the first couple of weeks after the assault, and Vicky had to lie close to me and reassure me that I was safe. Although the dreams were now less frequent, I still hated Joe with all my heart for making me feel like this.

"I'm going to get changed, then I'll get dinner started," I said, heading up the stairs. "You gals want anything in particular?"

"Whatever is fine," Mel said, not looking back from the TV.

"Oh, come ON!" Katie shouted as a blue shell crashed into her kart in the *Mario Kart* game they were playing.

"Alright, I'll check the fridge," I said, leaving them to it.

I made my way to the room I shared with Vicky, and knocked.

"Come in!"

"You decent, Vicks?" I called out: I'd been wary of walking in without making sure Vicky had clothes on since the first time I'd seen her wearing nothing but a pair of panties and a bra. She'd been amused at my embarrassment, saying it was no big deal since we were roommates and both girls — which had made me wonder what she'd have said if she'd found out I was not a girl, but a cis man pretending to be a girl.

"Yeah, come in!" she replied through the door.

I walked in. "Hi," I said.

Vicky was wearing a simple blue dress, which flowed around her while still hugging her chest and hips. I idly wondered how she managed to hide that kind of body when she had to go home for the holidays: hoodies, maybe. But still, to be unable to see Vicky for who she was . . . Cis people really can be oblivious.

"Hi. How was your day?" she asked.

"Same old, same old. Professor Markley is still pestering me for a final title for my paper."

"Just make one up, you can always change it later," Vicky replied. "Oh, by the way, you've got mail. Looks official." She pointed to my bed where a large envelope was sitting on the pillow.

It was addressed to 'Miss Lily O'Connor,' and emblazoned with the seal of the State of New York.

Hold on, was that . . . ?

I gingerly opened the envelope, being careful not to damage what was inside, and pulled out . . . two sheets of paper, stapled together. That was it? I'd expected something more.

Like I suspected, it was a court order: my name change.

I was officially Lily O'Connor.

I exhaled sharply; Vicky looked up from her cell to me. "Everything okay?"

I handed her the court order, and her eyes widened as she looked it over. "Lily, this is great! I'm so happy for you!" She wrapped me in a hug. "We have to celebrate!"

I smiled unsteadily. I wasn't entirely sure how to feel about having changed my legal name, especially since I would have to change it back soon, but Vicky didn't seem to notice my unease. "Let me text the others," I said.

I snapped a picture and sent it to our group chat, writing: *So guess what I just got in the mail . . .*

It took only a few seconds for the replies to start flooding in.

What! Anna wrote. *What what what! Amazing!*

Yeah!! It's great! Elanor added.

Nora sent a smiley face with starry eyes.

Vicky said we should celebrate, I wrote. *Are y'all free tomorrow night? We can go for coffee in the afternoon, and then there's a concert on campus.*

Yeah, of course, Vicky replied in the group chat. *Let's partyyyyyyy!*

Elanor and I are free, Anna wrote.

Me too, Nora added.

Great! I'll ask Mel and Katie too, I replied. *See you tomorrow!*

When I turned off my phone, Vicky gave me another hug.

"Oh, I'm so happy for you, girl," she said. "And a bit jealous. I can't change my name officially yet, because of my parents. So I'll just be content with vicarious joy."

I briefly thought how my parents would take me changing my name: not that I would ever find out — I fully intended to change it back before they could even notice.

I tightened my embrace. "Don't worry," I whispered. "Even if it's not your legal name, you'll always be Victoria to me."

Vicky reciprocated the hug, squeezing tight. "Thank you, Lily."

≣

". . . and I told him, well, even a stopped clock tells the correct time twice a day!" Anna concluded, and our group burst into laughter. "You should've seen the look on his face!"

We were having a coffee stop before the concert. It was just our usual group: Mel and Katie already had plans.

"Speaking of time, it'll be starting soon," Nora said. "Are you ready to go?"

"Yeah, almost," I said, standing up. "I just have to visit the ladies' first." I drained my coffee and gave her a peck on the cheek. "Wait for me."

She beamed a dazzling smile my way. "You know I will."

The bathroom was surprisingly busy: a few other girls were lining up for the three stalls, and as I joined the queue a couple more stepped up behind me. As I sat in the stall, I idly mused about how I no longer stood to pee — the last time I did must've been at least three months earlier — and relieved myself before pulling up my underwear, being careful to tuck, and leaving the cubicle.

It was weird, though. Only a few months earlier, I'd been nervous at the thought of going into the girls' bathroom, yet it now came so naturally to me I hardly thought about it.

As I washed my hands, another girl started using the sink next to me. I glanced at her in the mirror and almost did a double take.

It was Jillian. Jillian, Nora's ex-girlfriend. Jillian, the transphobe. Jillian, who absolutely hated my guts.

I hadn't seen her since January, at the clothing store. What were the chances we would meet again like this?

Jillian noticed I was staring at her and her eyes narrowed for a moment, then lit up in recognition.

"Oh, it's you," she said, surprisingly casually. "Lily, right? How are you doing?"

She was being . . . friendly, actually? How come?

"Fine," I said, not trusting my two-months-of-voice-training voice with anything further: there were a handful of other girls in the room, after all. How do you do, fellow cis? Nothing to see here. Don't look at me, please.

"Good," Jillian nodded. "You know, I almost didn't recognize you. You've really changed since last time. You can really see you're making an effort."

". . . Thanks."

"It's almost a shame that effort doesn't matter, though," she continued, still in her casual, almost-bored tone. "After all, you and I both know you're not a real woman."

Her words shouldn't have bothered me. At all.

I *wasn't* a real woman. I was just a man pretending to be a woman. I was just a fraud.

But after her voice had died down, I felt as though I'd been stabbed. My vision narrowed, my stomach dropped below my feet, and my head felt light, ears buzzing. My breathing became labored.

What's worse, as Jillian spoke several pairs of eyes swiveled around and landed on me. Looking at me. Staring at me. Piercing me. Studying me.

Judging me.

Suddenly, I had to be somewhere else.

Anywhere but there.

Without me telling them to, my legs started moving. I crashed through the door, and made a beeline for the café's front doors.

As I ran, I was faintly aware of some noises. My friends' voices.

"Lily? What's wrong?" Nora said.

Then, a roar, coming from Vicky: "You! What the *fuck* did you do to her?!"

"Vicky, no! Stop!" Anna exclaimed.

"Lily!" Nora said again, but I barely heard her. I barreled through the double doors leading outside, narrowly dodging someone coming from the other side. I stumbled, fell, bruised and scraped myself on the asphalt. Lost a shoe. Got up, tried to run — shook off my other shoe and started running again.

I crossed the road — barely hearing, as if from a great distance, the screeching of tires and honking of horns — and I was on the grass, still running until I fell again. Without any strength to lift myself back up, I cried my heart out for what felt like an eternity.

"—ly!"

A hand touched my shoulder; I shrugged it off.

"Lily!"

A pair of hands now, grabbing both sides of me. Holding me still, no matter how much I twisted and thrashed.

"Lily! *Look at me.*"

I opened my eyes and looked deep into Nora's.

"I—"

"Tell me five things you can see."

I hiccoughed. "W-what?"

"Tell me five things you can see, Lily," she repeated firmly.

I automatically looked around, searching for things to name. "Sky. Grass. Tree. Street. Cars."

Nora nodded. "Tell me four things you can hear."

I strained my ears. "Birds. Cars. Bicycles. People."

"Good," she said. "Tell me three things you can touch."

"Ground," I said, suddenly aware of the weight of the world below me. "Leg. Arm," I continued, touching my leg and arm.

"Now tell me two things you can smell," Nora continued.

I took a deep breath in through my nose. "Grass." Then I wrinkled my nose in disgust. "Car's exhaust."

"And now tell me one thing you can taste."

I licked my lips. "Coffee," I said.

"Very good," Nora said, looking deep into my eyes. She held my stare for a few moments, then exhaled. "Welcome back, Lily. You went away for a bit there."

I looked down at myself: I was a mess. My shoes were missing — I hadn't noticed losing them — and my hands, knees, and elbows were badly scraped; my tights were destroyed; and even though I didn't have a mirror handy, I was sure I looked terrible.

"Sorry," I said. "I just—"

"Shh." Nora put a finger to my lips. "It's okay, you don't need to apologize. I've only seen you like this once before, so clearly something happened."

I knew what she was referring to. When she'd seen me *like this* before.

"... Yeah, you could say so."

Nora gripped my hand firmly but gently. "Wanna tell me?"

I gulped, and nodded. "When I went to the restroom . . . Jillian was there."

"Oh."

"Yeah. She didn't recognize me at first, but when she did, she . . ." I paused, and took a deep breath. "She outed me. To everyone who was in there."

Nora's eyes narrowed. "Did she now?" she asked, a dangerous edge in her voice.

"'You're not a real woman,' she said. And then . . . then everyone just turned around, and looked at me, and they had *that look* in their eyes, and—"

"Hey," Nora said, putting a hand on my arm. "Stop, Lily. Don't go panicking on me again. You're safe now. You're safe. I'm here with you, and I won't let anyone hurt you. Jillian can't do anything to you now." She paused. "Though I may have to kick her ass when I see her again. No one misgenders my girlfriend on my watch."

There. A pang of guilt. It had been a while since I'd felt one of those, I'd almost forgotten what it was like.

"Please don't," I said. "I don't want you to get into trouble, Nora. Let's just leave her alone."

Nora just looked at me, and I could tell she was debating with herself whether to do as I was asking, or to go find Jillian and lay her flat.

"Please?" I asked again. "I really just want to forget about all this."

She held my gaze for a few moments, then sighed. "Alright. Your call, Lily."

"Thank you," I said. "Shall we go back? They're probably worried about us."

Nora got up from the grass, offered me her hand, and pulled me up too. Walking slowly, picking up my discarded heels along the way, we made our way back to the café.

Anna was waiting outside when we arrived. "There you are," she said, walking forward to meet us. "We have a problem."

"A problem?" I queried.

"Yeah," she nodded. "When you ran out of the bathroom we spotted Jillian coming out of there, too. And . . . And Vicky just ran toward her and punched her in the face."

"Good," Nora said.

"No, not good. Absolutely not good, Nora," Anna snapped. "Someone, I don't know who, saw the whole scene and called the cops on us. Campus police showed up a few minutes ago, they're talking with Jillian and Vicky right now. Elanor is inside, they're supporting Vicky, they thought they could help since they're in pre-law."

I felt my stomach churn; I felt terrible. Tears started welling in my eyes again.

"Let's go in," I said. "I wanna talk to them. Vicky and Jillian."

Without waiting for an answer, I strode back into the café. The place had been cleared out — all the customers were in one corner, and Vicky and Jillian were sitting in two chairs several meters apart from each other, being talked to by two cops. Well, glorified rent-a-cops. Security guards: that's what campus police are. Jillian was holding an ice pack to her cheek, and despite the situation I found myself smiling mildly. Fucking serves you right.

When she saw me walk in, Vicky started to get up, but Elanor pushed her gently back down into her chair. I approached them, but Elanor gestured for me to stay back; I could still hear what the cop was saying.

"So you realize what you did was a bad thing, right? Do you, Miss McPearson?" he asked sternly.

"... Yes," Vicky answered. "Yes, I do."

"Good," the cop nodded. "Alright. I'm going to leave you with a fine for now, but you still need to answer for your actions."

"How, exactly?" Elanor asked.

"You'll be contacted by the school's administrative office, and they'll set up a disciplinary hearing," the cop said. "At the meeting they'll look at all the evidence and decide what, if any, measures to take. You got all that?"

Vicky nodded hesitantly. "Yes, I understand."

"Then we're done here," he said, turned around, and walked away.

Apparently Jillian was done too, because she stood up from her chair and walked toward Vicky. "So, a disciplinary hearing," she said, looking her directly in the eyes.

Vicky just nodded in response.

"Good. I'll be there to testify about what you've done," Jillian continued. "And I'll see to it that you're expelled. This is a promise."

Without waiting for a reply, she strode dramatically out of the café, still holding the ice pack to her cheek.

"She can't do that, can she?" Anna asked from behind me. "She can't get Vicky expelled."

I thought back to what had happened with Joe. Even though he'd left Bradford McKinley before the hearing could take place, so didn't defend himself, the punishment he'd suffered for attacking me had been expulsion.

"I think she could, actually," I whispered.

Vicky whimpered. She was staring at the floor; her shoulders started shaking and she began to sob.

"I ..." She sobbed again. "I *can't*. I can't get expelled."

Anna crouched next to Vicky's chair and put a hand on her shoulder. "Come on now, Vicks. It won't—"

"I can't!" Vicky looked up from the floor and I saw utter despair painted on her face. "I just can't! I . . ."

She took a deep breath, hiccuped. Tears were streaming down her cheeks. "My parents don't know about me. They *can't* know about me. When I'm here at college, it's the only time I can be me. When I go back home for the holidays I have to be *him*. And . . . and it's crushing." Another sob escaped her. "I can only stand it because I know I'll be able to be me again when I come back here. If I get expelled, I . . . I'll have to be him for good. With no way out."

She shook her head, and locked eyes with me. "I can't be him. I refuse. If I have to be him, I . . . I'd rather die."

My eyes widened in horror. Did she just say . . . ?

"No," Elanor said. "Absolutely not. Stop with that talk right now, Vicks. We won't stand for it."

"Yeah," Nora said. "You haven't been expelled."

"Yet," Vicky replied, smiling bitterly.

"You haven't been expelled," Nora repeated, more firmly. "There's still the hearing. We'll think of something."

"Yeah, we will," Anna agreed, and gave Vicky's shoulder a reassuring squeeze.

Meanwhile, I looked at Vicky. My friend. One of my best friends. The person I was closest to besides Nora.

She was in trouble.

And it was all my fault.

21

Chosen Family

"THE DISCIPLINARY HEARING of Miss Victoria McPearson is now in session," Dean Anderson said, and banged his gavel. "I think all parties are present." He picked up a sheet of paper and read aloud, "Miss McPearson will be assisted by . . . Mx? Mx. Elanor Yates. Correct?"

"Yes, sir," Elanor answered.

"Okay. And the injured party, Miss Jillian Durand, will be assisted by Miss Heather Graham."

Elanor's counterpart — a short, blonde woman — raised her hand, and said, "Correct."

"Good. I think we can start by presenting the facts of the case."

I sat beside Vicky, holding her hand reassuringly, but I kept flashing back to the previous hearing I'd been involved with.

This hearing would likely be much longer: Elanor had worked tirelessly, barely sleeping over the previous few nights, to come up with a workable defense strategy, and they seemed confident enough. They'd promised Vicky to fight tooth and nail for her, and I believed them.

Jillian stood up and, followed by Heather, walked to the chair to the left of Dean Anderson; I glared daggers at her. I noticed she'd done her makeup carefully, to emphasize the bruise on her cheek, which was standing out proudly in all its blueness. It looked really painful, but I couldn't find it in me to feel even a shred of sympathy for her.

"Miss Durand, if you please," Heather said once Jillian had sat down. "Describe what took place three days ago, on Tuesday evening."

"I'd just finished classes for the day, and I stopped by Giovanni's to get a cup of coffee before returning to my dorm," Jillian said. "While there, I went to the restroom. As I was coming out of the bathroom, someone ran toward me and punched me."

"I have here a doctor's report." Heather pulled a sheet of paper from a folder. "No lasting damage, luckily, but the bruise will take a few weeks to fade completely." Dean Anderson took the report, and Heather continued. "And, Miss Durand, could you recognize the person who attacked you? Are they in this room right now?"

"They are," Jillian said, pointing at Vicky who shrunk into her chair. "They're sitting right there."

You absolute bitch. Vicks uses she and her pronouns and you fucking know *that,* I thought. Jillian was lucky looks can't kill, otherwise she'd have dropped dead on the spot.

"Please let the record show that Miss Durand has pointed to Miss McPearson," Heather said. "Do you have any idea why Miss McPearson would attack you?"

"None whatsoever," Jillian replied.

"No further questions."

Dean Anderson turned his eyes to our table. "Mx. Yates?"

Elanor took a deep breath and stood up. They'd worn a suit that day and they looked amazing in it, reminding me of legal dramas I'd seen on TV.

"We do not dispute Miss Durand's version of the events, Dean Anderson," Elanor said carefully, keeping their voice level. "What she described is exactly what happened. However, we intend to show that Miss McPearson's actions had some . . . mitigating circumstances to them."

"Do you have any questions for Miss Durand?" Dean Anderson asked after taking a moment to digest their words.

"Yes, actually," Elanor replied. "Just one. Miss Durand, had you ever met Miss McPearson before Tuesday?"

"Yes, twice," Jillian said. "Once back in November, and once in January."

"Okay," Elanor said. "No further questions."

"Miss Graham, do you have any other witnesses to call?" Dean Anderson said.

"No, sir," Heather replied.

"Alright. Then, Mx. Yates?"

"I would like to call Miss McPearson herself to testify," Elanor said, and Vicky made her way to the chair Jillian had just vacated.

"Miss McPearson, why did you attack Miss Durand?" Elanor asked directly; they'd coached both me and Vicky on the questions they would ask, and together we'd decided that straightforwardness was the best option. To show that we — that Vicky — had nothing to hide.

"I attacked her because . . . Because I thought she had attacked Lily."

"By Lily you mean Miss Lily O'Connor, who is sitting there," Elanor said, turning to point at me.

"Yes, that's right," Vicky answered.

"And why would you think that?"

"Lily came out of the bathroom just before Jillian. I mean, Miss Durand," Vicky said. "And she looked . . . Well, she looked terrible. Something had clearly happened to her. Something ugly. I'd only seen her look like that once before."

"When, exactly?" Elanor said.

Vicky locked her gaze with me before answering, and I could see an apology in her eyes. "When she was assaulted, two months ago."

The memory of Joe punching me, the feeling of being in danger with no way out, flashed through my mind. Thankfully, it was only a brief moment: I'd known the mention of my assault was coming, so I'd had time to mentally prepare myself and I was able to keep my fight-or-flight response under control. I still gripped the armrests of my chair tight enough to leave nail marks in the hard plastic.

"So, just to clarify," Elanor said. "You saw Miss O'Connor come out of the bathroom looking 'terrible,' and realized she'd probably been assaulted." Vicky nodded. "So when you saw the person you thought was responsible, you sprang into action to protect your friend."

"That's right," Vicky said.

"No more questions."

"I have a question," Heather said, standing up from behind her table. "Why would you think Miss Durand was the one who assaulted Miss O'Connor?"

"Because Miss Durand has a track record of being . . ." Vicky said; then she hesitated.

"Of being what?" Heather prodded her.

"Transphobic."

From my left, I heard Jillian scoff; I turned to glare at her again, even harder.

"First of all, you have no proof of that," Heather said. "And secondly, no assault even happened."

"But Miss McPearson thought it did," Elanor said. "Because of how Lily reacted."

"Miss Durand has nothing to do with what happened to Miss O'Connor. With whatever triggered her."

Elanor raised an eyebrow. "'Triggered' her?"

"Yes, triggered her enough to make her run away. Miss Durand did nothing to Miss O'Connor," Heather replied.

"Didn't she?" Elanor said, a smirk forming on their lips.

Heather hesitated. "Wait, what do you mean?"

"Did you have any other questions for Miss McPearson?" Elanor asked; when Heather answered in the negative, they continued, "Then, with Dean Anderson's permission, I would like to call Miss O'Connor to testify."

I swapped places with Vicky, stopping briefly as we walked past each other to share a reassuring smile.

"Dean Anderson, sir, I object," Heather said. "Miss O'Connor has nothing to do with what happened on Tuesday. Why are we listening to her?"

"Because she was involved," Elanor said, sounding like a kindergarten teacher patiently explaining a simple fact to a young child. "Seeing her flee the bathroom was what caused Miss McPearson to attack Miss Durand. And also, Miss O'Connor is privy to some information I believe Dean Anderson should be aware of."

Dean Anderson pursed his lips in thought, considering what Elanor had said for a moment. "You may ask whatever questions you have for Miss O'Connor, Mx. Yates," he then said.

"Thank you, sir." Elanor turned to me and I sat down, smoothing my skirt under me. I'd carefully chosen my clothes for the day: a skirt-and-blouse ensemble, with a light jacket, tights, and the low heels Nora had bought me. I'd done my best to look like a prim and proper girl, completely innocent and innocuous.

Elanor began our well-rehearsed script. "Miss O'Connor, did you know Miss Durand before meeting her in the bathroom last Tuesday?"

"How is this relevant?" Heather asked, but the dean silenced her with a glance.

"I did," I replied. "I met her for the first time last November."

"Interesting," Elanor said. "Would this be the same occasion at which Miss Durand and Miss McPearson first met each other?"

"I believe it was, yes. It was at my first GSA meeting."

"Describe what happened at that meeting, please."

"How is this relevant?" Heather asked again. "What's the point you're trying to make here?"

"I'm asking myself the same question," the dean said. "If you have a point, Mx. Yates, you better get to it quickly."

"Yes, sir," Elanor said. "I'll come right out and ask you directly, then: Jillian was transphobic at that meeting, wasn't she?"

"She was," I replied. At the same time, Jillian, who had until then sat in silence, stood up and shouted, "I was not!"

"Jillian," Heather said, placing a placating hand on her arm, which Jillian ignored.

"She was," I repeated. "I forget her exact words, but she said that being trans isn't a real thing, that trans people are just pretending, and that they can go back to being their original gender any time." I paused. "She was asked to leave the meeting because of that. Because of her transphobia."

"You have no proof of that!" Jillian shouted again, as Heather tried in vain to get her to sit down and shut up.

Elanor pulled out a sheet of paper from a folder with a flourish. "I have here a list of nearly a dozen people who were present at that meeting," they said, handing it to Dean Anderson. "And I also have signed affidavits, in which they swear that what Miss O'Connor described is exactly what happened. I'm sure if you call them to testify, they will confirm it directly."

Finding enough people to testify against Jillian for what she'd done in November had been easy enough: Elanor had asked Lena, Allie, and Patrick for their help, and they'd called up the members of the GSA.

"Then, when I, Vicky, and some other friends met Jillian again in January, by complete chance, she was transphobic to me again," I continued. "She said my friends were just 'humoring' me, as if I wasn't really a woman."

"You're—" Jillian began.

"Shut up." Heather cut her off.

"So Miss McPearson saw Miss O'Connor leave the bathroom in a panic, looking as if she'd been assaulted," Elanor said, without missing a step. "And then right on her heels comes another person, someone she knows for a fact is transphobic." They paused for a brief moment, then continued. "I would think that, in Miss McPearson's shoes, it would be quite reasonable to assume Miss Durand had attacked Miss O'Connor somehow." They turned to Dean Anderson. "Wouldn't you agree, sir?"

"But I did nothing to him!" Jillian said, pointing at me. "I mean her," she corrected herself after a second.

"Shut *up!*" Heather hissed.

"You did," I said. "You outed me to everyone in the bathroom. To every single person who was in there. 'You're not a real woman,' you said. And then everyone in the room turned to look at me. I felt their eyes on me." I paused for effect. "I felt *in danger*. That's what *triggered* me, Miss Graham," I spat out, staring directly at Heather, who at least had the decency to look away. "That's why I had a panic attack and ran away."

"Witness list. Affidavits," Elanor held several sheets of paper toward Dean Anderson, who took them without looking at them: he was looking at me instead.

That was what had kept them busy for the better part of the previous few days. I had no idea how, but Elanor had managed to track down four people who were in that bathroom at the time Jillian had outed me. Even though they had zero clues to start from, even though at first it had seemed hopeless, somehow they'd managed it. They'd conjured up a small miracle.

"Even if I said that, and I'm not saying I did—" Jillian said.

"You did," I replied.

"—they were still not justified in attacking me!" she exclaimed, pointing at Vicky. This time Vicky didn't shrink away, but instead glared at her. "Words aren't violence. You were never in any physical danger," Jillian continued, staring at me intensely.

Heather didn't say anything, she just closed her eyes and sighed deeply.

"Yeah, you're right, she wasn't," Elanor said as they grabbed another folder, a tinge of sarcasm in their voice. "After all, it's not as if people are assaulted, sometimes even killed, just for being trans. It's not as if someone in this very room has been assaulted for being trans. It's not as if we have proof of that in news articles like this one." They pulled out a sheaf of paper, stapled together, and dropped it on the table. "Or this one. Or this one. Or this one. Or this one," they continued, pulling out more and more articles. "Or even dozens of scientific papers that say the exact same thing." They turned and stared directly at Jillian. "You're a lesbian, Miss Durand, so you should know that outing queer people puts them in danger. Careless or malicious words put people in direct danger. In cases like this one, words are literally violence."

"So what, are you saying they shouldn't be punished for what they did?" Jillian said. "They fucking *assaulted* me! If the roles were reversed, you'd be shouting for their expulsion! You're only doing this because they're your friend!"

I laughed. "That's where you're wrong, Jillian," I replied. "Vicky is not my friend."

Jillian gave a start of surprise. "What?"

Elanor eyed me warily — what I'd just said was off-script — but I looked back at them for a moment, my eyes filled with determination.

"I said that Vicky isn't my friend," I repeated. I looked back at Vicky once again: what I was about to say was for her benefit, not Jillian's. "You have no idea what Vicks did for me. From the first time I met her she accepted me completely, without reservations. She never once questioned my identity: I said I was a girl, and that was good enough for her. Ever since then, she's been by my side. She's helped me with anything I needed, supported me in everything I did. She gave me resources I wouldn't other-wise have been able to access, at great risk to herself, and without asking for anything in return. When I was . . ." I suddenly felt my throat seize up, the memory coming back to me, but this was important, so I forged on. "When I was assaulted and couldn't stay in my dorm room, she offered me a place to stay, just like that, without blinking. Since then I've woken up many times in the middle of the night in a panic, and each time she's woken up too, and stayed by my side until I fell asleep again. She's done nothing but accept and support me, fully and completely. I wouldn't be half the woman I am now if it weren't for her. So no, Vicky isn't my friend." I paused for a moment, then concluded, "Vicky is my sister."

My voice almost broke on the last word: I felt wetness on my cheeks, and I was surprised to notice I was crying. I hadn't realized how emotional I'd been getting as I described everything Vicky had done for me. Vicky was openly weeping, but at the same time she was smiling: I returned her smile, took a deep breath, and turned toward Dean Anderson.

"Dean Anderson. Sir. Look. I know she made a mistake. But you need to understand that's all it was: a mistake. In the end, Vicky is a good person," I said. "And she doesn't deserve to be expelled."

"She does, actually," Heather said. "It's written down in plain words in the Bradford McKinley rules of conduct. No matter the circumstances, Miss McPearson attacked Miss Durand without any provocation. If that doesn't merit expulsion . . ."

I saw the dean moving his gaze slowly between everyone, unsure of what to do.

"Dean Anderson, sir," Elanor spoke up. "May I have a word? In private."

The dean looked at them for a moment, then beckoned them over. "You too, Miss Graham," he said. The three began speaking in hushed tones; after a minute or so the dean's eyes turned hard and he glared at Elanor, who had a cheeky smirk painted on their face, then they resumed talking. After a few more minutes, I saw Heather sigh deeply, shake her head, walk over to Jillian, and pull her away to the other side of the room.

I watched the two as they talked, Jillian growing more and more agitated, and Heather making several placating gestures. At one point, Jillian shouted, "I won't stand for it!" and Heather answered, just as loudly, "This is the best you're going to get, you idiot!"

Eventually, her face looking like she'd just sucked on an especially sour lemon, Jillian hung her head and nodded. Heather looked across the room to Dean Anderson and gave him a thumbs-up, but she wasn't smiling.

The hearing was quickly brought back to order. Since no one had any more questions for me, I was dismissed and I sat back down next to Vicky — after receiving a tight, teary hug from her.

"Alright," Dean Anderson said. "I have considered what happened, and I have reached a decision based on the totality of the evidence. While it's true that Miss McPearson's actions would normally merit expulsion, I have to recognize that there are significant mitigating circumstances around the event." He looked directly at Vicky. "Four months' probation, starting from the beginning of the next academic year. If you break another rule before this time is up, no matter how minor, you'll be expelled right away. If you don't, we'll forget about all this. Do you understand, Miss McPearson?"

Vicky nodded hesitantly. "Yes."

"Good. I don't think there are any objections . . . ?"

"No, Dean Anderson," Heather replied.

"Then we're done here. You're all dismissed," the dean said, and banged his gavel.

I smiled at Vicky and gave her hand a reassuring squeeze, as Jillian walked up to us. "You realize this changes nothing, right?" she said. "Neither of you—"

"Oh, *fuck off*," I snapped. "You know how much I care about your opinion, you miserable little shit? Somewhere between 'not at all' and 'minus infinity.' So just get lost, will ya?"

Jillian clearly hadn't expected me to talk back to her. "W-what?" she sputtered.

"You heard me. Go and fuck yourself. And not in the fun way." Without waiting for a reply, I grabbed Vicky and Elanor by the arm and pulled them toward Anna and Nora.

≡

"And then what did you say?" Anna asked.

Elanor took a swig of their beer and looked around at us. "Okay, okay. Then I said . . ." They slipped into a voice deeper than I'd ever heard them use. "I seem to remember you not wanting any negative publicity for the college. Well, I happen to have a friend who's a journalist, what do you think of this title? 'Trans woman expelled from Bradford McKinley for defending a friend from transphobia'. Wouldn't want that to get out, right?" They laughed, took another drink, and continued, "You should've seen his face!"

"Oh, I *did* see his face," I said with a grin, taking a drink. "I was sitting in a good spot, and I gotta tell you it was a spectacle."

"No, hold on a second," Nora said, gesturing with her bottle. She lowered her voice, and continued, "This is basically blackmail, isn't it? Are we sure this is right?"

She'd tried to keep a straight face, but in the end she couldn't — she burst out laughing on the last word, and we all joined her.

"No, of course it's not blackmail," Elanor replied, chuckling. "I didn't say anything at all. There's nothing on the record."

"Oh my God, I love you," Anna said, grabbing Elanor's face between her hands and kissing them deeply.

"Boy, I was having some doubts about going on to law school after graduating," Elanor said when they came up for air. "But you know what? This was way too fun and exciting. I'm definitely doing it."

"And I'll call you should I need a good lawyer . . . again," Vicky said, nudging Elanor's shoulder. "Thank you, Elanor. And thank you, Lily." She turned to me. "What you said in there was just . . . I never realized how much I needed to hear someone say something like that about me. Thank you."

"You're welcome," I replied. "I just hope I wasn't too out of line."

Vicky shook her head. "Not at all. I feel the same way. And you know you can always count on me, Sis. For anything."

I hugged her tight. "I'll go get some more beers," she said, and walked to the kitchen.

"Not too much, you're not supposed to be breaking any rules, remember!" Anna called after her.

"Quiet, you!" Vicky shouted back with a laugh.

I smiled at the exchange. God, I loved my friends. I was going to miss them very much when I eventually went back to being a man.

Suddenly, I felt a hand on my shoulder. I turned around and found myself looking into Nora's eyes, which were slightly clouded by alcohol. "Lily, listen, I've been meaning to ask something. For a while now."

I lifted a questioning eyebrow. "Yeah?"

Nora gulped. "I . . . My roommates aren't home tonight. Do you want to come over?"

Another eyebrow joined the first one: there was no mistaking what Nora's invitation meant.

Logically I knew I shouldn't.

But at that moment, maybe because of the booze I had in me, or maybe because of the euphoria of having managed to prevent Vicky from being expelled, logic gave way to instinct.

"Yes. Let's go," I said, standing up from the couch. I grabbed Nora's hand and we moved to the door. "Folks, Nora and I are going to . . . We're . . . Um."

Anna gave us a knowing grin. "Oh, just go, you two."

"Yeah, make yourself scarce," Elanor added.

"Have fun!" Vicky shouted from the kitchen.

"Yeah. See ya," I said.

I dragged Nora outside and closed the door behind us. "Well, Queen Nora? Shall we go?"

Nora grinned. "Of course, my princess. Follow me."

22

Eggshells

NEITHER NORA NOR I spoke for a long time. I could barely hear us breathing.

I wiped the tears from my eyes, likely smudging my makeup in the process, but I didn't care. Although the curtains were drawn, some light still filtered through. A glance at Nora's bedside clock told me it was a few minutes past five in the morning: nearly dawn. I'd talked for so long, without stopping, that the night was almost over.

As was my friendship with Anna, Elanor, and Vicky. As was my relationship with Nora. Considering everything I'd done, there was absolutely no way they'd want anything to do with me after today. They'd drop me like a hot coal. I'd be shunned and alone.

But that was exactly what I deserved.

All I had to do was wait for Nora to speak up. To say the words that would condemn me. To utter my sentence.

It was several long minutes before she made a sound, and when she did it was a deep intake of breath, and then a long, drawn-out sigh.

"Oh, you *complete dumbass.*"

. . . What?

There were lots of things I'd expected Nora to call me, but 'complete dumbass' was not among them.

"What?" I asked, somehow managing to find my voice.

"I can't believe you've been through so much and never thought to open up to me. Or anyone else, for that matter," Nora said. "You've been suffering alone for so long, and I never even noticed. I'm so sorry, Lily."

I stared at Nora. Why was *she* sorry? Why wasn't she screaming at me? Why wasn't she cussing me out? I was a liar. A deceiver. A terrible person. I didn't deserve to be treated well by anyone. I didn't deserve to be loved, not even by my girlfriend.

Was she even my girlfriend now? She was sure to break up with me after all this. Even if she somehow — how??? — managed to find it in her heart to forgive me for all the lies I'd told her, in the end she was a lesbian and I wasn't a girl.

"Nora, I—" I began.

"Lily," she cut me off. "This changes nothing. You . . . you've made a mistake." Her voice was doubtful, as if she didn't really believe the words that had just come out of her mouth. As if she didn't really believe the fact that everything I'd done had been a mistake. "But in the end, you're a good person. This doesn't change how I feel about you. And I doubt it will change how anyone else feels about you. Anyone whose opinion is worth listening to, anyway."

My mouth fell open. What? How? Why? Nora didn't . . .

"No!" I exclaimed. "Nora, no. Please. I . . ." I drew in a breath. "I've done so much. Don't lie to me. You hate me!"

"No, I don't," she replied calmly.

"Yes, you do! I deserve it! Hate me! I need you to hate me!"

Nora inclined her head and looked at me, her eyes meeting mine. I was startled to realize she was sad for me. "Why?" she said.

". . . Because! Because I've been lying to you! Because I've been deceiving you! This . . ." I gestured down at myself. "This isn't really me! I'm not the person you think I am!"

"You lied to me . . . how?" she asked. Her tone of voice was maddening: even, calm, as though she was genuinely curious. As though she wasn't judging me at all.

But she must have been.

"Well, for starters, I'm not a girl," I said.

Nora snorted, turned her head to the side, and covered her mouth with her hand — but I could see she was grinning widely in amusement. "Seriously, Lily? Have you taken a look in the mirror lately? I know you shouldn't judge a book by its cover, but when I look at you — not just at how you dress, but at how you move, at how you behave, at who you *are* — the word that comes to mind isn't 'man.'"

I flinched as if I'd been slapped.

Man.

Yes.

That's what I was.

I was a man.

So why did that word feel so bad?

"But . . ." I began. I gritted my teeth, squeezed my eyes shut. Powered through, despite feeling physically sick. "But I must be. I must be a man. Because I'm not a girl."

I opened my eyes again and looked at Nora, who clicked her tongue. "You know non-binary people exist, Lily," she said.

I scowled. "You know what I mean."

She conceded the point by inclining her head. "Okay. Then, leaving the question of your gender aside—"

"That's quite an important question!" I protested.

"Leaving the question of your gender aside," she repeated forcefully, "what else have you been lying to me about?"

"I . . ." I began, and then stopped.

I was coming up blank.

I fumbled in my thoughts, searching for an answer. Because that was what was important. I'd been lying. Constantly. Since the beginning. Since I decided to come out to Anna — no, to *pretend* to come out to Anna, because I hadn't really come out to her, had I?

Had I?

But if I'd been lying to everyone, if I'd been lying about everything, why was it so hard to think of a single lie I'd told? There were thousands of them, surely. Why couldn't I come up with one? One would suffice. But I couldn't.

"I . . ." I repeated. I looked pleadingly at Nora. "Don't do this to me," I whispered.

"I mean, were you lying when you told me you liked the dress I picked out for you? Were you pretending on Valentine's Day, when you said you enjoyed the time we spent together?" she asked, then her eyes turned hard. "Were you lying when you told me you loved me?"

"No!" I quickly answered. "God, no! Nora! No! Please, if you don't believe me about anything else, believe me on this. I've never lied to you about that. Not ever!"

"But you just told me you've been lying to me. 'About everything,' you said. So." She paused. "Have you been lying to me?"

"Never about my love for you. Never," I replied. "*Never*, Nora. I could never lie about that."

"What else, then?" she insisted. "You said you've been lying, so what have you been lying about? I mean, we've established that you think you're not a girl—"

"That's exactly it! Don't you get it, Nora?" I shouted. "That's what I've been lying to you about! To you and everyone else!" I punched the mattress in frustration. "God, it's like you're not listening to me. I'm not a girl! My name isn't even Lily, it's—"

"No," Nora said sharply, and my head snapped up in surprise. "I don't want to hear it. I don't want to know it. Whatever you were called before, that doesn't matter. You're Lily. That's who you are."

"No," I whispered. "No, I'm not. I'm not. I can't. I . . ." I sobbed. "I can't be Lily."

Nora bit her lip and looked at me for a long moment. "Do you want to be?" she asked quietly.

Do I want to be?

"I—" I began, and stopped. My mind started racing; my breathing got faster. I twitched, my head physically spinning and turning, looking desperately for a way out. I started to get up from the bed—

"Hey, no," Nora said, grabbing my arm to prevent me from leaving. "Lily—"

"Don't call me that!" I shouted. "I'm . . . I'm not . . ."

I was hyperventilating. My heartbeat pounded heavily in my ears. I desperately tried to pull my arm away, trying to free myself from Nora's grasp, but she was holding tight as if she was gripping a life preserver.

She grabbed my shoulder with her other hand and, with all her strength, turned my body to face her. She looked deep into my eyes; tears started welling up in them again.

"Nora . . ."

"Tell me five things you can see."

My mind responded almost automatically. I blinked, and my eyes darted around: the light from the window was brighter now, bathing the room in a dim penumbra.

"Uh . . ." I said. "Curtain. Clock. Bed." I hesitated. "Me. You."

Nora nodded. "Now tell me four things you can hear."

I listened carefully. "The birds outside. The bed squeaking." I took a deep breath. Slow, deliberate. Focused. "Me. You."

"Now tell me three things you can touch," she said with a kind smile.

"The bed. Me. You."

"And now, two things you can smell."

I breathed in deeply: Nora's scent — her perfume, her sweat, her *everything* — was almost overpowering, overflowing, coming in waves, mixing with mine. The whole room was filled with us.

"You and me."

Nora smiled, leaned in, and kissed me. "And one thing you can taste," she said, once she'd leaned back.

I licked my lips. "You."

Her smile became wider. "Good. Welcome back, my girl."

Girl.

The word did feel right, but to my half-panicking mind it was like a slap in the face.

"Nora . . . Nora, no. No. I . . . I'm not. I'm not a girl. I'm *not* a girl."

Nora looked at me for several long seconds, her stare bewildered and disbelieving. "Okay," she said after a while, letting go of me and raising her hands in mock surrender. "I get it. Alright, no problem. It's entirely fine. You can just . . . stop. You can stop taking hormones, switch up your clothes and presentation, give up on voice training, change your name again, and you can go back to being that guy."

A shock ran through my body. My stomach twisted and I had to hold myself back to avoid retching. I realized that I knew exactly what Vicky felt when she thought about having to go back to being her old self.

"No," I replied sharply. "No, I don't want to be that guy anymore."

"Hm. Understandable," Nora mused. "From what you've told me, from what Anna said, that guy was kind of a jerk. I mean, being friends with Joe? Spending time with him? Going along with what he said? What the hell? Who'd want to be that guy?"

I felt the need to speak up. To defend myself. To defend *him*. But when I tried to think of what to say, I once again came up empty.

"Alright," Nora continued. "But that's no problem at all, really. You don't have to be that guy, you can just be *a* guy. You know, a completely normal, run-of-the mill dude. You just have to—"

"No!" I shouted, without wanting to.

Nora stopped talking. She inclined her head to the side and looked at me curiously. "No?"

"No," I repeated, quieter this time, and lowered my eyes. "No. I . . ."

I gulped.

"I don't want to be a guy."

There was a moment of silence as Nora and I thought over what I'd just said.

"Lily. Lily, look at me."

Reluctantly, I tore my gaze from the bedsheets and looked up, deep into Nora's eyes.

"I get the feeling you've been walking on eggshells all your life," Nora said, smiling warmly at me, and placing a hand on my arm. "These past few months especially. Don't you think it's time to stop doing that, and just . . . stomp down? Stop pretending, and crush those eggshells entirely?"

"Stop pretending? What do you mean?"

"I mean admitting that you're a girl, Lily. Admitting it to yourself."

"But I'm not a girl."

"Why not?"

"Because . . . *Because*. You can't just say you're a girl. You can't just *be* a girl," I protested. "That's not how it works."

Nora's hand moved lightning-quick and clipped me lightly on the top of my head. "That's exactly how it works, you dumbass. You've been around queer people long enough to know that. And after all you've done, after all you've been through, after all you've just said to me, are you really going to go 'still cis, tho?' Seriously? Come on."

"But . . ." I began, then stopped. What was I even going to say?

"But?" she asked gently.

"But . . . I don't feel like I've earned it."

"Okay, first of all: it's your gender, you don't have to earn it. It's already yours. And second . . ." Nora paused dramatically. "Facts don't care about your feelings."

I blinked. Once, then twice.

"Nora, did . . . did you just . . . ?"

"Shh" She put a finger to my lips. "I'm going to ask you a question, Lily, and I want you to answer honestly."

I nodded.

"Who are you?"

"I'm Lily."

"You are, but you know that's not what I was asking. *Who are you?*"

The answer was on the tip of my tongue. I could almost taste it. But somehow, it still refused to come out.

What finally did it was Nora's expectant smile: faced with that, I found I just couldn't let her down. I couldn't let *myself* down. Not anymore.

"I'm a girl," I said.

Nora's smile widened. "And I'm *so* proud of you," she replied, wrapping me in a hug.

And I cried.

The floodgates opened and I cried my heart out. Everything I'd been through since my decision seven months earlier — everything I'd ever been through in my whole life — came pouring out. I cried, and cried, and cried. Basking in Nora's arms, safe in her embrace, I cried. And she cried along with me.

After what felt like hours, I stopped. We stayed there for a few more minutes, without speaking, just feeling each other breathing, each other's warmth.

Then we separated. Nora grasped my hands and looked at me, tears in her eyes, a wide smile on her lips.

"Are you okay, Lily?" she asked.

Lily. Yes, that was my name. Ever since I'd first heard it — after Joe, ironically, had first suggested it to me — it had felt natural. Without even realizing it, I'd started thinking of it as my real name.

Because that's what it was.

I was Lily, and I was a girl.

God, it was so simple. So clear. So evident. How did I not see it before?

"I think I am. No, sorry, I don't think I am. I *am*. Really."

Nora nodded. "I'm so glad. When you started talking, when you told me everything, I . . . I was afraid I would lose you. I was afraid I would do something wrong and push you away."

"No. No, Nora," I said. "You could never push me away. No matter how much you try. And I realize it's useless for me to push you away too." I smiled. "After all, I just tried to. I really tried. But you refused to let go."

"And I never will," she answered. "I'll never let go of you, Lily."

I smiled at her, and leaned in. We kissed. Deeply.

"And I'm really glad you've decided to come clean," Nora said, once we'd come up for air. "I'm willing to bet that if you hadn't, it would've kept eating you up inside. It's good to let it all out."

"And now I have to tell everyone," I said. "I'm really not looking forward to it."

Nora put her finger to her chin. "Well, not everyone. There aren't that many people who interacted with you directly. There aren't that many people who need to know. For all they care, you found out you were trans in November and decided to transition." She smirked. "No need to mention you were only doing it to try and own the libs."

"But what about our friends?" I asked. "What about Vicky and Elanor? What about Anna? I have to tell them. They deserve to know. I'm afraid of how they'll react."

"Psh, they're fine," Nora replied, waving her hand dismissively. "I think you've built enough trust and goodwill that they won't mind that much. We'll tell them you were both an egg and an idiot, and they'll understand."

"Are you sure?"

"I'm sure."

"Okay then." I flopped down in bed and stared at the ceiling. "Man, this night has been *a night*. It took a lot out of me. Physically and emotionally." I yawned widely.

"So what I'm hearing is you don't want to pick up from where we left off?" Nora said. I turned my head to look at her, and she pouted. "As I remember, we were just about to—"

She was cut off by a pillow smacking her in the face. "No," I said with a laugh. "No, not right now. I'm . . . too tired for that." I paused. "There'll be other chances."

"Oh, there will?" Nora replied teasingly.

For once, I didn't let her fluster me. "Yes, there will. I don't intend to let you off the hook that easily, Nora."

"I look forward to it."

"For the time being, we can cuddle. If you want."

"I do," she replied. "God, I do, Lily. I love you."

"And I love you."

We kissed one more time, then changed into our sleepwear. We slipped back under the covers, spooning: I thoroughly enjoyed the feeling of Nora's warmth on my back, her breath on my neck, and her arm draped over me.

It wasn't long until I fell asleep, a content smile on my lips.

"So ... um ... yeah," I said; my mouth dry. "That's pretty much it."

Nora, sitting beside me, gave my shoulder a reassuring squeeze; meanwhile Anna, Elanor, and Vicky, seated across from us, were giving me equally bewildered and disbelieving stares.

A waiter came by and set food and drinks down on the table; he hesitated, seemingly realizing just how awkward the atmosphere around our group was, and then left again without speaking a word.

The silence stretched further.

I could almost see the wheels turning in my friends' minds as they thought over what I'd said, and flashed back to every interaction they'd had with me over the previous seven months.

Again, silence.

I couldn't take it anymore.

"Please say something," I mumbled.

The silence was broken by Anna snorting loudly. She put her face in her hands and her shoulders started shaking. "Jesus H. Christ, Lily," she said, as she began laughing uproariously, soon joined by Elanor and Vicky. "Holy shit," she continued, gasping for breath.

"This is just . . . Holy crap," Elanor added. "I mean, I would doubt you, but you swore up and down that it's the truth, despite how far-fetched it is . . ."

"And it *is* the truth," Nora replied. "I believe Lily. I saw how she was this morning when she came out to me."

Vicky started laughing even harder; our table was getting weirded-out stares from the waitstaff and other patrons. "Yeah, it was a coming out, wasn't it? After all, this dumb baby . . ." She took a deep breath to calm herself down, but it failed and she was still laughing when she said, "I mean, I've heard stories about trans people with a thick eggshell, but *this* thick? Jesus, Lily, you were armor-plated."

"She was, wasn't she?" Anna said, starting to calm down. "I kinda knew it, I guess. I did tell you that you were a spiky egg when you first talked to me about being trans. I just didn't know the full extent of it."

"It's remarkable," Elanor said, also taking a deep breath. "Our friend is a big dum-dum, it seems."

Friend.

Was I still their friend?

"So, you forgive me? Despite everything?" I asked, with more than a bit of trepidation.

Elanor and Vicky both wiped their tears away and nodded. Anna, however, raised her finger. "Hold on, give me a sec," she said. She reached into her bag and retrieved a sheaf of paper, which she carefully and methodically rolled up into a cylinder. "Close your eyes."

I complied.

Anna whapped me upside the head with her makeshift paper club.

"There. Now I forgive you," she said.

"Ow," I complained, massaging my head and causing another bout of laughter to ripple through my friends.

"No, but seriously," Elanor said. "How is it that after seven months of 'lying', what made you break down was remembering a shitty eighties movie?"

"Well, I was a bit tipsy at the time, so I don't remember it clearly, but it was probably the fact that I love Nora so much—"

"Say it again," Nora said, smiling at me; I smiled back and gave her a peck on the lips.

"I love you, Nora," I answered. "But yeah, I love Nora, and I didn't want to force her into something she didn't want to be doing with someone she didn't want to do it with. Rape by deception, remember?"

"And while I appreciate the thought, that wouldn't really have been rape by deception, would it?" Nora interjected. "I was fully aware of who you are . . ." She raised a finger to stave off my objection. "Even if *you* weren't, *I* was, and that was something I wanted to do. I freely consented to having a relationship — including sexual relations when and where appropriate — with the girl I love."

"Say it again," I said.

"I love you, Lily, my beautiful girl," Nora said, and kissed me. Deeply. There was tongue.

After a while Anna started to make gagging noises, Elanor coughed discreetly, and Vicky muttered, "Seriously, you two. Get a room. Goddamn show-offs."

Without breaking the kiss, Nora glanced over at Vicky and sweetly gave her the finger.

"Liiiiiilyyyy, your girlfriend is being mean to me," Vicky said, pouting.

I pulled back from the kiss and swatted playfully at Nora. "Hey now," I said, in a mock-scandalized tone, "don't you be mean to my sister."

"Fiiiiine," Nora drawled.

"Good girl," I said and gave her a peck on the cheek.

"So, is this everything you had to say?" Anna asked. "Not that it wasn't important, and not that I don't enjoy hanging out with y'all, but I kinda have a project to get back to. Professor Markley is expecting the semi-final draft of my paper in the next couple days." She paused. "Wait, hold on, weren't you planning on writing a paper, too?"

"Uh … I was, actually," I replied. "It was going to be something about how transition is fake, actually, since even someone who isn't trans can do it, and use it to increase their social standing."

It took Anna a few moments to fully understand what my words meant, but then she started laughing again. "And I gather that by 'someone who isn't trans' you mean yourself, correct?" she said, guffawing. I nodded in confirmation, which only made her laugh harder.

"Swear to God, Lily, you're so dense it's an actual wonder you don't have your own gravitational field," Elanor said.

I pouted. "I'm getting better."

"In any case, what are you planning to do about that?" Anna asked, still chuckling.

"I've already gathered all the material, so I might as well write it," I answered. "But I'm going to approach the issue of transition a bit differently. I even thought about a title. *Not Just a River in Egypt: How Socially Ingrained Preconceptions Prevent People from Realizing Plain and Obvious Truths.* What do you think?"

"Sounds good," Vicky said. "If more on the psychological side of things, instead of social studies."

"I hope Markley will overlook that."

"So, anything else?" Elanor asked.

"Yes, actually," I replied. "I . . . I still have to come out to my parents. And I honestly don't know how they'll react. Could you . . . Could you all be there with me when I tell them? So I have some support whichever way it goes."

"Of course," Anna replied. "That's what friends are for, right?"

Vicky reached over, grabbed my hand, and gave it a reassuring squeeze. "And if anything happens, remember you'll always have a place to stay, Sis."

"When are you going to tell them?" Elanor asked.

"In two weeks," I answered. "They're driving down, so I won't have to lug all my things on a bus to go home for the summer. I've sent my dad a text, asked them to stay over for a day or two instead of going back right away. 'So you can do some sightseeing,' I said. This way, at least, they'll have some time to process things, to think it over before we have to go home."

"Alright. We'll plan this thing properly," Elanor said.

"We will." Nora put her arm over my shoulders and pulled me into a half-hug.

"Thank you," I said, looking around at each of them in turn — Anna, Elanor, Vicky, and Nora. "I don't know what I'd do without you."

"Don't worry, things will be fine," Anna said.

And maybe things would really be fine. Or maybe not. I had no idea what the future would bring, but I knew I could face anything coming my way because I had my friends by my side.

And, if nothing else, I knew who I was.

I was Lily.

And I was a girl.

EPILOGUE

I

Meet the Parents

"**I**S THAT THEM?" Vicky asked when I inhaled sharply.

"That's them," I replied, nodding stiffly. Nora redoubled her grip on my hand. "Okay. "Let's do this."

"Alright," Anna said. She and Elanor got up from their seats and walked across Giovanni's to my parents. I watched nervously as they greeted them, exchanged a few words, and walked back to us. We'd claimed one of the tables farthest from the door so we'd be able to talk without being interrupted.

As they got closer, I felt my body go as taut as a violin string. It was a good thing Nora and Vicky were sitting on either side of me, our backs to the wall, effectively boxing me in — and that they were holding fast to my hands. If they let go, I would probably have leapt over the table and run away as far and as fast as I could.

"Just breathe, Lily," Vicky said under her breath.

"You can do this," Nora added.

I kept staring ahead as my parents drew closer and closer, still talking with Elanor and Anna. By then I could make out their words: "... understand," my mother said. "Where is he? Why has he sent you to ... what was it you said? To 'fetch us.' What does that mean?"

My friends didn't reply. Instead, they stopped in front of our table and looked wordlessly at me. My parents followed their gaze, then froze when they spotted me.

My mouth was suddenly dry as the desert. I smiled nervously. Leaning heavily on all the training I'd done to keep my voice from wavering too much, I licked my lips and said, "Hi Mom. Hi Dad."

My dad's brow furrowed deeply, while my mom's eyes widened: their disbelief was evident as they took in my appearance.

I'd gone all out that day. *Clothes are armor*, Vicky had told me, and I wore my armor proudly. I had on the dress Nora had bought me, and the shoes we'd picked together. With Vicky's help I'd done my makeup carefully, not to hide my features but to enhance them — to make myself recognizable as me, but different, new and improved. I wanted my parents to realize who I was at first glance: I wanted them to see I was a girl.

I held my head up proudly to let them get a good look. They stared, their eyes wandering all over me, inspecting every square millimeter of my being. It took a long time, nearly a minute, before the silence was broken by my mother saying a single, shocked word.

"Dee . . . ?"

It had been a whisper, but oddly I found myself wishing it had been a shout. That way, at least, my wince at the sound of my old nickname would've been justified. "Yeah," I breathed out. "But it's Lily now." It was difficult to speak, I was having to grind the words out. "Why don't you sit down? This will probably take a while."

"Wh— But— How— *What?*" my mom sputtered. "Dee, what—"

"Lily," I replied firmly. "That's my name now." I paused. "Please sit down? I'm going to explain this, I promise. I'm going to explain every- thing. But let's all take a deep breath first."

"Maybe have a drink, too," Anna added. "Coffee good with everyone?"

"Just water, please," I said. "I'm already nervous enough. Mom? Dad? Will you have something to drink?"

They continued staring at me in shocked silence as they sat down.

"Just water for them, too," Vicky said; Anna and Elanor brought some to the table. I opened my bottle with shaking hands, took a deep gulp, and set it down on the table.

"Okay," I said. "I guess we should start with introductions, right? Hi." I gave my parents the best smile I could manage under the circum- stances. "I'm Lily. I'm your daughter."

"Since when?" my dad gruffly asked, rumbling the words out into his bushy, white-streaked beard.

I turned my attention to him. His brow was still creased and his wild mane of ginger hair framed his piercing green eyes, which felt as if they were staring into my soul.

"Since always," I said. "I've always been your daughter. I just hadn't realized it. So I don't blame you for not noticing."

He snorted out what might have been a half-laugh, then shook his head slightly. "That was not what I was asking. When did this start?"

I pushed down a wave of nausea at the memory of what had

happened the last time I'd been asked that question. I licked my lips which, despite the drink of water I'd just taken, still felt parched, and replied, "November."

"So it was already a thing when you came home for Christmas?" my mother asked.

"Kind of?" I said. "It's a long story. It will make sense in the end, I promise. But first, let's finish the introductions."

I looked at Anna, who nodded. "I'm Anna Suarez," she said. "I'm Lily's classmate."

"Elanor Yates," Elanor said. "I'm Anna's theyfriend—"

"Theyfriend?" my mom mumbled, as she and my dad exchanged a look.

"—and Lily's lawyer? Kind of?"

"You're a lawyer? Why does he need a lawyer?"

"She," they corrected her mildly. "And kind of, as I said. I'm still in pre-law, but I helped her get all the legal papers she required in order, among other things."

"What legal papers?" my dad asked.

"Let's just move on?" I said. "Nora?"

"I'm Nora Hartley," Nora said. "I'm Lily's girlfriend."

Both my dad and my mom nodded at that, but I didn't miss the split-second look of surprise on their faces.

"And I'm Victoria McPearson," Vicky said. "I'm Lily's . . . roommate."

"Vicky," I said, turning my head to look at her, "we've talked about this."

Her eyebrows pinched together. "I don't want to make things more complicated than they already are," she said.

"I'm not going to let you deny yourself, sorry." I looked at my parents again. "Vicky is my sister."

My parents' eyebrows rose toward the ceiling. "Your *sister*?" my mom said. "But . . . you're not related."

"Not by blood, no," I said, "but family isn't made by blood alone."

After a moment of hesitation, Vicky nodded in agreement. "We don't need to share genes or a surname; I chose Lily and she chose me." She passed an arm over my shoulders and drew me into a tight, protective hug. "That's all there is to it."

"And, as she said before, she's also my roommate," I added.

"Wasn't your roommate called Joe?" Mom said, then narrowed her eyes at Vicky. "Is *she* Joe?"

It took me a split second to realize what exactly my mother had asked, but then a laugh erupted out of me like an explosion, so loud it surprised even me. After a moment it turned into a coughing fit, and I bent over the table, half-laughing-half-coughing as Nora massaged my back and whispered, "Deep breaths, Lily."

"No, I'm not," Vicky said while I recovered. "Though it's a fair question, all things considered."

"But Joe is involved in all of this. He was, ironically, the one who set everything in motion," Anna said.

"Then why isn't he here now?" Mom asked, clearly puzzled, eyebrows pinched together.

"That's . . ." I said, catching my breath. "Um. It's a long story. I should probably start at the beginning. You see, Back in November, Joe and I had just returned to our dorm room after a party where we'd met Anna and Elanor. We were both quite drunk, and—"

"No, hold on, you were *drunk*?" Mom said, scandalized. "You mean, you drink alcohol?"

"I, uh . . ." I began.

"Come on, Beverly, it's perfectly normal." My father's deep, rumbling voice cut me off. "People drink in college."

"Yes, but he's still underage," Mom said.

"She," Nora said quietly.

"Not in most of the world," Dad rebutted. "It's weird that twenty-one is the drinking age in this country, if you ask me."

"So you approve of him getting drunk?"

"Her," Elanor murmured.

Mom turned her head and stared at them for a moment, then shook her head. "Whatever. Do you approve of *her* getting drunk, Maxwell?"

"I do not," Dad said, and he turned his eyes on me. "But making mistakes is part of growing up. I'm not going to blame him . . ."

He paused, held up a hand, and shook his head.

"I'm not going to blame her for getting drunk the first time she tries alcohol."

I decided that even though I was going to stretch the truth — my friends and I had agreed it was probably best if, for the time being, I didn't mention exactly why I'd decided to transition or when I actually realized I was a girl — I should at least be completely straightforward with my parents when it came to other things; like drinking, for one.

"Actually," I said, slowly and carefully, "that wasn't the first time I'd tried alcohol."

"It wasn't . . . ?" Mom asked.

"No. The first time I got drunk was when I was . . . thirteen? Probably?" I said, watching my parents' mouths drop. "I was drinking regularly by the time I started high school."

"You were?"

"It was beer, mostly," I continued, "bought with my allowance. It's actually surprising how cheap booze can be. But I also raided the liquor cabinet in the den a few times, refilled the bottles from the kitchen tap. You two only really drink wine, so you never noticed. There's a bottle of whiskey in there that's probably ninety percent water."

"The one I brought back from Ireland when we went to visit Grandpa and Grandma?" my dad asked, bewildered.

"Exactly," I replied. "It was . . ." I sighed. "It was the only way I found to . . . just numb everything down, stop the buzzing in my mind, and . . . manage."

"I . . ." Mom began to say, and then visibly gulped. "I had no idea. I never noticed. How could I not notice?" She put her face in her hands.

Dad put a comforting hand on her back. "Beverly . . ." he said.

"I don't blame you," I said. "I don't blame either of you. The fact you didn't notice my drinking, or that we never managed to really connect, is as much my fault as it is yours. But we can't change the past. What I would like . . ." I paused. Bit my lip: here comes the big ask. Would they accept me? I had no idea, but I had to forge forward. "I'd like to connect with you now, though. Now, and going forward. Starting with me telling my story. If you're willing to listen."

Mom looked up at me with tears in her eyes. "I am," she said, and Dad nodded in agreement.

"Alright," I said. "As I was saying, Joe and I . . ."

"No, wait." Mom walked around the table to stand next to Nora. "Would you mind . . . Nora, was it?"

"Yes."

"Would you mind swapping places with me, Nora? I'd like to sit next to my . . . my daughter, please."

Nora's face broke into a smile, and she sat in the chair my mom had vacated.

"Alright," Mom said, grabbing my hand. "Okay. Go on, Lily. I'm listening."

I steeled myself and began speaking.

As I told the (slightly redacted) tale of how I'd come to realize I was a girl, the grip my mother had on my hand became progressively tighter and tighter; and when I mentioned what had happened the last time I'd seen my former roommate, her eyes widened in shock.

"He *assaulted* you? Dee—"

"Lily," both my father and Vicky said quietly, before exchanging a look, Vicky's eyebrows lifted slightly in surprise — her expression mirrored mine, no doubt: that was unexpected to say the least, After a moment, though, she smiled at him.

"Lily, yes, sorry," my mom said. "Lily, what the hell? Why didn't you go to the police?"

"Because . . ." I began; good thing I'd decided to be almost completely honest with my parents, because what I was about to say wasn't going to be easy for them to hear. "Because if I did, you would've known. The news that I was . . . I was transitioning would've gotten back to you."

"Oh, sweetie," she said, and smiled sadly at me.

"I'm sorry we couldn't be there for you," my dad said.

"But it's still not fair," Mom said. "After what he's done to you, he gets away scot-free? And what if he comes back?"

"That will be the last mistake he will ever make, because I will put him in the ground," Dad growled under his breath.

Mom clicked her tongue in disapproval. "That's neither here nor there, Max. What if he *does* come back?"

"He probably won't," Nora said. "But if he does, we'll have advance warning."

"How do you know that?" Mom asked.

"I've kept tabs on Joe since he left," Nora explained. "Just to be safe."

"You never told me that," I said.

"I didn't see a reason to. You already had too many things to worry about."

"Thank you."

"But yeah, he moved back to Texas for a bit, but apparently his parents were fed up with him, for some reason..."

"I couldn't begin to guess why," Elanor commented flatly.

"...so they decided to send him overseas. They used their money to buy him a place at a university in England."

My eyebrows rose in surprise. "England?"

"Yes, the Royal College of Saint Almsworth. I think it's in Essex? Thereabouts? I have a friend there who's keeping an eye on him. Stephanie. I met her online. Nice gal, I think you'd like her."

"Give her my thanks, but tell her to be careful around Joe. You know what he's like. I don't want anyone else to get hurt like I did."

"I will."

"So what happened next?" my mom asked, giving my hand a comforting squeeze.

"Nothing much, really." I shrugged. "I moved out of my dorm room and into Vicky's place. It was all pretty much smooth sailing for me after that, especially with their help." I ran my eyes over each of my friends in turn, and I was rewarded with warm smiles from all of them. "They even helped me figure out what I needed to do to change my name."

"Change your name?" Mom and Dad exclaimed at the same time. "You mean, actually change your name?" Mom continued.

"Yes, *legally* change my name. We went down to the court in Syracuse and everything. In the eyes of the state, I'm officially Lily O'Connor, female."

"Oh," Mom said. "I ... Huh." She paused for a long while, and I could almost see the gears turn in her and my dad's heads. "So this is serious," she finally said, really quietly. "It's for real."

"I would hope this is for real," Anna interjected. "Do you think someone would come out, start hormones, switch up their gender presentation entirely, and even change their legal name, just for fun? Without putting some real deep thought into it?"

"No, you'd have to be really stupid to do that."

I glared at Anna, and she gave a self-pleased, cat-like smirk back to me.

We were all silent for a long while, until my mom said, "Well, this is a lot to take in. Really. I never would've guessed. Seriously, Dee— *Lily*," she corrected herself, then continued, "It's a bit of a shame, though. I've always liked the name—"

"Yeah, me too," I quickly said. "But it's not me, you know? Not anymore."

"Yeah, I get that. It's like changing your surname when you get married, isn't it?"

"Kinda. And I hope you'll forgive me for not telling you before changing my name. Or not asking you what name you'd have picked if I had been born a girl."

"You *were* born a girl, silly," Vicky said quietly, lightly slapping my shoulder.

"I don't mind," Mom said. "Lily is a nice name. And . . ." She took a deep breath, and let it out in a sigh. "As you said, we were never really close. And it's my fault."

"Mom . . ." I began.

"It's my fault," she repeated, more forcefully. "I never really paid that much attention to you, I was so caught up in my career and everything else."

"I'm sorry, Beverly, but . . . Wait, it's Beverly, right?" Anna interjected.

"It is," Mom replied.

"Bev, raising a child isn't on the mother alone, it's something both parents have to share, you and your husband both."

She caught my Dad's eye, "Maxwell," he said. "And the girl makes a good point, Bev. I've never expected you to focus only on . . . Lily. It's not just you who did her wrong."

"But—" Mom began.

"No buts. You had other priorities, like your career. And you were right to have them."

"They're right, Mom," I said. "Women don't have to be just wives and mothers, not if they don't want to."

Mom looked into my eyes; then after a long moment, she nodded. "You're right. But still, the point stands that I haven't really made an effort. Not to raise you right, but to *get to know* you." She squeezed my hand one more time. "But I'd like to put in the effort starting now. I never really knew my son, but I would very much like to know my daughter."

I found myself blinking back sudden tears. "Mom, I . . ." I said, then a sob escaped me.

"Shh," she said. "Come here."

Pulling lightly on my hand, she drew me into a firm but gentle hug. It was the first time I'd hugged my mother in a long while, and I found myself basking in the feeling while happy tears fell from my eyes.

"And I guess I have to thank all of you," Mom said, after finally breaking the embrace. "I'm really grateful for all you've done for Lily."

"It was our pleasure," Anna said. "Lily has been helping all of us in return."

"You will have to tell me and Dad all about that," Mom said, turning back to me. "We'll have plenty of time to talk once we're back home."

"Back home?" I asked, suddenly surprised.

"Of course. You *are* coming back home for the summer break, aren't you?"

"I, uh . . ." I said, then hesitated. "I am? Probably? I hadn't really made plans. I mean, I didn't know how . . . *this*," I motioned between me, my mom, and my dad, "would go."

"Understandable," my dad said gruffly.

"But I can stay here if it's a problem. I mean, I don't want to be a bother . . ."

"Why would you be a bother?" Mom asked, clearly puzzled. "It's your home. You'll always be welcome there."

"Okay," I said.

Truthfully, the idea of being back in my hometown made me nervous. The place wasn't rural by any stretch of the imagination, but it wasn't a big city either, and I remembered how some people — me included, sadly — talked about 'liberals' in general and queer people specifically.

My mom seemed to sense my hesitation. "Your friends can come too, if that makes you feel better," she said, then frowned slightly. "We only have the one extra bed in the guest room, though."

"We also have a fold-out couch," my dad interjected.

Mom turned to look at him in surprise. "We do?"

"The one in the den. I bought it before we got married and we never used it, so I guess you didn't know about it."

"Is it wide enough for two people?"

"It should be."

"Okay." My mother turned back to me, and continued. "So two of your friends can take the couch, and one can take the bed. And Nora can sleep in your room with you."

I was taken aback. "She can what?"

"She's your girlfriend, isn't she? You two sleeping together is pretty normal. It's going to be a bit of a tight fit, your bed isn't that big, but I think you'll manage."

"But no shenanigans," my dad added, raising a finger in warning.

Incredibly, I found myself laughing. "No shenanigans. Got it."

"So," Mom said, smiling brightly at me. "Will you come home for the summer, Lily?"

"Yes. I will."

11
Settling In

"**W**E'RE ALMOST THERE," I said, looking out of the window at the scenery. The countryside was slowly giving way to suburbs, which I knew would be turning into a city within a few miles. Being back felt nostalgic, as if a lifetime had passed since I'd last set foot in my hometown.

But then again a whole lifetime *had* passed. The last time I'd been there, I wasn't Lily yet.

"Seems nice," Nora said, "if a bit on the small side. How many people live here?"

"About fifteen thousand?" Mom replied from the driver's seat.

"Thereabouts," Dad agreed in a rumble.

"Huh," Nora mused. "That means it's only slightly smaller than Bradford McKinley and the surrounding city combined. Must be the atmosphere; it seems really quiet out here."

"It is," I said. "Nothing much ever happens."

"Something did happen," she said, and when I turned to look at her questioningly she gave me a roguish grin. "You were born here, so it can't be that bad."

I blushed and swatted at her. "Oh, you," I said with a half-laugh.

"If you're quite done flirting," Mom said, looking at me in the rearview mirror with raised eyebrows, "could you send Anna the location? We lost them a few miles back."

"You didn't wait for them?" I asked.

"Didn't see the point. We were almost there. We are there, in fact."

I fished my phone out of my purse as my mom flicked the turn signal on and turned into our driveway. "Done," I confirmed after a few taps on the screen.

"Alright," she replied, turning the engine off. "We'll put their car in the garage, I'll leave mine out here."

"Why?" Nora asked, opening the door and stepping out. "That's a three-car garage, looks like."

"Yeah, but there's Max's car in there, along with one of his projects."

"Projects?" Nora queried.

While Mom busied herself unloading suitcases, Dad walked to the right-most garage door. "Little hobby of mine," he explained. "I buy old cars, fix them up, drive them for a few months, then sell them at a small profit. Keeps my hands busy." He rolled the garage door up and gestured at the car inside. "This one's a . . ."

". . . a Fiat 850!" Nora exclaimed. "Where did you find this?"

Dad was clearly surprised by Nora being able to identify a decades-old foreign car on sight, but quickly recovered. "From a guy over at Fort Drum. He bought it in Italy when he was stationed there, brought it over when he came back. Only drove it a couple times before he blew the engine. It'd been sitting in his garage for five years before I bought it. Had to have it towed here."

"Cool, cool," Nora replied, nodding appreciatively at the car.

"Maxwell!" Mom called out. We turned around, and saw the Crown Vic that Anna, Elanor, and Vicky were riding in pull into the driveway. "For God's sake, stop nerding out and come help the girls with the luggage!"

"I'll get it!" Nora said and hurried over to her.

Dad looked at Mom for a moment, then chuckled. "Women, am I right?" he said, shooting me a glance; then he blinked. "Uh, I mean . . . Sorry."

Surprisingly, I found myself giggling. "No need to apologize, Dad."

The look he gave me was undecipherable. "Come on, let's not keep your mother waiting," he said after a moment.

≡

"Here you go," Mom said, setting the last of the luggage on the floor. "Do you need anything else, girls?"

"No, thank you, Mrs. O'Connor," Nora replied, sitting down on the bed beside me.

Mom smiled. "Oh, please, call me Beverly. Or Bev."

"Alright. Bev."

There was a slight pause as Mom looked at me. She clearly wanted to say something, but was hesitating, so I smiled at her. "Yes?" I asked, putting as much warmth into my voice as I could manage.

She inhaled and let her breath out in a sigh. "Do you maybe want to go shopping tomorrow? And then do something the day after tomorrow, and the following day, and the day after. I mean, it's okay if you don't want to," she added quickly, "but we could."

"Tomorrow's okay since it's a Saturday, but what about Monday?" I said. "Don't you have work?"

"Oh, I took a week off," she said with a shrug. "I had lots of vacation time saved up. I may have to go in for a couple hours if there's an emergency, but I'm free for the whole week." She paused. "You know, I thought we could spend time together. Get to know each other, since we . . . we never really did."

"That would be nice," I replied. "I'd like that."

Mom smiled widely. "I'll go see if your friends need anything," she said. "I'll call you when dinner's ready."

She left the room, keeping the door open behind her.

"Well," Nora said, after a moment. "She seems nice. Your dad, too."

"They do seem nice, don't they?" I replied; then my eyebrows scrunched together.

Nora nudged my shoulder with hers. "What's up?" she asked.

"It's just . . . I want this to work. I *really* want this to work."

"It seems to be going fine so far."

"It does. I . . . I don't know what to think, to be honest. I thought there would be more . . . resistance on their part. I guess I didn't expect them to accept me right away." I shook my head. "I don't know. Maybe I'm overthinking all this."

"You do tend to do that," Nora said, and laughed when I stuck my tongue out at her. "I wouldn't worry, though. Like I said, they seem nice."

"Right." I paused and leaned against her. "Thank you."

"For what?"

"For being here with me."

She pulled me close to her. "Always, Lily."

We were quiet for a few minutes, just enjoying each other's presence, then Nora spoke up again. "So this is your room, huh."

"It is," I nodded. "Home sweet home."

"Cozy," she said, looking around. "You have everything you need right here." She started wandering around, inspecting the room top to bottom. "And it's tidier than I imagined."

"What, did you think there would be piles of stuff just lying around?" I asked. "Well, too bad for you. I cleaned everything up before I left for college."

"Right." She opened a drawer and peered inside, then closed it again. "So where's the embarrassing stuff?" I raised an eyebrow at her. "Oh, you know. Childhood pictures. Angsty teenage poetry." She paused. "Porn mags."

"No porn mags, sorry," I laughed.

"Oh, what? Lily, you disappoint me. What red-blooded teen doesn't have a raunchy rag or twelve lying around?"

"I did look at them a few times, it's just . . . well, there are pictures of naked people in porn mags, of course."

"Of course."

"And, well . . . looking at naked women made me feel weird. Uncomfortable." I bit my lip. "Guess we know why that is now, don't we?"

"Yeah," Nora agreed, "And what about the men?"

I made a face. "Oh, no, yuck. Sorry, I'm definitely not into men."

"Oh?" she asked teasingly, and bent over at the waist. "And what are you into? This, maybe?"

She pulled on the collar of her shirt, exposing her collarbone and bra strap.

"Hmm . . . I dunno," I replied. "I really can't tell. Can I look at it more closely?"

"But of course," Nora said. I leaned back and propped myself up on the pillow and she climbed onto the bed and straddled me. "Is this close enough?"

"Yes, definitely," I said.

"Good," she said, leaning forward to kiss me deeply. Then she pulled back a bit and paused, gazing deep into my eyes from inches away. "You know, your bed looks comfortable."

"It is," I replied. "Believe me, it's very comfortable."

"I'm not sure. Maybe we should test it for a bit?"

"Do you think we have enough time before dinner?"

". . . Probably not, no," she said. "But we have enough time for this, at least."

She leaned forward and kissed me deeply again. When we broke apart, we both giggled and nuzzled our noses against each other.

"What's all this then?" Vicky's voice said; I looked up to see her standing in the doorway, a playful smile on her lips. "I seem to remember Beverly telling you 'no shenanigans', or did I imagine that?"

"It was my dad, actually, but you didn't imagine it," I replied, laughing and waving her into the room. "Are you all settled in?"

"Yeah," she answered. "Elanor and Anna too, I'm in the guest room while they're in the den. The fold-out couch is bigger than the bed, so they got it. What about you? Are you sure you're going to fit on this?" She pointed at my single bed. "It'll be tight considering you two have to sleep together."

"It's an excuse for me to hold Lily close," Nora said. I smiled and gave her a peck on the cheek.

Vicky laughed. "You two are disgusting. Seriously."

"That we are," Nora agreed.

"How is it, being back home as a girl?" Vicky asked. "Does it feel weird?"

"It does, quite a bit," I answered. "But it's good weird, not bad weird. You know how it is."

"I don't, actually."

It took me a moment to remember. "Right. Your parents . . ."

". . .don't know I'm a girl and *must not* know I'm a girl." She nodded, a sad smile on her lips. "I boymode when I'm there. The only people I know back home who *do* know are Emily and Josh, my two friends from high school. And I'm eternally grateful to them; being able to hang out with them as myself, as *Victoria*, makes going back for the summer bearable." She sighed. "I can't wait until I don't have to go back at all. Until I can break ties with my past completely."

"I'm sorry your parents are like that."

"I'm used to it. Your parents seem nice, though."

"Right? We were just saying that," Nora replied.

"Let's hope it keeps on being that way," I said.

"What do you mean?" Vicky asked.

"Their initial reaction was good. Better than expected, really. But what if they change their mind once they've had some time to think about it?"

"I don't think they will," Nora said.

"Yeah," Vicky agreed. "In my experience, if they're bad, they're bad right away."

"Still. Mom asked me to go shopping with her tomorrow, and . . . and I'm afraid it's going to be awkward. I mean, I've been her son for so long . . ."

"Want me to come with?" she asked.

"Would you?" I said. "It would really be a big help to have you there."

"Of course I will, Sis," she said, and she reached out to squeeze my shoulder.

"Meanwhile," Nora interjected, "I'm going to see if I can maybe talk to your dad a bit. Try to build a rapport with him."

"You don't have to do that, Nora," I said. "I mean, they're *my* parents. I'm the one who needs to have a relationship with them."

"I do, too," she replied. "After all, they're going to be my in-laws."

I froze. My eyebrows got lost in my hairline as I looked at her. Had she just said . . . ?

Vicky let out a low whistle. "Wow, Nora. That was smooth."

Nora grinned, while I just stared at her, entirely flabbergasted. "I . . . I . . ."

"Girls!" Mom called from downstairs. "Dinner's ready!"

"Coming!" Vicky shouted back. "Come on, you two, let's not keep your parents waiting."

Nora lifted herself from the bed; she offered me a hand and pulled me up too.

"You don't need to give me an answer right now," she said. "Just . . . think about it?"

"I will."

≣

"That was lovely," Anna said, wiping her mouth with a napkin. "Thank you, Mrs. O'Connor."

"Oh, do call me Bev. And you're welcome, dear," Mom said. "So, I was thinking about going shopping tomorrow morning. With . . . Lily."

I kept my emotions in check and didn't frown at the slight moment of hesitation she'd had when using my name. *It's only been a few days. Be patient, Lily.*

"Can I come with you?" Vicky asked. "I love shopping, and it's a good chance to see where my sister grew up."

Mom was clearly surprised by the request, but quickly recovered. "Yes, of course," she said. "You're more than welcome." She paused. "And what about you, Max?"

She looked at my father with slightly raised eyebrows; he glanced at me, then rumbled, "Think I'll stay home and work on the car."

"Do you want some help?" Nora asked.

Dad visibly hesitated: he looked Nora up and down. "You sure? I mean, you're a . . ."

He stopped speaking; Nora raised an eyebrow at him. "A lesbian?" she said in an amused tone.

". . . Was gonna say 'a girl', really."

"Girls can like this kind of stuff too," Nora said. "I study mechanical engineering at college."

"You do?" Dad asked; when Nora confirmed it with a nod, he continued, "Alright then. Do you have any work clothes?"

"I'll wear my best flannel."

"That's settled, then," Mom said, and she turned toward Anna and Elanor. "And what about you girls? What are you going to do?"

I saw Elanor's eyebrows pinch together slightly as Anna began, "We were thinking—"

"Elanor's not a girl, Mom," I said, cutting Anna off.

Mom was clearly taken aback. "She isn't?" she asked. "But the way she looks . . . I mean, I didn't realize she was a man."

"Not a man, either."

"I'm non-binary," Elanor said, giving me a grateful smile, then they turned to my mom. "I'm neither a man nor a woman, but a secret third thing," they said. "I use they and them pronouns."

". . . I'm sorry, but I'm not quite sure how that works," Mom said.

"It means that on a scale of zero to ten, where zero is a woman and ten is a man, I'm a letter," Elanor said; my mom's frown didn't clear. "Alright, how about this: if you have a gradient going from black to white, where black is man and white is woman, I'm purple." They paused and saw Mom was still deeply perplexed. "Okay, okay, let me see . . ."

"You're neither a gasoline engine nor a diesel engine, but you're an electric engine instead," Dad said, nodding.

"Ha!" Nora exclaimed. "That's a great analogy, actually. Good job, Maxwell."

Dad inclined his head, accepting the compliment with a mild smile on his lips.

"I'm still not sure I quite get it," Mom said.

"Don't worry, Mom," I said. "I had some trouble with it at first, too. You'll understand eventually."

"I do get it," Dad said. "You see . . ."

"Alright, I'm sorry, but before you get into this thing I think I'm going to go to bed," I said. "Today was very tiring. Good night, y'all."

"I'm coming with you," Nora said.

As we left the room together, I gave my mom one last glance: she still had a completely befuddled look on her face.

Nora and I managed to make it to my room and close the door before we broke down into giggles.

≡

"This is my favorite café," Mom said as we walked through the door. "I come here all the time, my office is just minutes away."

"What's your job, anyway?" Vicky asked as we set our bags by a table. "I realized I never asked."

"I'm an accountant," Mom replied. "I have my own firm, too; we serve pretty much all the businesses in town."

"Oh, that's cool! You must know your stuff."

"Yeah," Mom shrugged. "You girls take a seat, I'll go order and be right back. What will you have?"

"Just coffee for me," I said.

"Same," Vicky added.

"Alright."

She walked to the counter. After a moment I exhaled a breath, and Vicky nudged my shoulder. "How are you holding up?" she asked.

"Good," I replied. "I'm good. This is surprisingly fine."

"Shopping was good, wasn't it?"

"Yeah," I nodded. "Though I'm not sure I like how pushy she was."

"Pushy? Didn't see that. She seemed fine to me."

"Well, 'pushy' is probably not the right term. But she was always by my side, always trying to get me to try on something or other. Always trying to make conversation with me. This," I gestured vaguely, "is the first time she's let up on me since we left this morning."

Vicky hm-ed pensively. "Yes, I see."

"I understand that she's . . . trying to make up for lost time? I guess? But after a while, it can be too much."

"Do you want me to tell her?"

"Not just yet. I want to see if she keeps doing this before saying anything. I don't want to risk ruining my relationship with her, you know?"

"I get it," she replied, then looked up as Mom returned to the table.

"The waitress will be right over with our orders," she said. "What were we saying? Jobs?"

"Yeah, we were discussing that. Well, you know what I do, right? Full-time student, majoring in social studies education."

"Good to hear you haven't changed your major as well as your gender," she giggled. "And what about you, Victoria?"

"Aerospace engineering," she replied. "Just finished my second year."

"Oh really? Sounds difficult."

"Not really?" Vicky shrugged. "I find it easy enough. But it can be complicated sometimes. You know how they say, 'It's not rocket science' to mean something easy? Well, what I'm studying *is* rocket science. Lots of math and physics and chemistry to keep in mind."

"Chemistry?" I asked.

"For propellant. Rocket fuel."

"I know what propellant is," I said with a smile. "I played KSP."

"You did? Cool."

"And what about your parents?" Mom asked. "What do they do?"

I felt Vicky stiffen and her smile froze on her lips. "They . . . My dad's a teacher, sort of. School district superintendent. Mom's a homemaker."

"Right. I was thinking, could you maybe give me their number? I'd like to talk to them."

Vicky's voice was choked when she answered. "What for?" she forced out.

"To ask them for pointers. After all, you know. We both have trans daughters."

"That might not be the best idea, Mom," I said. "Vicky's parents aren't exactly accepting of her."

Mom sat up in her chair, clearly taken aback by the revelation. "They aren't . . . ?"

"They don't know she's a girl. And it's better to keep it that way."

"Huh," Mom said. "Okay."

I felt Vicky squeeze my hand; when I turned to look at her, she smiled in gratitude.

"Here you are, ladies," the waitress said, placing a tray on the table. "Three coffees and three croissants."

I turned an interrogative look towards Mom, and she said, "The croissants here are really good, I wanted you to try them."

"Thank you," I said to the waitress.

"You're welcome," she said, then narrowed her eyes at me. "O'Connor? That you?"

I looked at her carefully. She was about my age, and the hair on the right side of her head was buzzed short, coming down to her shoulder on the left. She had two rings in her right eyebrow, half a dozen studs in her right ear, and her left arm was covered in an intricately designed tattoo. She looked familiar, but I wasn't sure where or when I'd seen her before.

". . . Yes?" I hesitantly replied.

"Wow. Almost didn't recognize you there. You've *changed*, girl." She paused. "It's girl, right?"

"It is. Sorry, I don't remember your name."

"Rachel, Rachel Petersen. We were in high school together."

That name rang a vague bell. "Right. Sorry, I didn't place you at first. I . . . I think I was kinda dissociating all the way through high school? If that makes sense."

"It does. Gender stuff will do that. And we never really talked that much. I thought you were kind of a dick, to be honest."

Well, that was direct, wasn't it? I winced. "Sorry."

"Apology accepted. It's water under the bridge anyway. I'm glad to see you've figured yourself out."

"You . . . don't seem to mind," I said, looking at her warily.

"Of course I don't," she replied, and pointed at a pink, purple, and blue pin attached to her apron. "Weirdos stick together."

"Right."

"So do you wanna go out sometime?"

I blinked. "Wait, what?"

"Yeah, you're cute. Wanna go out sometime?"

"Thank you for the compliment, but I have a girlfriend."

"Alright," she said, shrugging, and turned to Vicky. "Is this her?"

"No, I'm her sister," Vicky replied, and extended a hand to her. "Victoria, nice to meet you."

"You too," Rachel said, shaking her hand. "Do *you* wanna go out sometime?"

Vicky laughed. "No, thank you."

Rachel clicked her tongue, disappointed. "Bummer. But can't blame a girl for trying, can ya now?"

"Rachel!" a man's voice called out. "Stop hitting on customers and get back to work!"

"Whoops, gotta go," she said with a smile and a wink. "It was nice to see you again . . ."

It took me a moment to realize what she was waiting for. "Lily," I said.

"Lily. Nice name."

"Rachel!" the man called again.

"Coming, Gramps!" Rachel grabbed her tray and went back to the counter.

"That was . . . odd," Mom said. "I'd seen her before, but I had no idea she was . . . *like that.*"

Vicky and I looked back at Rachel and shrugged. "She's not that odd," Vicky said. "Queer people tend to be weirder than the average, especially when they have someone like them to talk to freely."

"Right. Hold on, that was rude of me, wasn't it?"

"What was?" I asked.

"To say *like that.* After all, you are like that too, aren't you?"

"I guess. Maybe people are just not used to having us queers around. You're not used to us being visible."

Mom bit into her croissant and nodded pensively. "Right. We're not," she mumbled.

⣿

"Here we are," Mom said, setting down the bags next to the front door. "We'll put these away later, we're already running a bit late. I'm going to go make lunch."

"Can I help?" Vicky asked.

"Yes, of course," Mom replied. "It's just setting the table and heating up leftovers from last night, though. I can manage."

"Still."

"Alright. Lily, can you tell Max and Nora lunch will be ready in ten minutes?"

Leaving Mom and Vicky to prepare, I made my way through the house to the garage. The door was ajar, and I stopped before going through it, hearing muffled voices.

"... See here?" Nora was saying. "This side is a bit narrower than the other side, so it's difficult to slide the thing through. But if we tighten the bolts beforehand then loosen them from the other side, it's easier."

"Yes, I see. I never considered doing that," Dad replied. "I'm just now realizing that, in all these years, I've done this the hard way. You're a clever girl, Nora."

"Thanks. So, shall we get to it?"

Before they could start doing whatever they were doing, I knocked on the door, pushed it fully open, and went through. "Dad? Nora?"

Nora turned to look at me, smiling brightly. She was wearing a flannel shirt with the sleeves rolled all the way up, and her hands were dirty with grease, as were my dad's; they both had a few stains on their faces, too. "Lily! Hi!" Nora said. "How did it go this morning? Did you have fun?"

"I did," I said. "Mom said lunch will be ready in ten."

"Oh, I better clean myself up, then."

She walked past me, stopping to give me a peck on the cheek as she went, and disappeared through the door to the house.

"So," I said after a few moments, turning to Dad.

He looked back at me, but didn't say anything.

The silence stretched. Awkwardly.

"Mom said lunch's almost ready."

"Yeah, heard you the first time."

"Alright."

Another long moment of silence.

"I . . . I'll go help Mom and Vicky," I said, and turned to go.

"Lily . . ." Dad said.

I turned back to him. "Yes?"

He opened his mouth as if to say something, then, after a moment, he shook his head. "Nothing."

". . . Alright."

"I'll go wash my hands." He walked past me, not meeting my gaze, and left the garage through the door.

I stared at his back as he walked off, and briefly wondered if I should call out to him, ask him to tell me what was on his mind.

But what if you don't like what's on his mind? a voice in the back of my head said. *What then?*

No. Better to leave it for now. He would talk to me eventually.

I hoped.

III

Coming Around

EVERY DAY SINCE I'd arrived home was the same as the one before. Mom would ask me to go somewhere with her, and Vicky would tag along.

On the fifth day, I was halfway tempted to tell Mom no: being with her almost twenty-four seven was seriously starting to give me anxiety; she was more than a bit overbearing. But in the end, I decided to acquiesce to her request once again, since I had yet to reach my breaking point. "Alright, let's go," I said. "Where are we going? Shopping again?"

"It's a surprise," Mom said, touching her finger to her lips.

I was puzzled, and about to inquire further, when Anna asked, "Can I come along?"

"Yes, of course," Mom said. "You and Elanor are both welcome."

"Just me; Elanor wants to go somewhere else."

"I've read there's a retrogaming store the next town over," Elanor piped up. "I want to check and see if they have a copy of the first *Ace Attorney* game."

"Which they've already played many times over, mind."

"But I don't have a physical copy. An original cartridge for the DS. It's the only one missing in my collection."

"Nerd," Anna said, nudging Elanor in the shoulder.

"And proud of it," they rebutted.

"But yeah, just me today."

"Alright." After mulling it over, I turned to my dad. "What about you, Dad? Do you want to come into town with us?"

Dad looked at me in surprise. "Me?"

"Yeah," I replied. "Want to come with us?"

There was a long pause, and I couldn't glean what he was thinking by the look in his eyes. In the end, though, he said, "Kind of you to offer, but I want to keep working on the car a bit more."

"We don't have a deadline," Nora interjected. "We have all the time in the world. You can go."

Dad shook his head. "I want to finish the thing we were working on yesterday."

"What thing? We weren't working on—"

"I'm staying home," he said, his voice hardening a bit. Nora looked at him for a moment longer, then loudly clicked her tongue.

"So I guess it's me and you, Lily, and Vicky and Anna," Mom said. "Unless you want to come too, Nora?"

"I'll stay here with Max, if you don't mind," she said, looking at my dad, who didn't meet her eyes.

"Alright. I think we're going to stay out a bit longer, too," Mom replied. "Grab a bite to eat — there's a new restaurant I want to try — and come back in the afternoon. You okay to make lunch on your own?"

"Yeah, sure," Nora said.

"I'll go get ready," I said. Finishing my mug of coffee, I left the kitchen, making my way to my room. When I closed the door, my shoulders slumped.

Still no luck getting through to my dad. I'd tried several times a day, but each time I talked to him he gave very brief answers without meeting my eyes.

It was a bit weird, since he seemed to be getting along with Nora just fine, and to a lesser extent with Vicky, Anna, and Elanor. I was the only one he refused to talk to.

No, not refused, that wasn't the right word: he was *avoiding* me. He did his utmost to avoid engaging me in conversation. I didn't know what to make of it; I was beginning to think he hated me. Which would make sense — I was the one who'd, figuratively, taken his son away from him.

If he kept this up I'd probably have to rethink my relationship with him entirely: maybe even cut ties with him. His behavior was starting to give me a lot of anxiety, something I definitely didn't need in my life. But I would burn that bridge if I came to it.

I got on with preparing myself for one more day with Mom. It was probably going to be exhausting, but I had to do it if I wanted to have a relationship with her.

☰

"Here we are," my mother said, stopping the car. "And just in time, too. Seriously, service at that restaurant was so slow . . ."

"Just in time for what?" Anna asked; Mom ignored her question and got out of the car. We all followed as she walked across the parking lot to a nondescript, two-storey building.

"What's this place?" I asked. "I don't think I've been here before."

"This is my office," Mom replied, pointing at a plaque next to the door which had *O'Connor, Montoya, & C., Accountants and Auditors* written on it in bold letters.

"Alright," I replied. "And what are we doing here, exactly?"

"You'll see," she replied cryptically, ushering us into the building.

We climbed a flight of stairs and opened a door, where we were met by a woman with straight black hair and deep brown eyes, who smiled widely at me. "Hi! You must be Lily, it's so nice to meet you!"

". . . Likewise?" I replied. "I'm sorry, who are you?"

"Cassandra Montoya," she replied. "I'm Beverly's partner." She turned to Mom, and continued, "It's incredible, she looks so much like you."

"She does, doesn't she?" Mom replied. "She's beautiful."

I felt my cheeks redden at the compliment as Cassandra turned back to me. "I've met you before, actually, but you probably don't remember me," she said. "You used to play with Nate, my son, when you were very little. He's a few years older than you."

"Sorry, I don't really remember. How's he doing?"

"He's good. He's with CBP, at Massena."

"Is everything ready, Cassie?" Mom asked.

"Of course. I've asked everyone to go to the meeting room."

"Good. Let's do this, then. Come along, Lily."

I looked at her in puzzlement, but followed her through a door and down a corridor; Anna and Vicky brought up the rear, while Cassie walked next to me.

"So, are you excited for your big day?" she asked.

My confusion increased. "Big day? What do you mean?"

Her smile disappeared. "You . . . don't know?" She looked at my mom, who'd stopped in front of another door. "Bev, haven't you told her?"

"No, I wanted this to be a surprise," Mom replied.

"Uh . . ." Cassie said. "Beverly, I don't think—"

"Good afternoon, everyone!" Mom exclaimed, opening the door and walking through. "Thank you for coming!"

She grabbed my hand and dragged me in along with her: it was a meeting room with about a dozen people in it.

"I asked you all to take some time off your work because I wanted to introduce someone to you," Mom continued. "This is Lily, my daughter. She used to be my son, but now she's my daughter, and I wanted you to meet her."

She pushed me in front of her, and all eyes turned to me.

"Do you want to say a few words, Lily?" Mom asked.

I felt the blood drain from my face as I stared at the assembled crowd like a deer in headlights.

"I . . . Uh . . ." I stammered.

"Jesus fucking Christ, Bev," I heard Cassandra hiss behind me.

"Uh . . ." I said again.

Vicky and Anna were instantly by my side. "Do you need to get out of here?" Vicky whispered, but she wasn't looking at me; she was glaring daggers at my mom, who looked puzzled by my reaction.

I nodded, feeling very light-headed.

"Let's go," Vicky said, grabbing my hand and pulling me toward the door.

"Sorry, everyone, I guess she's a bit nervous!" Anna called out loudly. "We'll be right back!"

"Wait, what's happening?" my mother said, looking at Anna, and then at me. "Lily?"

My friends ignored her as they guided me out of the room.

"There's a café near here, right? One Beverly goes to a lot?" Vicky asked. I distantly realized she was talking to Cassie, who was coming along on our precipitous retreat.

"Yeah," Cassie answered. "Let's go."

"What's going on?" Mom asked. "I'm coming—"

"No!" Cassie snapped. "*Stay*, Bev. Give us some space. Give us ten minutes."

I heard, more than saw, Mom stop dead in her tracks. The crowd murmured at the scene we'd just put on, but I didn't care. I was feeling so dazed that I just went along as my friends and Cassie guided me down the street.

Rachel looked up at us from the counter as we entered. "Lily! Hi . . ." she said, then trailed off. After a moment, she said loudly, "I'm taking my break now, Gramps!"

Walking briskly, she rounded the counter, grabbed my arm, and pulled me across the café, sitting me down at a table near the back. "I'll be right back," she said, as Vicky, Cassie, and Anna sat down too.

"What the fuck," Cassie whispered. "I can't fucking believe Bev did that. She didn't give you any warning? Any at all?"

"None," I replied, shaking my head. "I had no idea she . . ." I gulped. "Thank you," I said to Rachel as she set a tall glass of ice water in front of me.

"On the house," she said, sitting down at the table. "You look like you need it."

I took a deep gulp of the cold liquid, holding it in my mouth for a few moments before swallowing. "Fuck," I breathed out. "That was . . . terrifying."

"I'll bet," Anna said. "It must have been a shock, especially considering . . ."

She trailed off. "She's had some bad experiences with stuff like this," Vicky explained when Cassie looked at her for an explanation.

"Right," Cassie said. "I'm so sorry, Lily, I had no idea. She asked me to help her with the announcement, but I honestly thought you'd agreed to it. I didn't think she would surprise you like that."

"And you know what's the worst part? Now we have to explain to her why her well-meaning surprise was actually bad," Anna said, looking up and away from the table.

I followed Anna's gaze, and saw Mom walk into the café. She looked around and, when she spotted us, strode over to us.

Vicky stood up.

There was an intense anger in her eyes as she looked at my mother, a fire I'd never seen there before. "Listen here, you—"

"Vicky. Victoria. Please," Anna cut her off, moving between Vicky and Mom. When Vicky turned and glared at her, she didn't back down, but continued, "She made a mistake, yes, a huge mistake, but she's not a villain. Take a deep breath, Vicky. Calm down. Please."

It took a few moments, but Vicky sat back down. Anna let out a small breath of relief, turned to my mother, and nodded. After a brief hesitation, Mom sat down too. "Can anyone tell me what just happened?" she asked.

"You hurt Lily," Vicky snapped.

"Vicky," Anna hissed.

"I did not!" Mom replied at the same time: she sounded scandalized, as if the mere thought she could hurt me was a deathly insult.

"You did," Vicky replied. "Not on purpose, no, but you did. You hurt Lily. Right?"

She turned to me, and I hesitantly nodded.

"I . . . I didn't," Mom said, but her protestation was weaker this time. "I didn't hurt Lily." She paused, then added, almost in a whisper, "I'm her mother. I wouldn't hurt her. No parent would hurt their child."

Vicky stared at her for a second, then reached up to flip her hair to the side. She bowed her head and pointed. "Do you see this?" she asked.

My eyes widened: running across her scalp, discolored but clearly visible because of the millimeter-wide patch of hairless skin around it, was a thin line about three inches long — a scar. "Vicky, what—"

"Courtesy of my father. I told him I'm a girl — the first and last time I told him that — and he threw a glass at me. Fifteen stitches. It still hurts sometimes."

Her voice was tight. Controlled.

She straightened up and flipped her hair back into place.

"That was also the only time I went to the hospital. I slipped and hit my head on the corner of a table, apparently. When we were alone the doctor asked me if that was what really happened, but I was too scared to tell him the truth. But that was not the only time my dad hit me." She raised both hands, fingers splayed. "I need more than these to count them. I don't even remember them all. And my mom . . ." She grimaced. "My mom just watched. A few times, after the fact, she told me, 'See, this is what happens when you make him mad.' Because it was my fault, of course. And there is absolutely zero doubt in my mind that my father would kill me if he knew I'm . . . *like this*." She motioned down at herself. "They'd never find my body. He told me that."

"Vicky, I . . . I had no idea," I whispered. "You never told me."

"I don't like talking about it." She smiled sadly, then locked eyes with my mom. "Parents can and do hurt their children. My father hurt me, and you hurt Lily." She raised her hand to stave off Mom's oncoming objection. "Not physically, of course. It was nowhere near as bad, and it wasn't intentional. But you did hurt her."

Mom held Vicky's gaze for a few moments, then slowly nodded. "How did I hurt her?" she asked.

Vicky smiled thinly, seemingly pleased my mother had listened to her. She looked at me and inclined her head, giving me the go-ahead to speak.

"You told everyone in the office about me being trans without asking me first," I said, rasping the words out — despite having just had a drink, my throat still felt dry. "I might have wanted to do it differently, or not at all."

She seemed to consider my words. "Yes, I see your point. It's just . . ." She sighed. "I wanted everyone to know I support you. I wanted everyone to know I'm proud of you, Lily."

"That's exactly the point, Mom," I replied. "It's not about what you want. It's about *me*."

"It is, isn't it?" she said. "I'm sorry, Lily. I just didn't stop to consider things. It's just that . . ."

She put a hand to her eyes.

"Mom . . ." I began.

She raised her other hand to stop me. "When I saw you again at college . . ." she said, her voice choked. "When I saw *you*, I realized just how much I'd messed things up. I didn't pay enough attention to you, or I would've noticed there was something wrong with you. And I couldn't help but wonder just how many things I've missed. And I was determined not to miss anything else, ever again."

I reached across the table and grabbed her hand; she grasped it tightly, as if it was a piece of driftwood in an empty ocean. "And I'm grateful for it," I said. "But . . . there's a big gap between 'no relationship at all,' and 'everything everywhere all at once,' you know? We can take things slow, at our own pace."

"Right," she said. There were tears in her eyes, but she was smiling. "Promise me you'll tell me when I'm being too much again? Because I probably will be."

"Yeah," I laughed. "I promise."

"Good." She paused. "You're not coming back to the office, are you?"

I quickly shook my head. "No way in hell," I said. "Having to explain myself to a bunch of people I've never seen before in my life? Absolutely not."

"Right. I really screwed up, didn't I?"

"You did," Cassie said. "Seriously, Bev."

"Guess I'll go back there and tell everyone what I did," Mom said. "I can just picture it: 'Hey, everyone, it turns out I'm an inconsiderate idiot.' It will be great."

"Don't worry, I'll help you," Cassie said. "If anyone asks, I'll tell them exactly why you've been an inconsiderate idiot. In vivid detail."

"I deserve it." Mom turned toward Vicky. "Thank you for setting me straight, Victoria."

She held out her hand toward Vicky who, after a moment's hesitation, grasped and gave it a squeeze. "No, thank *you* for listening."

"You've been an incredibly good sister to my daughter, Vicky," Mom said. "I'm really glad she had you by her side when I wasn't there for her. And I'm sorry your parents can't see you for the wonderful young woman you are: I know I would be proud to call you my daughter. It's seriously their loss."

Vicky smiled a sad smile back at her. "I don't mind. I have all the family I need right here."

☰

After we separated from Mom and Cassie, Anna, Vicky, and I made our way home. It was only mid-afternoon, but I went straight to the garage and asked Nora to come to my room right away. ("No, Dad, we're not going to do anything.")

We changed into our pajamas and lay down in bed, hugging closely.

I took the chance to scream into Nora's chest. A few times.

"Bad day?" she asked when I was done.

"Seriously bad. But also good."

I explained what had happened with Mom in detail, and she was at first puzzled, then she frowned in barely repressed anger, and then, finally, she smiled.

"Nothing is ever simple in your life, is it, Lily?"

I pouted. "Hey, come on. It's hardly my fault this kind of thing keeps happening to me."

She gave me a kiss on the forehead. "I'm glad things are going along fine with your Mom," she said. "Looks like your fears were misplaced: she does care about you."

"Though I sorely wish she'd asked before doing what she did."

"She probably will from now on."

"True that."

I didn't say anything else, but Nora seemed to sense I was still tense and upset. "What's up?" she asked.

"It's Dad. He . . ." I shook my head. "I have no idea how to even begin to talk to him. Every time I try, he clams up. Completely refuses to hold a conversation. Which is weird, he seems to be doing fine with you."

"He *is* surprisingly chatty when he's talking about something that interests him," she replied, then she quickly added, "But I don't mean that he—"

"He's not interested in me, is he?" I cut her off. "I'm probably just a nuisance to him: that's why he won't talk to me. After all, he and Mom had a perfectly good life out here before I came along with my . . . my being a girl and everything."

"That's not true, Lily," Nora said, leaning down to kiss the top of my head. "I'm sure he does care about you. Just like your mom does."

"He has a weird way of showing it," I replied bitterly.

Nora was silent for a long time. When she spoke again, she asked, "Are you free tomorrow?"

"Of course I am," I answered. "I mean, Mom will probably want to go somewhere with me again, but after what happened today, I don't think she'll make a fuss if I tell her no."

"Okay, good. Well then, here's what we'll do."

Following Nora's instructions, the following day at breakfast we told everyone we would be leaving Nora and Dad home to work on the car again, while I would be heading out on the town with Mom, Vicky, Elanor, and Anna. They, however, left on their own when Dad went upstairs to change into his work clothes, while I made my way to the garage with Nora.

"Alright, what now?" I asked. "Because I don't think Dad will speak to me even if I help you two with this."

I nodded to the car, and Nora shook her head. "You're not going to help us with the car, Lily. I have a plan."

"A plan?"

"I'm planning on doing something pretty sneaky. It's something that could very easily backfire and make your relationship worse—"

My eyebrows lifted slightly at that.

"—but which, on the other hand, I believe will *not* backfire and will make your relationship better. Do you trust me, Lily?"

I didn't hesitate. "I do."

"Alright." Nora reached through the car's window, tugged something, and the trunk — which was in the front of the car — unlatched with a clunking noise. She pulled it fully open, and smiled. "Climb in."

I looked at her, askance.

"Don't worry," she said with a laugh. "I'm not going to lock you in."

"Alright," Assisted by her, I climbed into the trunk — it took some finagling, the space inside was tiny — but I managed to find a somewhat comfortable position to lie down in. Nora grabbed a screwdriver and placed it on top of the latch to prevent the door from closing completely, then lowered it again.

"Don't make any noise," she said, "or this won't work."

Once the door was fully lowered, only a fraction of an inch remained between it and the car's body; I could barely see the inside of the trunk in the low light that filtered through the crack. Still, I tried to relax and breathe quietly.

A few minutes passed before I heard the garage door open. "You got here quick," Dad's voice said.

"I wanted to check the tools before we started," Nora replied.

"Alright."

I heard footsteps approaching the car, and the creaking of the engine compartment being opened.

"You know how to change a timing belt on one of these engines?" Dad asked. "See here where—"

"You haven't been talking to Lily," Nora said.

There was a moment of silence. A *long* moment of silence. Then a heavy sigh.

"No, I haven't," Dad said.

"Max. Seriously? We've talked about this."

I held my breath as I strained my ears.

"I know."

"And you said you would talk to her."

"*I know*," Dad snapped. "Sorry," he added after a moment. "It's just . . . it's not that easy, you know?"

"What's not easy?" Nora asked. "You just need to talk to her."

"Yeah, but . . . what do I say?" Dad rebutted. "We were never close, even when she was a boy. And now that she's a girl, it's even harder."

"Why is it so hard?" Nora insisted.

"I don't know. Maybe I'm scared? I'm afraid I'll fuck this up again, like I did before."

"Max, you—"

"Don't tell me I didn't fuck it up," Dad cut her off. "Because I did and I know it. I mean, I didn't even notice she was getting drunk every weekend! And now I'm supposed . . ." Another sigh. "I'm supposed to just start over with her, when the only thing I want to say is, 'I'm sorry?' How the hell do I do that?"

"Max . . ."

"I'm a complete failure," Dad said. "I failed at raising her. And I care about her so fucking much, but I can't find the words to tell her."

There was silence, then I heard footsteps approaching the trunk.

"Alright, I think that's enough," Nora said. "You hear that, Lily?"

There were two loud bangs, as Nora knocked on the trunk. I jumped and banged my head on the metal. "Ow . . ." I complained as she pulled the trunk's door open, exposing my presence.

"Lily . . . ?" Dad said.

I looked up at him and smiled sheepishly. "Uh . . . hi, Dad."

"I'm really sorry for tricking you, but you're both fucking useless at this," Nora said. "Pardon my French. But like father, like daughter, I guess. I'll leave you two to talk."

She walked around the car and out through the door that led to the house, pulling it closed behind her.

I looked at Dad.

Dad looked at me.

"So," I said.

"So. Uh . . ."

A pause.

"Do you need a hand getting out of there?"

"Thank you." He offered me his hand, helping me climb out of the trunk.

Another pause.

"Did you really mean it? Everything you said?" I asked.

". . . Yeah," he said. "I'm sorry, Lily. I know I should really have talked to you, but— oof." He breathed out as I threw myself at him, clamping him in a tight hug.

"Thank you," I whispered.

He reciprocated the hug, holding me close. "I love you, Lily. And I'm proud of you. I'm sorry I didn't say it before, but . . . you know how I am with words."

I blinked to clear away the tears that were clouding my eyes. "I don't mind."

We kept hugging for several long moments, then broke the embrace. "Come with me," Dad said.

I followed him out of the garage. Nora was leaning on the wall just outside the door, and she blinked at us in surprise when we walked through it. "What, you're already done?"

"Yeah, we're already done," I said, and nudged Dad in the shoulder. "He's a man of few words, but we understood each other perfectly."

"Good. I'm glad."

"Thank you, Nora," Dad said. "You're a gem."

She grinned. "Glad I could help."

"Come along now, join us."

Dad walked past Nora, and we both followed him to the kitchen. "Don't go anywhere now," he said as he left the room. "Take a seat."

He was back a few minutes later, carrying three glasses and . . .

"Whiskey?" I asked.

"I was planning on sharing this with you when you were old enough, on an important day," he said. "Your graduation, or maybe your wedding day. I think this is the best time."

"Thanks, Dad." I replied with a smile.

"Though you've beat me to the punch," he said. "This is the bottle you got into. The one I brought back from Ireland." He held it up to the light and looked at it closely. "Still looks sealed. You did a good job."

"Lily's a resourceful gal," Nora said with a laugh.

"I'd prefer it if she used her resourcefulness for something else from now on," Dad said, joining in the laughter. He uncapped the bottle, filled the three glasses halfway, and grabbed one of them, raising it.

"A toast. To my beautiful and amazing daughter."

I grabbed my glass and clinked it against his.

"Cheers," Nora said.

"Cheers," Dad replied.

I took a sip and made a face. "Doesn't taste very good."

"Of course it doesn't," Dad replied. "It's probably ninety percent water."

IV
Bootlegging

"Thanks for dinner," I said, leaning back in my chair, a satisfied smile on my lips.

"Yeah, it was great," Nora agreed.

"Glad you liked it," Dad replied, and he jabbed his thumb toward the kitchen door. "There's more if you want it."

"No, thank you, really. I couldn't eat another bit."

"We'll have plenty of leftovers, then."

"You really need to give me the recipe for that stew, Max," Anna said. "It's one of the best I've ever tasted."

"Of course it is," Nora said. "He's a chef."

Anna's eyebrows rose toward the ceiling, as did Elanor's. "Really? You don't seem the type," they said.

"Now what exactly do you mean by that?" Dad said with a grin. "The beard, maybe?"

"It's the whole thing, really. The beard, the hair, the fact you spend most of your free time working on cars," Elanor replied. "Overall, you just don't fit the . . ." They paused. "Um."

"The stereotype?" Vicky asked, with a half-smile.

Elanor nodded, embarrassed. "The stereotype, yes. Sorry. I should know better than to judge a book by its cover."

"I'm not offended," Dad said. "Anyway, I'm not a chef. I'm a cook."

"Oh?" Vicky said. "What's the difference?"

"Chefs are all fancy-pants, white outfit, funny hat. They come up with recipes, often have their own restaurant. Me, I'm not that special. I just cook short-order at a diner."

"At the best diner in town," Mom piped up. "Don't sell yourself short, Max."

"I'm not selling myself short. My food's not even that good."

"It is," Nora rebutted.

"It absolutely is," Anna said.

"It is, a hundred percent," Vicky added.

"See? They think so, too. Majority rule. You're a good cook. Suck it up," Mom teased him.

Dad didn't say anything, just grumbled under his breath and looked away, but I could see that under his beard, his cheeks had taken on color.

Mom stood up from the table. "Come on, I'll help you clear the table and put away the leftovers."

"Oh, I'll help too!" I said.

Vicky stood up as well. "Me too."

"Kind of you to offer, Vicky, but you're a guest," Mom said. "I could never make a guest work."

"Bev, I've been staying here for more than two weeks now. I'm going to feel guilty if I keep on doing nothing while you, Max, and Lily do all the work." She paused. "And besides, Lily is my sister. Family helps each other out, right?"

"Right." Mom smiled at her. "Okay, if you insist. Could you grab the plates and bring them to the kitchen?"

Vicky nodded; while Anna, Elanor, and Nora moved to the living room, Mom, Dad, Vicky, and I worked quickly, and in a few minutes we'd cleared the table, put away the leftovers and started the dishwasher.

"We're heading to bed," Mom said. "Are you going to stay here for a bit longer?"

"Yeah," I answered.

"Alright. Don't stay up too late."

As my parents went to their room, Vicky and I joined the others in the living room. Nora had claimed the couch and I joined her, leaning back against her while Vicky flopped down into one of the armchairs; Anna and Elanor were comfortably draped over the other.

"Listen, Lily, I was meaning to ask," Vicky said, tucking her legs underneath her. "Have you sorted out your HRT situation yet?"

"What do you mean?"

"Are you going legit? Like, going to Planned Parenthood or wherever, getting an official prescription, and having your insurance pay for it. You could do that, since you're out to your parents and all."

I hesitated. "I . . . haven't really broached the subject with them?"

"I don't think they'll have any problem with it," Nora said. "They're cool."

"No, what I mean is if I tell them I'm going legit, I'm going to have to tell them I *wasn't* legit before. That I was DIY-ing my hormones."

"Oooh, yeah," Anna said. "Yeah, I can see how that could be a problem."

"Probably not? I still think they're going to be cool about it," Nora said.

"Still," I said. "I'm not sure I want to tell them yet. I think I still need a bit more time to prepare myself and to think how I want to tell them."

"Right," Vicky said, smiling at me. "So I still need to get cypro and E for you from Canada."

"If it's not too much trouble."

"No trouble at all, I was planning on doing a pill run next week anyway."

"I'm coming too," I said.

Vicky paused and turned to look at me. "You're . . . ? No, Lily." She shook her head.

". . . No?"

"No."

"Why not?"

"Because . . ." she began. "Um, you see . . ."

She stopped talking again, but Nora spoke up. "Because it's dangerous," she said. "That's why you don't want Lily to come, right, Vicky?"

Vicky nodded wordlessly.

"Dangerous?" I asked, twisting my body so I could look at Nora.

"I mean, it's basically bootlegging. Smuggling. If you get caught, you're in trouble. Legal trouble."

"Probably just a fine, though," Elanor said. "Estrogen isn't a controlled substance, and neither is cypro."

"Yeah, but testosterone is," Vicky said; when I gave her a curious look, she explained, "I'm buying T for some transmasc folks at the GSA, too. Worst case scenario if I get caught with that, I could end up in jail."

"Well then we'll end up in jail together, because I'm coming too," I said, folding my arms and giving her a defiant look.

"Lily—"

"You're not going to talk me out of this, Sis," I said. "You've put yourself at risk for me so many times. Let me put myself at risk for you for once. We're sisters, after all."

After a moment, Vicky's face broke into a smile. "Yeah. Thanks."

"I'm coming, too," Nora said. When we turned to look at her, she continued, "What? I go where Lily goes."

"Me too," Elanor said.

"And me," Anna added.

Vicky looked around the group and then sighed. "Alright, okay, fine. We're all going."

"We can make a day trip out of it, instead of just going there and back again," Elanor said. "It'll be fun."

"Yeah. I've never been to Canada," Nora said. "I'm glad I brought my passport."

". . . Oh," I said.

Vicky gave me a curious look. "What do you mean, 'Oh'?"

"I . . . don't have a passport."

"You don't?" Anna said. "Lily, you've lived most of your life not fifty miles from the border, and you didn't think to get a passport?"

"Well, I do have a passport. But it's my old one, I didn't get it changed yet, so it's no longer valid."

"Oh, no, it's valid," Elanor said.

"It is?" I asked, surprised.

"It totally is," they nodded. "It doesn't expire just because you have a different name and gender now. Though you may get some weird looks at the border."

"Been there, done that," Vicky commented with a hint of bitterness in her voice.

"That's right, you still have your old name on your passport too, right?" Nora asked. When Vicky nodded, she continued, "Heading out or coming back?"

"Both. It never got super bad, just a few smirks and snide comments, but cops are the same everywhere. Plain or maple-flavored, it doesn't matter: bacon is bacon."

"I'm sorry," I said.

"That's why most trans people get their documents updated as soon as possible," Elanor commented. "I'm surprised you haven't thought of doing that, Lily."

"Um. Well, you see," I said, "I didn't do it right away after changing my name, because . . ."

I let the sentence hang in the air, and Anna said, "Because you thought you were going to change your name back, right?" I nodded, and she laughed. "Oh, you're just so precious. A perfect dumb egg."

"I'm not an egg!" I protested.

"Not anymore."

I grabbed one of the pillows from the couch and lobbed it at her.

≣

I looked out of the window as we drove over the St. Lawrence River, the morning light glinting off its blue waters. We'd set out at dawn, so we'd be able to spend as much time as possible in Canada.

"It's beautiful," Mom said from the front seat.

Vicky, in the driver's seat, nodded. "It really is."

"I don't get why we're going through Massena, though. Wasn't Ogdensburg closer?"

"A bit, yeah, but Massena has more lanes and is less busy. We'll more than make up for the distance in time saved at the border."

"Do you go to Canada often?"

"A few times a year. What about you?"

"The last time was years ago. It's nice to spend a day just doing tourist stuff, it's been too long."

I bumped my shoulder against Nora's, sitting beside me in the back seat, and glared at her. *Good job, dear.*

She shrugged her shoulders apologetically in a way I knew meant: *Yeah, my bad. I shouldn't have mentioned to Bev we'd be going to Canada. But what was I supposed to do? Tell her, "No, sorry, you can't come," when she started making plans? You didn't.*

She had a point, but I still kept looking at her sternly.

"Everything okay, Lily?" Mom asked, turning to look at me.

"Yeah, everything's fine."

"Can you give me your passports? We're coming up to the border."

Nora and I handed our passports to Mom as Vicky slowed the car to a stop and rolled down the window. Out of the corner of my eye, I saw the other car — the one Dad, Anna, and Elanor were riding in — pull into the next lane over.

"Good morning," a bored-looking cop said, barely suppressing a yawn. "Passports, please."

"Here," Vicky said, handing them over. The officer began leafing through them. Then he stopped, peering intently at them.

"Troy McPearson?" he asked, looking at Vicky.

She visibly cringed. "Yes," she said, through gritted teeth.

"Huh." The cop turned his eyes to me through the back window. "And—"

"Is there a problem, officer?" Vicky asked pointedly.

The man's gaze returned to Vicky, and a smirk formed on his lips. "No, no problem at all. Have a good day, *sir*."

He handed the passports back to Vicky, who rolled the window up and drove on as soon as the bar raised.

"Well, that was unpleasant," Mom snapped, quirking her mouth in clear distaste. "I'm of half a mind to stop here and give him an earful when we come back through."

"Don't," I said, reaching out and placing a hand on her shoulder.

She turned in her seat to look at me. "But, Lily . . ."

"It's not worth it."

Mom held my gaze for a moment, and then smiled sadly. "It's not easy being yourself, is it?"

"Yeah," I breathed out and looked at Vicky. "You okay?"

"I'm fine," she said, her voice tight. "I'm used to it."

"Can't you do anything about it?" Mom asked. "Can't you change your name?"

"I still live at home when I'm not at college. If I change my name now, it's possible my father will get wind of it and throw me out. Or worse." She set her jaw and stared straight ahead, a look of determination on her face. "Next year. After I've graduated I won't have to go home any longer. I can find a job, change my name and gender, and give him the middle finger. But not until then."

‡

"I'm here," Vicky sat at the table beside me.

"That took you a bit," Dad said. "Was there a line?"

"No, but I ran into a friend as I was coming back from the restroom," she replied. "I stopped to chat with him."

"Everything good?" I asked.

"Yeah, everything's fine. He was a bit surprised that we met this far into the city, since he lives in the outskirts. It's my first time in Ottawa proper, actually." She looked around. "It's a nice town. I like the ambience."

"This is our favorite restaurant," Mom said, exchanging a smile with Dad. "It still looks the same, though I can't vouch for the food. It's been years since we've last been here, maybe they've changed management."

"I don't think you can go wrong with poutine," Anna said.

"Yeah, but that's a Québec dish, isn't it?" Elanor replied.

"It is," Dad nodded. "You have to go further east to find real poutine. To Montréal, at least."

"It's a shame we don't have more time today, or we could do that," Nora said.

"There'll be other chances."

As our food arrived, I bumped my shoulder against Vicky's. When she turned to look at me, I raised my eyebrows in an unspoken question. She nodded, and I nodded back.

☰

"There's the border." Vicky pointed ahead.

"Good," Mom said from the back seat — we'd swapped places for the return journey — stretching her limbs. "Just a bit longer, and we'll be home."

"Let's hope they don't hold us too long," I said, exchanging a glance with Vicky.

We stopped in front of the booth, and a CBP officer looked up at us. He had black hair and tanned skin, and his name tag read MONTOYA. "Good evening," he said. "Passports, please."

Vicky wordlessly handed them over. He looked at Mom's and Nora's before flipping open mine; he stared at the picture inside, then set my passport aside and opened Vicky's. His lips pursed in thought.

"Well," he said, looking at Vicky and then at me. "I honestly have to say, I would never have guessed. You two look really nice."

"Thank you," I said, trying to paint a smile on my face.

"Where are you headed? Going back home?"

"Yeah."

"I see." He paused. "Why did you go to Canada? Do you have any . . . business there?"

"What do you mean by business?" I asked.

"I mean, do you have any clients there? Two beautiful girls like you . . ."

He let the sentence hang in the air, and I understood. "No," I said. "We had a day out. As a family."

He glanced at Mom and Nora, who were looking at him from the back seat. Nora was piercing him with a glare, but Mom's eyes were narrowed as if she was studying him.

"As a family, huh," the man said.

"Yes, sir. It's been a nice day, but very long," Vicky said, voice weary. "We woke up early this morning, and we're quite tired. We'd be grateful if we could just get through so we can get home and rest."

"Hmm," he mused, and he tapped our passports a few times against his hand. "Not yet. I need to inspect your vehicle."

Out of the corner of my eye, I saw Vicky freeze, and I felt the hair rise on the back of my neck. "Inspect our vehicle?" Vicky asked.

"Precisely," the officer said. "Please drive over there and—"

"Nathan?" my mother exclaimed from the back seat.

The officer stopped, arm halfway raised, and his head perked up. "Yes?"

"Nathan Montoya? Is that you?"

"Yes . . . ?" he repeated, looking at her warily.

"Oh my God, you've grown so much! It's been so long!"

". . . I'm sorry, who are you again?"

"I'm Beverly. I work with your mom."

"Oh." There was a long pause and when Officer Montoya spoke again, his voice was noticeably strained. "Hi, Mrs. O'Connor. How are you?" he said, smiling a careful smile that didn't quite reach his eyes.

"Oh, I'm good, I'm good. Couldn't be better. You know, I just spent a day in Canada with my family, so . . ."

Montoya's smile was frozen on his lips. "That's nice, that's nice," he said.

"You know, I really *do* have to tell Cassie I've seen you. It's such an incredible coincidence," Mom continued. "And you're being so very helpful."

The blood drained from the cop's face. "Yeah," he said. "Yeah. Alright."

He handed our passports back to Vicky, who passed them over to me. "You can go now. Have a good evening."

"You have a good evening too, officer," Vicky said, trying and failing to keep the gloating out of her voice. She rolled the window back up, and we drove off.

"You're going to tell Cassie, aren't you," I said.

"Oh, you bet I'm gonna tell her," Mom replied.

"Good."

We made it a quarter of a mile further along the road before Mom spoke again. "Alright, what's in the trunk?" she asked.

Vicky and I exchanged a glance. "I don't know what you mean," I said.

"Don't even try that with me, Lily," she said. "I saw you two freeze up when he said he wanted to search the car. What's in the trunk?"

Seeing no point in continuing to deny it, I said, "Hormones."

Mom gave a start of surprise. "Hormones . . . ?"

"Yes, hormones. You know, the ones I take. Because I'm trans."

"I . . . Huh," Mom said. She was quiet for a moment, the noise of the engine filling the silence, then she asked, "You don't get them from a doctor here in the US?"

"I mean, I could. I didn't until now, because if I did they'd show up on your insurance statement. And then you'd know. But now that you know about me, I could do that." I paused and looked at Vicky. "Some people don't have that luxury."

"Oh," Mom said. "Oh, I'm sorry, Victoria."

Vicky looked at her through the rearview mirror. "You're . . . not mad?"

"No. I would be, except . . . I get it. I've talked with you enough to know you have a good head on your shoulders, and you don't do anything unless you've thought it through. If you say that's the only way you can get hormones, I believe you." She paused. "I just wish there was something Max and I could do for you."

"It is how it is. But I'm glad we didn't get caught: you and Lily getting thrown into jail would've been a terrible birthday present."

It took a moment for me to realize what she'd just said. "Wait, it's your birthday?!"

"Yeah?"

"*When?*"

"Next Saturday."

I stared at her, mouth agape. "Why didn't you tell me?"

"It's not a big deal." Vicky shrugged. "I've never really celebrated it. Didn't have anyone to celebrate it with. And, I mean, what's there to celebrate anyway? I'm a year older. Hooray."

Her voice was flat, devoid of emotion. I reached out and put a hand on her arm. "Vicky—"

"You don't need to do anything, Lily," she said, taking her hand off the steering wheel and placing it on mine. "Really. You've given me enough just by being my sister."

But despite what Vicky said, by the time we parked the car, I'd decided.

I was going to make sure she would never forget this birthday.

V
Many Happy Returns

I HELD THE sign a bit higher as I watched the passengers disembark from the Greyhound.

"I think that's them?" Nora said, as a boy and a girl, both about our age, stepped off. They looked around, and the boy pointed at us when he spotted us.

"Definitely them." Alright, Lily: big smile, and concentrate on your voice — you want to make a good first impression.

"Hi!" the girl said, pointing at the sign. "I think you're waiting for us."

"I think so, too." I offered her my hand. "Lily O'Connor, nice to meet you."

"Emily Wilson," she replied, shaking it. "This is my boyfriend, Josh."

"Josh Woods, nice to meet you," he said.

"Nora Hartley."

"Shall we be off? We still have a bit of a way to go," I said, once the introductions were over. "We've parked just around the corner."

"Lead the way," Emily said.

"I was quite surprised when I got your call," Emily said as we drove. "How did you even get my number?"

"I looked through Vicky's phone," I replied, and smiled. "Please don't tell her."

She laughed. "Don't worry, I won't."

"I'm really glad you could make it. We're quite far from North Carolina, the trip must've been long."

"Yeah, little bit. But we honestly had nothing better to do, we were just lazing around at home. A spur-of-the-moment weekend trip is a welcome distraction."

"I'm sure Vicky will be happy to see you," I said. "Thank you."

"You're welcome."

"I'm glad to see she's made some good friends," Josh interjected. "I was honestly a bit worried about her."

"We're more than friends, actually," I said. "I consider her my sister."

"Really?" he said; he seemed honestly surprised.

"Really. She's helped me so much. I wouldn't be half the girl I am if it weren't for her," I replied, as Nora reached over and rubbed my arm.

"Huh," Josh said. "It's honestly incredible how far she's come."

"You were in high school together, right?" Nora asked.

"Different years, but yes," he nodded. "Did she tell you she tried to attack us at prom?"

I raised my eyebrows, looking at him through the rearview mirror. "She did?"

Emily scoffed. "Come on, Josh, it wasn't really an attack. We were never in any danger. She was way too drunk to be a serious threat, even though it was a bit scary."

"I'll bet," I said. "I've never been on the receiving end of her temper, but I know how she can be when she has to protect someone she cares about."

Emily made an appreciative noise, smiling to herself. "Glad she's taking my advice to heart," she said.

"She thinks of you as her friends, you know. She's never talked at length about her high school days, but she's mentioned you a few times."

"Good, because I think of her as a friend too."

"Even after she attacked you?" Nora said.

"Water under the bridge," Emily said. "She apologized for that, and for everything else she did. I'm more than willing to let bygones be bygones, especially since I think we all know dysphoria can make us do dumb things."

That elicited a laugh from Nora. "Oh, you have no idea," she said. I pierced her with a glare and she blew a kiss at me.

"Oh? Do tell," Emily said.

Josh cuffed her shoulder lightly. "Emily."

"What? I'm sensing there's an interesting story here, is all."

"You're a terrible gossip, you know?"

"But you still love me."

"I do."

"So, yeah, what's the deal?" Emily turned back toward me.

"Maybe later, or tomorrow," I replied, flicking on the turn signal and pulling into a parking lot. "We're here."

"Oh, boo. Fine."

We walked the short distance to the café, and I pushed the door open.

"Oh, hi, Lily," Rachel said when she saw us.

"Hi, Rach. Is everything ready?"

"Yeah, I've set you up in the other room. Your parents are already here, and so is the cake."

"Thank you."

"Oh, by the way, nice top."

"I have a name, you know," Nora said, and she turned to Rachel. "I'm Nora, nice to meet you."

My mouth fell open; I felt my face go red, and I stared at my girlfriend, sputtering incoherently as she smirked at me.

"Ha! Got ya," Rachel said. "You should see your face, it's amazing."

"She's so cute," Nora agreed, raising her hand for a high five; Rachel obliged.

I pouted. "Bullies. The both of you."

"Stop complaining, here they come," Rachel said. I followed her gaze, and through the café door I spotted Vicky, Elanor, and Anna walking toward us. They were talking among themselves and they hadn't noticed us yet. "Do you need a couple more minutes to finish setting things up?" Rachel asked.

"Yeah."

"I'll send them your way in five, then," she said.

"Thanks again, Rach," Nora replied as we hurried to the back of the café.

There wasn't much left to set up: Mom and Dad had taken care of decorating the cake with candles, which we quickly lit. Nora pulled the curtains, filtering out most of the light coming from outside: with the lights in the room switched off, the effect was warm and cozy.

We took up position around the table, facing the door. Just in time — it opened almost immediately and Elanor and Anna walked into the room, followed closely by Vicky.

". . . the point, Anna," Vicky was saying. "I don't get why Taylor—" She stopped abruptly, blinked, and took in the room. "What . . ."

"Surprise!" we shouted in unison. "Happy birthday!"

"Wh— What?" Vicky stammered. "What is—"

"Happy birthday, Vicky," I said, stepping forward and hugging her.

"Lily. Lily," she said in a disbelieving tone. "Lily. I thought I told you . . ."

"Yeah, told me I didn't need to do anything," I replied, squeezing her tight. "But I wanted to do something. And don't even try to say you don't deserve this." I broke the hug and stepped back, "because you do deserve it, Sis."

"Thank you." I held out my hand and she let me guide her to the table.

"I really hope we got the number of candles right," Mom commented. "You're turning twenty today, right?"

"She is," Emily said.

Vicky gave a start and looked at her, noticing her presence only at that moment because of the darkened room. "Emily?!" she exclaimed. "Josh?"

"Hi, Vicky," Emily said with a smile. "Happy birthday."

Vicky looked at the two of them for a moment, mouth agape, then asked, "What are you doing here?"

"Lily called us," Emily said, nodding toward me. "And when she mentioned your birthday was coming up . . ." She shook her head. "I can't believe you didn't tell us. Seriously, girl."

"I . . . I didn't think you'd be interested."

"Why wouldn't we be interested?" Emily rebutted. "We're friends. I wouldn't miss this for the world."

Beside her, Josh nodded in agreement; Vicky bit her lip. "Thank you," she said, and started blinking rapidly.

I laughed. "Oh, come on, don't you start crying now," I said. "You still need to make a wish and blow out the candles."

"Alright." She held up a hand, signaling us to give her a moment. "Alright. Just . . . give me a sec."

It took about half a minute for Vicky to recover, but then she smiled and stepped up to the table.

"Okay," she said. "I wish—"

"No no no," Nora said, quickly waving her hands. "Don't tell us, just think it."

"Otherwise, it won't come true," Anna added.

"Okay." Vicky closed her eyes briefly, then opened them again, took a deep breath, and blew out the candles, plunging the room into darkness as we cheered and clapped.

Nora and Anna moved to the windows and pulled the curtains back, letting the afternoon light back in.

"Thank you all. Seriously," Vicky said as Mom and Dad busied themselves cutting the cake into slices and doling it out onto plates.

"Oh, you haven't seen anything yet," Nora said. "We still have to give you your presents."

"... You got me presents?"

"Of course we got you presents. It's your birthday. Birthday means cake and presents."

Vicky gave a wry smile. "Yeah. Yeah, of course. Oh, thank you," she said, as Mom handed her a plate.

"The first slice goes to the birthday girl," Mom said.

"And the second to the birthday girl's sister," Dad added, giving me my own slice.

"We didn't know what flavor you liked, Vicky, so we got a Sacher. Hope we didn't pick wrong."

"No, you didn't," she replied with a laugh. "Can't go wrong with chocolate. And this one," she added, slicing off a piece with her fork and holding it up, "seems very good. Just look at the layers, they're perfect."

"It's from a bakery here in town," Mom said. "That's where we always get our cakes."

Vicky raised an eyebrow and glanced at Dad, who chuckled as he handed a plate to Emily. "Nah, I'm completely useless at baking," he said. "What about you?"

"I've always wanted to try it, but never did," Vicky answered. "According to my father, baking isn't manly, so I didn't want to risk it."

"Maybe we can practice together from now on."

"... What do you mean?"

Dad opened his mouth to say something, but I cut him off. "Does everyone have a slice? Good. Bon appétit!"

"This would've gone well with a glass of white wine," Mom

commented, putting down her fork. "Shame they didn't allow us to bring a bottle."

"That's because everyone in this room besides us is underage, Bev," Dad replied. "They probably didn't want to risk a fine. Besides, I thought you didn't approve of underage drinking," he added, his lips creasing into a smile.

Mom waved her hand dismissively. "Whatever. A single glass never hurt anyone. In any case," she continued before Dad could say anything else, "it's time for presents! I'll go first. This is for you, Victoria."

She handed Vicky a large, neatly wrapped package. Vicky opened it. "*Materials Engineering for Aircraft and Spacecraft*," she read from the front cover.

"I looked through the college website and saw this is the recommended textbook for a class you have next year," Mom said.

"I'll be sure to put it to good use."

"And this is from me," Dad said, giving Vicky his gift: a worn paperback edition of *2001: A Space Odyssey*. "One of my favorite books, I bought this way back in the day," Dad explained. "I hope you haven't read it. I also have the sequels if you want to borrow them, even though they're not quite as good."

"Thank you, Max," Vicky said. "I'll let you know what I think of it."

Then it was my turn: Vicky carefully unwrapped the small package I gave her, and held up a fine silver chain on the end of which a pendant shaped like half a heart hung. "I have one too," I said, showing her my own pendant: the two could join together to form one whole heart. "We match."

I got a smile and a hug as a reward.

Emily gave Vicky a fountain pen ("From my collection. Happy birthday, Vicky") and Josh gifted her a bottle of fountain pen ink ("From *my* collection"). Anna gave Vicky a dress, Elanor gave her a matching hat, and Nora a makeup set in matching shades: they'd clearly coordinated with each other.

When all was said and done, Vicky was smiling widely, looking around the group. "Thank you, everyone. Seriously. This was the best birthday I could've asked for. I'm really thankful to have you all in my life." She looked at me. "Especially you, Lily. I don't know what I did to deserve having you as a sister."

She reached out with a hand, and I grabbed it and gave it a squeeze. "I feel the same way. But we're not quite done yet," I said. "There's still one last present you need to open." I turned to Elanor, and asked, "You did bring it, right?"

"Of course, just give me a second." They left the room briefly, came back with a manila envelope, and handed it to me. "Next time I'd appreciate having a bit more time, though," they chided me. "I had to call in a couple favors. You were lucky my Pol Sci professor likes me and has enough connections to make this work on such short notice."

I gave Vicky the envelope. "Here. This is from me, Mom, and Dad."

Vicky glanced at Mom and Dad, then took the envelope from me and gave it a curious look. "What is it?" she asked.

"Come on, open it," I said.

She untied the string that was holding the envelope closed, and pulled out several sheets of paper. "These look official," she said, her forehead creasing. "What *are* these?"

I took a deep breath before answering.

"They're adoption papers."

Vicky froze.

Her eyes ran over the text, but otherwise she wasn't moving. She seemed to have even forgotten how to breathe. It took her a minute to find her voice and fill the silence.

"They're what?" she asked, her whisper barely audible.

"Adoption papers," I repeated. "As well as name and gender change papers."

She looked up at me, bewildered. ". . . They're *what*?" she asked again, even more quietly.

"This was Lily's idea, but Max and I agreed to it," Mom said.

"I've gone through it all with my professor to make sure everything is in order," Elanor said. "The papers haven't been filed, of course; they haven't even been signed, since they need your signature."

"Oh, you can use the pen I gave you for that!" Emily piped up.

"Did you know about this?" Josh asked.

Emily shook her head. "It's a coincidence, but a lucky one."

"Once you've all signed the papers, filed them, and gone through the confirmation hearing, in the eyes of the government you'll officially be Victoria O'Connor, female," Elanor said.

Dad nodded. "Our daughter."

"My sister," I said.

Vicky was still staring at me wide-eyed, disbelief evident on her face. "But my father . . ."

"He doesn't need to know about this," Nora said. "Right, Elanor?"

"Right," Elanor nodded. "You're a legal adult. In this state, adult adoption doesn't require you to notify anyone."

"And if he somehow does learn of it and tries to do anything to you, I'll put him in the ground," Dad said.

"And I'll help you with that," Mom added. "No one tries to hurt my daughter and gets away with it."

I didn't look at them: I was focused on Vicky, who was still looking deep into my eyes. I couldn't decipher the emotions I saw in hers, but I offered her my best smile, the one I reserved for my closest friends — and for family.

"So what about it, Vicky? Will you be my sister?" I asked.

It was as if my words had shaken her from a dream. She shook her head, her eyes moist. Slowly, very carefully, she slid the documents back into the folder, then enveloped me in a fierce hug.

"You enormous idiot," she whispered, then hiccoughed. "We're already sisters. But yes." She tightened the hug. "Yes. Absolutely. Yes."

We held each other and cried tears of happiness together for several long minutes before pulling apart.

"Your makeup is a mess," I said.

"Look who's talking," she said, chuckling. "But seriously, Lily." She looked around the group, her eyes pausing briefly on Mom and Dad, who smiled at her, and then she looked back at me. "Ever since I started at Bradford McKinley, there's been a moment I've always dreaded: when the school year is over and I have to go home. But I don't have to do that anymore."

She held out her hands and I grabbed them.

"I don't have to go back home," she said, "because I am home."

I gripped her hands tighter.

"Welcome home, Vicky."

Afterword

THANK YOU FOR reading this book. Some of you might have read it before; if so, thank you for reading it again!

When Kate approached me with the idea of publishing an updated and revised edition I was immediately enthusiastic about it. After all, while this isn't one of the first books I published, I feel like I've developed a bit more as a writer since putting this book up for sale. During my re-reads (yes, authors do re-read their books, believe it or not) I found several things I wanted to tweak and adjust. Not too much, but enough to bring it up to my current standards.

The thorough editing Kirstyn gave it helped, too.

The substance, however, hasn't changed: it's still a book that's very dear to my heart, and one I've enjoyed writing. And I hoped you've enjoyed reading it, too. Or enjoyed again. Reenjoyed? Is that a word? It is now!

As always, here come the thank-yous, so here goes. Thank you to Kate for taking a chance on this, and for Kirstyn for putting her editor's pencil into action. Thank you to my sister Laura for designing the cover, and then re-designing it to fit the new edition. Thank you to Alyson for being a friend and an inspiration and allowing me to steal a few things from her. Thank you to my friends in the Department for enabling me, and thank you to my patrons for supporting me and for tolerating my delays. Thank you to my family for always been there for me and for fuelling my passion.

And thank you to you who are reading these words now.

Until next time.

ABOUT THE AUTHOR

AFTER DECADES OF dreaming up and narrating stories for herself and for her family and friends, Zoe decided to turn pro and share her tales of the world as a way to distract herself from her day job and other assorted bleakness. When she's not writing she lives somewhere in Europe with two humans, a cat, and a turtle.

NTITHESIS PRESS is a small, radical press dedicated to amplifying Trans and Queer voices, preserving our histories, and challenging systems of oppression through storytelling. We believe in the transformative power of narrative to combat erasure, foster solidarity, and celebrate the vibrant diversity of trans and queer experiences. We believe that it is vital that our stories are shared and in doing so, preserved.

We publish Queer and Trans voices for Trans and Queer audiences, not books designed to apologetically make us palatable for cis-het audiences.

Through books, archives, and community collaboration, we strive to ensure that Trans and Queer stories are not only heard but remembered — because our histories are sacred, our voices essential, and our futures worth fighting for.

≡

PATREON SUPPORTERS

Penelope Moore
Jade Allen
Diana G
Erin Banneret

www.ingramcontent.com/pod-product-compliance
Lightning Source LLC
Chambersburg PA
CBHW011926050726
47591CB00009B/2366